Silent Voices

Also by Ann Cleeves

Raven Black
White Nights
Red Bones
Blue Lightning

Silent Voices

A Vera Stanhope Mystery

Ann Cleeves

Minotaur Books

A Thomas Dunne Book
New York

For Tim

This is a work of fiction. All of the characters, organizations, and events portrayed in this novel are either products of the author's imagination or are used fictitiously.

A THOMAS DUNNE BOOK FOR MINOTAUR BOOKS
An imprint of St. Martin's Publishing Group.

www.thomasdunnebooks.com
www.minotaurbooks.com

ISBN 978-1-250-03358-1 (hardcover)
ISBN 978-1-250-03359-8 (e-book)

Minotaur books may be purchased for educational, business, or promotional use. For information on bulk purchases, please contact Macmillan Corporate and Premium Sales Department at 1-800-221-7945 extension 5442 or write specialmarkets@macmillan.com.

First published in Great Britain by Macmillan

First U.S. Edition: May 2013

10 9 8 7 6 5 4 3 2 1

Acknowledgements

I'm grateful as always to the old team—Julie, Catherine, Helen, Roger, Jean, Rebecca, Sara and her associates worldwide. Thanks also to the new team—Elaine, Paul, Brenda and David— who have helped me look at my characters in a different way.

Chapter One

Vera swam slowly. An elderly man with a bathing hat pulled like a fully stretched condom over his head went past her. He wasn't a strong swimmer, but he was faster than she was. She was the sloth of the swimming world. But still she was almost faint with the effort of moving, with pulling the bulk of her body through the water.

She hated the sensation of water on her face—one splash and she imagined she was drowning—so she did a slow breaststroke with her chin a couple of inches from the surface of the pool. Looking, she suspected, like a giant turtle.

She managed to raise her head a little further to look at the clock on the wall. Nearly midday. Soon the fit and fabulous elderly would appear for aqua-aerobics. The women with painted toenails, floral bathing costumes and the smug realization that they'd be the last generation to retire early in some comfort. There'd be loud music, the sound distorted by a tortuous PA system and the appalling acoustics of the pool, so it would hardly seem like music at all. A young woman in Lycra would shout. Vera couldn't bear the thought of it. She'd swum her regulation ten lengths. *Well, eight.* She couldn't do self-deception if her life depended on it. And now, her lungs heaving, she really felt that her life did depend on it. So sod it! Five minutes in the steam room, a super-strength latte, then back to work.

The swimming had been her doctor's idea. Vera had gone for a routine check-up, prepared for the usual lecture about her weight. She always lied about her alcohol intake, but her weight was obvious and couldn't be hidden. The doctor was young, looked in fact like a bairn, dressed up in respectable adult clothes.

'You do realize you're killing yourself?' She'd leaned forward across the desk so that Vera could see that the perfect skin was uncovered by make-up, smell a discreet grown-up perfume.

'I'm not frightened of dying,' Vera had said. She liked making dramatic statements, but thought this one was probably true.

'You might not die, of course.' The doctor had a clear voice, a bit on the high side to make for pleasant listening. 'Not immediately at least.' And she'd listed the unpleasant possible symptoms that might result from Vera's over-indulgence. An old-fashioned school prefect laying down the law. 'It's about time you started making some difficult lifestyle choices, Ms Stanhope.'

Inspector, Vera had wanted to say. *Inspector Stanhope.* Knowing that actually this child would be unimpressed by the rank.

And so Vera had joined the health club in this big out-of-town hotel, and most days she squeezed an hour from her day and swam ten lengths. Or eight. Never, she thought self-righteously, fewer than eight. She tried to choose a time when the pool was empty. Early mornings and evenings were impossible. Then the changing room was overrun by the young, the skinny, tanned women who plugged themselves into iPods and used all the equipment in the gym. How could Vera expose her eczema-scaly legs, her flabby belly and cellulite in front of these twittering, giggling goddesses? Occasionally she would peer into the room that looked like an updated torture chamber, with huge machines and heaving, writhing bodies. The men were gleaming with sweat and she found herself fascinated by them, by the slippery muscles, the heavy shoulders and the trainer-clad feet pounding on the treadmill.

Usually she came to the health club in mid-morning, dashing away from work with the excuse of a meeting. She'd chosen a place that was some distance from work; the last thing she wanted was to be recognized by someone she knew. She hadn't told her colleagues she'd joined, and though perhaps they'd picked up the smell of chlorine on her skin or hair, they knew better than to comment. Now she reached the edge of the pool and stood up to catch her breath. It would be impossible to heave herself out as she'd seen the youngsters do. As she waded to the steps, one of the staff moved the line of floats into the middle of the pool to mark off the area reserved for aqua-aerobics. She was just in time.

The steam room smelled of cedar and eucalyptus. The steam was so thick that she couldn't make out at first if anyone else was there. She didn't mind sharing the room with other women—at least nobody here could see the detail of her ugliness. They might sense her bulk, but nothing else about her. Oddly, though, she felt vulnerable if she was alone here with a man. It wasn't that she feared attack or even an inappropriate touch, the possibility that some nutter might expose himself. Only a swing door separated them from the noise of the pool. A scream would bring one of the staff. And she'd never been much scared by nutters. But there was an intimacy here that disturbed her. She felt that if she struck up a conversation she might reveal herself in a way that she would later regret. Almost naked, drugged by the heat and the smell, this was a place where an encounter might lead into disclosed confidences, difficult territory.

She saw that she was sharing the steam room with a woman, who sat in the corner, her knees bent, so that her feet rested on the marble bench. Her head was tilted back and Vera thought she seemed completely relaxed. Vera envied her. Complete relaxation was a state she rarely achieved. The child-doctor had suggested yoga and Vera went for one session, but found it excruciatingly boring. To hold a pose for what seemed like hours, to lie flat on one's back while thoughts and ideas charged around one's head, sparking a need for action. How could that possibly be relaxing? Vera lowered herself carefully onto the marble, slippery with condensation, but still made a sound like a wet fart. No response from the tactful woman in the corner. Vera tried tipping back her head and shutting her eyes, but thoughts of work intruded. There was no specific case to trouble her. It had been unusually quiet since Christmas. But there was always something: a niggle about office politics, the memory of a lead that should have been followed. It was at these times of physical stillness that her brain was most active.

She opened her eyes and shot a jealous glance at the woman in the corner. The steam seemed less thick and Vera saw that she was middle-aged rather than elderly. Short curly hair, a plain blue costume. Slender, with long, shapely legs. Only then, as a hidden draught cleared the mist again, did Vera realize that her companion was too still and her skin was too pale. The object of Vera's envy was dead.

Chapter Two

Out in the pool area the aerobics class had begun. There was music, though only the thumping bass beat was discernible. Vera looked over the swing door. In the water the women were twisting their bodies and waving their hands in the air. She bent over the body and felt for a pulse, knowing as she did so that she wouldn't find one. The woman had been murdered. There were petechiae in the whites of the eyes and bruising around the neck. She knew it was wrong, but a little voice in Vera's head shouted in excitement. Now she hesitated. The last thing she wanted was to create mass panic. Neither was she prepared to greet medics or colleagues in a black bathing costume, which gave her the appearance of a small barrage balloon. She needed to dress first.

A young woman in the uniform dress of yellow polo shirt and yellow shorts was collecting sponge floats from the side of the pool. Vera waved her over.

'Yes?' A badge strung around the woman's neck on a bit of nylon string said she was called Lisa. She droped the floats into a pile, gave a professional smile.

'There's a dead woman in the steam room.' The background noise was so loud that Vera had no anxiety that she'd be overheard.

But the girl had heard her. The smile disappeared. Lisa stared at her, speechless and horrified.

'I'm the police,' Vera said. 'Detective Inspector Stanhope. Stand there. Don't go in and don't let anyone else in.' Still no response. Lisa continued to stare. 'Did you hear me?'

Lisa nodded—still, it seemed, unable to speak.

The changing room was almost empty because the class was continuing. Vera pulled her mobile from the locker and phoned Joe Ashworth, her sergeant. For a moment she considered lying. *I was having coffee in the bar and the staff called me down when they found the body.* But of course that wouldn't do. She'd sweated in the steam room, sneezed. Her DNA would be there. Along with that of a countless number of health-club members. Besides, how many times had she ranted about the small lies told by witnesses to hide embarrassment?

With her free hand Vera pulled on her knickers. Once the class was over, people would be queuing up to use the steam room and she wasn't sure the little lassie in yellow had it in her to stop them.

Ashworth answered.

'I've got a suspicious death,' she said. No need after all to go into how she came to be involved. She sketched in the details. 'Get things moving and get yourself down here.'

'Why isn't it natural? Heat, exertion, you'd think heart attack. Maybe someone at the health club's been watching too many cop shows on the telly? Put two and two together and come up with five?'

'The poor woman was strangled.' Vera knew it was wrong, but she expected somehow that Ashworth could read her thoughts, was always irritated when it was clear he couldn't. Besides, would she really have called him out for a heart attack?

'I'm just down the road,' he said. 'In that fancy garden centre to pick up a present for my mam's birthday. I'll be there in ten minutes.'

She ended the call and continued dressing. Somehow her skirt had fallen on top of her costume and had a damp patch at the back. Looked as if she'd pissed herself. She swore under her breath, walked back to the pool area, avoiding the footbath and aware of disapproving glares. This wasn't a place for the fully clad. She needed to find a manager, but she didn't want to leave the scene. The aerobics class was reaching its climax. A conga of prancing ladies—with one or two gents—circled the pool. The music stopped and the conga fell apart in a laughing, chattering heap. Lycra-woman shouted into her microphone that they'd all done very well and she looked forward to seeing them next time.

Vera snatched her moment, and the microphone, from the hand of the instructor. Paused for a second. She'd always enjoyed being the centre of attention. Was aware that she was considered at times a figure of fun, but minded that less than being ignored.

'Ladies and gentlemen.'

They stared, disturbed it seemed by this change to routine, by this woman who was so obviously out of place. What was going on? A demonstration perhaps? The Fat People's Democratic Front insisting on the right to be unhealthy? This, at least, was how Vera judged their reaction. But she had her clothes on and that gave her a sense of superiority. From here she could see the wrinkled necks and the bingo-wings; she looked down on the untinted roots of their hair.

'I'm Inspector Vera Stanhope of Northumbria Police.' Glancing up, she saw Joe Ashworth emerge from the changing rooms with a man in a suit whom she took to be part of the hotel management. He'd been even quicker than she'd expected. 'I regret to say that there's been a sudden death in the club and I ask for your cooperation in the matter. Please return to the changing rooms. Once you're dressed, you'll be asked to wait in the lounge for a short while until we take a few details. We'll inconvenience you as little as possible, but we might need to contact you further.' She looked across the water at Ash-

worth and his companion. Both nodded to show they too
had understood what was expected of them.

The pool emptied slowly. They were all curious and
excited. Like a bunch of school kids, Vera thought. At least
there'd be no complaints about their being kept waiting
for statements to be taken. They had too much time on
their hands and not enough excitement in their lives. It
was hard to believe that one of them might be a murderer.

Ashworth moved around the pool to join her, followed
by the suit. The stranger was young, eager to please, small
and bouncy and round. She'd worried that the hotel management might be obstructive: murder might not be good
for business; but this man seemed as excited as the pensioners in the pool. He stood on the balls of his feet and
rubbed his hands together. It seemed to Vera that he was
thinking what a good story he'd have to tell his lass when
he got home that night, and hoping that his picture might
appear on the local television news. These days everyone
wanted their moment of fame.

'This is Ryan Taylor,' Ashworth said. 'Duty manager.'

'Anything I can do, Inspector?'

'Aye. Rustle up some tea and coffee. Lots of it, and
serve it in the lounge. With biscuits. Sandwiches. We'll be
keeping folk hanging around for a long time and it's
already lunchtime. Best keep them sweet.'

Taylor hesitated.

'You can charge them for it,' she said, catching his
drift. 'The fees at this place, they can afford a couple of
quid for a fancy coffee.'

His face brightened. The death of a strange middle-
aged woman wasn't so much a tragedy for him, she
thought. More a marketing opportunity. She expected him
to leave them, but he just moved a couple of yards away
and talked into the walkie-talkie he had clipped to his belt.

Lisa still stood just outside the steam-room door. She
was pale. Vera wondered if she'd opened the door and
looked inside. A young lass like her, Vera would have

expected a reaction more similar to that of the manager. Death wouldn't be real for her. It would be the first scene of a TV drama.

'Have you touched anything?' Vera asked. 'No problem, like, if you have. But you need to tell me. Fingerprints. You know.' But the outside of the door would be the only place they'd get fingerprints, she thought. No chance inside with all that steam. The fingerprint powder would turn to sludge.

At last Lisa did speak. A small, timid voice. 'No,' she said. 'I didn't touch anything.'

'Are you all right, pet?'

The young woman seemed to pull herself together, smiled. 'Yeah, sure.'

'Been on duty all day?'

'Since eight this morning.'

Vera pulled a pair of latex gloves over her hands. Joe had given them to her earlier. He was a real Boy Scout, Joe, and always prepared. Looking down at her fingers, she was reminded of the old man in the swimming cap. Would she recognize him with his kecks on? Maybe not. She opened the steam-room door. 'Take a peep,' she said. 'Don't worry. It's not that gruesome. But I'd like to know if you recognize her. Could save us a fair bit of time.' Behind Lisa's head Joe Ashworth was frowning and shaking his head, all disapproval and indignation. He seemed to think women were delicate flowers who couldn't survive without his protection.

'I don't really know any of the names,' Lisa said. 'You don't in the pool. If you're running a class, that's a bit different.'

'Still, you should be able to tell us if she's a regular. She might do one of your classes too.'

Lisa hesitated, then looked inside.

'Have you seen her before?' Vera demanded. What was it with the lass? Vera couldn't be doing with these weak and wilting young women.

'I'm not sure. They all look much the same, don't they?' And Vera supposed they did. Just as all the skinny young women looked the same to her.

'Can we get this steam switched off?' Vera didn't know what damp and warmth did to a corpse, but she didn't suppose it would help preserve it. 'Without going in there, I mean.'

Taylor bounced over to her. 'Sure, I'll organize it now.' He hesitated. 'Is there anything else I can do to help?'

'I'm assuming she died here this morning,' Vera said. 'I mean, the place would have been cleaned overnight. Someone would have noticed if she was in the steam room then.'

'Sure. Of course.'

But the words seemed forced to her. 'Really? This is a murder inquiry. I'm not fussed about your hygiene regime.'

'We've been having problems with our cleaning staff. A couple of the regular girls are off sick. I brought in a temp, but he's not brilliant. I'm not saying he didn't clean in here, but it wouldn't surprise me if he'd sloped off early.'

'Where did you get him from?' Vera tried not to sound too keen, but felt a spark of interest. New member of staff. Dead punter. Didn't necessarily mean there was a connection, but it would make life a whole lot easier if the temporary cleaner had a conviction for killing middle-aged women. Or if the victim turned out to be his estranged wife.

'He's the son of our receptionist. University student home for the holidays.'

'Right.' She should have known life couldn't be that simple. 'I'll need to talk to him. And to all the staff who were on duty.' She thought she'd rather do the staff interviews. Leave the jolly old buggers to Ashworth, who had the patience of a saint. 'You'll have a record of all the health-club members who checked in today?'

There was an entry system with swipe cards. She assumed each card had an individual chip and didn't just activate the turnstile.

'Aye,' he said, but again he didn't sound too convinced. 'All the IT is done from headquarters in Tunbridge Wells. I assume they'll have the records.' Vera thought she'd get Holly onto that. It'd be a boring kind of job, hanging on the end of the phone while some geek worked his magic with the computer. Holly, her most recently appointed DC, was young and bonny and bright and, even without seeing her, the geek would want to prove how clever he was. Holly was also known to get a bit above herself, and Vera occasionally gave her boring jobs to put her in her place.

'There's no way a non-member could get into the pool area?'

'In theory,' Taylor said. 'Unless she was a guest of someone who *does* belong to the club. Then we'd ask the member to show her own card at the desk and sign the guest in.'

Vera replayed her own visits to the club in her head. She was always in a hurry, often swiped the plastic card upside down so that the turnstile wouldn't work, and dropped her towel because she was flustered, holding up the people behind her. But there was usually a yellow-clad woman at the nearby desk to put her straight.

'You said "In theory",' Vera said. 'What about in practice? How hard would it be for an impostor to get in?'

'Not hard at all. You'd have to know the set-up, but there are ways round the system.'

'Such as?' Something about the round little man was starting to irritate. It was his good humour, she thought. Nothing seemed to rattle him. Happy people really got on her tits.

'Well, you could claim to have forgotten your card. People do that all the time. We'd ask you to sign in, but we'd never check your signature against a members' list. Karen on the desk would just click you through.'

'So you could sign it as anything?'

'Pretty much.'

'How else could you get round the system?'

'Borrow a card from a mate. We're pretty sure that happens all the time, especially with younger members. Each card has a photo, but we don't usually look at them. It's there for its deterrent effect as much as anything.' He seemed quite unconcerned that the system was being abused—to find it rather a joke.

'Great,' Vera said. 'Bloody great.' But really she was already intrigued by the complications of the case. She was a good detective. She didn't often enough get the chance to prove it.

Chapter Three

Connie waited outside the church hall in the spring sunshine. There were primroses in clumps on the bank on the other side of the lane. One time she'd have thought this idyllic: the sun, the kids' voices coming through the open windows of the hall, birdsong from the bushes along the burn and from the trees marking the boundary of the churchyard. After a winter of snow and rain, it was good just to see the blue sky. But now she felt the tension that came with every trip to pick up Alice. Other mothers were wandering along to collect their children from playgroup. Connie always made sure she got to the hall first. She couldn't cope with the turned faces, the occasional false, pitying smile, then the accusing silence that lasted just as long as she walked past the waiting women to join the queue.

The playgroup leader opened the door and Connie went in ahead of the crowd. Best just to pick up her daughter and get out of there. Alice was sitting on the mat, back straight, legs crossed. She caught sight of her mother and beamed at her, but her posture remained just the same. Connie wanted to say: *Don't try so hard, sweetie. Don't care what they all think of you.* But Alice wanted to be popular with the other kids and she wanted to please the middle-aged women who ran the group. It was only at night that her control gave way. Then she wet the bed, was tormented by nightmares and climbed trembling in beside Connie to sleep. In the morning she refused to talk about the night terrors. Connie had never found out the exact cause of the scary dreams, but she could guess. She was haunted herself by memories of being chased down the street by a flock of reporters.

'Alice, your mummy is here.' It was Auntie Elizabeth. The play leaders were known collectively as 'the aunties'. Elizabeth was plump and pleasant. The vicar's wife. Connie thought she was itching to get inside Connie's house and inside her head. Maybe she thought her faith gave her permission to be curious and to poke around in other people's lives. Connie could understand the compulsion: she'd spent her working life being nosy too. But she knew that the woman looked out for Alice and she was grateful for that. The child shot to her feet and ran over to her mother. The kids must have been playing outside in the sun, because her freckles seemed brighter and there was a patch of mud on the knee of her jeans. For a moment Connie wondered if she'd been pushed, imagined bullying, the resentments and cruelties of the mothers played out by the children. She couldn't think that way, though. It would lead to paranoia and madness.

She took Alice's hand and led her to the table where the paintings, the handprints and pasta collages had been laid out to dry. The other mothers had gathered around Elizabeth and, while Alice found her own creations, their conversation filtered into Connie's consciousness.

'No Veronica today?'

Veronica wasn't an auntie, but chair of the playgroup committee. She stalked through Connie's dreams. A slender predator with a Marks and Spencer cardigan and bright-red lips. Often she was in the hall when the mums turned up, soliciting unpaid fees, cakes for the next bring-and-buy.

'No.' Elizabeth's voice was calm and easy. Connie was never sure exactly what the vicar's wife made of Veronica. 'I need to talk to her too. I'll call into her house on my way home. This lovely weather, she might have decided on a day in the garden. I think Christopher's working away at the moment.'

Connie automatically took the paintings Alice had handed to her. 'Lovely,' she said. 'We'll put them up in the kitchen when we get home, shall we?' Her voice was distracted; she was listening for more news of Veronica, and for once was happy to linger in the hall. But now the conversation had moved on to the allocation of school places, to some social function in the pub. Veronica was forgotten and Connie walked away, still holding Alice by the hand, without speaking to anyone.

Connie had rented the cottage by the river when she'd left the city, just desperate to get away, not really caring where she went. It belonged to friends of Frank's parents. They couldn't be arsed to do holiday lets any more, Frank had explained. And they didn't use it themselves; they were both still working. They'd bought it as an investment, a way of saving for their retirement, before the bottom dropped out of the housing market. Frank had even offered Connie a place in his house when things blew up. For Alice's sake, he'd said hurriedly, in case Connie got the wrong idea. He'd moved on after the divorce, had a new woman in his life. But they were welcome to his spare room until the reporters got pissed off with camping outside her gate. She'd been so desperate at that point that she'd almost accepted. Perhaps Frank had realized he might end up with a couple of unwanted lodgers, because the offer of the cottage in the Tyne valley came soon afterwards. Connie imagined him on the phone to all his mates. *Help me out here. You must know of somewhere she can stay. Yeah, she might have brought it all on herself, but no reason Alice should suffer. I'll have to let them crash here if I can't come up with something else.* He did still use words like 'crash'. He was artistic director of a theatre in Newcastle and his new woman was a young designer.

The house, known as Mallow Cottage, was pretty from the outside. Traditional stone, with a tile roof and a small garden leading to a burn, which joined the river just beyond a small bridge. Inside it was dark and damp, but Connie could cope with that. The first couple of weeks had been great. She'd enrolled Alice into the playgroup, began to make friends of a sort. Women, at least those who asked her in for coffee, let their kids come to the cottage to play with Alice. Connie had decided to use her maiden name. She'd been divorced for a while, so Frank's surname had no relevance for her. Maybe she could slide into anonymity, perhaps even find work again now that the publicity had died down. After all, she needed the money. She couldn't live off her savings and Frank's charity forever. And back at work, perhaps the nightmares would leave her.

Then there'd been an article in a national newspaper, commemorating the first anniversary of Elias's death. A photo of Connie, looking frightened and tearful coming out of court. And suddenly there were no callers at the cottage for coffee. Except Elizabeth, whose motives were purely professional. And no invitations for Alice to go to tea. The whispers had started, the sideways glances. Some women made attempts to be friendly in a breathlessly curious sort of way, but Connie became aware of a campaign led, she soon realized, by Veronica Eliot. *If you make friends with her, it's as if you condone what she's done. Is that what you want? Do you want people to think you're like her? I don't know how they can let her keep her daughter.* The words were childish and petty, could have been spoken by the leader of a gang of eight-year-olds in the playground, but were effective. It was a sort of mob rule. People didn't stand up to Veronica. And then Connie was met by silence in the queue at the playgroup door, icy glares when she went to the post office to collect her child benefit.

The old Connie would have stood up to her. *Look, you stupid cow, give me a chance to explain.* But after a year of police enquiries and reports and court appearances, all the fight had gone from her. Besides, it seemed immoral that she should feel sorry for herself. She'd given up that right after Elias had died. So she slouched around the village, expecting no contact or kindness. She grew thin. Sometimes, she fancied she'd disappeared altogether, and only Alice could see her. Her only solace was the half bottle of wine she allowed herself in the evening when her daughter was asleep. She was almost grateful for the nights when Alice wet the bed and climbed in with her; then she had someone to hold on to.

They had just gone outside when the visitor arrived. Perhaps he'd been there all along, looking down from the bridge, hidden from them by the tree. On one of his trips to the cottage Frank had slung a thick rope over the bough of the apple tree that stood in the corner of the small garden at the top of a bank. Alice used it as a swing. She'd be at school in September and was big and strong for her age. Physically fearless. She'd grip the rope and run and then, kicking away from the ground, she'd be in the air, almost over the river. Connie knew better than to comment. She couldn't impose her fears on her daughter. But she turned away briefly so that she didn't have to look at that moment when Alice went flying, bit her lip to stop herself shouting out. *Take care, sweetie. Please take care.*

Alice was playing on the swing now. The apple blossom was in bud, the new leaves a startling bright green, blocking the view of the road. Connie was drinking the coffee she'd made after lunch. Then Alice called out 'Hello!' to someone Connie couldn't see, and the stranger appeared at the gate. He stopped there, looking in at them. Connie's first thought was that this was a reporter who had tracked them down. That had been a fear since they'd moved to the valley. The man was young with the easy smile of a natural charmer. Definitely a reporter. Over his shoulder was a rucksack that could contain a camera. Though the knitted hat gave him the look of a rambler, so perhaps he was walking along the river bank.

'Can I help you?' Her words were so sharp that Alice, who'd just swung back to the ground, looked up at her, surprised.

He seemed a little shocked too. The smile wavered. 'I'm sorry. I didn't mean to disturb you.'

Not a journo, Connie thought. Journos didn't apologize. Not even the charming ones. She gave a little wave of her hand, her own apology. 'You surprised me. We don't get many visitors.'

'I'm looking for someone,' he said. His voice was educated.

'Yes?' The caution had returned. Her body was tense, ready to repel him if he asked for her by name or made a move to come through the gate.

'Mrs Eliot. Veronica Eliot.'

'Ah.' She felt relief and curiosity too. What could this man want with Veronica?

'Do you know her?'

'Yes,' Connie said. 'Of course. She lives in the white house at the end of the lane. Just over the crossroads. You can't miss it.' He paused for a moment before turning away and she added: 'If you're driving, there's a lay-by just down the track where you can turn round.' No reason now not to be helpful, and she was curious. She hadn't seen a car.

'No,' he said. 'I don't drive. I came on the bus.'

'Blimey, that's brave! Do you hope to get back tonight?'

He smiled. She thought now it was hard to age him. Certainly younger than her, but he could have been anything between eighteen and thirty. She knew Veronica had a grown-up child, a model offspring of course, reading history at Durham. But his friends would surely know where Veronica lived.

'There is supposed to be a bus back to Hexham in a couple of hours,' he said uncertainly. 'And I can get a taxi if all else fails.'

'Are you a relative?' She realized this was the first *normal* conversation she'd had for months and she hoped to prolong it. How pathetic, she thought. That things have come to this!

He hesitated. The simple question seemed to have thrown him. 'No,' he said at last. 'Not exactly.'

'I don't think she's in,' Connie said. 'The car wasn't in the drive when I walked from the village earlier. And I heard that her husband Christopher is working away. Would you like to come in for a cup of tea to wait? If Veronica's been out for lunch, she'll be back soon and we'll see her car pass from here.'

'Oh, well, if it's not too much trouble.' And he opened the gate and walked into the garden. Suddenly he seemed less nervous, almost arrogant. Connie had a sudden moment of panic. What had she done? She felt that she'd invited disaster across her threshold. The young man sat beside her on the wooden bench with the peeling white paint and waited politely. She'd offered him tea, so he expected her to provide it. But the kitchen was at the back of the house and she wouldn't be able to keep an eye on Alice from there. Connie thought it would be impossible to leave her daughter here with a stranger.

'Alice, come with me. You can be waitress. Fetch the biscuits.' She hoped she had biscuits, because the word worked its magic and Alice trotted obediently after her into the house.

They prepared a tray. Teapot and cups, milk jug and sugar basin. Juice in a beaker for Alice. *I've lived in the country too long. Next thing I'll be in the WI.* But that wasn't much of a joke. Veronica Eliot was chair of the WI, and of course Connie would never be made welcome, even if she wanted to join. They processed out into the garden. Connie carried the tray and Alice followed with a few biscuits on a flowery plate. But when they walked round to the sunny side of the house with its view of the lane and the river, the white bench was empty. The young man had disappeared.

Chapter Four

When Vera was a child, the Willows had been a grand hotel, family-owned and famous throughout the county. One of the few memories she had of her mother was of the three of them there for a lunch. Her mother's birthday perhaps. It would have been Hector's idea; her father had always liked the grand gesture. She couldn't remember what they'd eaten. She suspected now the food wouldn't have been very good. Post-war British. An overcooked slab of meat and vegetables turned grey in the boiling. But it had had a faded glamour. There had been a woman in a long dress playing a grand piano in the corner. Hector had ordered champagne in a loud, showy-off voice and her mother had drunk two glasses and become giggly. Hector, of course, had drunk the rest.

Originally it had been a large country house and there was still a drive that wound through parkland. It had been built on a bend in the river, so there was a feeling almost that it was on an island, especially at this time of the year when the Tyne was swollen from melted snow. There were coppiced willows that marked the boundary and stood now with their roots in water. Local history said that one of the archaeologists who'd done much of the early work on Hadrian's Wall had lived there, and in the library and lounge there were faded sepia photos of excavations, men in plus fours, women in long skirts.

More recently the hotel had been taken over by a small chain with a head office in the south. The basement had been turned into the health club, and any sense that it was a place only for the very wealthy or the glamorous had disappeared. They'd let in Vera, for goodness' sake! But it still had pretensions. In the dining room gentlemen were expected to wear a jacket and tie. The furniture was old and shabby, but once it had been good.

In the health club now there was still an air of excitement and of chaos, but Vera felt in control, happier than she had for months. Sod all that exercise—what she needed to make her feel really alive was interesting work.

Billy Wainwright, the crime-scene manager, had turned up to take control of the scene. The room was clear of steam, but all the surfaces were damp with condensation. 'You do realize this is about the worst crime scene I've ever visited? No chance of fingerprints on these surfaces. Half the population of Newcastle could have walked through here without leaving a trace.' As if, somehow, it was Vera's fault. Billy Wainwright, famous in the service for his bonny wife and his serial adultery. A genius at his job, but a complete rat of a man. Vera stood well out of the way, but, looking in through the open door as he was working, she got a better view of the dead woman. A classic Willows Health Club member. Well groomed, middle-aged, but with the body of a younger woman. She saw a locker key pinned to the strap of the woman's bathing costume.

'What's the number on the key, Billy?'

He lifted it carefully with fat gloved fingers. 'Thirty-five.'

She'd expected Taylor the duty manager to have left them. Surely he would have important things to do. But he was still at the poolside, oddly incongruous in his suit and shiny black shoes. The walkie-talkie was back at his ear. She strode across to him, waited impatiently while he finished his conversation.

'Sorry,' he said. 'Just trying to rearrange a few meetings to keep the lounge free for your witnesses. We're hosting a conference of personnel managers.'

'I assume you have a pass key for all the lockers.'

'Yes.'

'Well, can you get it for me.' Why was she so sharp with him? He'd been helpful enough. Perhaps it was his reluctance to leave them to their work. His obvious thrill to be involved in the investigation, even if only as an observer. I'm allowed to feel excited, she thought, because it's what I do with my life. He's just some sort of voyeur.

Now, at last he did walk away from the pool and through the changing rooms to the desk beside the turnstile. Upstairs in the lounge they could hear excited conversation, the clatter of coffee cups. Ashworth had pulled in some uniforms to help him take statements, but it was obviously going to be a slow process. As Vera had suspected, most of the elderly members were treating this as free entertainment; they were in no hurry to leave. Taylor spoke to the woman at the desk.

'Can you give me the locker pass key, pet?'

It was as if he was speaking to a child; Vera thought that if Taylor was that patronizing to her, she'd have thumped him. The woman at the desk was older than him, could have been well past forty, but fighting it. Black hair and heavily mascaraed eyes. The name-tag said she was Karen.

'Is your lad the temporary cleaner?' Vera asked.

Karen had turned to take a key from a hook on the wall behind her. 'Why? What's he got to do with this?'

'Probably nothing. But I need to chat to him. Is he on duty today?'

Karen put the key on the counter. 'He does lates. He won't be in until four.'

'No rush,' Vera said easily. 'I'll catch up with him then.'

There was a uniformed female officer guarding the changing-room door and at that point Vera sent Taylor away. 'No point taking up any more of your time. I can manage from here.' She thought he was going to argue with her, but he caught himself just in time and smiled instead. She watched the light catch the polished heels of his shoes as he disappeared up the stairs.

Vera recognized the officer guarding the door, but couldn't remember her name. 'Is it all clear in there?'

'Aye.'

'Billy Wainwright taken a look?'

'For all the good it'll do, he says.' The woman smiled fondly and Vera wondered what it was with the man. He wasn't even much of a looker. He was sympathetic, she supposed. A good listener. Perhaps that was the attraction.

'I've been in the changing room already,' Vera said. 'So there's no real problem with contamination if you let me in.'

The policewoman shrugged. Vera was the boss and, besides, it wasn't her problem.

Inside the changing room the television high on the wall was still on. Sky News with pictures of the US President and his First Lady visiting somewhere exotic. African children in starched white shirts and women wrapped in brightly coloured batik cloth. The dead woman's locker was close to the one Vera had used that day. She pulled on a fresh pair of gloves. The lock was stiff and for a moment she wondered if she'd get it open, then she put her shoulder to the door, pushing it until the mechanism caught. The door swung towards her.

Vera looked inside, without touching anything at first. The clothes were neatly folded. A floral skirt, a white shirt, almost as crisp as those worn by the children in the newsreel, a navy cotton sweater. White lacy underwear, as fresh as if it had been newly bought. How did women do that? Vera's turned grey after the first wash. And she would never have bought anything so glamorous. Under the clothes, a pair of sandals. You could tell they'd be comfortable, the leather soft, but stylish too, with a small heel, the leather plaited and fastened at the ankle. Not the sort of thing Vera would wear in a million years.

On the television the weather forecast was being read by a young woman in a breathy voice. The next few days would be unusually mild and sunny for the time of year. 'Beautiful spring weather.' Vera turned briefly and saw a photograph of fat lambs and catkins. The people who ran the smallholding next to her house were still lambing. It was always later in the hills this far north.

No handbag. That seemed odd to Vera. Wouldn't every woman have a handbag with her? Even Vera carried her stuff in a canvas shopping bag. There was a purse, though, tucked inside one of the sleeves of the navy jersey. Had the woman left her bag in her car because it was too bulky for the locker? A bunch of keys was attached to one corner of the purse by a metal clip. Opening it, she found the woman's health-club membership card. The photo was small and grainy, but was clearly of the victim. There was a name.

Jenny Lister. Aged forty-one. Vera would have guessed her as a couple of years younger than that. The address was a village in the Tyne valley, Barnard Bridge, which was about five miles away. Very nice, Vera thought, and pretty much what she would have expected. But why would anyone want to murder a middle-aged woman from an affluent community in rural Northumberland?

She flicked through the contents of the purse. A couple of credit and debit cards in the same name and twenty pounds in cash. One of the credit cards was labelled Mrs Jenny Lister. So there was a husband, or at least had been once. If the couple were still living together, he was probably at work. Vera looked at her watch. It had already gone three. Perhaps the couple had sat down for breakfast together, discussed their day. Now he would have no idea what had happened to his wife, no concerns for her safety. Unless, of course, he'd followed her and strangled her.

*

Upstairs in the lounge, Ashworth and his colleagues had almost worked their way through the members of the aqua-aerobics class. He was using a small office, calling people in one at a time to take their contact details, and to ask if they'd been into the steam room or noticed anything unusual. The plate on the office door read *Ryan Taylor, deputy manager.*

'Who's the manager?' Vera asked, distracted for a moment. 'The big cheese?'

'Woman called Franklin. She's away on leave. Morocco.'

'Very nice.' She said it automatically, but Vera knew really she'd hate foreign travel. She came out all blotchy in the heat.

Ashworth was on his own, catching up on the notes from his most recent interview.

'We've got a name,' Vera said. 'Jenny Lister. Lives out at Barnard Bridge.'

'Worth a bob or two then.' Ashworth looked up from the sheet of paper.

'I thought I'd head out there now. She might still have school-age kids. I'd rather tell them what's happened immediately than have them phoning round her friends to find out where she is, causing lots of noise and fuss.'

'Fine,' Ashworth said. 'Do you want anyone to go with you?'

'I think I can find the way by myself.' Vera knew it wasn't her place to be ferreting round the dead woman's home and family. She'd been told at appraisal after appraisal that her role was strategic. *You should learn to delegate, Inspector.* But she could do this better than anyone else in her team, so what point was there in delegating to an inferior investigator?

'What do you want me to do when I've finished here?'

'Talk to the staff,' Vera said. 'I was going to do it, but I'd rather get out to the family home. There's that lass Lisa. She seems a little jumpy to me, could be there's something on her mind. The woman on the desk is called Karen. She's got a son, a student who's working here as a temporary cleaner over his Easter holiday. Have a word with him. We need to check that he cleaned the steam room last night. There's still a chance the body was here all night. Not likely, because you'd have thought someone would have reported the dead woman missing, but he needs talking to anyway. See if anyone remembers the victim. Taylor should be able to reproduce the photo from the membership card. They take them here when you join, so they'll have them saved somewhere on the computer.'

'You a member?' Ashworth stifled a grin.

Vera ignored the question. 'Show the photo to the staff, see if they know her. And get Holly to find out from her computer geek what time Jenny checked into the club this morning.' She slid the car keys from the keyring that had been attached to Jenny's purse. 'And when you've chatted to the staff, see if her car's still here. Best take a CSI with you. They'll treat it as a crime scene. I think the victim's bag might still be inside. If so, let me know.'

'I'll let the wife know I'll be late then.' The words were meant to be sarcastic, but Vera took no notice.

'Aye. I'll meet you back here if I finish in time. Otherwise I'll give you a ring. Meeting first thing in the morning at the station. They've set up an incident room?'

'Holly's looking after that. Charlie's been helping me take statements here.'

Vera nodded. She thought she'd better let Holly out to see some action the next day. She wasn't a hard boss. Not really. She knew it was important to keep her troops happy. Walking across the car park, she realized she was starving. She'd picked up a cheese pasty from Gregg's before going swimming and it was still in the bag on the passenger seat of the car. A bit greasy and tepid after sitting in the sun all day, but no meat in it, so nothing to go off. She ate it with relish and set off south and west towards the Tyne.

Barnard Bridge was west of the hotel, on the way to Cumbria. It was in an area unfamiliar to Vera. She'd grown up in the hills, and most of the crime in her patch occurred in the city or in the post-industrial villages on the south-east coast of the county. This was rich farming country. The cottages in the villages and small market towns had been bought up by professionals looking for the good life, environmentalists who seemed to square their green credentials with the commute along the A69 into Newcastle, Hexham or Carlisle. It was a place of farmers' markets, independent booksellers and writers. A little bit of southern England planted in the north. Or so Vera thought. But she had a chip on her shoulder the size of Kielder Forest. What would she know? She'd never felt comfortable with the intellectual classes.

Chapter Five

The house was more modest than Vera had been expecting, part of a terrace on the main street running through the village. She parked right against the pavement. It was five o'clock and the place was quiet. The Co-op on the corner was still open, but there was nobody about. This was teatime for kids, and the commuters from the city would still be at work or on their way home. She knocked on the door, not really expecting an answer, but almost immediately there were footsteps inside, the click of the Yale being turned.

'Forgotten your key again?' The words were spoken before the door was properly opened. There was laughter behind them. 'Really, Mum, you are the limit.' Then the girl saw Vera, paused and smiled.

'Sorry, I was expecting someone . . . Can I help you?'

'Is your mum Jenny Lister?'

'Yes, but I'm afraid she's not here.'

'I'm with Northumbria Police, pet. I think I'd best come in.' She saw the panic that was the inevitable result of a police officer turning up unexpectedly on the doorstep. The girl stepped back to allow her in, and then her questions followed Vera down the narrow hall.

'What's this about? Has there been an accident? Have you come to take me to the hospital? Shouldn't we leave now?'

*

Vera took a seat at a table in the kitchen at the back of the house. The walls were yellow and the low sun lit them up. Again this wasn't what Vera had been expecting. She'd imagined Jenny as a stay-at-home wife, kept in idleness and luxury by a hard-working businessman, but this looked more like a student house. The kitchen looked out over a small garden, the Sunday papers were still on the table, and a bottle of red wine stood on the counter, half drunk, a cork stuck back into the neck.

'Is it just you and your mam?' Vera asked. There were photos pinned on a big cork noticeboard on one wall. The victim with this girl, both of them smiling into the camera. No doubt then as to the identity of the dead woman, and Vera felt suddenly very sad about that. She looked like a nice woman. No reason why decent women shouldn't join health clubs too.

'Yeah, my dad left when I was a kid.' The girl had red hair, that opaque cream skin that often goes with it. She was wearing jeans and a long cotton top with flowers on it. Bare feet. She was so skinny it was hard to put an age on her. School sixth form maybe. But pleasant and polite. None of that adolescent rage you read about. She was still standing, leaning against the windowsill, looking outside.

'Sit down,' Vera said. 'What's your name, pet?'

'Hannah.' The girl chose a seat opposite to Vera's. 'Will you please tell me what all this is about.'

'There's no easy way of telling you this, I'm afraid, hinny. Your mother is dead.' Vera leaned across the table and took Hannah's hands in hers. No point in saying how sorry she was. What good would that do? She'd been younger than this lass when her own mother had died. But at least she'd had Hector. Hector had been a self-centred bastard, but he'd been better than no one.

'No!' The girl looked at her almost as if she pitied Vera for having made such a ridiculous mistake. 'My mother's not ill. She's fit for her age. She swims, does Pilates, dances. She's just taken a flamenco class.' She paused. 'A road accident then? But she's a dead careful driver. Neurotic. You've probably got the wrong person.'

'Does she belong to the health club at the Willows?'

'Yes, I bought her membership. She was forty the birthday before last. I wanted something special, did a guilt trip on Dad and squeezed the money out of him.' The girl seemed finally to believe what she had been told, stared at Vera in horror.

'She didn't die of natural causes.' Vera looked at her to check she understood what she was saying, watched the silent tears roll down the perfect cheeks. The girl seemed unable to speak and Vera continued: 'She was murdered, Hannah. Someone killed her. This is hard. Too hard for anyone to bear, but I have to ask you questions. It's my job to find out who killed her. And the sooner I know all about her, the sooner I can do that.'

'Can I see her?'

'Of course. I'll take you to the hospital myself if you like. But that won't be possible until later this evening or maybe tomorrow.'

Hannah sat opposite Vera with her back to the window. The sun lit up her hair, like a halo.

'Would you like me to ask your father to come round?' Best do this by the book.

'No. He's in London. That's where he lives now.'

'How old are you, Hannah?'

'Eighteen.' She answered automatically, too stunned to question Vera's right to ask.

A responsible adult then. No need for a minder. Not legally. But all the same, she just looked like a bairn. 'Is there anyone else you'd like with you? A relative?'

She looked up. 'Simon. Please get me Simon.'

'Who's he, then?'

'Simon Eliot. My boyfriend.' She paused. Then, despite her sadness and confusion, she corrected herself, taking a small comfort from the idea. 'My fiancé.'

Vera felt like smiling. It seemed like they were playing mothers and fathers. Who got married that young any more? But she kept her voice serious. 'Live local, does he?'

'His parents have the big white house at the other end of the village. You'll have passed it on the way in. He's a student in Durham. Home for the Easter holidays.'

'Why don't you give him a ring? Ask him to come round. Or do you want me to speak to him?' Vera was thinking the lad's parents would look after Hannah if there was nobody else. At least until they could contact the father and bring him back from London. Hannah already had her mobile out and was punching out the numbers. At the last minute, as it started ringing, she passed it back to Vera. 'Do you mind? I can't talk about it. What would I say?'

'Hello, you.' A deeper voice than Vera was expecting, warm and sexy. It came to her suddenly that nobody had ever spoken to *her* like that.

'This is Inspector Vera Stanhope from Northumbria Police. There's been a sudden death. Hannah's mother. Hannah asked me to contact you. I wondered if you'd come round. She needs someone with her.'

'I'll be there.' The phone went dead. No messing. Vera was glad Hannah hadn't taken up with a fool.

'He's on his way,' she said.

While they waited for him, Vera made tea. She was desperate for a cup, and the pasty hadn't done much to stop her hunger. This was a house where there'd be biscuits. Possibly even home-made cake.

'What did your mam do for a living?' She'd plugged in the kettle and turned back towards Hannah, who was still staring into space. There was no indication in the house, no clues for Vera to pick up, but she thought something arty. The things in the house—the furniture, crockery, pictures—wouldn't have cost much, but they were put together with flair.

Hannah looked up very slowly. It was as if the question had taken hours to get through to her brain and she had only just remembered what had been asked. 'She was a social worker. Fostering and adoption.'

Vera had to readjust her ideas. She'd never thought much of social workers. Either interfering busybodies who wouldn't let folk get on with their own lives or ineffective wimps. A social worker had come to visit when her own mother had died, though she'd called herself something different then. Child Welfare Officer, that was it. Hector had charmed her, said of course he'd be fine to look after his daughter, and that had been the last they'd seen of the woman. And even though Hector had been hardly what anyone would call a model father, Vera wasn't convinced having a social worker involved would have improved things. She was saved the need to answer because there was a brief knock on the front door, then Simon let himself in. *He must have his own key.* The thought flashed into her mind as she watched the young man take Hannah into his arms. Though it was hardly relevant because Jenny hadn't been killed at home, it made him seem somehow part of the family and the idea of the couple being engaged seemed less ridiculous.

He was dark and big and towered over Hannah. Not conventionally good-looking, Vera thought. Slightly overweight, nerdy glasses, impossibly big feet. But there was a charge of attraction between them, even in this moment of the girl's grief, that took Vera's breath away and gave her a dark and destructive pang of jealousy. *I've never experienced that in my life, and now I probably never will.* He sat on one of the kitchen chairs and took Hannah onto his lap and began to stroke the hair away from her forehead, as if she were a small child. The gesture was so intimate that for a moment Vera was forced to look away.

The student dragged his attention from his girlfriend and gave a little nod to Vera. 'I'm Simon Eliot, Hannah's fiancé.'

'What did Jenny make of your engagement?' She had to pull them into conversation, and it was impossible to ignore the relationship between them. It would have been impossible too, surely, for Jenny to ignore it.

'She thought we were too young.' Hannah slid from Simon's knee and took the chair beside him, though her hand still rested on his leg. 'We wanted to get married this summer, but she asked us to wait.'

'And did you agree?'

'In the end. At least until Simon gets his MA. Another year. It seems like a lifetime, but in the scheme of things . . .'

'Why marry at all?' Vera asked. 'Why not just live together like everyone else?'

'That's just it!' For the moment Hannah seemed to have forgotten her mother's death. Her eyes gleamed. 'We're not like everyone else. What we have is so special. We wanted a special gesture to reflect that. We wanted everyone to know that we intend to spend the rest of our lives together.'

Vera thought that Hannah's parents had made similar promises when they married, but that relationship had hardly survived their daughter's birth. They'd probably started off with ideals too. But Hannah was young and romantic, and it would have been cruel to disillusion her. Now, this student was all she had to cling on to.

'But Jenny had nothing against Simon?'

'Of course not! We all got on together very well. Mum was just over-protective. Since Dad left there'd only been the two of us. I suppose it was hard for her to accept that there was someone else in my life.'

Vera turned to the man. 'And your parents. What did they make of the prospect of your marrying so soon?'

He gave a little shrug. 'They weren't over the moon. They'd have come round.'

'Simon's mother's a snob,' Hannah said. 'A social worker's daughter wasn't quite what she had planned for him.' She smiled to show there was no ill will.

There was a pause. It seemed to Vera that they'd all been colluding in avoiding discussing Jenny Lister's murder. For a moment they'd wanted to pretend that nothing dreadful had happened, that the worst thing going on in their lives was a vague parental uneasiness about an early marriage.

'When did you last see your mother?' Vera asked, keeping the same tone—nosy neighbour.

'This morning,' Hannah said. 'At breakfast. I'd got up early to have it with her. I'm on Easter holiday, but I wanted to do some serious revision for my A levels. Prove to Simon's parents that I do have a brain, even though I'm planning to go to art school instead of a fancy uni.'

'Did she discuss her plans for the day?'

'Yes, she was going for a swim on the way into work. She does a lot of evenings, so she doesn't have to start at nine.'

'Do you know if she had anything specific at work to get in for?' Vera thought she'd get a better idea of time of death by finding out when Jenny was in the health club than by anything the pathologist would give her.

'A meeting at ten-thirty, I think. She was supervising a student and had scheduled a session with him.'

'Where was Jenny based?'

'The area social-services office in Blyth.'

Vera looked up, a little surprised. 'That's a long drive every day!'

'She didn't mind it. Said it was good to put some distance between her and work, and anyway she covered the whole of the county, so some days she was doing visits this way.' There was a moment of silence, then Hannah looked directly at Vera. 'How did she die?'

'I'm not sure, pet. We'll need to wait for the results of the post-mortem.'

'But you must know.'

'I think she was strangled.'

'No one would want to kill my mother.' The girl spoke

with certainty, the same certainty with which she'd pronounced her love for the man sitting next to her. 'It must have been a mistake. Or some psychotic. My mother was a good woman.'

Leaving the house, Vera thought goodness was a concept she didn't entirely understand.

Chapter Six

There were times when Joe Ashworth thought he was a saint to put up with Vera Stanhope. His wife certainly thought he was mad to tolerate the late nights and the early mornings, the abrupt summons to Vera's house in the hills at a moment's notice: 'Just because she doesn't have any family responsibilities, no life away from the job, it doesn't mean you can just drop everything and run away to her.' Ashworth had tried to make a joke of it, 'At least you can't be worried we're having an affair!' Because Vera was twenty years older than him, overweight and her skin was rough with eczema. His wife had frowned then and looked at him over the mug of hot chocolate she made each evening to help her sleep. There was no problem about her putting on weight. She'd only just stopped feeding the baby, and the kids kept her active. 'Maybe you don't fancy the inspector, but she might have designs on you!' Ashworth had laughed at that, though the thought had made him uncomfortable. Sometimes his boss had a way of staring at him through half-closed eyes and he wondered what she was thinking. Had she ever had sex? It was hardly something he could ask her, though at times her questions to him were personal, verging on the rude.

Now she'd left him in charge at the health club and the hotel while she buggered off up the Tyne valley to nose around into the victim's private life. Not her job at all, and something she could have left to a junior member of the team. His wife occasionally suggested that he should apply for a different post—if not promotion, then a sideways move to give him greater experience. Times like this, Ashworth thought it was a sensible suggestion.

He saw Lisa, the young lass Vera had co-opted to help her, in the hotel lounge, which was empty finally; all the health-club members had been interviewed and sent away, and a big notice on the hotel door said that the club was closed for business for twenty-four hours 'Due to Unforeseen Circumstances'. He believed Vera had been thoughtless with Lisa—making the girl peer into the steam room to look at the body, just to save herself a few minutes in the identification, was unprofessional and unkind.

A young woman with a Polish accent seemed to be in charge of the lounge. She wore a black dress and flat shoes. 'Can I get you some refreshment?' He asked Lisa if she'd like a coffee and, when her latte arrived, with small round home-made biscuits on a plate, Lisa sat, bent forward, her hands wrapped round the glass. There was a smudge of foamed milk on her upper lip. She must have seen him looking at it, because she blushed and wiped it away with her napkin.

The lounge was set out like the drawing room in one of the National Trust houses Joe's wife had made him go to, before the kids had come along. Polished dark-wood floor with a square carpet in the middle. The carpet was red and woven, almost as hard on the feet as the floor itself, so threadbare that in some places there was no pattern left. Pictures in big gilt frames on the walls. Mostly portraits, men in wigs and women in long dresses. Big leather chesterfields against the walls and chintz-covered chairs grouped around tables with fragile legs. At one end there was a huge fireplace, but without a fire today, and the big radiators were cold too, so there was a chill as soon as you walked in. The room had a background smell of dust.

Now the remnants of the pensioners' coffee and sandwiches were scattered on white china plates over the tables. There were coffee pots and bowls of lump sugar.

Crumbs and crusts had ended up on the floor. At the other end of the room a middle-aged woman was starting to clear up the debris.

'Thanks for sticking around,' he said. By now Lisa's shift should be over. They were sitting in a corner, and his words seemed to echo around the space.

She slid her eyes up to look at him. 'That's all right.'

'The dead woman's called Jenny Lister,' he said. 'Does that mean anything to you?'

She shook her head. 'She never came to any of my classes. But mostly I do the over-fifties stretch-and-tone, and she looked a bit young for that.'

'Aye,' he said. 'Sorry the boss made you look at her.'

'Though she didn't look *that* old,' Lisa went on. 'She might have gone to Natalie's mums-and-babies class. It's not unusual to get new mothers in their forties. Not these days. You should check with her.'

'Were you on duty at the pool all morning?'

'No,' she said. 'We only have trained lifeguards in after nine-thirty, when the off-peak membership starts. Before that it's the keen swimmers. They sign a disclaimer form. There's usually someone around, but we're short-staffed at the moment. I popped in a few times, but I didn't see or hear anything unusual.'

There was a moment of silence and she looked up at him bleakly. Ashworth felt he was floundering. What would Vera Stanhope do now? She'd thought this lass was worried about something, and usually she was right about people. 'What's it like working here?'

He saw the question had surprised Lisa. What relevance could that have to the murder of a middle-aged woman?

She looked at him suspiciously. 'It's OK. Usually.'

'This is between ourselves,' Ashworth said. 'I won't pass anything you say on to your boss.'

'He's all right.'

Perhaps she's not really anxious, Ashworth thought. *Perhaps she's just a sulky, uncommunicative teenage girl.* He'd had younger sisters and could remember them driving his mam and dad crazy with their silences and their moods.

'So is there anything you think I should know, anything odd or unpleasant that might be important to our investigation?' He spoke briskly, but resisted the urge to raise his voice.

Lisa put down her latte and looked uncomfortable. She twisted a strand of hair between her fingers. 'Things have been going missing,' she said. 'Just in the last couple of weeks.'

'What sort of things?'

'Purses, credit cards, watches.'

'From the changing rooms?' *Why hadn't Taylor mentioned that? It might have provided a motive of a sort, if Jenny Lister had walked in on the culprit.*

'Once or twice,' Lisa said. 'But more often from the staffroom. That's why Ryan could get away with not reporting it. He didn't want the fuss, you see. He didn't want people cancelling their membership because they thought someone was thieving. Not with Louise, the general manager, being away.'

And that's why he didn't mention it to me.

Lisa looked up at him again. 'They think it was me,' she said. 'Not Ryan, he's OK. Fair. He knows I wouldn't do anything like that. But the rest of the staff. I've heard them talking. It's because my dad's been inside and I live in the west end. You just have to give your address and you get blamed. But it wasn't me. I like this job. I'm not going to screw it up.'

Ashworth nodded. The council estates in the west end of Newcastle had been notorious when he was growing up, still had a reputation for crime and gangs despite the private housing that had gone up around it. He thought that Vera had been right again. 'Any idea who might have been stealing?'

She paused. She'd have been brought up not to grass.

'I'm not going to charge in with the handcuffs,' he said. 'But you work here. I'm just asking for your opinion.'

He saw her take that in and watched her give a little smile. Maybe people didn't ask her opinion very often. She considered.

'Things started going walkabout around the time Danny started working here.'

'Danny?'

'Danny Shaw. The temporary cleaner. I heard Ryan tell that fat lady detective about him. He's a student. His mam works on reception.'

'What's he like?'

She paused to choose her words and folded her arms across her chest. 'A bit kind of sly. He tells you what you want to hear. And not a great cleaner. But then I don't think men do clean very well, do you?' Ashworth was thinking she'd probably got that bit of wisdom from her mother, and in fact that it could have been an older woman talking, when she shot him a look. 'But he's fit, mind. All the girls here fancy him something rotten.'

'Any of them been out with him?'

She shook her head. 'He plays them along, all flirty and flattering, but you can tell it's just a game with him. He thinks he's better than us.'

'What about you then?' Ashworth asked, jovial as if he was about fifty-five and her uncle. 'Have you got yourself a nice lad?' And he hoped she had. He hoped she'd be happy.

She went all serious on him again. 'Not yet. I saw what happened to my mother. Married when she was seventeen and three kids by the time she was twenty-one. I'm taking my time. I've got my career to think about.' She sat, straight-backed with her hands on her knee, until he smiled at her and told her she could go.

Karen Shaw, the receptionist, was about to leave. She was sitting behind her desk, staring at the clock on the wall opposite, and as soon as the minute hand hit the hour she was off her chair and packing her magazine and putting her cardigan over her shoulders. Ashworth wondered why Taylor had kept her there all afternoon. Perhaps he'd just forgotten about her. Or perhaps Vera had told her to stick around until the end of her shift.

'Have you got a moment?'

She glared at him. 'A day like this, all I want is to get home to a deep bath and a big glass of wine.'

'You've hardly been rushed off your feet! There've been no customers this afternoon.'

'No,' she said. 'I've been bored out of my tiny mind.' She pulled her bag onto her shoulder. 'Look, it's not challenging work at the best of times. Today I've felt like screaming.' He could feel the energy fizzing around her.

He gave her his best smile, the one his mam said would charm the birds from the trees. 'Tell you what, give me half an hour of your time and I'll buy you that glass of wine.'

She hesitated, then grinned. 'Better be a small one then. I'm driving.'

She led him upstairs to the hotel bar. The whole place had an empty, rather eerie feel. Ashworth was reminded of a horror movie that Sarah had forced him to watch on the telly one night. She had a taste for the macabre. He imagined an axeman appearing in the empty corridors. Only Jenny Lister hadn't been killed with an axe.

The room was smaller than the lounge and the style was different. Ashworth imagined men in white jackets and girls in flapper dresses with headbands and long cigarette holders. There were shelves with cocktail glasses, and a silver cocktail shaker stood on the curved wooden bar. Behind it a spotty adolescent sat on a high stool, reading the sports page of the *Chronicle,* spoiling the atmosphere. All the staff, it seemed, had been told to continue working as if there hadn't been a murder by the pool. The boy obviously resented their interrupting him. 'Sorry, the hotel is closed.'

Karen flashed him a smile. 'I'm staff and he's fuzz.'

They sat at a table near the window looking out over the garden towards the river, she with a glass of Chardonnay and he with an orange juice. He saw that the lawns had been cut, but the borders were wild and overgrown. It occurred to him, in another uncharacteristic flash of whimsy, that they could look like lovers—the younger married man and the lively divorcee, both looking for fun or passion or companionship. Didn't such people meet in hotels like this? For the first time he could almost understand the attraction of such an affair, the excitement.

'I can't be long. My husband will be expecting his tea on the table.' Shattering the fantasy. Why had he assumed she'd be divorced?

'How long have you worked at the Willows?'

She pulled a face. 'Two years.'

'You don't enjoy it?'

'Like I said, it's pretty tedious. But I'm not qualified to do anything else. I thought I'd spend my days as a kept woman. Maybe I'd find anything that involved sucking up to a boss a bit hard to take.'

She paused, but he didn't interrupt. He could tell she liked an audience. She'd keep talking.

And she did: 'My husband has a property business. He bought up a bunch of cheap Tyneside flats before the boom, did them up to a basic standard and let them out to students. But lots of the work was done on credit. He always thought he'd be able to sell on, if things got tight.'

She paused again and this time he did stick in a few words. Just to show he was listening. 'But when things got tight, nobody wanted to buy . . .'

'Yeah. Suddenly the cash dried up. It was a shock to the system. No more holidays abroad, no new flash cars. We even had to sack the cleaner.' She grinned at him to

show she was mocking herself, the whole crazy lifestyle.
It was clear that she hadn't been brought up to money.

She continued more seriously: 'I mean, we survived,
but it wasn't easy. Then Danny went off to uni and we had
his fees to pay. He's our only son and we didn't want him
to go short. Jerry was working his bollocks off, so the only
thing to do was for me to get off my backside and get a job.
I'd been a member of the Willows Health Club, so when I
saw this post advertised I thought: *That'll do for me.* And
it's OK. But I hadn't reckoned on the boredom factor.'

She stared out of the window. He saw Keating, the
pathologist, arriving at last. He'd been delayed on another
case, and Jenny Lister was still waiting for him in the
steam room.

'Did you know the woman who died?'

'I recognized the face. Wouldn't have known the
name.'

'What do you remember about her?'

'She was always in a hurry and she never stayed long.
And she was polite. Always gave me a smile and a wave,
even when she was just swiping her card through the bar-
rier. Treated me like a person, not just a bit of the
machinery.'

Now Ashworth had to come to the sensitive bit. A
woman was going to protect her son, wasn't she? Whatever he'd done. 'You got a holiday job here for Danny?'

'Yes.' And already she was on the defensive, looking up
at him as if to say: *So what? No harm in that, is there?*

'How's he liking it?'

'He's a young lad. He'd rather be in bed or out with his
mates. But it was his idea. He wants to go travelling in the
summer and he knows we can't pay for it. So it's down to
him.'

'We'll have to talk to him,' Ashworth said. 'He cleaned
the pool area. He might have seen something.'

'You don't need my permission to do that. He's nearly twenty. An adult. He'll have started his shift now, if they've let him into the hotel.'

Ashworth knew that they'd let Danny in and that he was sitting in Taylor's office. He was next on the list for interview.

'What do you know about the thieving that's been going on here?'

She drained her glass and set it on the table, kept her voice relaxed. 'That sort of thing goes on everywhere, doesn't it? Petty. There's all sorts work here. Can't see what it might have to do with murder.'

'But it'll have caused bad feeling. Gossip. Not nice to think that one of your mates might be stealing from you.'

She shrugged. 'I try not to listen too much to gossip.' Once again she gathered up the big squashy bag. 'If there's nothing else, there's a deep bath and a chilled glass waiting for me at home. One's never quite enough for me.' He stayed where he was and watched from the window until she emerged from the main door of the hotel. She took a mobile phone from the bag, hit a button and put it to her ear. At the car she turned and he could see that she was frowning and talking furiously. He'd have bet his police pension that she was speaking to her son.

Chapter Seven

At the Lister house, Vera tried to persuade Hannah to move in with Simon's parents, at least for a few days, but the girl refused. 'I want to stay up all night and cry. I'll probably get very drunk. I couldn't do that anywhere but in my own home.'

'We can arrange for a liaison officer to camp out with you then.'

'No,' Hannah said. 'Absolutely not. I couldn't bear it.'

She moved back to the window and stared down at the garden, which was all in shadow now.

'You'll stay with her?' Vera directed the question to Simon. The girl took no notice of them.

'Of course,' Simon said. 'I'll do whatever she wants.'

He stood behind the girl and wrapped his arms around her. They seemed not to notice Vera's leaving.

On her way out of the village, Vera saw the white house Hannah had described as Simon's home, and on impulse she pulled into the gravel drive. She still thought of Simon and Hannah as hardly more than children and she'd feel happier if an adult were involved in the girl's care, or at least aware of what was going on. Besides, perhaps Simon's mother and Jenny Lister had been friends. The woman might have useful information.

Vera saw as soon as she drove past the high yew hedge that the garden was immaculate. The daffodils and narcissi were past their best, but still there was colour everywhere: clumps of blue grape hyacinth and forget-me-not and deep-purple hellebores. The lawn had even had its first cut of the season. *Either the woman's a fanatic or she has paid help.* Vera couldn't bear tidy gardens, and she was more interested in growing food than flowers. She let dandelions grow in damp patches and picked the leaves for salad on the rare occasions when she fancied a healthy meal. Her neighbours were ageing hippies who were pleased not to have order in the next-door garden. Vera wondered briefly what they'd make of this.

There was a twitch at an upstairs window. The noise of the car had attracted attention. Vera wondered if news of Jenny's death had spread throughout the village. Had Simon told his mother on his way out that his girlfriend's mother was the victim? Possibly not, Vera thought. He'd arrived so quickly to look after Hannah that surely he wouldn't have had time for any conversation. Nobody appeared at the door. Simon's mother—if that were the person upstairs—wouldn't want to be thought a woman who peered out of windows. Or perhaps she just hoped the visitor would drive away?

Vera rang the bell and then there was the sound of footsteps on the stairs and an open door.

'Yes?' The woman was tall. She was in her fifties, perhaps the same age as Vera herself, but as well groomed and tidy as the unforgiving garden. Dark hair curled away from her face, grey trousers, a white cotton shirt and a long grey cardigan. Lipstick. Was she on her way out, or did she always wear it? Vera stood on the doorstep and thought how odd some women were.

'Can I help you?' The woman was losing patience. She was confused, Vera could tell. The car Vera was driving was large, new and rather expensive. One of the perks of her rank. Mrs Eliot would consider it the sort of car to be driven by a successful man. Yet Vera was large and shambolic, with bare legs and blotchy skin. She never wore make-up. Vera looked poor.

'I'm from Northumbria Police. Inspector Stanhope.' Somewhere at the bottom of her bag there was a warrant card, but best not go there. She might find that bit of bacon sandwich discarded from breakfast yesterday.

'Oh?' The woman seemed preoccupied but not scared, which was often the response to an unexpected knock from the police. *What have I done? Has there been an accident? Has anything happened to my husband, my daughter or my son?* Simon's mother took in the information and seemed almost excited. Perhaps, after all, she had heard of her neighbour's murder. Though there was no grief, or pretence of grief.

She held out her hand. 'Veronica Eliot. Are you here about Connie Masters? She changed her name, but I recognized her at once. I knew there'd be charges brought eventually.'

The name was vaguely familiar to Vera, but she refused to be distracted.

'I'm here about Jenny Lister.'

The woman frowned. Confused? Disappointed? 'What about Jenny?'

'So your son didn't tell you?' Then, when the woman shook her head. 'Look, pet, why don't you let me come in?'

Veronica Eliot moved aside, then let Vera into a large entrance hall. On the wall facing the door was a painting that drew Vera to stare at it. A small watercolour of stone gateposts with a grassy track curving away between them. Vera thought the track was inviting. You'd want to follow it. But in the painting it didn't seem to be leading anywhere. On the gateposts were carved birds' heads. Cormorants, maybe. Long necks and long beaks.

'Where's that?' Vera asked.

'It's the entrance to Greenhough, my grandfather's house,' the woman said.

'Very grand.'

'Not any more. There was a fire in the Thirties. The only thing left now is a boathouse. And those gates.'

Veronica deliberately turned her back on the painting. She led Vera down a cool corridor and into the kitchen. *Servants' quarters*, Vera thought. *So that's how she thinks of me.* Without being asked, the inspector took a seat at the head of the table. 'Jenny Lister's dead. Murdered. That's why your lad's run off: to take care of Hannah.'

The woman's face gave nothing away. Another small frown that expressed distaste rather than shock. Slowly she sat down too. The chairs were pale wood to match the table, upholstered in grey. Expensive and classy enough, if you wanted a kitchen that looked like a businessman's boardroom. The appliances were all at one end, half a mile away, and were stainless-steel and very big.

'I see,' Veronica said at last. 'One of her clients, I suppose. I've really never understood why anyone would choose to become a social worker. Think of the people you have to deal with. Look at Connie Masters.'

That name again. Vera made a note to check it out when she finally got to the office. Social workers had never been her favourite people, but now, in the face of this woman's attitude, she had an urge to defend Jenny Lister.

She was forming a comment when Veronica spoke again: 'It's sad of course, but at least now there'll be an end to the ridiculous idea of a wedding!'

'You don't like Hannah Lister?' Vera was surprised. She'd taken to the girl immediately, had thought: *If I had a son and he'd taken up with a lass like that, I'd be pleased as Punch.*

'Oh, she's nice enough, but they're both so young. And I always thought Simon could do better for himself. He's at Durham. There are some lovely young women at his college.' She looked wistful.

My God! Vera thought. *Hannah's right. She's a real old-fashioned snob. I thought the species had died out years ago.*

'And Mrs Lister approved of the engagement, did she? That wasn't the impression I had from Hannah.'

'You could never tell with Jenny. Typical social worker. Sitting on the fence. She *said* she thought they were too young, but I don't think she did enough to keep them apart. During the holidays Simon practically lives there. Hannah's still a schoolgirl. Jenny seemed to realize how ridiculous the relationship was, but she still encouraged Simon into the house.'

'What does your husband make of the relationship?' Because there must be a husband, Vera thought. Someone to make the money, to keep Veronica in expensive cosmetics and smart new furniture.

'Oh, Christopher works away a lot. He's seldom here. He's only met Hannah a couple of times.'

'Did Hannah and Simon meet at school?'

'No. Hannah was at the comprehensive in Hexham.' Veronica almost sniffed. 'We sent Simon to the Royal Grammar in town.'

'That must have cost you a bit.'

Vera made the comment under her breath and Veronica pretended not to hear it. She continued: 'They met through music. There's a scheme for young musicians at the Sage. Simon started giving Hannah lifts home after rehearsals. Then there was a music tour of northern Italy and they came back besotted with each other. They've been living in each other's pockets ever since.'

Vera thought of some of the youngsters she came into contact with at work: the druggies and boozers, the thieves and the fighters, the mothers on sink estates sick with worry. She thought Veronica Eliot had little to complain about. 'Any idea why someone would want to kill Jenny Lister?' she asked suddenly. Because so far she'd come across nothing near to a motive. Before Veronica could begin another rant about social-services clients, Vera added, 'She worked with kids apparently, so at the moment we don't think the murder is work-related. How did she get on with folk in the village? What did people make of her?'

Veronica appeared to consider. 'We didn't really mix in the same circles. She probably wasn't around much. She was at work all day and she had a long commute. I think it's important to contribute if you live in a small community. You know the sort of thing: parish council, playgroup committee, board of first school governors. I'm on them all.'

It must be nice to have the time. But Vera knew she'd rather stick pins in her eyes than become one of those professional rural committee members.

'Are you a member of the Willows Health Club?'

If Veronica was surprised by the question she didn't show it. 'No,' she said. 'Not my sort of place, actually. It was a lovely hotel once, but it's definitely gone downmarket since the chain took over. I was taken there as a guest when the club first opened, but I found it rather tacky.' She pursed her lips with distaste. 'They actually expect members to take their own towels.'

Despite her immediate dislike of the woman, Vera supposed it was over-optimistic to consider that Veronica could be a suspect. The inspector would be delighted to take her to the police station, make her wait with the regulars at the desk and question her in a stinking interview room, but of course Veronica would never strangle anybody. She'd bring them down with her superior looks and supercilious words.

'Can you point me in the direction of someone who knew her well?' Vera hoped there was someone outside her immediate family who was sorry Jenny was dead, someone who would drink to her memory and tell stories of the good times they'd shared together.

'Really, Inspector, I don't think I can help you. Jenny and I knew each other because our children are friends. We had nothing else in common.' She stood up and walked out of the kitchen and down the corridor. Vera followed. 'Of course you could try Connie Masters. I suppose they met through Jenny's work.' She gave a little triumphant smile, hesitated at the door in the hope of some response and, when none was forthcoming, she closed it and locked it carefully.

Vera was so intrigued that she was tempted to bang on the door to demand information about Connie Masters. But that was clearly what Veronica had been hoping for, and Vera refused to give her the satisfaction. Instead she got into her car and drove away slowly, hoping the scatter of gravel wasn't chipping the paintwork on her flash new car.

At the crossroads at the edge of the village, she paused to take her bearings. In the cottage squatting in the low ground next to the river on the other side of the road an upstairs light was switched on. It made her realize that it was later than she'd thought. Looking at the clock on the dashboard, she supposed that Ashworth would have finished at the Willows and would already be on his way home to his neat little box on a neat little housing estate just outside Kimmerston. She'd catch up with him in the morning. In the cottage, silhouetted against the light behind, she saw a woman and a child, and was overwhelmed by a sudden sense of loss for a childhood she'd never experienced. The woman in the cottage stood with her arms wrapped around the girl as if protecting her from the world outside the window. Hector hadn't meant to be cruel, but he'd been careless and Vera had been left to fend for herself.

Chapter Eight

Ashworth wasn't on his way home, as Vera had supposed. He was in the steam room, still looking down at Jenny Lister's body, standing next to Keating the pathologist. The doctor was a rugby-playing Ulsterman usually given to plain speaking. Today, though, his tone was rather whimsical. It seemed he'd been in the hotel before. 'We looked at the Willows as a possible venue for my daughter's wedding. The grounds would have been glorious, but inside . . !' He paused, distracted by his first view of the victim. '. . . rather sad, don't you think? Impossible to keep up a place this size these days.'

'The boss thought she'd been strangled,' Ashworth said. Danny Shaw was waiting in the manager's office, and he didn't want the lad giving up and going away. He didn't have time for small talk.

'I'd say the boss is quite right. Not manually, though. Look at that mark. Fine rope or wire. Rope more likely, because the skin's not been cut.'

'Was she killed here or moved after death?' Ashworth knew the questions Vera would want answered.

'Here, I'd say, though you'll have to wait for the post-mortem before I can be certain.'

'Thanks. Can I leave you to it? I'm still trying to interview the possible witnesses.'

Keating must have picked up the trace of complaint in Ashworth's voice. 'Where's the sweet and beautiful Vera?'

'Gone to inform the next of kin.'

'Bear with her, Joe. She's the best detective I've ever worked with.'

Ashworth was embarrassed. He wouldn't have wanted Keating to think he was disloyal. 'I know.'

Danny Shaw sat in the manager's office. Ashworth saw him through a window in the door, leaning back in his chair, nodding his head to the rhythm of music coming through his iPod. But something about the way the boy moved made Ashworth think this was a pose. The boy was too self-conscious, and not as cool and relaxed as he was trying to make out. He was wearing black combats and a loose black T-shirt, and looked to Ashworth a classic student. As soon as the door opened he took out the earplugs and straightened, half rose from his chair in a gesture of respect. Polite enough, Ashworth had to concede. He didn't much like students on the whole. Envy, maybe; he wouldn't have minded three years of sitting on his backside reading books. Then he remembered what Lisa had said about Danny: *He tells you what you want to hear.*

'Sorry to keep you waiting,' Ashworth said. 'But your mam will have let you know I was on my way.'

The boy looked bewildered. So perhaps it hadn't been Danny that Karen had been speaking to so earnestly on her mobile in the hotel car park after the interview in the bar.

'Did you know Jenny Lister, the woman who died?' Best get to the point, Ashworth thought. His Sarah would kill him if he turned up really late. She couldn't sleep until he got in, and the baby always woke in the night. One o'clock, regular as clockwork, and again at five unless they were lucky.

'They don't let me loose on the members.' Danny laughed. 'I'm just the cleaner.'

Ashworth put a blown-up photo of the victim on the table. 'But you might have seen her around.'

There was a moment's hesitation as Danny glanced down. 'Sorry,' he said. 'I can't help.'

'Tell me how your job works,' Ashworth said. 'Talk me through a regular shift.'

'I'm on lates. Start at four. First off, based in the men's changing rooms. It's a busy time, people coming in straight from work, so it's about keeping the place clean and tidy, mopping the floors where people come in from the pool, checking the toilets and showers. Then, when the health club closes at ten, I clean the pool area and gym.' He managed to imply that the job was beneath him.

'And that's what you did last night?'

'Yes, just the same as usual.'

'And you checked the steam room and sauna?' Ashworth had to ask, though Vera had phoned him after speaking to Jenny's daughter. They knew now that Jenny had still been alive for breakfast that morning; there was no possibility that her body had been in the steam room all night.

'Of course.' He smiled, challenging Ashworth to question his commitment to his work. Ashworth decided not to play.

'See anything out of the ordinary?'

'Like what?'

'I don't know.' Ashworth tried to keep his voice patient. 'Like signs of a break-in, or that there was still someone in the place.'

'You think the murderer might have got in the night before?'

'We don't have a specific theory at this point. We have to explore all the possibilities.'

There was another moment of silence. Danny seemed at least now to be taking the question seriously. 'I certainly didn't see anybody. I mean, I'd have called security. The hotel does lots of weddings at weekends, some con-

ferences. Late at night you get pissed people thinking it'd
be fun to go skinny-dipping when nobody else is around;
once I caught a couple of lads hiding away in the showers
before we locked up, but we do a thorough check that the
place is empty. There was nothing like that last night.'

'Can you walk me through the changing rooms?' Ashworth found it almost impossible to visualize the changing
rooms and the business side of the health club. He knew
Vera had been in to find the victim's identity card, but it
wouldn't hurt for him to have a quick look.

'Sure.' The boy got to his feet—glad, it seemed, to be on
the move. Because he'd been slouched in the chair, Ashworth hadn't realized how tall he was. Standing, he
became a gangly, loose-limbed giant.

Ashworth followed him into the ladies' changing
rooms. There was a smell of chlorine from the pool and
something else faintly cosmetic. There were bays of lockers all along one wall, with wooden benches underneath
them and again between the bays. The tiled floor was
clean and dry. For a moment he longed to be out of this
antiseptic, artificial atmosphere. He hadn't had a breath of
fresh air since Vera had summoned him at lunchtime.

'Is this where the thieving was happening?'

'What thieving?'

'Are you pissing me about, lad?' Usually he minded his
language when he was working—and when he wasn't—
but something about this boy got under his skin. 'I'd heard
stuff had been stolen from the changing rooms.'

'Oh, that. I'm not sure much was actually taken. Most
of the members are getting on. They forget where they
put something and they put it down to theft.'

'What about the stuff that went missing from the
staffroom? Are you putting that down to senile dementia
too?'

'I wouldn't know about that.' Danny had given up his
attempt to be pleasant and looked like a petulant

teenager. 'I don't go into the staffroom much. Crap coffee and crap company.'

Ashworth shook his head and let the boy go.

He couldn't find a CSI to come with him to look for Jenny Lister's car. They had better things to do, they implied, than wander round in the dark with him. Once he'd tracked it down, he could give them a shout and they'd tape it.

Outside it was still clear and the moon lit up wisps of mist over the river. There were a few parking spaces very near the house and then a larger car park hidden by trees closer to the gate. He walked down the row of cars by the hotel, clicking the fob of the key Vera had given to him. Nothing. He had a small torch in his jacket pocket and felt stupidly proud to be so well prepared. In the big car park it was very dark. The lights from the house didn't reach there and the trees blocked out the moonlight. Again he walked past the scattered vehicles pressing the fob, thinking that perhaps Jenny had got a lift and this was a waste of time, until there was a click and the flash of headlights and he was standing by her car.

It was a VW Polo, small, but only a year old. He shone the torch through the windows. No handbag on the front or rear seat, or as far as he could tell on the floor. He took his handkerchief from his pocket and used it to open the boot. He'd rather face the fury of the CSIs than the wrath of Vera. Still no bag. He wasn't quite sure what that meant.

Walking back to the hotel, to let the CSIs know which car was Jenny Lister's, his phone went: his wife, calling to ask if he intended staying out all night.

He'd just pulled into the drive at home when his phone rang again. This time it was Vera Stanhope. He sat in the car to take the call. Sarah would have heard his car, but she didn't like work conversations in the house.

'Yes?' He hoped he sounded as tired as he was feeling. He wouldn't put it past her to send him out again.

Her voice was loud. She'd never really got the hang of mobiles, yelled into them. She sounded as if she'd just woken up after a good night's sleep. Murders took her that way, invigorated her as much as they excited the pensioners he'd spent all afternoon interviewing. Once, after a few too many glasses of Famous Grouse, she'd said that was what she'd been put on the Earth for.

'Connie Masters,' she said. 'Name mean anything to you?'

It did vaguely, but not in enough detail to satisfy her and he knew that once he'd chatted to his wife and shared the details of her day, he'd be up most of the night, his laptop on his knee, checking it out for the other woman in his life.

Chapter Nine

Connie hadn't watched the news on TV since the day Elias died. She was always frightened that she might catch a glimpse of herself: pale and inarticulate at that first press conference, or running down the steps of the court in the rain at the end of the case, knowing even then that this was nowhere near over. Her preferred viewing now was light and escapist; she watched documentaries about celebrities, or selling houses or moving to the sun. Every evening, once Alice was in bed and asleep, she would pour herself a glass of wine, eat a supper that took no preparation and lose herself in the inanities on the screen. She had survived another day. Alice had survived another day. That alone was worth celebrating. Boredom was a small price to pay.

It was almost ten when her ex-husband phoned. So few people called her these days that the sound was a shock. She found that she was trembling.

'Yes?' There had been threatening phone calls, but they'd dwindled away to nothing. Perhaps the newspaper article commemorating Elias's death had stirred things up again.

'It's me.' Then when she didn't answer. 'Frank.' A sharp bark, as if she were deaf or very old.

'Yes,' she said. 'I know. What do you want?' She supposed it was about taking Alice away on holiday. He'd been talking about camping in France in June. She'd agreed of course, she couldn't deprive her daughter of a treat like that, but all the time there was a niggle at the back of her mind. A very un-adult envy. *Why can't I come too?*

'I wondered if you'd heard. About Jenny Lister.'

'What about her?' Jenny had never been her favourite person. On the surface friendly enough. Supportive. But underneath quite ruthless. Steely even. Given to principles.

'She's dead. Murdered.'

Connie's first reaction—absolutely appalling of course—was that it served priggish Jenny Lister sodding well right. Then that this might make life very awkward. What if the business with Elias was raked up all over again? Only then came a moment of guilt, because deep down she knew that Jenny had dealt with her as well as any manager would, and that with someone else in charge of the case the experience would have been no different.

Frank was still talking. 'I'm sorry if I disturbed you. But I thought you'd want to know.'

'Yes,' she said. 'Thanks. I hadn't heard.' She replaced the receiver. The television was still yattering away in the background and she turned it off. Then all the noises came from outside: the burn running over the pebbles at the end of the garden, and the leaves of the apple tree against the upstairs window. And the voices that were inside her head.

She shivered. She could smell the damp in Mallow Cottage now, imagined it oozing through the stone floor and running down the lime-washed walls, green and slimy like the stones in the burn. She went upstairs, pulled the duvet from her bed and took it down to the living room, poured another glass of wine, one more than her usual daily allowance. Curled up on the short sofa, her duvet tucked around her, she relived her memories of Jenny and Elias, grieving for both of them as best as she could. Not doing a good job of it, but at least making an attempt for the first time. She was still there when it was getting light, and by then the wine bottle was empty.

Jenny Lister had employed her. Connie had got into social work in her late twenties after a spell, ironically, working on a local paper. What had attracted her? The usual ideals, she supposed. The romantic notion that she might make a difference in people's lives. Throughout the training she'd had an image of this family held together through her support: a tousle-haired boy and a girl with big sad eyes climbing on her knee, thanking her for helping their mummy and daddy. All crap of course, but she'd always needed a bit of praise to keep her going. Jenny had been quite good at the praise thing, at least at the beginning.

Once a month they'd have supervision sessions in Jenny's office. Real coffee and nice biscuits—sometimes home-made. Jenny was one of those superwomen who baked at weekends and went to the theatre and read proper books. The sort of woman Frank's new lover might grow into. And Connie would talk through her caseload. They were part of the child-protection team—the most exciting and dramatic area of social work. No incontinent old ladies or smelly, schizophrenic men for them. Jenny was in charge of fostering and adoption, of assessing and training prospective adoptive parents, but most of Connie's work was following up kids on the 'at risk' register. Some of them would end up being fostered or adopted of course, but while Jenny chatted to nice middle-class foster parents in leafy suburbs on her home visits, Connie's took her to the skankiest estates in the North-East. All dog shit and graffiti, and not a tousle-haired boy or sad-eyed girl in sight. Sometimes she thought Jenny didn't have a clue what it was like.

At first during supervision Jenny said all the right things: 'Sounds as if you've developed a really good relationship with that mum, and a great idea to go with her to the toddler group.' And: 'Absolutely right to insist on talking to the class teacher.' So Connie would come out, high on caffeine and approval. Later, though, Connie's caseload increased and the visits to families became more routine, so the clients sometimes blurred in her head—was Leanne the one with the headlice or was that the flat with the Rottweiler chained in the kitchen? Then Jenny frowned more often, and Connie found herself on the defensive. She always made sure her notes were in order—she'd been a journo, hadn't she? She could tell a good story—but sometimes, visiting the flat where the teenage mother had moved in with that aggressive bloke with the weird stary eyes, she was overwhelmed with relief when there was no answer to her knocking. And even though she thought she'd caught a glimpse of a woman's face at the bedroom window, she jotted *No response* in her diary and moved on to the next call of the day. She wasn't paid enough to put up with a load of abuse. On this estate even the cops hunted in pairs.

It had been a relief when she'd found out she was pregnant with Alice. Had she become pregnant just because it gave her an excuse to have a break from work? Frank hadn't been overjoyed when he'd first heard the news. She'd cooked him a meal, lit candles, bought flowers and all he could say was: 'Hardly brilliant timing, babe.' He'd just taken over as artistic director of the theatre, had taken a pay cut when he gave up his work as a lecturer at Newcastle College. Perhaps he'd already started to screw his new little woman. Perhaps that was why he'd looked so uncomfortable.

She'd supported his decision to leave the college, even though it meant she'd have to stick at the social work, even though the thought of going into work every day, climbing the concrete steps to the bare and mucky flats, facing pathetic mothers and slobby fathers made her feel ill when she woke up every morning. She'd understood what it was like for him to do a job he hated. And she hadn't had the courage to scream: 'What about me? How do I escape?' Had she guessed how close she was to losing him, that one more demand would send him into the arms of the skinny designer about whose work he raved? But at least the pregnancy meant she could take maternity leave, catch her breath. Push the panic away for a while. She could order her world, buy a pram and lay Babygros out in a row on the painted white chest. Frank had felt obliged to spoil her, had become attached, despite himself, to the baby kicking inside her stomach.

When she returned to work, Jenny had been solicitous. She'd cooed over the pictures of Alice. 'Are you sure you want to do this? Lots of new mums find it too stressful, too close to home. There are other branches of the profession, just as satisfying, but not so demanding.' *Incontinent old ladies. Care in the community.*

Connie had refused to take the offered escape route. Why? Pride, and because the alternative would be even worse. Because she thought motherhood had given her an insight, an empathy she'd been lacking before. She'd explained this to Jenny, in a stumbling, halting way, and got a huge smile as a reward. 'Fine then. Let's just go for it.' And the following week Connie had been introduced to Elias's mum.

Mattie had been frail and screwed up. She'd spent most of her life in care, rejected apparently by her student single mother, surviving temporary foster parent after foster parent. Never, for some reason, placed for adoption. It seemed none of the breakdowns in placement had been down to Mattie; from all accounts she was pliable, eager to please. At sixteen she'd been found a flat. Not on a brutal estate, but in a small new housing-association development. That had been down to Saint Jenny, who'd fought Mattie's corner from the start. At seventeen the girl discovered she was pregnant. When Connie first met her, Elias had been six. Totally gorgeous to look at. Obviously mixed-race with coffee-coloured skin and black hair. It wasn't tousled, but very curly; still, he was the child of Connie's student fantasies, the child she would rescue, whose saviour she would become. The boy's father played no part in the story.

Mattie had survived without much social-services support while her child was a toddler. She took her baby to the Sure Start nursery close to her home. He had regular check-ups at the clinic. If anything, the records showed, she was an over-anxious mother, neurotic even. Compared with the drug-taking, irresponsible teenage mums with whom the health-care professionals often dealt, she was a doddle. A delight. Not the sharpest tool in the box, they said, but a devoted mother.

Then Mattie fell in love. Connie never discovered quite how the couple met. She asked, but Mattie blushed and stammered and said: 'Oh, you knaa, we just kinda bumped into each other.' And the man, the object of her worship, was never really around for Connie to ask. Maybe a dating agency? The small ads of the local paper? Though Connie had never seen Mattie read, except a picture book in a stumbling way to Elias, because at the Sure Start she'd been told it was a good thing to do. Perhaps Michael Morgan had seen her in the street and picked her up. She'd grown into a bonny young woman, if you liked your females helpless and waif-like. *And if Frank was anything to go by, many men did enjoy that sort of look.*

Everyone agreed Michael was weird. But harmless, everyone had also agreed that at first. Connie was only assigned the case because Jenny was careful, and had a personal interest in Mattie and because, as Jenny said, *All the research shows if you bring a strange man into a family you change the dynamic. Best just keep an eye until things settle down.* And probably because she thought Connie could do with an easy caseload on her return from maternity leave.

Jenny had frowned again when Connie said Michael was weird. 'In what way weird?' Maybe it was because the word was so loaded with judgement and Jenny was a good liberal, or maybe she always frowned when she was puzzled, and she genuinely wanted Connie to explain.

Connie had struggled to articulate her feelings. 'He's well educated, works in that complementary-therapy centre in Tynemouth. Acupuncture. I wondered why he'd take up with Mattie and the baby.'

'Someone looking out for lost souls?' And Jenny had laughed. 'We social workers know all about that.'

'He hardly speaks.' Connie had felt the need to continue, to express her unease about the man. Making it sound as though she'd done an in-depth assessment, when she'd only met him the once. 'He just sits there, smiling. I wondered if he was on something. Or if he's ill. Mad.'

'No criminal record.' And Jenny had frowned again. 'But let's keep an eye on the situation. Trust your instinct, eh?'

So Connie had continued to call, glad of the excuse to go actually, because Mattie's flat provided an oasis of calm in the round of visits to swearing parents, flats that smelled of piss and worse, babies whose bums fell out of stinking nappies. These days Mattie made herbal tea in big mugs with sunflowers printed on them. Her home had always been tidy, but now there were books on the shelves. No fiction, but volumes on religion and complementary medicine. And there were rugs on the floors, flowers in a vase. But no toys, Connie noticed. No mess. By now Alice was a toddler and their house looked as if a hurricane had passed through. She mentioned it to Mattie, who'd looked unflustered. 'Michael doesn't like clutter,' she'd said. The next time Connie went, she chose a time when Elias would be home from school. He was sitting at the table doing homework, looked up when Connie went in, but didn't smile. Still no toys.

Frank had left six months after Alice's second birthday. His departure was completely unexpected to Connie. Recently there'd been no rows. He was occasionally irritated by the chaos into which their domestic life had descended, but knew better than to blame her solely for that. She'd thought things were fine, was even starting secretly to plan another baby. Perhaps he'd managed to live with her reasonably harmoniously because he knew one day soon he'd leave, because the skinny designer consoled him during the long Saturday afternoons when Connie played with Alice and did the ironing, the afternoons when he told her that he was rehearsing the cast. Rehearsing, she supposed now, for a life of conjugal bliss.

Connie had held things together for the sake of Alice and to keep up appearances at work. No way was she going to break down in Saint Jenny's office. She didn't need pity. 'An amicable split,' she told her colleagues. That was the same day Elias's class teacher rang Connie to express her concern about the boy.

Chapter Ten

'There was a case conference,' Vera said. She was holding a case conference of her own in the incident room at Kimmerston. All the team were there: Joe Ashworth, her right-hand man; her teacher's pet, the beautiful Holly; and old man Charlie, bleary-eyed and scruffy. And Billy, the crime-scene manager, who had, Vera thought at times, more sense in his little finger than the rest of them put together, despite his wayward cock. 'Seems to me that's what social workers do when they can't decide what action to take.'

The weather had changed and it was more like winter again, still almost dark outside and rain dribbling down the windows. Vera pulled her attention back into the room. She hadn't slept much, but felt charged with energy, could feel it running through her big awkward feet and tickling her fingers.

'The teacher's concerns were a bit vague. Elias was coming to school tired and hungry. There were outbursts of temper and he wasn't that sort of kid. A couple of times he peed his pants. She knew social services were involved, so she got in touch with Connie Masters. Any other situation she'd probably just have had a word with the parents.'

'No sign of abuse?' Holly was wearing smart jeans and a tight black sweater. Vera always noticed the younger woman's clothes, fuelling the irrational envy just like picking at a scab.

'Not physical abuse,' Vera said. 'No bruises or burns. A younger child and they'd have called it "failure to thrive". Just a sort of listlessness, a change of personality.' She thought abuse came in many forms.

'What came out of the case conference?' Joe Ashworth was good at feeding her questions; he wanted to move the meeting on. He looked tired. But then he'd been up most of the night too, digging into the Elias Jones case.

'Everyone decided there was no reason to take dramatic action. Connie Masters would visit a bit more regularly— she was only calling in three or four times a year. She'd talk to the lad on his own and to the mother. The teacher would investigate what was going on at the school. It could be that the boy's change of behaviour had nothing to do with the situation at home. Maybe a bit of bullying or a falling-out between friends in the playground.'

Charlie coughed and spluttered into a grey handkerchief that might once have been white. Vera looked up at *her* class. 'So at this point everything done by the book, you see. All decisions and actions recorded. Exemplary social-work practice.' She waved her fingers in the air to indicate quotation marks. The last phrase had been taken from the committee of inquiry's report.

'Where does the victim come into it?' Charlie asked.

'Jenny Lister.' Vera emphasized the words, glared at him to make sure he'd got the point: the woman deserved the dignity of a name. 'She was Connie Masters's boss. She chaired the case conference. She'd known Elias's mum since she was a bairn, because Mattie Jones had been in and out of care all her life too.' She looked at Ashworth, inviting him to take over the story. He walked to the front of the room. *Eh, lad, is this what you want? To be in charge and push me out, like some cuckoo shoving its overweight foster mam out of the nest.* She wasn't sure whether to be proud of him or annoyed by his cockiness.

'So it was left to Connie Masters to follow up with the family. But she was falling apart at the time too. Her husband had just left her and she had a toddler to bring up on her own. A lot was made of that in the inquiry. It wasn't felt that she was entirely objective when it came to working with Elias's family.' His tone was verging on the self-righteous. He could get that way at times, and it made Vera want to give him a good slap. Just because he had the perfect wife and kids, he thought everyone should be able to do it. But she let him continue.

'Connie Masters arranged to take Elias out. Sold it to him as a treat. They'd take a picnic out to the coast, stop for fish and chips on the way home. She thought a full afternoon away and he'd be more likely to open up to her.'

'Was that normal?' Holly interrupted, turned in her seat to make sure they were all taking notice of her. 'I mean, for a social worker to spend all afternoon on one child. If there was no real reason for concern. I thought they're all supposed to be snowed under with work.'

'This was a special child,' Ashworth said. 'A favourite, if you like. And like I said: Mattie was known to them, almost like family herself. Maybe they felt a special responsibility for her son.'

He showed no irritation at the interruption, but went on as if it hadn't happened. 'So there was an afternoon out at the seaside. Longsands, Tynemouth, with a bucket and spade, egg sandwiches and fizzy pop. Elias had a great time, making sandcastles, kicking about a ball. Connie asked him about his mam's boyfriend: "What about Michael? Does he take you out?" But no response. Not even: "He's OK." Elias just refused to discuss him.'

He paused and for a moment they could hear the whir of a printer in another room, the rain on the window, the rush-hour traffic building up below.

'Then, just before they were about to leave the beach, Connie suggested they went for a paddle. "We can't go to the beach and not get our feet wet!" Elias was reluctant, but she took him by the hand and led him to the edge of the water. When it ran over his toes, he shrieked and she thought the cold had startled him. Then a slightly bigger wave came and splashed him, and he really freaked out apparently. Panicked, clung to her, and she had to carry him back up the beach to the dry sand. She tried to get to the bottom of his anxiety. Was he worried Mattie and Michael would be angry about his damp clothes? There was no problem—she'd explain it was her fault. But he went all silent on her again and closed down completely. When she dropped him back at the flat, she felt she'd achieved nothing at all.'

'And you got all this from the report, did you?' Holly asked, sceptical. She was ambitious and there was always an element of rivalry in her dealings with Ashworth.

Ashworth looked at her. 'Yeah,' he said. 'Pretty much. Masters was a journalist before she went into social work and she knows how to tell a good story.'

They fell silent again and Vera thought they were there, on the beach with the kid, and they were all thinking: *What would I have done?* And the honest ones would have known they'd have done nothing. A lad who was a bit of a wimp, scared of being splashed by water. Hardly grounds for taking him away from his family. The courts would laugh in your face. She was scared herself when water got in her face.

Ashworth went on to tell them what Connie Masters did. 'A couple of weeks later she called into the family in the evening. No appointment. Elias was in bed, so she didn't see him, but that wasn't what she was there for. The school was supposed to be looking out for him and she wanted a chat with the mother and the guy who had become, in effect, Elias's stepdad. Apparently it was all very civilized. On the surface. Michael was at the table writing—work apparently—and Mattie was washing up the tea things. Masters noted that Mattie seemed rather subservient and eager to please.'

Charlie looked up. 'One time,' he said, 'there'd have been nothing unusual about a man working and the woman making his tea.' He coughed again and settled back into an angry silence. Everyone knew his domestic situation was fraught and they took no notice.

'Another thing she noted,' Ashworth continued as if Charlie had made no comment. 'The telly had gone. When she was on her own with the boy, Mattie had liked the telly, talked about the soaps as if the characters were real people. Masters asked about it. She thought maybe it had gone for repair or they were waiting for a new one. "Michael doesn't like the television," Mattie said. "He thinks it dulls your mind." No real answer to that one.'

Listening in her corner, Vera thought there were times when that was just what you wanted. To dull the mind. Whisky was her drug of choice, but she could see that television might work for some folk, the endless reruns of *Morse* or *Midsomer Murders*, the makeover shows and the talent contests, they might get you off to sleep at night.

'So they had their meeting,' Ashworth went on. 'Mattie Jones, Connie Masters and Michael Morgan. Masters explained that they were concerned about Elias. He was losing concentration at school, subject to mood swings. Had they noticed any change in him at home? And Mattie—less than articulate at the best of times, according to Masters, a frail beauty who was hardly more than a child herself—only shook her head and looked sad.' Ashworth looked directly at Holly. 'And those words were taken straight from the inquiry notes. Michael said he'd tried to make friends with the boy. "But I'm not very good with children. Too self-centred, I'm afraid." Then he added, surprising Masters, who wasn't expecting such an immediate result, "Look, if it's awkward, maybe I should move out. I don't want to make things difficult for Mattie and Elias. That's the last thing I'd want." And Morgan was as good as his word. He was gone by the weekend, promising to stay in touch with Mattie, but going back to the flat that he'd never really given up at the complementary-therapy centre.'

Vera pushed her backside off the windowsill where it had been resting. It was time for her to take over now. Leave it to Ashworth, and they'd be here all day.

'So the professionals all heaved a sigh of relief,' she said briskly, 'and thought the problem was solved. If anything *was* going on with the kid, then the cause of the trouble had been removed. Jenny Lister was the only one to counsel caution. She said Connie couldn't assume Michael Morgan was at the root of the child's anxiety, and told her to continue regular visits. Mattie was a damaged individual and still needed supervision and support. She sent an email to that effect to all the professionals who'd attended the original case conference. But Connie got distracted by the rest of her caseload: families with problems that seemed more urgent. And her own personal life was a shambles. She made a couple of flying visits to Mattie, who said everything was OK, but she didn't see Elias again. It seemed that nobody spoke to Michael after that meeting at the flat. During the investigation that followed his death, it became clear that Elias was still having problems at school, but because of Jenny's email, the teacher assumed Connie was involved with the family and was dealing with it. Almost exactly a year ago, the child died. He was drowned in the bath. Mattie drowned him. At first she said it was an accident, but during the first interview with police she admitted that she'd killed him. She blamed him for Michael walking out. And maybe she thought that if the boy wasn't there, her man would come back to her.'

Vera looked around the room. She saw that she had their full attention. There were no facetious comments, no eyes rolled towards the ceiling to show they'd lost patience with all this talk. Usually they wanted action, but the death of a child affected them, made them quiet and still.

'The officers investigating the child's death spoke to Michael. It seemed bathtime was always a trauma for the boy. In interview, Mattie admitted that she used water as a punishment, held Elias's head under until he choked.' Vera kept her voice even, but imagined the scene in her head. Mattie whispering so that her lover couldn't hear: *Michael doesn't like clutter. Michael doesn't like noise. Be a good boy and this'll never happen again.* 'It was hardly surprising he was freaked out by an unexpected wave at the seaside. In the court case her defence team tried to persuade the jury that the death was a repetition of the earlier incidents and she hadn't meant to kill her son.'

Now the team members were furious, full of righteous indignation. 'Didn't the boyfriend try to stop her? How could a mother do that to her son?'

Vera answered the last question first. 'The psychologist's report talked about Mattie's low IQ. Michael was the first man to show her any kindness and she was in love, head over heels, crazy for him. The psychologist was surprised at the use of water to exercise control over the boy. It's not a normal form of punishment. She thought it likely Mattie had been treated the same way herself, perhaps by one of her foster parents or in residential care. Mattie might even have thought it was a normal way to behave.'

The room fell silent. 'Michael claims he had no knowledge that Mattie was mistreating her son,' Vera went on. 'The CPS must have believed him. They never prosecuted.' Then there was a release of tension, some chortles of derision. Nobody had much faith in the judgement of the CPS.

She looked at Ashworth. She'd stolen his thunder for long enough. Let him take over now.

'The press blamed Connie Masters,' he said. 'She was suspended, then sacked. Took her dismissal to an industrial tribunal, but they upheld the social-services department decision. Jenny Lister's memo clinched it. She'd instructed Masters to maintain her involvement with the case, not to focus exclusively on Michael.'

Ashworth paused. Vera wondered if he'd done amateur theatrics when he was at school. He could do a dramatic pause as well as anyone she knew. Almost. Nobody was quite as good as her when it came to summing up the essence of a case.

'The important decision, of course,' he said, looking around, making sure he had the full attention of his audience, 'is whether this has any relevance to Jenny Lister's murder, or if it's entirely a coincidence.'

Chapter Eleven

Ashworth sat in Connie Masters's cottage. It was dark and dreary, full of second-hand furniture, everything shabby. The middle of the morning, but they still needed the standard lamp in the corner switched on. And the carpet could have done with a good clean. Joe and his wife furnished their home from Ikea, or Habitat if they could run to it, pale wood and lots of light, the occasional splash of colour.

His head was still full of the morning briefing. After the discussion of the Elias Jones case they'd gone over the pathologist's report, listed possible suspects at the Willows. Vera had found the method of strangulation interesting. 'Thin rope. Clever. Nowhere much to hide a murder weapon in swimming trunks or a costume, but you call ball the rope up into a fist and nobody would know you had it with you. That would make this a premeditated crime, wouldn't it? And the killer must have known Jenny always used the steam room after a swim. He could have been in there waiting for her.' Then she'd stopped, hit her forehead with the palm of her hand, one of her theatrical gestures, which made Joe think she'd been considering the possibility from the start. 'What about the nylon string the staff wear round their necks to hold their name badges? Could something like that have killed her? Can we get a sample for comparison?' Now, in the gloomy cottage, Joe tried to leave the briefing behind and concentrate on the present.

He'd found Connie in the house on her own; her daughter was apparently in playgroup in the village hall. 'I've only got half an hour,' she'd said as soon as he'd introduced himself. 'Then I'll have to go and collect Alice.' Defensive, not really wanting to let him through the door.

But she had allowed him in and now they sat drinking coffee. She looked tired, grey. Ashworth had glimpsed a couple of empty wine bottles on the kitchen bench and wondered if she was a boozer.

'Are you telling me it's a coincidence?' he said. 'That you moved in just down the road from Mrs Lister by chance?'

Usually he avoided confrontation in interviews. It wasn't his style, and besides he found that a quiet and sympathetic approach gave better results. But in this case he'd found himself running out of patience, first with Danny, the student cleaner, and now with this woman. Looking at her, he found it hard to put the images of Elias Jones's drowned body out of his mind. She hadn't committed the murder, but she'd allowed it to happen.

She looked up at him, stung by his tone. 'Yes, that's exactly what I'm saying. I didn't even know she lived in the village.'

'You worked with the woman for six years and you didn't know where she lived?' He allowed the incredulity into his voice, and the question came out hard, high-pitched.

'Look, I'm a city girl.' Connie looked at him over the coffee mug, set it on the table in front of her before continuing. 'Grew up in London, came to Newcastle as a student. Lived in a flat in Heaton, then when we were married we got a tiny house in West Jesmond. I knew Jenny lived in Northumberland somewhere, out in the wilds. On the rare occasions we socialized—team nights out, that sort of thing—it was in town. Why would I know she lived in Barnard Bridge? Do you know where your boss lives?'

A rhetorical question, but Ashworth answered it in his head. *Oh, aye, I know. The number of times I've dropped her back there when she's been too pissed to drive. Or when she's summoned me at a moment's notice to talk over a case.*

'You can't think I killed her?'

Ashworth thought this had really just occurred to Connie. The idea cut through her depression and her hangover. She stared at him now, clear-eyed and horrified.

'Some folk would think you had a motive. If it hadn't been for her, you'd still have a job. You wouldn't be stuck in this place living off benefit, all the world calling you names.'

'No!' Connie stood up to make her point. 'That was down to me. If I'd followed best practice, if I'd made one phone call to Elias's teacher, if I'd made the effort to visit in the evening when I knew I'd catch him in with Morgan, I'd still be working and I wouldn't have had my picture all over the newspapers. I didn't kill Elias. His mother did that. And Jenny Lister didn't get me the sack. I managed to cock up my professional life all on my own.'

'She could have backed you up a bit more, twisted the story to get you out of bother.'

Connie smiled and he saw for the first time that she was an attractive woman. 'Nah,' she said, 'that was never going to happen. Not Jenny's style.'

'Where were you yesterday morning?' He was starting to be convinced by her story, but he wasn't going to let that show.

'What time?'

'Between about eight and eleven-thirty.'

'I was here until nine, when I took Alice to playgroup. That starts at nine-fifteen. I drove her up to the hall and dropped her off, then went into Hexham for an hour. A treat to myself. Window-shopping and a decent coffee. Not quite the same as going into Newcastle, but all I could manage in the time. It was a nice day, so I brought the car back here and walked into the village to collect Alice.'

Ashworth looked out and saw that the rain had stopped. The sky—what you could see of it through the dripping trees—was starting to lighten. 'Where did you park in Hexham?'

'Next to the big supermarket, just up from the station.'

'I don't suppose you kept the parking ticket?'

'I didn't have a parking ticket!' She was starting to get annoyed now and he liked her better this way: fiery, standing up for herself, rather than listless, all the energy sucked out of her. 'There's free parking there, though it's a bit of a walk into town. I save on the parking and buy myself a coffee instead. Those are the kind of calculations I have to make, living on benefit and the pitiful maintenance my husband contributes for his daughter.'

'Did you meet anyone you know?'

'I don't know anyone out here in the sticks.'

'You see,' Ashworth went on, all reason and calm, 'Jenny Lister's body was found in the Willows Health Club. That's about halfway between here and Hexham. Not very far at all. You'd have passed it on your way into the town. Another coincidence, maybe?'

'Yes, Sergeant,' she said. 'Another coincidence.' She paused. 'I've been to the Willows a couple of times. If you have dinner in the restaurant you can use the pool. That was in the old days, while I was still married, before we had Alice, when a drive into the country on a summer night was a treat.' She got to her feet and Ashworth thought she was going to call the interview to a close, but she went into the kitchen and fetched the jug of coffee that had been keeping warm on the filter machine. She topped up his mug without asking and refilled her own. He liked milk and sugar, but she didn't offer those and he didn't ask.

'Tell me about Jenny,' he said. 'What sort of woman was she?'

'Efficient,' she said. 'Honest. Private.'

'Did you like her?'

Connie thought about that. 'I admired her,' she said. 'She never let anyone get in close enough to know if we liked her or not. Nobody at work at least. That was her survival technique, I guess. Some people in social services work the other way: all their mates are people in the same business, who understand the stress and frustration. Jenny always said she wanted to leave her job at the office door. Maybe that was why she chose to live so far away from base.' She paused before continuing. 'Jenny was always convinced she was right. Always. She listened to the arguments, but once she'd made up her mind about a situation you couldn't shift her.'

Ashworth thought he had colleagues like that too. And there were plenty of people in the police service who didn't like to mix work and home. Most of his mates were cops and that was easier because they could get the jokes, share the tension, but some officers didn't want to know once the shift was over. It made them a bit isolated, outsiders in the team. Had Jenny come across in that way: aloof, maybe even patronizing?

'Did she talk about her family at all?'

'I knew she had a daughter, but that was only because Jenny had a photo of a girl on her desk and I asked about her. And when my husband left, Jenny said the same thing had happened to her, when her child was very young. Apart from that, nothing.'

'You can't think, then, who might have wanted to kill her.'

'Oh, I'm sure she had threats,' Connie said easily, 'over the years. We all had those.'

'What do you mean?'

She looked at him as if he were stupid. 'Our work involved removing children from their families, usually against their will. Of course there were people who hated us. We were challenging their ability to be parents, violating their homes, making them look incompetent or cruel to their neighbours. What do you think the reaction was like? Often it was violent and abusive.' She paused for a moment. 'But do I think one of Jenny's clients killed her? Absolutely not. Most of them live chaotic and disorgan- ized lives and that's why their children are at risk. No way could they plan a murder like that. They couldn't even get to the Willows, never mind blag their way inside the health club. I don't know who killed Jenny Lister, but I'd be astounded if it had anything to do with her being a social worker.'

She gathered up the mugs and took them into the kitchen, came back into the tiny living room to put on out- door shoes. Ashworth followed her outside. He wasn't sure it was healthy, living on this low, damp land so close to the water. The garden was overgrown. In a corner rhubarb was starting to sprout, and a few celandines were growing in the long grass. 'Do you think you'll be living here long-term then?' He couldn't see it. Like she'd said, she was more of a city girl.

'God, no!' She pulled a face. 'But I was desperate to get away from the press, and Frank, my ex, knows the owners. I don't think I could face a whole winter here.'

At the small gate, which was green with lichen and soft with rot, she paused.

'There was a stranger in the village,' she said. 'Yesterday afternoon. Just after lunch. It's probably not important. He wasn't looking for Jenny.'

'Why don't you tell me all the same?'

She looked at her watch to check that she had time to wait for a couple of minutes and was reassured.

'It was a bit odd. We went outside to sit after lunch— there was the first real sun of the spring—and there he was. Alice spotted him on the bridge. He said he'd come on the bus. He was looking for Veronica Eliot. She lives in the big white house by the crossroads. I told him she'd been out when I walked past. I suggested that he wait and offered him tea.'

'Why would you do that?' Ashworth disapproved of risk-taking at the best of times. A woman living on her own, it was surely crazy to invite a stranger into her home.

'I'm not sure. I was lonely. I'm a pariah here since they found out about Elias. I wanted some adult company and he seemed OK. But I wasn't going to leave Alice alone with him, so I took her in with me to make the tea. And when we got back, he'd disappeared. Like I said: odd. But maybe he saw Veronica's car turn into her drive. Or maybe he just thought better of hanging out with a mad, desperate housewife and her child.'

Connie gave a small, sad smile and hurried away down the muddy track.

Chapter Twelve

Once the team briefing was over, Vera sat for a moment in her office. She wanted to sort her thoughts. She'd sent Ashworth to Barnard Bridge to talk to Connie Masters. Holly and Charlie were back at the Willows, interviewing the hotel staff members who had been absent the previous day. It seemed to Vera, looking down at the street where the weekly market was already busy, that the choice of the health club as a setting for murder was most significant. Why kill the woman there, when the culprit could be caught at any time? There must have been other, less complicated places to commit the crime. Jenny's killer must have known she belonged to the club, or he had followed her there. That implied a stalker, a crime that was premeditated, planned over a long period. Otherwise, Vera thought, the motive was more trivial and banal, and Jenny had been killed because of something she'd witnessed on her visits to the Willows. No planning at all. Murder often happened for the pettiest of reasons, and those crimes were especially tragic.

She phoned the landline number for Jenny's house in Barnard Bridge. Simon Eliot answered.

'How's Hannah?'

'We didn't get much sleep,' he said. 'I thought I'd call her doctor. Explain. She was talking all night and she needs to rest. Maybe he can give her something to knock her out tonight.' He paused. 'She wants to see her mother.'

Not her mother, her mother's body. Something quite different.

'That should be fine. I'm tied up, but I'll arrange for someone to pick you up.' Vera had already decided she'd send Holly. Maybe Hannah would talk more to someone closer her own age.

'I'm not sure she wants me there,' Simon said. 'I think she'd like to say goodbye on her own.' Vera caught the pain in his voice.

'That's a good thing surely,' she said. 'Give you a bit of time to yourself. No point you cracking up too.' She paused. 'I'd like to talk to some of Jenny's friends. Seems there was nobody she was really close to at work, so I'm assuming there must have been people in the village. Your mam didn't know. Can you help?'

'Anne Mason,' he said. 'She's a teacher at the primary school up the valley and lives in a barn conversion not far out of the village. They went to the theatre, out for meals. They did the flamenco class together. I think she's away at the moment. It's the Easter holidays. She and her husband have a holiday home in Bordeaux and they go there whenever they can. Jenny went with them sometimes.'

'Don't suppose you have a mobile number for her?'

'I don't, but Hannah might. I'll check.' There was silence on the other end of the line. 'There's nothing I can do to help her,' he said at last, a cry from the heart.

'Nothing anyone can do at the moment, pet.' And Vera gave him Holly's name, said she'd be in touch when they had a time for Hannah to go to the mortuary.

Vera had arranged to meet Craig, Jenny's area manager, for lunch in Kimmerston. He had to be in the town anyway and that was the only window in his day. That was the way he talked: buzzword bingo brought to life. There was a partnership meeting, he'd said on the phone. Inter-agency stuff. That was his working life now, all strategy and politics. He never actually saw a client in his life. Vera thought he sounded bloody pleased about it. *I should*

be like that, all strategy and politics. That's what the bosses
want of me. But, God, think how boring that would be.

He suggested they meet in a wine bar in Front Street.
She'd walked past it a few times, but had never been
tempted in. She knew exactly how it would be: over-
priced and poncy. And full of beautiful people who would
stare at her, thinking she was a *Big Issue* seller who'd wandered in from a night on the pavement. She got there
deliberately a little late so that she wouldn't have to wait
on her own for him to arrive, and saw him immediately,
a guy in his forties, wearing a suit, reading the *Indie*. A
briefcase on the floor beside him. Vera had never carried
a briefcase in her life. The place was almost empty—it
was still early for the lunchtime rush—so they wouldn't
be overheard.

When he saw her approaching she noticed the surprise and disappointment on his face. Perhaps he'd been
hoping for a Helen Mirren lookalike. These days, people
expected senior female officers to walk straight out of
Prime Suspect. He got up to shake her hand and she realized he was very tall. There weren't many men who
dwarfed her.

'This is terrible,' he said. 'Jenny Lister was the best
social worker I've ever met. I'm not sure what we'll do
without her. Her team is in pieces.' He looked down at her
bleakly. 'I'm not sure what *I'll* do without her. She kept the
whole show on the road. Officially my deputy, but actually she was the one who kept me straight.'

That made Vera warm to him. Underneath the jargon
and the ambition he was human after all. When he
ordered a bowl of chips to go with his smoked-salmon
baguette she liked him even more.

'So she was good at her job?'

'The understatement of the year.' He dipped a chip
into a bowl of mayonnaise. 'If she'd wanted to, she could
have gone to head up a social-services department. She
was organized, an excellent supervisor, scarily clever.'

'So why wasn't she promoted?' Vera had never quite believed in saints. What was it about Jenny Lister that she'd stayed in the field instead of taking the opportunity to become a manager?

'She didn't want it,' he said. 'She said she didn't need the money or the aggro. And she'd miss working with clients and foster parents. She'd miss the kids.'

'Did you believe her?'

The man looked up, shocked. 'Of course! Jenny Lister didn't lie.'

Not true, Vera thought. *We all lie. We wouldn't survive otherwise. It's just that some of us do it better than others. Jenny Lister must have been a magnificent liar.*

The man continued. 'She loved being the most talented social worker in the place. Perhaps she knew management wouldn't be her thing. She wouldn't have wanted to be second best.'

'What about her background?' Vera asked. 'Was she local?'

He looked up from his food. 'Yes, born-and-bred Northumberland. Went south to university, but lived the rest of her life here.'

'Are her parents still alive?' *Maybe Jenny had confided in them if they were local. Maybe they'd have Hannah to stay for a while.*

'No,' he said. 'She never talked about it, but my wife's a local-history buff and came across the story in an old copy of the *Hexham Courant*. Jenny's dad was a solicitor, seemed he was defrauding his clients. He took his own life before the case could go to court. The mother lived for a good few years after that, but she was never the same apparently. She couldn't stand the shame. I think she lived in residential care somewhere on the coast. She died about ten years ago. I remember Jenny going to the funeral.'

Another woman with a crook for a father, Vera thought. Perhaps she and Jenny would have had things in common after all.

On the way back to the station, pushing her way against the market-day flow of people on the wide pavement, Vera's mobile beeped to show she had a text. She'd never really understood the text thing. Why not phone and leave a message? Really she needed specs, but was too vain and too disorganized to go for an eye test, and here in the busy street she couldn't be arsed to try to read it. She'd be flattened by the elderly farmers and the county ladies walking in the opposite direction. In her office, she made coffee before checking her phone. The message was from Simon Eliot. Of course, that was the way the young communicated. *Jenny's friend Anne just home from holiday. Happy to talk to you.* Then a phone number.

She was about to phone Anne Mason when there was a call on her landline. It was Holly, just back from taking Hannah to the mortuary, speaking in a sort of stage whisper. 'Is it OK if I stay with her, boss? She's in a real state. She's only a kid.' Was there a touch of accusation in the tone? As if Vera was a heartless beast for not taking better care of the girl?

'Sure, if she wants you there.'

'She's so knackered I'm not quite sure what she wants, but she's asked if I can hang around.'

'That's great then. See if you can get her to talk. So far all we have on Jenny Lister is that she's a cross between Saint Teresa and Gandhi. With about as much of a love life.'

'Yeah,' Holly was enthusiastic, glad to have something to get her teeth into. 'Her husband left when Hannah was a baby. There must have been men in her life since then. I mean, that was years ago.'

She seemed not to realize there was anything cruel in

the comment, and Vera let it go. Vera had never had a man in her life. What would Holly have made of that?

Anne Mason lived halfway up a hill looking down over the valley, where Barnard Bridge village ran the length of the burn. Vera didn't much like this sort of barn conversion— a massive structure that left you with echoing spaces and an exposed roof. The design reminded Vera of a church, and where would you put all your junk if you didn't have an attic? She could see Anne's place from the beginning of the narrow lane, which branched off the main road a couple of miles out of the village. The lane ran along the Tyne for a while and her view was hidden by woodland. Then the car emerged into open countryside and she saw the building again, the milky sun reflected from the glass that had replaced the wide barn doors.

Anne Mason didn't seem to be the sort of woman who would collect much junk. She was slight and fine with small hands, sensible short grey hair. She was still wearing the cotton trousers and walking boots in which she'd travelled.

They sat in stylish Scandinavian chairs looking down at the valley.

'We got Simon's phone call when we were driving up the A1. I can't believe it. Jenny of all people.' There was a rucksack on the polished wooden floor close to the door. Occasionally she would glance at it and Vera could tell that, despite her friend's death, it irked her not to be unpacking immediately. She was a woman who would hate untidiness, unfinished business. Unbidden, a phrase from the Elias Jones report came into Vera's head: *Michael hates clutter.* The women weren't soulmates then. Jenny's house had been comfortably cluttered; it wouldn't have bothered *her* to go off to work with a couple of mucky plates on the counter.

'Where's your husband now?' Vera asked. If Jenny had gone on holiday with them both in the past, the man might have something useful to contribute.

'He's gone to collect our dog from the kennel.' Anne gave an apologetic grin. 'We don't have children. The dog's our baby.'

The lower floor of the barn was open-plan, a big wood-burning stove at one end and the kitchen at the other, all shiny black granite and stainless steel.

'What does he do for a living?' *This place wasn't bought on a teacher's wage.*

'He's an architect. This was his project.' She smiled again, waited for the anticipated compliment.

'Lovely,' Vera said, with no attempt to pretend that she meant it. 'Now, what can you tell me about Jenny Lister? I understand that you were close friends.'

'Very. We met about ten years ago. I was teaching in Hannah's primary school—I'm still there, for my sins. Jenny joined the PTA. We'd share lifts back to the village after meetings, took to calling into the pub for a drink afterwards, and found we had lots of interests in common: film, theatre, books. The friendship developed from there.'

'How often did you meet?'

'At least once a week. Wednesday was our night. We were both so busy that it was easier to keep one evening free. Sometimes we'd go out—we'd always do the RSC, for example, when they came to Newcastle; occasionally there'd be something we'd fancy at the Sage. Recently we took a six-week basic flamenco course, great fun, though Jenny was much better at it than I was. Usually we'd just stay in the village. Supper here or at her house. A walk in the summer, if the weather was good.' Anne suddenly looked stricken, and Vera saw that she was thinking there'd be no more companionable Wednesday evenings. Nothing to look forward to, to break up the week. Then no doubt she'd felt guilty for being so selfish. Vera had always thought guilt an overrated emotion.

'Did she talk to you about the Elias Jones murder?'

'Not in any detail. She was very professional about her work. When there was all the publicity—the stuff in the papers laying into social workers—I could tell she was having a bad time. I asked her once why she did it. I mean, teaching isn't the easiest job in the world, but you'd have to be mad to go into social work, wouldn't you? You get all the blame and none of the credit.' Anne paused, and looked out of the huge glass window towards the village. 'Jenny just said she loved it. It was the one thing she was good at. Not true, of course: she was good at lots of things. She was a brilliant mother.' Another pause. 'And a wonderful friend.'

'What *did* you talk about then?' Vera was struggling to imagine it. These two middle-aged, middle-class women spending all that time together. Wouldn't they just run out of things to say? She'd never had that sort of friendship. She was growing quite close to the hippy-dippy neighbours who had the smallholding next to her house in the hills. Some evenings they got pissed together on her whisky and their dreadful home-made wine. She'd help them when the sheep needed clipping or the hens had escaped. But to spend hours, just talking . . .

'Recently, I suppose, it was me talking and her listening.' Anne seemed strained suddenly, and Vera thought now that she'd been tense throughout the conversation. It wasn't just that her best friend had been murdered. Perhaps she was that sort of woman – nervous, anxious. Perhaps that was why she'd chosen to spend her professional career teaching well-brought-up bairns in a pleasant rural school. She wouldn't manage stress of any kind.

Anne took a deep breath and continued, 'Recently my marriage has been going through a bad patch. Sort of mid-life crisis, I suppose. I was attracted to a new member of staff at school. Nothing happened, not really, but feeling like a besotted teenager unsettled me. Jenny made me see how ridiculous I was being. She said that John and I had just built this place, spent years getting it perfect and, having achieved it, everything seemed like an anticlimax. I was just looking for something exciting. I'm sure she was right.'

God, Vera thought, *what self-indulgent drivel. I'd rather spend time with an honest criminal any day than with this introspective woman.*

'She was going to come to France with us this time, but she decided not to. She said John and I needed some time to ourselves. She was that sort of friend.'

'What about *her*?' Vera said briskly. 'Did she have any men friends?'

'I'm not sure.'

So, it seemed the confidences had all gone one way. Jenny had been happy to listen to her friend talking about her adolescent crush, but had given nothing in return. Discretion, it seemed, was a part of her personal as well as her professional life. What secrets did she have to hide?

'Recently I thought there might have been someone,' Anne said suddenly. 'She cancelled one of our Wednesday nights at the last minute, without a proper excuse. And she seemed very happy. Glowing.'

'Didn't you ask her what was going on?' Now Vera was really starting to lose patience. This woman was sounding like a soppy story from a magazine.

'She said she was in a relationship, but she couldn't talk about it,' Anne said.

'Where did she meet her mystery lover?' Vera couldn't help herself. 'The flamenco class?'

'No!' Anne seemed shocked by the thought. 'No, really, I don't think so. And if she had, why wouldn't she tell me?'

'Why all the secrecy then?'

'I thought maybe she'd started seeing a colleague.' Anne looked awkward. 'Or a married man.'

So, not such a saint after all.

Driving down the narrow track towards the village, Vera was pleased. It was as if she was rediscovering the Jenny Lister of the welcoming little house and the charming daughter. Vera had always been more comfortable with sinners.

Lost in her thoughts, she had to stop suddenly to let a tractor past. She pulled off the road and saw the gateposts with the carved cormorants' heads that she'd first noticed in the painting on Veronica's wall. The vegetation had grown up around them and they wouldn't have been visible from the road. On impulse Vera switched off the engine and got out of the car. She walked down the grass track between the pillars, through a spinney of alder and birch. There were wood anemones and violets, the colours very bright in the shaft of sunlight that shot through the trees. Then the woodland stopped and she saw where the house must once have stood.

There were still the remains of a formal garden, wide terraces and a walled patch where vegetables had been grown, where the skeleton of a greenhouse still leaned against the wall, but the brick and stone of the house had all been removed. Old dressed stone would be worth a fortune here in the Tyne valley. Why had the land never been sold? Did Veronica own it, or some other branch of the family? This would be a developer's dream location. Perhaps it was in a conservation area and building was prohibited.

Grand stone steps led through the middle of the grass terraces. She walked down them, feeling as if she'd walked onto a film set. There was a series of statues on either side. Chipped and covered in lichen, they were mostly of strange mythical creatures. Some were hidden by ivy and a few had disappeared under a tangle of bramble. On one of the terraces there was the huge empty bowl of a fountain.

Looking down towards the river, she saw a pool. Trying to remember far-off geography lessons, Vera thought that perhaps the course of the river had changed over time and this lake had been left. Beside it, quite intact, was the boathouse, about which Veronica had spoken. It was made of wood that had recently been varnished; a deck on stilts was built out over the water. No boats were kept inside it now; the window was glazed and there were red-and-white curtains. A couple of dinghies, upended, lay beside it. Vera imagined it would be the perfect spot for grand family picnics, pictured Veronica presiding over a wicker hamper, trying to recapture the glory of her grandfather's home.

Walking back to the car, she felt almost sorry for the woman.

Chapter Thirteen

Outside Connie Masters's cottage, Ashworth hesitated for a moment to look at her car; it was pulled into the verge, so the cow parsley and the long grass had been flattened. A silver Micra seven years old, with a distinctive bump on the offside wing. He wrote down the registration number. If there was CCTV at the car park where she'd claimed to have left it in Hexham the previous day, it might be possible to rule her out of the inquiry altogether.

He checked his voicemail. Vera had left a message saying she was meeting Jenny Lister's boss for lunch. No orders or requests. Maybe she was mellowing with age. Then he rang back to the station to ask for the CCTV tapes of the Hexham car park to be picked up. Giving his own orders. *God, am I turning into Vera Stanhope?* The idea made him smile. Nobody else on Earth was anything like Vera.

At the Willows he met Charlie, who was on his way out, saw him from a distance leaving the hotel, his back bent and his hands in his jacket pocket. A posture like that, Ashworth thought, he'd have chronic back pain by the time he was sixty. Standing by Charlie's car, chatting, Ashworth was aware that they were visible from the public areas in the hotel. Even though they couldn't be overheard he felt awkward, as if he were on a stage and being stared at by a hostile audience, and he kept the conversation brief.

'Any joy?'

Charlie shrugged. 'I showed Lister's photo to the workers who came on duty this morning. A couple vaguely recognized her as someone who used the swimming pool, but nothing more than that. You'd have thought one of them would have had some contact with her, had a bit of a chat. The records showed she came swimming at least once a week.'

'I don't know. These places are all very impersonal.' Joe Ashworth had joined a gym the year before, in his local-authority leisure centre, though, not a smart place like this. He'd been there for an hour each session, but plugged into his Walkman, he'd hardly spoken to the other people. Unconsciously he ran a hand over his belly. Definitely running to flab. Since the new baby he hadn't had much time for getting fit.

'I reckon she must have been killed more than an hour before the body was found,' Charlie said. 'After nine-thirty, there's an off-peak membership deal and that's when all the older people turn up. Before then it's the serious swimmers. They do lengths up and down the pool before work. Concentrated stuff. You get the impression they wouldn't notice anything happening outside the water, and they don't usually have time for the sauna or steam room.'

'And before nine-thirty there isn't the same staff supervision.' Ashworth remembered his conversation with Lisa.

Charlie got into his car and wound down the window to have a fag before driving away.

Inside, Ashworth went straight to Ryan Taylor's office. Both the hotel and the leisure club were open again now, though the place seemed quieter than Ashworth might have expected. Perhaps murder wasn't good for business after all. A young woman was vacuuming the carpet in the lobby. No sign of Danny, but then he didn't start until the afternoons. Ashworth wondered how the student spent his days. At home catching up on work for university, or out with his friends?

He thought again how cool the murderer must have been to have killed Jenny while all the other people were just feet away, even if they were ploughing up and down the pool. Or was the killing opportunistic? A madman after all, just wanting to feel the exhilaration of taking another life.

Taylor was on the phone, his office door ajar, and Ashworth waited for him to complete the call before tapping on the glass and walking in. The manager was frowning.

'That was another cancellation,' he said. 'A conference booked in for next week. They said they couldn't take the risk of bringing clients here. What's wrong with them all? Do they think the murderer's still here, prowling the corridors and waiting to get them?'

'Maybe not.' Ashworth took a seat. 'But they ought to know you've got a petty thief causing problems. Why didn't you tell me about the stealing?'

'You can't think that's relevant to the killing.' Taylor fiddled with the knot of his tie, looked out of the window, refused to catch Ashworth's eye.

'That's not for you to judge. I need to know what's been going on here.'

'A few things had gone missing.' Today Taylor seemed to have lost his boyish energy. He was tired, washed-out. Were the cares of management finally getting to him? 'Mostly from the staffroom. It happens. I'm on top of it.'

'What are you doing to stop it?' Taylor didn't answer and Ashworth continued: 'So you were just hoping the problem would go away?'

'Look, another few days and Louise, the manager, will be back from leave. She's paid to deal with staff problems. Let her sort it out. I don't have the authority to hire and fire.'

'That's not quite true, is it?' Ashworth tried to sound sympathetic. 'You hired Danny Shaw, and the thieving started with his arrival. Tricky for you when you don't have any proof either way.'

'That was a temporary appointment in an emergency.' Taylor was starting to get rattled—not, Ashworth thought, because of these questions, but because he knew he'd have to justify himself to his boss when she returned. 'Danny goes back to university in less than a week.'

'And you don't want to upset his mum,' Ashworth said. 'Seemed like a strong woman. I wouldn't want to cross her.' And that was true enough, he thought, remembering dark-haired Karen with the quick tongue and the angry eyes.

They sat for a moment in silence.

'You do see how important it could be?' Ashworth said at last. 'If Jenny caught someone stealing, they could have killed her to shut her up.'

'You wouldn't kill someone over something as small as that?' Taylor was defensive now, flushed, a schoolboy being reprimanded for some foolishness, not having the sense just to sit and take it.

'Oh, believe me,' Ashworth said, 'it happens.' And into his mind came pathetic acts of violence: a broken glass slashing through a face to the bone because of an imagined insult, a woman beaten to death because her ironing hadn't come up to scratch, a small boy drowned in a bath because his mother fancied herself in love. 'So I need to know exactly what's been going on here: what items have been taken and when. And I need you to tell me who you think is behind it.'

In the end Taylor was more helpful than Ashworth had expected. At least he'd recorded every incident, every complaint brought to him, entered it in a rolling report on his PC.

'So who's the culprit?' Ashworth asked after he'd read through the printout, seen the list of stolen cash, the watches, the earrings and beads. There was no individual item of great value, but it added up. 'You must have your suspicions. Do you think Danny's behind it?'

'I don't see that. He's a bit of a lad and not a brilliant cleaner, but he's not stupid. He's got too much to lose for the sake of a couple of bits of tat that would make a few quid sold on. No, I don't see him as a thief.'

'Who then?'

Taylor looked awkward. 'The other staff think Lisa's the culprit.'

'Because she lives in the west end and her dad has a criminal record.' Ashworth hoped Lisa hadn't been sneaking into the staffroom, slipping her hand into pockets and handbags. He'd liked her, and he believed his judgement about people was OK. Vera always laughed at that and called him naive. *We're all capable of violence, Joey, if we're pushed to it. Even you.*

'Not just that,' Taylor said. 'She keeps herself to herself. She's a bit prim. The others meet up outside work, drinking, partying. She never does. They'd rather blame her for the thefts. Easier than thinking it might be one of their mates.' He paused. 'I did wonder . . .'

'Yes?'

'If it was all a set-up to get rid of her. It's weird how sometimes they take against people. They make her life hell, actually. Petty digs. Insults. I can't think of any one thing that she might have done to offend them. It's just like they want someone to hate. The women are the worst. Like they blame Lisa for anything that goes wrong in the place. Like Lisa doesn't have any feelings. I think she's amazing for sticking it out.'

'Is that why you didn't tell me about this yesterday? Because you thought it was the staff making trouble for Lisa? That it was just a trick to get her the sack?' Ashworth wondered if maybe Taylor fancied the girl, if she brought out the protective male in him. Or was he embarrassed by the petty cruelties of his colleagues?

'The thing with Lisa has been horrible. I don't think there's a ringleader. No one person stirring up bother; it's more a strange sort of herd mentality. It's kept me awake at nights. Louise, my boss, won't do anything about it. She wants to be part of the gang too. Pathetic! I was hoping I might deal with the problem while she was on holiday, but I only seemed to make things worse.' He looked up at Ashworth, relieved at last to be able to confide about the problem that had obviously been haunting him. 'When that woman was killed yesterday I was pleased. Dreadful, isn't it? But I thought it would give them all something else to gossip about. Take the heat off Lisa for a while.'

'When did all this nastiness against Lisa start? Since Danny began working here?'

'God no! Long before that. On her first day at work. Something she said, or something in her attitude, just turned them against her.'

'And you really think they might have orchestrated the thefts to force her out?' It seemed to Ashworth to be ridiculously far-fetched. But if you had a load of people cooped up in a place like this, bored by their work and by each other, perhaps they would create a drama just to bring some excitement to their working lives. A conspiracy to make them feel they belonged.

Taylor shrugged. 'Or to get rid of me. I'm not their most popular person either.'

'Why are you so interested in Lisa?' Ashworth asked. 'Are you going out with her?' He still wondered if the man was exaggerating the problem, his judgement clouded because of a romantic attachment.

Taylor laughed, glad to relieve the tension. 'Hardly! I'm already spoken for. My partner's called Paul and we share a flat in Jesmond. I don't fancy Lisa, but I like her. She's a bloody good worker. And brave. She needs somebody on her side.'

Chapter Fourteen

Connie flattened herself against the wall of the post office to let a livestock lorry down the narrow main road of the village. There was a campaign to get a bypass for Barnard Bridge, but nobody really thought it would happen. Outside the hall, waiting again for the end of playgroup, she thought: *Twenty-four hours ago I was standing here and I didn't know Jenny Lister was dead.* She ran through her conversation with the young detective. Had she hit the right tone? It was important that he believed her. She couldn't stand the idea of more publicity, of having to face the same intrusive questions from prying officials. She hadn't told him everything of course, that would have been impossible. Even now, she hated the idea of appearing a fool.

Veronica Eliot made her way along the street, looking very much the country lady in smart brown trousers and a tweed jacket. She'd parked her car outside the old school. Even from a distance Connie could make out the signature, rather incongruous red lips and red nails. A vampire in cashmere and green Hunter wellies. *Why do I hate her so much?*

As Veronica approached, Connie braced herself for the icy stare or the barbed comment, the chin in the air as she stalked past, but instead the older woman stopped. She hesitated, uncertain for the first time since Connie had met her. It was still early and there were no other parents around, nobody to witness the meeting.

Connie took a brief moment of pleasure in the woman's discomfort and said nothing.

'You'll have heard about Mrs Lister.' For Veronica, this was tentative. It didn't sound like a challenge, or even an attempt to fish for information, which was what Connie had been expecting. She'd felt sure Veronica would have noticed the strange car outside her cottage, and Ashworth was so obviously a detective that Veronica must have guessed there'd been a visitation from the police. She'd want to know all about that.

'Of course,' Connie said. 'It was on the local news last night.'

'You must have known her. She'd have been a colleague of yours?'

'Yes.'

'Such a terrible shock,' Veronica said, at last recovering something of her poise. 'I didn't know her well, but our children are friends. Have you heard if the police have made any headway in their investigation?'

So she was fishing after all. Or was it just that her desire for gossip outweighed her dislike of Connie?

'They'd hardly be likely to confide in me, would they?' Connie felt some of her old strength returning and gave a little laugh to prove it.

'I suppose not, but I thought you'd still have friends in social services. They might have some idea what's going on—' Veronica broke off as a group of mothers walked towards them, then added hurriedly: 'Look, why don't you come to lunch. Nothing special. Bring your little girl.' And she hurried away to greet the gathering women, without waiting for an answer. Watching her, Connie thought she looked like one of the wading birds you see on the beach, her head tipping forward to prod the mud, not for worms, but for information. She didn't acknowledge Connie's presence again during the ritual collection of the children, but Connie wondered if the only reason she was there was to have offered the invitation.

She was determined not to go. How dare the woman issue what was close to a summons and expect her just to fall in with the request. But holding Alice by the hand and leading her back through the village, she found herself overwhelmed by curiosity. Not just about what Veronica might want of her, but about the woman's life and family. That social worker's compulsion, the need to delve into other people's lives. And lunch had been offered. Connie hadn't been shopping for days and there was nothing much to eat in the cottage. She saw Veronica drive past in her Range Rover and wondered what it would be like to belong to her crowd, to be provided for by a rich husband, to live in a big house and drive a big car. There was a moment of envy. *I want some of that.*

She'd only seen the house from the lane and it felt like an intrusion to go through the big wooden gates and up to the front door. It wasn't very old or even very grand. A solid square box, built—Connie would guess—in the Fifties, rendered and whitewashed, the silhouette softened by creeper growing along one corner, impressive only because of the large garden. It would have looked more in place in a smart city suburb. A pretend country house for a pretend country lady. Connie felt a moment of superiority: at least her tiny cottage had authenticity. It had been there for hundreds of years and had grown out of the landscape. It was mouldy and dark, but it had style.

Alice was quiet. Playgroup always wore her out. She didn't even ask why they weren't going straight home. What would Connie have answered? *Mummy wants to know her enemy.*

The front door opened and Veronica was standing there. Did she want to hurry Connie inside before her friends could see that they were fraternizing? Was fraternizing even a word you could use for women? Lack of sleep and the events of the previous day had left Connie light-headed. She felt as if she'd been drinking and other strange thoughts chased through her mind. Nobody knew

she was here. One woman from the village had been murdered already. Was she the next intended victim? She
found herself smiling at the idea of Veronica as killer, at
the image of the sharp red nails ripping into soft flesh.

'Thank you for coming along.'

Veronica had got her way and now she was concilia-
tory. Connie walked into a hall with a polished parquet
floor, flowers in a big copper bowl on a little table, paintings. In pride of place the graduation photograph of a dark
young man in cap and gown.

'I've put out some lunch in the kitchen.' And an effort
had been made. There was a salad—'the first leaves from
the cold frame'—cold meat, a local pâté and Northumberland goat's cheese. A loaf from the Rothbury bakery.
White wine chilling in the fridge. For Alice, little sausages,
carrot sticks and a home-made cake. Had Veronica spent
the morning planning this, or was her larder always
packed with goodies?

*She wants more than bits of gossip to pass on to her
friends.*

But despite herself, Connie found she was feeling
grateful for the attention. Her fight had gone. She could
think of nothing nicer than sitting here in this light, white
kitchen drinking cold wine while Veronica found old toys
for Alice to play with: Dinky Toys that had belonged not
just to her son but to his father, a wooden jigsaw puzzle
and a bucket of plastic bricks.

'Is your husband still working away?' It was the ordinary stuff of conversation, but Veronica looked at her, as
if she were searching for a deeper meaning to the question, some slight or sarcasm. She must have been
reassured because she answered almost immediately.

'Yes, a conference in Rotterdam.'

'But your son's home for the Easter holidays?' Connie
thought the art of social intercourse wasn't so hard after
all. The skill was coming back to her.

Again there was a pause, a quick appraising glance. No answer this time, but Veronica had a question of her own. 'Did you know Simon, my son, was going out with Jenny Lister's daughter?'

'No!' Connie took a while to process the information. The photo on Jenny's desk had been of a slight, red-haired child, but of course now she'd be older, a young woman. 'How dreadful all this must be for her! I never met her, but I had the impression that she and Jenny were very close.'

Veronica reached over and poured a little more wine into her visitor's glass. 'I suppose you went to visit Jenny. You were almost neighbours after all.' Connie saw she was drinking very little herself.

'No! I didn't even know she lived in the village.' *If I say it often enough, will people believe me?*

Veronica did seem to believe her, because suddenly she relaxed and gave a thin, wide smile, a red crescent tipped on its back. 'Ah, so you weren't good friends then.'

'I don't think Jenny made friends with anyone she worked with. A deliberate choice to keep home and work separate.'

'Very wise. That's my husband's philosophy too. I know hardly anyone from his office.'

She sounded wistful and Connie thought how bored and lonely Veronica must be. Her son independent and no longer needy, her husband never at home. No wonder she haunted the playgroup committee and the WI. How else could she believe herself useful? Connie almost felt sorry for her, then she remembered the hostile glares from the playgroup mothers, the snide remarks. She couldn't forgive so easily after all.

Veronica continued: 'I host dinner parties, of course, for his clients, but that's rather different. That's just an extension of his work. As if he'd moved the office here for the night.' At last she poured herself a full glass of wine. A pale light from the garden shone through it and gave it a greenish tinge. 'I don't mind. I'm glad to support him.'

'Work followed me home rather uncomfortably over the past couple of years.' Connie turned her attention from the glass to Veronica. She'd decided she wasn't ready to let this woman off the hook entirely, that after all she couldn't exchange months of catty comments for a peaceful lunch. 'There was no rest from it and no escape. I'd hoped there'd be some respite after I moved here, but of course the scandal followed me. People who only knew part of the story were very unkind.'

'People felt very strongly,' Veronica said. 'They always do when there's a child involved.' The response was sharp and swift.

'I made a mistake at work.' *Why did she feel the need to justify herself?* 'Other people, who earn a load more money than I ever did, make mistakes at work, but they don't get their picture all over the newspapers.'

'But a child died!' It came out as a wail and Connie thought this was more personal. Veronica's campaign against her hadn't just been the interference of a busybody. Had she lost a baby, had a miscarriage, a stillbirth? Alice, startled by the noise, looked up from her game. Seeing the women, still apparently in friendly conversation at the table, she returned to it.

'Yes,' Connie said quietly. 'A child died. And I've thought about that every day since. I didn't need you to remind me.'

They sat for a moment in silence. Outside, the sun slid from behind thin cloud and there was a startling light, brilliant on the damp grass, making all the colours garish and unreal. Veronica stood up and opened a window and the sudden sound of a blackbird outside seemed almost deafening.

'I worry about Simon,' she said. 'I don't want him caught up in all this. He has an academic career ahead of him. He insists on staying with Hannah at the house. I've invited her here, but she says she wants to feel close to her mother. That seems morbid. Her father has said she should stay with him, but she won't go.'

Connie didn't know what to say. *I'm the last person to give you advice about your child.* Alice, suddenly bored, got up from the floor and climbed onto her mother's knee. She put her thumb in her mouth and was almost asleep. Connie stroked her forehead. She was aware of Veronica watching them, almost greedily.

'How lucky you are!' Veronica said. 'It's a lovely age.'

Conventional words, but with such force behind them that Connie felt uncomfortable. She could tell Veronica longed to hold a small child in her arms. She was about to come out with something easy and meaningless: *Perhaps there'll be grandchildren before too long.* But even as the words were forming in her head she knew they would be no consolation. Veronica wanted a child of her own. Flesh and blood, immediate and not once-removed. Subconsciously Connie found herself holding Alice a little tighter.

'Let's have some coffee!' Veronica got to her feet and the tension was broken. Connie thought she was letting her imagination run away with her. It was the stress of the past day, and it had never been a good idea to drink at lunchtime. Now Alice was properly asleep. Connie shifted her weight so that she had a hand free to hold the mug. The smell of the coffee was wonderful, reminded her suddenly of her first holiday in France with Frank. A cafe in the Cévennes. Heat and dust and a post-sex languor.

'I'm so glad we had this conversation.' Veronica was sitting very close now, her face poking forward, with the prodding, wading-bird mannerism Connie had noticed earlier. 'I'm so glad we've sorted things out.'

Connie was confused. What had been sorted?

'You must come again. Bring Alice to play in the garden. And if you need a babysitter, you only have to ask.'

Connie finished the coffee and stood up, setting Alice on her feet. 'Come on, sweetie, it's time to go. Wake up, or you'll never sleep tonight.' She felt the need to escape the house, and the woman whose switch of attitude was incomprehensible. At the front door she paused. She wanted to end the encounter with a normal exchange, not the sense that she was running away.

'By the way, did that man find you?'

Veronica frowned. 'What man?'

'Yesterday lunchtime someone turned up at the cottage, asking for you. Young, charming. I wasn't sure if you were in, but I pointed him in the right direction.'

'Oh.' With a supreme effort Veronica turned on a smile. 'I expect it was a friend of Simon's.' But before that, Connie had seen her look at Alice with the same hungry desperation.

Chapter Fifteen

Late afternoon Vera called the whole team together for a meeting in the incident room. Tea, and iced buns from the bakery over the road. So much was going on in this case that she needed to keep a fix on the strands of the investigation. Once, she'd been interviewed for the *Police Gazette* and asked for the most important attribute of a good senior detective. She'd answered 'concentration'. If she couldn't keep the various possible scenarios in her head, she couldn't expect her staff to keep on top of things.

Holly had been reluctant to come in when Vera had phoned her: 'I think I should stay here. Hannah's falling apart and we've developed a great relationship.'

Vera had insisted. 'You're doing her no favours if you make her dependent on you. Great for your ego, but a bastard for her. And we have to know what you've found out from her. You can go back later if you have to, but get a family liaison officer to take over tomorrow. They're trained for that work, and you're not.'

So Holly was there, an overnight bag at her feet, a badge that she was needed. *Loving* feeling indispensable, Vera could tell, despite the warning. Charlie was already into his second bun, a smudge of icing on his nose, crumbs down the front of his jacket. And Ashworth was frowning as he checked through his notes, looking almost grown-up. Vera wasn't sure his extra family responsibilities were good for him. He'd lost his sense of fun, his joy in his work. She'd lost her playmate.

'OK,' she said, calling them to attention, poised in front of the whiteboard with the thick, black marker in her hand. 'Let's see what you know. Holly? Have we found out any more about Jenny's private life? I see the search team's been through the house. Any news on that?'

Holly pushed her hair away from her face and pretended not to like the attention. 'Hannah doesn't know anything about a recent boyfriend. She says there've been men in the past. One guy who worked for the National Park. According to Hannah, he was besotted, but Jenny dumped him about a year ago. Hannah was surprised; she'd thought her mother was keen too. Since then, nothing.'

'You've got the name of this man?' Vera knew Holly would have. Holly was ambitious and knew better than to leave herself open to criticism.

'Sure. Lawrence May. Age: late forties. Divorced. No kids. They went walking and birdwatching together.' Vera thought Hector, her father, might have known him. Hector had been keen on birds too, but best of all he'd liked killing and stuffing them. When she'd taken over his house in the hills she'd found the freezer full of corpses waiting for his attention. As a taxidermist on the shady side of legal, he'd have seen May as the enemy. A lily-livered robin-stroker without any idea of what the countryside was all about.

'Spoken to him?'

'Not yet.'

Of course not. She'd been too busy playing Mother Teresa with the girl.

'Get onto it first thing tomorrow.' Vera looked at the plate of buns and saw it was empty. Her fault. She should have known better than to leave it within reach of Charlie. 'Did the search team turn up anything interesting from her home or her office?'

'The team found her laptop at home,' Holly said. 'If she's still in touch with Lawrence May, there should be emails. There was an electronic diary on it, but that was mostly work. IT is sorting through the rest now.'

'We still haven't found her handbag,' Vera said. 'A woman like that, surely she'd have a handbag. Probably a briefcase too. Holly, can you ask Hannah? She'd know what her mother usually carried her stuff around in.'

Holly nodded, but Vera could tell that her mind wasn't on such mundane details. She was still thinking about bringing comfort to the girl.

'According to her best mate, there was a new man in her life,' Vera said. 'A secret lover. If she'd started going out with May again, no reason surely why she'd keep it secret.'

'Unless she just wanted to see how it worked out before going public,' Joe Ashworth chipped in. Sometimes Vera thought he represented her feminine side. He had the empathy and she had the muscle. Well, the bulk. Muscle, she had to admit, was sorely lacking. 'She wouldn't want to make a fool of herself, announce they were an item again, only for it all to fall apart.'

'The friend thought the new bloke might be married,' Vera said. 'Something to keep in mind. We haven't got much else as a motive.'

'Except for the Elias Jones case.' Charlie still had his mouth full. 'Lots of hatred stirred up over that.'

'So let's look at that again.' Vera wrote the child's name on the whiteboard. 'How far have we got with it? Joe, you spoke to the social worker, the one that was pilloried in the press. Connie Masters. Do we think she killed her boss?'

'She claims she didn't even know Lister was living in the village.'

'And do we believe her?' *Come on, Joe. Commit your-self.*

'Yeah,' he said and she wanted to cheer. Joe Ashworth spent so much of his time sitting on the fence that he should have a blister on his arse. 'At first it seems impossible—a place that small and they've not bumped into each other—but Masters has only been living there for a few months, and Lister would be out all day at work. The times when she might be around, in the evenings, Connie Masters is at home with her bairn.'

'They didn't socialize at all when they were working together?' Holly liked her evenings in the pub with the lads when a case was closed. Liked being fancied.

'Apparently not. Not Jenny's way of working. She liked to keep home and the office separate.'

'Still seems a bit of a coincidence . . .' Holly pushing it.

'The boss asked me what I thought, and I'm telling you.' They glared at each other, the two bright kids in the school vying to be top of the class.

'Have we tracked down Michael Morgan yet?' Vera asked. Sometimes the rivalry between the younger members of her team amused her, but now she needed them to pull together and focus. Then, when everyone looked at her as if they didn't have an idea what she was talking about, she added sharply: 'Mattie Jones's boyfriend. The man she fell for, the man she'll have us believe she killed for. The man who became a sort of stepdad to Elias. So far, all I know about him is that he was weird. I might be wrong here, but aren't we looking for weird? Do we know if he's still sticking pins into people for a living? I guess he'd have to have a basic knowledge of anatomy if he trained as an acupuncturist. Might come in handy if you wanted to strangle a fit, healthy woman. I don't suppose we've checked if he was a member of the Willows.'

She was glad that they looked sheepish, though she was as guilty as they were of having forgotten about Mattie's lover. She'd concentrated, as they had, on Jenny Lister's private life.

'I want that information first thing tomorrow,' she said. 'Address, recent employment history and cross-check with the Willows' membership. But don't make contact yet. We need to know more about him first. I have the impression he's a slippery kind of character. I'll maybe take a trip to Durham and chat to Mattie before we make a move on him.'

'She's not there.' She hadn't been sure Charlie had even been listening, but now he chipped in, a great smirk all over his face.

'What do you mean?'

'Mattie Jones isn't in Durham nick.'

'Where is she then?' Vera glared at him. All the female lifers in the region were sent to the high-security wing in Durham. And Vera couldn't stand her team playing games at her expense.

'Hospital.' Charlie was almost apologetic now. 'Appendicitis. She was taken in as an emergency the day before yesterday. Picked up some sort of infection and she's still there.'

'I'd best buy a nice bag of grapes then. She'll be ready for a visit.'

There was a moment of silence. Vera was suddenly aware of how tired everyone was. A day into the investigation and there was already too much information. Nothing here was simple. She needed to raise the energy level and hold their attention. Maybe they could all do with a swim or a workout at the gym. She grinned at the thought of Charlie on a treadmill.

'The Willows,' she said. 'What do we have from there?'

'I reckon Lister must have been killed before nine-thirty,' Charlie said.

'The pathologist won't be that specific.'

'Don't care,' he said. 'Nine-thirty the cheap deal starts, and that's when all the wrinklies and the yummy mummies turn up. They stand around chatting as much as swimming. Most of the old folk blind as bats without their specs in the pool, which is why it took so long for anyone to realize the woman was dead, but the killer wouldn't have known that. Before nine-thirty it's the business people, in for a quick swim before work. No lifeguard on duty, according to Joe. I chatted to the staff. Hardly any of the early-morning swimmers use the steam room. They're in too much of a rush.'

'Makes sense,' Vera conceded. Sometimes you had to throw Charlie a scrap of praise to keep him motivated.

'There've been reports of petty thieving.' This was Ashworth wanting to move things to a close. Vera saw him take a quick look at the clock on the wall. His missus always gave him a hard time when he wasn't back in time to see the kids before bedtime. 'Could be a motive, if Lister saw one of them stealing.'

'Who's the main suspect?'

'They've accused Lisa, the lass from the west end, but the assistant manager reckons she's just a scapegoat. My money's on Danny, the student. The thefts only started after he got the temporary work, and he's an arrogant sort of bastard. You could see he'd think he'd get away with it. His boss thinks he wouldn't risk his future career for a few trinkets, but I'm not so sure. He's a chancer.'

Vera suddenly longed for a drink. Beer, she thought. There were a few cans of Speckled Hen left in the larder at home. If he behaved himself, she might even give one to Joe Ashworth. Her place was on his way home. Almost.

'Seems to me we have three separate areas of enquiry,' she said briskly. 'First, Jenny Lister's private life. We need to trace her secret lover. Why was she so desperate to keep him secret? If he's married, we could be looking at a jealous wife. Then there's the Elias Jones case. Is it relevant to the present investigation? If so, how? And finally, the thefts at the Willows. Doesn't seem much of a motive, but people have killed for less.'

She winced at the cliché, but her team seemed happy enough with her summary. They'd have been happy whatever she'd said. They were bored now by all the talking and just wanted to get out of the room.

*

Ashworth took less persuading than she'd expected to come back with her for a drink. Perhaps he preferred to arrive home when the chaos of bath and bedtime was over, when the house was quiet and he could have his wife to himself. Joe liked to think of himself as a perfect family man, but everyone was allowed his little self-deception. It was a still evening, and dusk when they arrived at Vera's house. She got out of her car and smelled gorse flowers and damp foliage and cows. If Hector had given her nothing else, he had given her this house and she would always be grateful to him for that. During this investigation, with all the talk of parenting, she'd found herself thinking about him, and it came to her suddenly that he was an easy scapegoat. She blamed him for all the ills in her life and that might not be quite fair. Hector might be the cause of *most* of them, but not all.

She lit the fire already laid in the grate, not because it was particularly cold, but because the rest of the room was a mess and it would give them something to look at. And because she knew Joe liked it. Her neighbours had bartered half a lamb for a load of apple logs with a guy in the Borders and had donated her some of the wood; she'd arrived home one night and found the logs neatly stacked in the lean-to at the back of her house. The couple were capable of these acts of kindness and she was grateful they were there, happily tolerated the occasional solstice party when dozens of odd people set up camp on the field in front of her house, turned a blind eye to their dope-smoking—even when it happened, thoughtlessly, in her home.

Vera left the curtains undrawn and fetched beer from the kitchen, a loaf of bread on a board, a lump of cheese. They sat on the two low chairs, their feet to the fire. Vera thought this was as happy as she would ever get.

Ashworth broke into her thoughts. 'What do you make of this Elias Jones connection? Important or just a distraction?'

She considered for a moment, felt the metallic taste of beer and can on her tongue. 'Important anyway,' she said. 'I mean, even if it doesn't provide a direct motive. Because it tells us a lot about Jenny Lister.'

'Like?'

'She was efficient, organized. A control freak. She didn't like mixing home and work. Principled. Principles don't always make you popular. If she caught someone doing something she considered wrong, she wouldn't keep quiet about it.'

'You're thinking about the thefts at the Willows?'

Vera took time to consider that one. 'Maybe, though it seems very petty. More likely something going on in the village.' She was thinking about Veronica Eliot and her pristine house and her model family. Nothing was ever that perfect, so what, exactly, was happening under the surface?

Ashworth looked at his watch.

'It's all right, Joe,' she said indulgently. 'You're safe to go home now. The bairns'll be in bed. Tomorrow, prise Holly away from the daughter and see if one of you can track down Jenny's secret lover. A village that size, someone will know. They'll have seen a strange car, bumped into them in Hexham.'

He stood up. His face was red from the fire. Or maybe the dig about the children had struck home. 'What about you?'

She didn't move. He could find his own way out. 'Me, like I said, I'm going hospital visiting.

Chapter Sixteen

Mattie was in a side-ward; a female prison officer sat in the corner with a pile of fashion magazines on her lap and a bag of Maltesers in her hand. *God*, Vera thought. *I bet the woman can't believe her luck. All this time off the wing!* The officer looked about the same age as the patient in the bed, she was a dirty blonde and big-busted, the buttons straining on her white uniform shirt. Easy-going, the sort who'd really enjoy a good night out and a couple of days sitting on her arse with a load of trashy reads and chocolate.

'Hiya!' Friendly too. Vera was pleased about that. Whatever Mattie had done, Vera didn't like to think of her terrified and friendless in hospital. 'The sister said you'd be coming. I'll make myself scarce, shall I, so you can have a chat? Tell you the truth, I'm desperate for a tab.' Her eyes were inquisitive, but she set the magazines on the chair and disappeared, her craving for nicotine stronger than her curiosity.

Vera pulled the chair closer to the bed. The woman lying there looked very young. There was a fan on the bedside locker, but she was still flushed and feverish. 'She's still got a nasty temperature,' the sister had said. 'Was hallucinating in the night about all sorts. But the antibiotics seem to be starting to work this morning.'

'What sort of hallucinations?' Might be the temperature, Vera thought. But it could be guilt or fear. Nothing like guilt to bring on nightmares.

'Oh, you know, monsters and devils. The usual stuff.'
And the sister had laughed. She'd seen it all before.

Mattie seemed to be dozing now. Vera called her name
and she opened her eyes, blinked, confused.

'Where's Sal?'

'She the prison officer?'

Mattie nodded her head.

'Gone to get a fag. I just need a few words. My name's
Vera Stanhope.'

'You a doctor?' She had a little-girl voice too. You'd
never think she was old enough to have had a child at
school.

Vera laughed. 'Nah, pet. I'm the fuzz.'

Mattie closed her eyes again, as if she just wanted to
shut Vera out, as if she preferred her dreams of monsters
and devils.

'I'm not here to cause bother,' Vera said. 'Just for some
information, for a bit of a talk. I think you can help me.'

Mattie looked at her. 'I told the police everything the
first time.'

'I know you did.' Vera paused. 'Have you seen the
news lately?' There was a television on a stand on the
wall, but it was coin-operated, the NHS making money
where it could.

Mattie followed her gaze. 'Sal got it to work for me. She
used her own cash. But we haven't watched the news.'

Of course, Vera thought. Mattie would like the kids'
cartoons, and for Sal it'd be *Britain's Next Top Model* and
Wife Swap.

'Jenny Lister is dead,' Vera said. 'You remember
Jenny?'

Mattie nodded. Her eyes seemed very big. 'She came
to visit me in prison.' A tear rolled down her face. 'What
happened?'

'She was murdered.'

'Why are you here?' Mattie seemed wide awake now, even tried to sit herself up a bit. 'That had nothing to do with me.'

'You knew her,' Vera said. 'I'm talking to the people who knew her. That's all.'

'You can't blame me.' Now the words were hysterical and so loud that Vera was worried they'd attract attention from the nurses' station. 'I was locked up. I couldn't get out if I'd wanted to.' And Vera saw that she probably wouldn't want to. She would feel safe in prison, segregated probably on a wing for vulnerable offenders, comforted by kind prison officers like Sal and by the daily routine of education and meals. Besides, it seemed Mattie didn't even know the date of Jenny's death. She'd been in hospital, not in prison, when it had happened.

'No one's blaming you,' Vera said. 'I need your help. That's why I'm here.'

Mattie looked confused. The idea that someone might need her was obviously alien. She'd always been the needy one.

'I liked Jenny. I wish she wasn't dead.' A pause followed by another wail, an outburst of self-pity. 'I'll miss her. Who'll come to visit me now?'

'When did you last see her?'

'Last Thursday.' The answer came quickly.

'You're sure?' Vera had expected some vague date in the past.

'She always came on Thursday.'

'Every week?' Vera was astounded. For a busy woman, this was surely above and beyond the call of duty.

'Thursday. Afternoon visits.'

'What did you talk about on Thursday afternoon when she came to visit?' Vera thought it couldn't have been much of a conversation. Whatever had dragged Jenny to Durham jail every week, it hadn't been the scintillating chat. Was it guilt? Had the social worker blamed herself for the death of the boy and Mattie's imprisonment?

'The same stuff as usual,' Mattie said.

'And what was that?' Vera found her sympathy was running out. She felt like shaking the lass, telling her to sharpen up her act, that Vera had a murderer to catch. Next time, she thought, she'd send Joe Ashworth to interview Mattie Jones. Vera had managed to toughen him up a bit over the years, but he was still a soppy bugger.

'About me,' Mattie said with a touch of pride. 'About my childhood and that.'

'A sort of therapy session?' Vera wondered what had been the point of that. This woman was locked up. She wasn't going to murder anyone else in the near future. Why hadn't Jenny Lister saved whatever skill she had in poking around in other folk's brains for the clients who needed her?

Mattie looked puzzled. The concept of therapy had passed her by. 'It was for her book,' she said.

'What book?'

'Mrs Lister was writing a book about me.' The woman smiled, a child given a sudden treat. 'It was going to have a photograph of me on the cover and everything.'

The prison officer appeared at the door. Even from where she sat, Vera could smell the smoke around her. She was carrying a cardboard mug of coffee and a can of Coke. 'Everything all right in here?' she asked breezily. She put the Coke on the bedside locker next to the fan. Another gesture of kindness that Vera failed to notice at that moment.

'Did you know about this?'

'What?' The officer was immediately defensive and Vera softened her tone.

'That Mattie's social worker was planning to write a book about her, about the Elias Jones case?'

The officer shook her head. 'Mattie got regular visits from her social worker. We all thought that was dead kind, because no other bugger came to see her.'

Vera turned back to the patient, who'd managed to reach the Coke and was ripping the pull-tab from the can.

'Michael never came to see you then?' she asked. 'You never got a visit from him in prison?'

Mattie was very still for a moment, poised with the Coke halfway to her mouth. Then she shook her head.

'Did you ask him to come? Have you spoken to him on the phone? Is he still working at the same place?'

Too many questions, Vera saw at once. Mattie couldn't take them all in. Vera was about to start again, more slowly, when the young woman answered, moving awkwardly in the bed as she spoke.

'He told me he's got another girlfriend. She's having his baby. He told me I shouldn't bother him again.'

'Did you tell Mrs Lister about all that?' Vera leaned forward. She could do gentle and maternal when the situation demanded. And here they had a possible motive. If Michael Morgan was about to become a father, social services might want to be involved. They might consider the child at risk.

'I was upset,' Mattie said. 'I'd used my phone card to speak to him and he told me about the baby. He hadn't liked my boy and he'd said he never wanted a baby with me, but he made one with his new lass. It wasn't fair. That afternoon Mrs Lister came, and I started crying and telling her all about it.'

'When was that?' Vera asked. 'How long ago was that, Mattie?'

Mattie shook her head. 'Not very long,' she said.

'Was it Mrs Lister's last visit to you? The one before?'

But Mattie couldn't say. She began to cry quietly, not this time for the dead social worker, but for herself, abandoned by the man with whom she'd fancied herself in love.

Sal shifted uneasily, protective of the young woman in her charge, but wanting to help. 'Mattie got upset around the time of the anniversary of Elias's death,' she said.

'That was when she contacted Morgan again. I think some of the other girls had seen it on the local news and had been having a go at her.'

Vera flashed a smile at her. 'Thanks, pet.' She turned away from the bed and lowered her voice. 'If Mattie remembers anything about the social worker, get in touch with me. I need to catch her killer.' She fished a card out of the canvas Sainsbury's shopping bag she used as a brief-case and scribbled her personal mobile number on the back. 'Jenny Lister was a good woman.'

But walking down the wide, gleaming corridor of the flash new hospital, she wondered if that was true. If Jenny Lister was planning a book on the Elias Jones case, she was abusing her client's trust for her own gain. The true-crime books about famous murders sold in thousands, and one by a social worker involved in the case would attract huge publicity. Jenny Lister could become a wealthy woman. It seemed so out of character for the person she'd thought she was getting to know that Vera could hardly believe it. But why would Mattie make up something like that?

Vera drove fast up the A1 and, just after turning off towards Hexham, she phoned Holly. 'You still in the Lister house?'

'Yes.' Just from the one word Vera could tell she was defensive and sulky. Ashworth would already have been in touch and would have told her to move out.

'How's Hannah this morning?'

'Still pretty shell-shocked and numb, but at least she slept last night. The doctor gave her a sleeping pill and Simon persuaded her to take it.'

'Is he still there too?'

'He's just left,' Holly said. 'His father's just got back from working overseas and he's gone home to see him. His mother's cooking a family lunch. There was a three-line whip.' A pause. 'Look, boss, I really think I should stay. Hannah shouldn't be left on her own, and the FLO can't get here until this afternoon.'

'No problem,' Vera said. 'I need to chat to her anyway, so you pack up your stuff and be ready to leave. I'll be there in half an hour.' *I must be a truly horrible person*, she thought, passing a timber lorry, *for that exchange to have given me so much pleasure.*

Hannah still seemed doped up when Vera arrived. She sat in a rocking chair by the kitchen window, staring at the blue tits pecking at a string of peanuts hanging from the bird table. Holly gave her a big hug before she left, but Hannah hardly responded. Vera thought Holly wouldn't have liked that: she was kind-hearted enough, but she needed emotional payback.

'I don't know about you,' Vera said. 'But I'm starving. Is there anything to eat in this place?'

Hannah turned in her seat, but only shrugged. She looked as if she'd lost pounds just in the two days since her mother had died, and she'd been skinny to start with. Vera thought Holly would have done better to spend her time cooking a proper meal for the girl than to sit around feeding off her grief.

The freezer was well organized and everything labelled. Jenny Lister, superwoman. Vera found a tub of home-made soup and a bag of wholemeal rolls. She set the soup whirring round the microwave and stuck the rolls in the oven to thaw and crisp. Her sort of cooking. She ignored Hannah while she set the table and then called her to come for her lunch.

'I'm not really hungry.' Hannah looked at her with blurred, unfocused eyes.

'Well, I am, and your mam will have taught you it's rude to sit and watch a person eat.'

Hannah got up from the rocking chair and joined Vera. She sat with her elbows on the table as Vera ladled soup into a bowl. It smelled delicious—of tomato and basil—and, despite herself, the girl dipped in her spoon and reached out to break off a piece of bread.

Vera waited until the soup had gone before she started talking.

'Did you know your mother went to visit Mattie Jones in prison?'

Hannah looked a bit brighter now, sharper. 'She didn't talk much about her work.'

'Mattie Jones is the young woman who killed her child. You'd have seen about it on the news. It was a big case. Your mother didn't mention it at the time?'

A pause. 'I *do* remember. It was one of the few times I'd seen Mum get angry. She got up and switched off the television. She said she couldn't stand the way the media demonized the people involved—Mattie and the social worker. The reporters made everything seem so simple, and this case wasn't simple at all.' Hannah shut her eyes and there was a little smile. Vera could tell in that moment that her mother had become alive for her again.

'Did Jenny ever talk about a book she was writing?'

Hannah smiled again. 'She was always talking about her book, but I don't think she'd started writing it.'

'What do you mean?' Not wanting to put the girl under pressure, not wanting to give away how important the answer might be, Vera raised herself to her feet and filled the kettle.

'It was her dream. To be a writer.'

'You mean stories, and that?' Still with her back to Hannah, Vera dropped teabags into mugs.

'No! She said she'd never be any good at fiction. She wanted to do a sort of popular guide to social work. Real cases—the individuals disguised of course—to bring it alive for the reader. So people could understand the strains and the dilemmas that social workers face.'

Vera set a mug of tea in front of Hannah, ferreted in a tin for a couple of biscuits.

'I think she started writing it,' Vera said. 'Researching it anyway. Are you sure she didn't work on it at home?'

'Not sure, no. We both led our own lives. She spent quite a lot of time working here on her laptop. Maybe she wanted to start her book in secret. You know what it's like when you talk about your dreams. People have expectations, put the pressure on. I can imagine her completing it, even waiting before she got a deal with the publisher before telling me. Then it would be: *Ta-da, look what I've done!* And a bottle of fizz to celebrate.' Hannah looked up, her eyes as feverish as Mattie's had been. 'But now it'll never happen, will it?'

'Would she have written it straight onto the laptop?' Because there was no record of any document of that kind saved. The techies had already been through the material on the computer.

'No, probably not. She was a great one for longhand. She still wrote letters! Real ones, every Christmas, to all her friends and the ageing aunts. It was one of the pieces of advice she gave me about essays at school: *Anything tricky, write it out first. There's a direct line between the brain and the pen.* It never worked for me, but it would have done for her.'

'So we're looking for a notebook somewhere.' Vera was talking to herself more than the girl, but Hannah answered.

'Yeah! A4, hardback. She bought them from an old-fashioned stationer's in Hexham. Used them all the time for work. Why? Is it important?'

It could help us find out who killed your mother. But Vera didn't say that. She just smiled and made more tea.

'Did Holly ask you about your mam's handbag?' They were still sitting at the table, the teapot between them.

'I don't think so.'

Of course not. Anger and satisfaction mixed. She'd have an excuse for bollocking Holly when they next met.

'We haven't found it yet,' Vera said, 'and it could be important. Could you describe it to me? And did she use a briefcase?'

'It was big enough for her to get all her files in, so she didn't need a briefcase.' Hannah gave a sudden smile. 'She loved it. It was made of soft, red leather.'

'These notebooks you're talking about, she'd have carried them in the bag too?'

'Probably.' Hannah was losing interest now. She was staring out of the window. 'Do you think Simon will be back soon?' As if the boy could somehow save her from her sadness, as if he was the only person who could.

Chapter Seventeen

Joe Ashworth thought it was all very well for Vera to give her orders, but prising Holly from the Lister house hadn't been easy. In the end there'd been a compromise: she said she'd go as soon as the family liaison officer turned up in the afternoon. Which meant that in the morning he was on his own in Barnard Bridge and, while Vera had said *someone* would know about Jenny's lover, tracking that person down hadn't proved easy either. Ashworth had grown up in one of the pit villages in south-east Northumberland—though there hadn't been many pits left even when he was a small child. It was the sort of place where kids played in the streets and their mams sat on the doorsteps, watching them and gossiping. He had no problem digging out secrets on his old stomping ground. Vera said he was like a magician, that he could conjure confidences from thin air. But there was no magic to it. He'd wander into the nearest social club, slip into the dialect that marked him out as one of their own, and soon the barmaid would be telling him what he wanted to know. Or directing him to someone who could help. Everyone liked telling stories, and Joe was a good listener.

This place was different. He arrived just before nine, thinking that he might catch the young mothers as they dropped their bairns off at school, forgetting of course that there was no longer a school in the village. It had been converted into a swanky house, two big cars parked where once the playground had been. There was the playgroup that Connie Masters's daughter attended, but that only ran for three days a week. He looked at the notice outside the village hall. Not today. The main street was empty of pedestrians, though there was a steady stream of traffic and the vibrations of the lorries seemed to churn in his head and stopped him thinking clearly. The baby had woken a couple of times in the night and the lack of sleep didn't help.

In the post office, which served also as a shop, a couple of pensioners queued at the counter. He waited until they'd paid their bills and one had sent his letter to a grown-up child in Australia, before chatting to them. Two elderly men who'd lived in the village all their lives.

'But it's not the same, you knaa. One time I'd be able to tell you the name of every man, woman and child in the parish. Now half the houses have people I've never seen.'

Ashworth felt his confidence return. Ex-collier or ex-farm labourer, folk were all the same. One of the men lived next door to Jenny Lister. He'd already talked to a police officer, he said shyly, when prompted by his friend. They'd called on everyone in the street the day before. A nice enough lad, but you could tell he was in a hurry. They'd invited him in for tea, but he'd not had the time.

'Well, I have all the time in the world,' Ashworth said. 'And I could murder a cup of coffee.'

The men looked at each other and Ashworth sensed a problem. They didn't want to be inhospitable, but neither felt they could invite him home. Cuthbert lived well out of the village, and Maurice had been banished for the morning so that his wife could clean and bake in peace. She'd be embarrassed if he turned up with a stranger when she wasn't prepared for visitors. They had adjoining allotments and had planned to spend their time there. Ashworth thought they'd probably had adjoining desks at school. Cuthbert and Maurice. Cuthbert the talker, the leader. He'd made it to farm manager on one of the big estates, still lived in a tied cottage. Maurice was quieter and spoke with a bit of a stutter. His left arm didn't seem to work so well. He was the Listers' neighbour.

Again, Cuthbert took charge. They could go to the caff, he said. Nothing on the allotment that couldn't wait. And Maurice agreed, as he always would. The caff was right by the river. It had a big new sign outside that read 'Tyne Teashop'. Fancy, old-fashioned lettering, gold on a green background. At the door the men paused. Ashworth could tell they'd never been inside before, that even Cuthbert was a bit nervous.

'This a new place?' Ashworth asked. 'Looks OK. And it's my treat of course.'

Things were a bit more relaxed then, and Ashworth could understand that too. His mam had always been in charge of the money in their house; she'd watched over the bank statements every month and given his father his spends on Friday teatimes.

'It used to be a bakery,' Cuthbert said. 'Then Mary retired and some lass from the south bought it up. My wife came in once and said never again. Tourists' prices.'

They took a table by the window. A middle-aged woman came to take their order. There were five different sorts of coffee on the menu and Maurice seemed a bit flummoxed by that, so Cuthbert ordered cappuccinos for both of them. 'Mo had a stroke not so long ago,' he said. 'Sometimes his speech isn't what it was. But the four of us had a grand holiday in Italy when we first retired, the galleries and that, and I know what he likes.' Spoiling Ashworth's preconceptions of two elderly yokels who'd never left the Tyne valley.

'Anything to eat?' The owner was pleasant and, from her voice, Ashworth judged she'd come from no further south than York.

They went for a selection of mixed fancies. The woman served them, then disappeared into the kitchen, and Ashworth could gently bring them back to the subject of Jenny Lister.

'You must have known her since she first moved in?' He directed his questions to both men. Maurice didn't seem to mind having Cuthbert speak for him, but Cuthbert turned back to his friend and let him answer.

'Aye, the lass was still a baby. My Hilda used to help out, babysitting. We never had bairns ourselves and she was glad to do it.'

'You got on, then?'

'Oh, they were lovely neighbours. Jenny brought my Hilda to visit me in the hospital when I had the stroke. Every evening for a week.' Maurice bit into a dainty cake with pink icing, licked his stubby brown fingers.

'I have to ask some personal questions,' Ashworth said. 'There'd be things Jenny wouldn't want spread about the village, and I know you'd respect that. But this is different. This isn't just tittle-tattle. It might help us find out who killed her.'

They nodded. Very serious, pleased to be useful again.

'We think she had a boyfriend,' Ashworth said. 'But nobody knows who he is. Did you see anyone come to the house?'

Maurice shook his head slowly. 'Only the lass's friends. And they were canny too, mind. You read things about young people today, but they always had a word and a bit of a joke. The woman who teaches in that school in Effingham called in sometimes, but I never saw anyone else. Not that I remember.' He looked up at Ashworth with a crooked smile. 'Not that my memory's what it was since the stroke.'

'Would Hilda know?'

Cuthbert began to chuckle and choked on the last crumbs of his cake. 'Of course Hilda would know. She's to the Tyne valley what that spy place in Cheltenham is to the security services.'

'But not a gossip,' Maurice stammered. 'Not really.'

'Well, she knows more than she lets on.' Cuthbert was indulgent. 'That's certainly true.'

'Would she talk to me, do you think?' Ashworth was certain he could winkle information from the formidable Hilda. Old ladies loved him. 'I mean, I wouldn't want to disturb her if she's busy, but you can tell how urgent it is.'

Maurice hesitated.

'Come on, Mo!' Cuthbert said. 'A chance to talk to a bonny lad like this. She'd jump at it. You'll be in more bother if you don't take him to see her. Besides, she'll have all the vacuuming done by now, and the washing'll be on the line. She'll be sat watching some nonsense on the telly with a cup of coffee.'

Maurice smiled his lopsided smile and got to his feet.

Hilda hadn't quite finished the housework. When they arrived she was mopping the kitchen floor. They stood in the hall and saw her wide bottom, swaying to the movement of the mop.

'What's all this about?' Fierce, but concerned too. Maybe she thought Maurice had been taken ill again.

'It's about Jenny Lister,' Cuthbert said.

Hilda gave him a sharp look that Ashworth couldn't quite interpret. She made them stand in the hall while she finished the floor, then took them straight into the small living room, leaving the door open so she could shout through to them from the kitchen. It could have been Ashworth's nana's house. Gleaming dark-wood furniture, and everywhere lace mats. On the wall embroidered samplers. A smell of beeswax and peppermint. The window was small and covered with a net curtain that let in very little light.

'Tea or coffee?' She'd emptied her bucket and was polishing the floor dry.

Maurice grinned at Cuthbert. It seemed they'd made the right decision.

The coffee was very weak, instant made with warm milk, but there were home-made flapjacks and scones still warm, with so much butter that it drizzled over their fingers as they ate. The cakes in the tea shop had been hardly a mouthful.

'Who's this then?'

'He's the police.' Maurice looked at her anxiously.

'Well, I guessed that much!' She turned to Ashworth. 'I suppose you have a name.'

So he introduced himself and answered her questions about where he'd been born and where he lived. It seemed she'd worked at Parson's as a secretary when she was younger and had known one of his aunts.

'What do you want to know then? I'm guessing it'll be about Jenny Lister.'

'Whatever you can tell me,' Ashworth said. 'We don't always know the best questions to ask.'

Hilda took off her apron, sat on a high-backed chair and folded her hands on her lap. When she spoke it was with the concentration of a *Mastermind* contestant answering questions on her specialist subject. 'Jenny Lister moved into the village in . . .' a very brief pause '. . . 1993. The summer. Hannah was a baby, and Jenny was still on maternity leave.' Another pause and a little sniff to show she disapproved of the concept. *A touch of jealousy?* Ashworth wondered. *If I'd had bairns, I'd have stayed at home and looked after them myself.* 'The father, Jenny's husband, had gone back to London, where he'd come from.'

The same sort of history as Connie Masters, Joe Ashworth thought. *Her man left her while she had a young child. Was the shared experience relevant? Or would the stress of holding together a marriage, a new child and a stressful job be too much for most relationships? Maybe it happened all the time.* His wife hadn't worked since their first child had been born. He couldn't imagine how he'd survive if she were out all day. It seemed strange to him that he'd never realized how much he depended on her holding the show together.

Hilda continued. 'Jenny was what they called a generic social worker in those days. She dealt with everything. Then there was a change in the system and she specialized in children. She ended up as the fostering and adoption officer.' She looked at Ashworth through small, square spectacles. 'But you'll know that already.'

He nodded. 'All the same, it's useful to have someone sum it up.' The other men might as well not have been in the room. Maurice seemed to be dropping off to sleep. The lorries rolling past the window provided a background rumble.

'She had a boyfriend,' Hilda said suddenly. 'Lawrence. Worked as a ranger with the National Park. Nice enough. We invited them round to dinner one night. Before Maurice was taken ill, we liked to entertain. Still do, but only close friends these days.'

'What happened with this Lawrence?'

'I don't know. They were talking about setting up home together, and the next thing I heard they'd parted.'

'Did Jenny ever talk to you about it?'

'She wasn't one for weeping on folks' shoulders,' Hilda said. With the apron removed, Ashworth saw she was rather stylishly dressed. A pleated skirt and a yellow cotton blouse. A smart woman, in every sense of the word.

'But you'd have been the nearest thing she had to a mother.'

'I saw her in the garden soon after it happened. She looked dreadful. Pale as a ghost, and you could tell she'd been crying. I asked her in for coffee. She told me they'd split up. I made a comment about men—you know how you do when someone's upset: "Don't worry about it. Most of them are commitment-phobic." Something of that sort. But she said Lawrence wasn't like that, and it had been *her* decision to stop seeing him.'

'Did she say why? Was there someone else?'

'Aye.' Hilda looked up at him. 'Someone completely unsuitable. Her words not mine. "I know it's wrong, but I can't help myself. He makes me feel alive." That's what she told me.'

'Did she tell you any more about him? You do realize how important this might be?'

'She was ashamed of the relationship.' The dumpy little woman looked up at Ashworth to make sure he understood what she was saying. 'It didn't seem healthy to me. You should never have to apologize for your choice of man. Maybe she'd met him by chance, had what they call a one-night stand. Or I wondered if she'd come across him through work.'

'A colleague?' Ashworth could tell how that might be frowned upon, but surely sleeping with a social worker wasn't necessarily a matter of shame.

'More likely a client, don't you think?' Hilda was speaking to Ashworth now as if he were an equal, almost as perceptive as herself. 'I could see that happening. She'd feel sorry for someone, try to help him, then get too emotionally involved.'

Ashworth could see how that might happen too, and why it would have to be a secret. It would probably be against the rules of her profession, and Jenny would also be afraid of appearing a fool. The cool professional tangled up with some loser. How would that look?

'It could have been a married man,' Ashworth said. 'Someone local, someone you know maybe, so she wouldn't want to tell you about him.' The idea of Jenny falling for a client made more sense to him, but he had to explore other options.

'Maybe.' Hilda seemed unconvinced. 'But people don't seem too bothered about having affairs these days. I don't know that Jenny would have been *that* upset. Besides, if it had been someone local, I might well have heard about it before now.' Implying that there was no doubt about it.

'Cuthbert says he doesn't know half the folk who live in the village these days.'

Hilda gave a wicked grin. 'Aye, well. Cuthbert doesn't belong to the WI.'

Chapter Eighteen

The morning after her lunch with Veronica Eliot, Connie Masters woke feeling washed out and tired. She drove to Hexham to shop for food, but returned home without even stopping in town for coffee. Outside a newsagent's in the main street there was a blown-up headline: TYNE VALLEY SOCIAL WORKER'S DEATH. THE INVESTIGATION CONTINUES. No link had yet been made to Elias Jones, but Connie thought it was only a matter of time before the press picked up on it, until they'd hunt her down again.

Alice had woken several times in the night, troubled by the old nightmares. She trailed listlessly round the supermarket, hanging on to Connie's hand, and when they got home she fell asleep straight after lunch on the sofa in the living room, watching children's television. Connie covered her with a quilt and let her sleep. In the quiet house, with the background sound of running water, she imagined herself back in the social-services office where she'd been based, trawling through the conversations she'd had with Jenny Lister in the months either side of Elias's death. Trying to find an answer for the new murder, one in which she played no part.

Jenny's room at work had been small. One wall was covered with drawings and paintings done by the children she'd placed into foster care. Pictures of smiling stick-children, a big pink heart. *Molly loves Jenny*. There were plants, living and flowering, not dead like the ones in the open-plan office shared by the rest of the team. Walking into Jenny's room had been to step into a place of colour and civilization. They might talk there about misery, but Connie had felt it first as a place of sanctuary, then as a place for confession. And even as a child, she'd lied about her sins.

'Tell me about Michael Morgan.' Jenny had smiled in an encouraging way. It had been the supervision session after Morgan had offered to leave Mattie and the child. They'd been sitting in the comfortable chairs, facing each other across the tiny coffee table. Of course Jenny organized her room informally before staff meetings. She wasn't one for the hierarchy of sitting behind a desk to talk to her team.

And Connie had blustered a little, reluctant to tell Jenny that actually she'd only really met the man twice. Once briefly when he'd just moved in, when she'd had the impression of stillness, intensity, that had led her to describe him as 'weird'; and that last occasion when he'd offered to move away from the family. She'd deliberately chosen times to visit Mattie when he wasn't there. Ostensibly thinking that Mattie might talk to her more freely if Morgan wasn't around, but really because Connie was unnerved by him. When he was in the room she felt she had no control.

She set up her excuse first. 'Of course I try to see Mattie on her own as much as I can. I think he really has a hold over her.'

'But you must have gained some idea?' Jenny frowned. Her frown always gave the impression that she was a little disappointed in the staff member seated in front of her, that they hadn't quite reached her exacting standards.

'He's charismatic.' The words had come out of Connie's mouth without her truly realizing the implication of them. But once out, she knew it was true. She'd only met the man twice and couldn't describe him— couldn't, for instance, have made up one of those Identikit pictures the police showed on *Crimewatch*—but she had a sense of him. A man who knew what he wanted and thought he would get it. A man who would command attention in whatever company he chose to appear.

'In what way?' The frown had disappeared and Connie now saw she had Jenny's complete attention.

Connie shook her head, frustrated that she couldn't quite find the right words. 'It's how he looks at you. Compelling. And it makes you think you'd tell him everything he wanted to know. Like a priest almost, at confession.' Connie had been brought up a Catholic, had rejected all that as soon as she could think for herself of course, but was still haunted by its power.

'What made a man like that take up with Mattie?' They'd discussed this before, but Jenny had seemed suddenly more focused on the man than ever before. 'He's obviously educated, and as you say he has a certain attraction. A control issue, do you think? He wants a woman who will be subservient to him.'

'Maybe.'

And Jenny had leaned forward. 'I think I should see him. I'm not questioning your competence, not at all, but he could be dangerous, not just to Mattie and Elias, but to other young inadequate women and their children. I'd like to make my own assessment.'

Occasionally Jenny had done this: she'd dipped into one of her team's cases to satisfy herself. The control freak in her, the team had decided, not liking it, because inevitably she came up with something they'd missed, but admiring her thoroughness.

Now, in the dark cottage, with the river running outside the window, Connie tried to remember what the outcome of that decision had been. Had Jenny arranged a meeting with Morgan?

Certainly, it had never been discussed during the court case or the disciplinary hearing, Connie had been clear about that. Surely, if Jenny had met Morgan, she would have kept a record of it. She might even have been called as a witness, asked to give her assessment of the man and his influence on the single mother. Mattie's barrister had tried to implicate Morgan in Elias's death: 'This was a controlling man. He gave Ms Jones the impression that if she got rid of her son, he would return to her. One might almost say that he was inciting a mother to kill her son.' The judge had pulled him up on that statement, and Morgan seemed to have made a good impression on the jury. Connie hadn't been in court while he gave evidence, but she'd spoken to people who had been there, who'd said he'd seemed really caring and kind. Charming, even. What had Jenny made of him? Now, Connie was fascinated. *Why didn't I ask her while I had the chance?*

The room suddenly got darker and Connie was aware of a figure blocking the light from the small window. Someone was outside, looking in. A woman, big, untidy, with a round moon face. Connie decided it was one of those travellers who appeared sometimes, selling dishcloths or lucky heather. She hurried to the door before the woman knocked and woke up Alice, and was surprised at how much milder it was outside than in the room.

'I never buy anything at the door.' Best to be firm from the start, before you started getting the sales pitch.

'Eh, pet, I'm not selling.' The woman grinned. Stood, solid as a rock, refusing to budge from the doorstep.

'I don't need religion either.'

'Nor me.' The woman sighed. 'My father was a scientist, of sorts, and I was brought up to despise the Church. But I always found it a tad appealing all the same. Forbidden fruits, you know what it's like.'

'Well, what do you want?' By now Connie was so exasperated that she forgot the sleeping Alice and raised her voice.

The woman put a finger to her lips, a parody and a rebuke. 'We don't want to wake the little one. I saw her through the window. Sweet. Shall we talk out here? My name's Vera Stanhope. Detective Inspector, Northumbria Police. You had a word with my colleague Joe Ashworth yesterday.'

'You're a police officer?' Connie was astonished. And not just a police officer, a senior detective!

'I know, pet. Hard to believe, isn't it? But we're not all pretty little boys like Joe.' She sat heavily on the wooden bench under the window and patted the seat to indicate that Connie should join her. 'Leave the door open and we'll hear if the little girl wakes up.'

And to her surprise, Connie did as she was told.

'Jenny Lister,' Vera said.

'I've already told your sergeant everything I know.' *But was that true? Details were dribbling back into her mind. Like the fact that Jenny had mentioned going to see Michael Morgan.*

Vera looked at her with clear, steady eyes. 'Oh, surely not everything,' she said. 'Anyway, things move on. There are new lines to investigate, new questions arise.' She paused. 'Did you know Jenny was planning to write a book about the Elias Jones case?'

'No.' It wasn't the question she was expecting. She wondered if this woman was entirely sane. But thinking about it, the idea of Jenny as a writer wasn't surprising. Jenny had been convinced she was right about everything, and might see it as her duty to pass on her wisdom to the world.

Vera nodded and continued immediately.

'Did you know she visited Mattie Jones every week in prison? Even when the lass was on remand?'

'No. Not really.' This time the answer was less emphatic and Vera picked up on the hesitation.

'You were still working with Jenny before the case went to trial. Surely she would have told you?'

'I was moved from the case as soon as Elias's body was found,' Connie said. 'Standard practice, even before the disciplinary hearing.'

'But you were based in the same office,' Vera persisted. 'You must have met in the tea room, bumped into each other in the Ladies. You'd have thought she'd tell you what she was up to.'

Connie shook her head. 'Not Jenny's style. She was discreet. I was no longer involved in the case.'

'You don't seem surprised. About the prison visits.'

'No.' Wood pigeons were calling in the trees on the other side of the river. They reminded Connie of childhood holidays in the country, long summer days. 'Mattie was more than a client to Jenny. She'd known her for years. Jenny would have felt she'd let her down.'

'So it would have been a kind of penance?' *Religion creeping in again.*

'Yes,' Connie said. 'Perhaps. Something like that.'

'This book . . .'

'Really, she didn't say anything to me.'

'Apparently,' Vera paused, clearly choosing her words carefully, 'she was quite evangelical about it. She wanted to tell the world what the social worker's life was really all about. The human face. The moral dilemmas. Get away from all the tabloid stereotypes. Does that make sense to you?'

This time Connie paused. 'Yeah, that sounds like Jenny. She could be quite priggish.'

Vera beamed. 'Hallelujah! I never believe in saints. Someone's telling the truth about the woman at last.'

Connie looked up, surprised, caught Vera's eye and grinned too.

'Did you know Michael Morgan had found himself another girlfriend? That she was having a baby by him?' Vera asked. 'At least that's what he told Mattie. He could just have been trying to get her off his back, of course.'

'Were they still in touch?' Connie hadn't expected that. She'd thought Michael had walked out of Mattie's life, once and for all, before the murder.

'She was in touch with *him*. She phoned him from the prison, sent him visiting orders. She was besotted, after all. And some women have no pride.' Vera stretched her legs out in front of her. She was wearing sandals and her feet were rather grubby. 'That would have started alarm bells, wouldn't it? Michael Morgan involved with another woman and child?'

'Yes, of course. Though he was never charged. No evidence that he'd witnessed abuse or instigated it. Social services would have to be careful. They'd take advice from lawyers.'

'What would the procedure be?'

'I'm not sure.' It seemed to Connie that *that* life, the life of emergency case conferences and the bureaucracy of the 'at risk' register, was part of a former existence. She no longer understood it. 'An informal visit to start with, I suppose. Contact with the woman's GP and midwife, to alert them to a possible problem.'

'Who would do that? Who would be in charge of the new case?' Vera turned to Connie and waited for the answer. Connie could sense how much it mattered to her, felt her own heart beating faster, in time with the detective's.

'I guess it would be somebody senior because of the sensitivity. But you could easily find out. There'd be records.'

'I know I could, pet. But I'm asking you. You knew them all. You were in the thick of it.'

'They might ask Jenny,' Connie said at last. 'Because she knew Michael Morgan already.'

'She *knew* Morgan?'

The violence of the response made Connie backtrack. 'I'm not certain about that. You'll have to check. But she talked about meeting him. It was after he'd left Mattie's flat, but before Elias died. She said she wanted to assess him for herself, to judge the risk that he might pose to the family.' A pause. 'I was a bit pissed off actually. I thought she didn't trust me.'

'She never came back to you? Never told you if that meeting took place?' The detective remained still, but Connie could sense a new energy about her, a sharpness. An excitement.

'No, but Elias died soon after. We had other concerns then. Like I say, you'll be able to check. Jenny's record-keeping was legendary.'

Now Vera heaved herself off the seat, dusted bits of lichen from her skirt. She shook Connie's hand, clasping it in both of hers. 'Best keep this conversation secret,' she said. 'Safer, eh?'

'I'm hardly likely to go to the press!' Connie wished now that Vera would stay. She would have liked to share a pot of tea with her. The woman was entertaining.

'Aye, well, take care of yourselves, all the same.'

And the woman stamped down the track to her big, flash car, leaving Connie feeling abandoned and uneasy.

Chapter Nineteen

The family liaison officer had arrived at the Lister house almost as soon as Hannah had finished washing up. Vera had half-heartedly offered to do it, but Hannah had refused. She needed, Vera thought, to feel that this was her place still. That it didn't belong to strange police officers.

'What are your plans, pet? Will you stay on here?'

Hannah turned from the sink and looked confused, as if the question had no meaning. Then the doorbell rang and it was the FLO, and while Hannah was obviously sorry it wasn't Simon standing there, she seemed relieved by the interruption.

Outside on the pavement Vera took a deep breath; she felt more of a sense of escape and liberation than she would coming out of Durham jail. She phoned Ashworth. 'Where are you?'

'Doing the house-to-house again.' He lowered his voice. 'The plods that did it the first time round missed stuff.'

'Anything useful?'

'Well, I can't go into details now.' Vera imagined him in one of the houses in the street. He'd have excused himself from the lounge to take the call, would be standing in a narrow hall, the residents on the other side of the door straining to hear every word.

'Give me half an hour,' she said. 'I want a word with the ex-social worker you took such a shine to. Then I'm planning a visit to Michael Morgan and I want you along.

Charlie can carry on there. I've sent Holly to talk to Lawrence May, the guy who was Jenny's boyfriend.'

On the way to Connie's cottage she drove past the Eliot place. There was a new car on the drive of the white house, something low and sporty. The master of the house had obviously returned, and inside the family was probably celebrating with a special lunch, while Hannah mourned for her mother.

Vera had grown up in the hills and these low places, shut in by trees, gave her the creeps. She wouldn't want to live so close to the river; imagined floods, biting insects, disease. Even the lambs seemed overfed and fat.

When she talked to Ashworth after her interview with Connie, he said he wanted to take his own car to Tynemouth, the town where Morgan lived and practised. It was miles away, right on the coast, and he could go straight home from there. He'd had enough late nights. His wife would kill him. Vera insisted he go with her. 'We can't go into this cold. This could be it, man. We need at least the chance to talk it through.'

'Couldn't it wait until the morning? Give us a chance to prepare properly for the interview?'

But, standing outside the shop in the weak spring sunshine, Vera knew she couldn't wait a whole night before confronting Morgan. It would kill her. Sometimes she had this reckless streak. Impulsive. The sensible thing would be to wait, to consider all the angles; she couldn't do it.

'If it's a late finish, I'll drop you home,' she said. 'Then pick you up in the morning. It wouldn't be the end of the world if you have to leave your car here overnight.'

And he had no argument to that. He climbed into the car beside her. She thought he was as eager as she was to talk to Morgan. He just had to go through the motions of putting his family first.

'So what did you get from the house-to-house?' Vera knew she was a good driver. Instinctive. These small roads could be tricky if you didn't know them, but she couldn't afford to hang around. Then she sensed Ashworth tense beside her and put her foot on the brake, reduced the speed a bit. She needed him to concentrate. She listened to his account of the conversation with Jenny's neighbour.

'She thought Lister had fallen for one of her clients?'

'She wasn't that certain,' Ashworth said. 'Just that it was someone unsuitable.'

'But she wouldn't have plucked the idea of a client out of thin air!' Vera was excited now. 'Jenny might have said something, dropped a hint that made Hilda think that way. And it stuck in her mind, even though she couldn't remember the original comment.'

'Maybe.' Vera saw that Ashworth thought she was making too much of it. He was her restraining influence. Sometimes, she thought, he was her conscience.

'Connie said that Jenny met Michael Morgan,' Vera said. She kept her voice calm. Didn't want Ashworth to think she was over-reacting. 'Apparently she wanted to do her own assessment of the man.'

'You think Lister was having an affair with Morgan?' His voice was sharp and incredulous.

'I'm keeping an open mind,' she said. 'But if the bastard killed her, I'll have him.'

Tynemouth was a pretty little town, with a wide front street and bonny Georgian houses. A castle and a priory, both in ruins. Tea shops and posh frock shops and a converted church on one corner, called the Land of Green Ginger, where you could buy antiques and books and fancy children's clothes. In the evening the bars and the restaurants pulled in the younger crowd, but this time of day, so early in the season, it was the haunt of elderly ladies and middle-aged couples walking hand in hand, window-shopping. The same sort of clientele, Vera thought, as the Willows Health Club.

They found Morgan's place in a narrow terraced street just off the sea front. *Tynemouth Acupuncture* in discreet letters on a classy brass plaque next to the freshly painted door. It seemed he must live in the flat upstairs. The window was open and they could hear music. If you could call it music. Something electronic and repetitive. The clinic was shut.

Vera rang the bell and at last they heard light footsteps on an uncarpeted floor. She'd been expecting Morgan, but the door was opened by a young woman, who was hardly more than a girl. Long, straight dark hair, a skimpy printed dress worn over leggings, little flat pumps. The dress was loose and floaty and could have been concealing an early pregnancy.

'Could we speak to Michael Morgan?'

The girl smiled. 'I'm sorry, he's tied up at the moment, but I could make an appointment for you.' She spoke as if meeting the man would be a huge treat for them. More educated and less flaky than Mattie, but a similar type, Vera decided. Frail and drippy.

'He's here then, is he?'

'Michael's meditating,' the girl said. 'He can never be disturbed when he's meditating.'

'Bollocks.' Vera flashed her a smile. 'We're police, pet, and I know he'd be delighted to help us with our enquiries.' She nodded Ashworth past her up the stairs. 'What's your name then?'

'Freya.' Now she seemed just like a schoolgirl. 'Freya Adams.'

'We'll need to speak to you in a little while too. But disappear for half an hour, there's a good lass. Buy yourself a glass of pop and a bag of crisps and we'll see you back here then.' Vera shut the door, leaving the girl on the pavement. She thought maybe she should have been more tactful. Sometimes adrenalin got her that way, made her too slick and clever for her own good.

Two rooms of the flat must have been knocked through to make a long narrow space, with windows at either end. Vera walked straight into it at the top of the stairs. The floors had been stripped and waxed and were honey-coloured. There were thin muslin curtains, wall hangings in gold and saffron, the only furniture a futon, a low table and one wall covered in bookshelves. The music came from a system on one of the shelves. 'Can we switch that off?' It never did any harm to establish your authority immediately, and the persistent wailing made her want to scream. There was silence.

Morgan and Ashworth were standing close to the window that looked over a small garden at the back of the house, in the middle of a conversation. Vera had been expecting hostility: she'd be really pissed off if two strangers came into her house and started shouting the odds. But Morgan seemed only faintly amused. He was better-looking in the flesh than his photos had led her to expect: a striking face with very blue eyes. She'd checked out all the old newspaper pictures of him, but wouldn't have recognized him in the street; he'd shaved his head since the trial and now had the look of an Eastern monk— the image, she guessed, he was aiming at. He came up to her, arm outstretched to shake her hand. 'And you are?'

'Vera Stanhope. Detective Inspector.'

He was wearing loose cotton trousers and a cotton shirt with no collar. The sort of gear her hippy neighbour went in for. It came to her that this man could well have come to the next-door parties.

'I was just explaining to Mr Morgan that we're sorry to disturb him,' Ashworth said.

'And I've told him that I'm always pleased to help the police in any way I can.' Morgan nodded for them to take a seat. The futon was as uncomfortable as Vera had known it would be. It creaked. It hadn't been made for someone of her weight, and she wasn't sure if she'd make it to her feet unaided at the end of the interview.

'Would you like tea?' The man smiled at them. 'I have camomile, peppermint . . .'

'Just a few questions,' Vera said. 'We'll not take up too much of your time.'

He smiled again and sat on the floor facing them. The movement was fluid, very graceful, and it came to Vera, unbidden, that he'd be very good at sex. The physical stuff. Was that part of his attraction? She felt a moment of panic, of the old regret that time was slipping past. Then something close to lust.

There was a silence. Ashworth and Morgan waited for her to speak. Morgan was looking at her as if he understood her discomfort, with compassionate blue eyes that held her attention. *Sod him! Did she need his pity? She might want his body, but that was something quite different.*

'Is it right that you've got that lass of yours pregnant?'

She felt that Ashworth relaxed as soon as she'd spoken. This was what he'd been expecting, a full-on attack.

'I think we both had something to do with that. But, yes, Freya's going to have a baby. We're delighted.' He gave a slow smile and though Vera despised his attitude, she still couldn't take her eyes from his face.

'But Mattie's not, is she?'

'What's this about, Inspector? Why are you here?' The tone was still easy.

Vera ignored the question. 'What I don't get, Mr Morgan, is what you saw in Mattie. I mean, she's a bonnie lass, but not your intellectual equal, I'd say. Or was that part of the appeal? That she'd never answer back?'

Morgan frowned. 'You're right, of course. It was a mistake to get involved with Mattie. I'll always regret it. She became fixated, obsessed. It really wasn't something I encouraged. And I much prefer my women to have minds of their own.' He gave a little smile, which was almost a challenge to Vera: *I'd much prefer someone like you.* But that was nonsense, of course. Nobody wanted her. Morgan turned away and said in a soft voice, 'I'll always feel guilty about Elias dying, that I should have foreseen it or done something to prevent it.'

'So how did you hook up with Mattie?' This was Ashworth, less aggressive, asking the question as one man to another.

'I suppose I started off feeling sorry for her.' Morgan leaned forward, his elbows on his knees, showing again how flexible his body was. Vera was aware of the shoulder muscles under the flimsy cotton shirt. 'And it's always flattering to be needed. I thought I could make a difference in her life. A terrible arrogance, I see now.'

'Where did you meet?'

'That was quite by chance. A cafe in Newcastle. She didn't have quite enough money to pay for her coffee and I offered her a few pence. She was ridiculously grateful. I'd saved her the embarrassment of having to walk away.' He looked up at them, very earnest, willing them to understand. 'There was simplicity about her that I found awesome. A real inner beauty.'

'Not quite the full shilling though, is she?' Vera broke in. 'I mean, what would you talk about, those long boring nights in her flat?'

He shook his head, despairing of her crassness. 'She was desperate to learn,' he said. 'I've always thought that I might make a teacher—not in the conventional sense, of course—and in talking to her about my beliefs and ideals they became clearer to me.'

Self-centred prat. Vera was pleased she no longer found him appealing. She saw the brown marks between his teeth, that there was a hair growing from a mole on his neck.

'But you screwed Mattie up, didn't you? Deprived her of the things that held her together: the telly, her friends in the street, the games she played with her lad. Was she always going to be an experiment? You never moved her in here, did you, like your classy new girlfriend? Basically she was just your bit of rough.'

Vera saw Morgan had been glad of the excuse to leave Mattie and move back to Tynemouth. He must have celebrated after Connie's visit. It gave him an escape route and it made his desertion look like self-sacrifice: *I'm leaving for the sake of your son.*

Vera thought Mattie would have done better to drown him than the boy.

Morgan continued in the same reasonable way. 'I didn't understand how disturbed she was. I never thought she'd kill Elias in the hope of getting me back.'

'When did Jenny Lister come to visit?' Vera asked. Soon Freya would be back, and she wanted to catch the girl before she had a chance to talk to Morgan. It was time to move things on.

For the first time he didn't have an immediate answer.

'She *did* come to visit you?'

'She came here a few times,' he said. 'I heard about her murder. I'm so sorry she's dead.'

'Bit of a coincidence,' Vera said. 'Death following you around wherever you go. What did she want with you?'

'To assess me.' He gave a small smile. 'That's what she said.'

'Was this before you took up with Freya or after?' Vera found from somewhere a blast of anger. *He very nearly had me conned. He's a clever bastard.*

'The first time was before Elias died. I think she wanted to make sure I no longer had any influence over the family. I convinced her of that.'

'Jenny fell for your charms then, did she?'

'She believed me. Charm didn't come into it.'

'When did you last see her?'

There was a pause. Outside in the street some young people were laughing and jeering, pulling Vera's attention away from the room for a moment. In the distance she saw Freya approaching.

'Well? It was recently, wasn't it? Within the last two weeks. She'd found out from Mattie Jones that your young lassie was expecting a baby. She wanted to warn you from playing the same games with her as you did with Mattie.'

'I don't play games, Inspector.'

'When did you last see her?' Vera bellowed and the sound seemed to echo around the uncluttered room.

He gave a little nod. 'You're quite right. It was ten days ago, just a week before Jenny was murdered.'

'And what did she want with you?'

'She spoke to Freya, who confirmed that she was here under her own free will, that we love each other. But I'd guess love is a concept you don't understand, Inspector.'

'Did you have a relationship with Jenny Lister, Mr Morgan?'

He threw back his head and laughed.

Outside, the girl was almost at the door. Vera stood up suddenly, fury giving her the impetus to rise from the futon.

'I want an answer!'

'Of course there was no relationship, Inspector. Ms Lister was a rather beautiful woman. But not my type.'

Vera stamped out of the room, leaving Ashworth to follow.

Chapter Twenty

Ashworth thought Vera had seriously messed up the interview with Morgan. Sometimes that happened to her: she let a witness get under her skin, play with her head. Then she completely lost focus. They should have taken time to prepare for this meeting, and now they were leaving with important questions left unanswered. After Vera had clattered down the wooden stairs to the street, Ashworth spent a few moments talking to Morgan, thanking him for his time. On the next occasion he'd come back here on his own. He thought the man still had information to give. Morgan was clearly a pervy bastard, but unlike Vera, Ashworth thought *he* was sufficiently professional not to let his personal opinion get in the way.

By the time he reached the pavement the two women were walking away from him towards the main street. The spring sun was very low now and he saw them as silhouettes, Vera's bulk and the girl's figure slender, willowy, reminding him suddenly of the iconic outlines of Laurel and Hardy at the end of their movies. Turning back towards the sea, he saw a dense, grey bank of fog on the horizon, and a huge tanker emerging from the mouth of the Tyne.

In the street, he kept his distance. The women were already in conversation and he didn't want to interrupt. They turned into a new cafe bar, and there Ashworth joined them. It was the sort of place his wife might have enjoyed. Unpretentious, solid furniture: scrubbed kitchen tables and wooden chairs, on the wall blackboards show-

ing the menus, mostly local food, fish and lamb. Maybe
he'd bring Sarah here next time they were down the coast.
There were a couple of highchairs in the corner so they
obviously welcomed bairns.

'This is Joe,' Vera said. 'My right-hand man.'

'I should go back.' The girl still seemed unsure, ill at
ease. She hadn't yet fallen under Vera's spell. 'Michael will
be wondering where I am.'

'No rush.' Vera took a seat, set her enormous hands flat
on the table. 'He'll be meditating. You said he wouldn't
want to be interrupted while he was in the middle of med-
itation.' And of course Freya had no answer to that. 'I'll
have a pint, Joe. They stock that ale they make in Allen-
dale. And something to nibble on, because I'm feeling a
bit peckish. What about you, love? I suppose you're off the
alcohol, with the baby on the way.'

'Michael and I don't drink anyway.' Freya sat primly,
her hands in her lap.

'Good for you. Orange juice then. Or would you rather
have an ice cream?'

The girl regarded Vera suspiciously. Joe thought his
boss should cut out the flip remarks, but Freya answered
anyway. 'Orange juice would be fine.'

When Joe returned from the bar, they were still sitting
in an uncomfortable silence.

'Did you know that Mrs Lister had been murdered?'
Vera asked. She'd stopped being playful and her voice was
serious and low.

'Mrs Lister?' Freya seemed genuinely confused.

'The social worker that came to talk to you about your
relationship with Michael.'

'Oh her! I think I only knew her first name.'

'Michael was on first-name terms with her, was he?'

Ashworth thought this was Vera back to her sure-
footed best, but the girl didn't answer. The waiter brought
their drinks, a basket of bread, a bowl of olives.

'Had you heard that Jenny Lister was dead?' Vera asked again.

'No.' It was impossible to tell from the flat response whether or not Freya was telling the truth. She reached out, took a piece of bread and spread it with butter, but left it uneaten on her plate.

'That's why we're here, talking to you and Michael.' It seemed now that Vera was the most patient woman in the world. 'You both saw her soon before she died.'

'So, we're like witnesses.' Freya's face lit up, the last reaction Ashworth would have expected. But people often had a voyeur's excitement when they were close to a violent death, as if it conferred a degree of celebrity on them. He hoped she had friends she could phone or text about her part in this drama. A mam she could call on when she went into labour. He hated to think of her alone in the flat with that man.

'Exactly,' Vera said. 'You're witnesses. So you don't mind answering a few questions?'

'Of course not. I thought you were just here to have a go at me about Michael. Because he's a bit older than I am.'

Vera shot a look at Ashworth, but let that go. 'How often did you meet Jenny Lister?'

'Only once,' the girl said. 'Though Michael had seen her before. He'd gone out with that terrible woman who killed her son, and social services had been involved then.'

'He told you about that?'

'Of course he did,' Freya said. 'Michael and I don't have any secrets. It sounded dreadful. Michael really loved the kid. He was devastated about what had happened. Then there were all the rumours, people thinking he was involved in some way.'

'Bad for business.'

Ashworth thought Vera had gone too far, but Freya took the comment at face value. 'Yeah, really bad! His regulars stuck by him of course, but he's only just starting to pick up new clients.'

'It didn't put you off? The fact that he was linked to the Elias Jones case.'

'No! If you really love someone, you stand by them, don't you?' She looked at them, demanding their agreement, but neither could quite meet her eye.

'If we could go back to Jenny Lister,' Vera said gently. 'You met her about a week ago?'

'Yes, something like that.'

'Where did you talk to her?'

'She came to the flat,' Freya said. 'I think she must have phoned to make an appointment because Michael knew she was coming. He asked me to get back from college early so I'd be in.'

'Where are you studying?' Ashworth couldn't help interrupting. He was glad Freya still had a life of her own. Lectures and gossip. He wanted to pack her up into his car and take her home to her parents.

'Newcastle College. I'm doing drama and English A levels. Acting's my thing.' She smiled self-consciously. 'I've already got an agent, actually.'

'Won't the baby get in the way of all that?' Vera was glaring at Ashworth, cross that he'd disrupted the flow of the conversation. He gave a little shrug of apology. 'I assume it is Michael's baby?'

'Of course! What do you think I'm like?'

'Didn't you consider a termination?'

Great, Vera, Ashworth thought. *Dead tactful. Let's talk about her getting rid of her baby in a public place, where anyone could walk past and listen in.*

But the girl seemed unfazed. 'Michael doesn't believe in abortion. And he said that we'd look after the baby together. He believes I'll be a great actress. He wants me to fulfil my potential, live out my dreams.'

There was a moment of stunned silence. 'Well, we all want that, don't we, pet? I want to become Chief Constable and win *Miss World.'* Vera drank from her beer, gave a little sigh of distracted contentment. Ashworth, thinking of the chaos in his home, the pressure of home and work, wanted to weep for the girl. 'How did the interview with Jenny Lister go?'

'Fine.'

'A few details would be good.'

'First she talked to Michael and me together.' Freya sat back in her chair, and for the first time Ashworth could see the small, rounded belly. 'About our attitudes to a baby, how it would disrupt our lives. Michael would have to accept that things would change, that there'd be clutter, mess, noise. How would he cope with that? Practical stuff, like had I registered with the doctor and antenatal classes. Then she asked Michael to leave us alone and she talked to me.'

'Michael didn't mind that?' Vera asked.

'He's very protective,' Freya said. 'But I told him it was OK. That was when the social worker asked more personal things, prying actually. About our relationship, my background, all that.'

'What do your parents think of Michael?' Again Ashworth found it impossible to keep quiet. No way was *his* daughter going to end up with some pervy man old enough to be her father. He'd make sure of that. What was Freya's family thinking of?

'My parents don't give a shit actually. They moved to Spain, bought a bar. Act as if they're twenty again. No responsibilities, pissed every night.'

'Living the dream,' Vera muttered, only loud enough for Ashworth to hear.

'That social worker was a patronizing cow,' the girl went on. 'I had teachers like her. The ones that talk to you as if you're daft, as if they always know best. You could see how she might wind someone up so they lost their temper and killed her.'

'Where did you meet Michael?' Ashworth asked. Outside in the main village street the shops were closing for the evening. The light had faded. The mist had seeped in from the sea and they could hear the foghorn at the mouth of the Tyne. From the metro station the first commuters were coming home from work. The waiter lit the candle on their table and the sudden flare of the flame lit up the girl's face.

'At the Willows,' she said, brushing her long hair away from her face. 'You know, the smart hotel on the other side of town. He used to run a clinic once a week in the health club. I've been working as a waitress there at weekends since I was fifteen. We met at the beginning of December, the staff Christmas party.'

Chapter Twenty-One

Vera sat alone in the house that had once been her father's. Nights like this, a few glasses in to a bottle of Scotch, she could still imagine him there, lording it in the only comfortable armchair close to the fire. Or at the table, spread with plastic sheeting, his hand up the backside of some dead bird, preparing to stuff it, his eyes narrowed in concentration. That smell of dead flesh and chemicals.

'Taxidermy. Art and science combined,' he'd say.

And theft. And murder. Because he'd taken rare birds from the wild, killed them to the order of collectors as barking mad as he was, and she'd never shopped him. What had that made her? It came to her now that this case was all about families, the weird ties between kids and their parents. *Blood and water,* she thought, remembering Elias, drowned by the mother who claimed to love him.

She'd grown up with Hector's insults, mocking, masked as humour: 'Your mother was a beautiful woman. I only ever collect beautiful objects. Oh, Vee, whatever happened to you? Where did you spring from? Must be my side of the family, eh? Let's hope you have my brains.'

Only I didn't even get the brains, she thought now, throwing another log onto the fire, watching it spit, the bark peel and split. *I should have checked for a connection between Michael Morgan and the Willows. Basic policing.*

All the way north in the car she'd ranted at poor Joe Ashworth. 'Do I have to think of everything? I asked for a staff list. For cross-checks between all suspects and the health club. Charlie was supposed to be doing it. What's the idle bastard been up to?' Driving too fast through the fog, enjoying seeing him grow pale, wincing when they almost hit an oncoming vehicle, his mouth clamped shut.

Finally she'd provoked the reaction she'd hoped for. He'd cracked, lost it too. 'Just because you don't have a life worth saving, you don't have to take me down with you. I have a wife, kids. People who actually care about me. And if you spent your time supervising your team, like an SIO should, instead of doing their work for them, you'd know what Charlie had been up to.'

She'd dropped him off at the end of his street, with a curt arrangement to collect him the next morning: 'Make sure you're ready. I don't want to hang around while you're changing a nappy or kissing your brood goodbye.' No invitation to come back to her house for a drink first, although she'd been looking forward to that all afternoon: the chance to put things into perspective, to relax with the one man she'd ever really been close to. She'd had it in mind since suggesting that he leave his car in the Tyne valley.

How sad is that! It was her father sneaking inside her head again. *He's young enough to be your son. Do you really think he gives a tinker's curse for you?*

She got to her feet and went to the window. The fog hid all the lights in the valley. It was as if she was marooned, alone in the world. Unsteadily she carried the bottle and her glass into the kitchen. If she had another drink now, she knew she'd be up all night, and she had to show the ghost of her father that she was good at her job. That she knew what she was doing.

Kimmerston police station and the morning briefing. Ashworth had been ready when she'd arrived at his neat little house in the tidy estate of wannabe executive homes; he'd appeared through the front door before she'd even left the car. And she'd been gracious. Had apologized, which was almost unheard of for her. So now there was an uneasy truce between them.

She looked around the room at her team. 'We've cocked up big-style.' Vera thought that was noble of her, the 'we'. 'How did we miss the Morgan/Willows connection?'

'Because he isn't really a staff member,' Charlie said. 'He uses the room in the health club, pays a nominal rent for it because they think he pulls in punters for the other stuff. But he's self-employed, so he wasn't on the staff list they sent, and he's not officially a member.'

He was nervous, which pleased Vera no end. So nervous that the hand holding the polystyrene coffee cup was shaking and there was a tremor in his voice. She thought Ashworth would have been on the phone to Charlie as soon as he got in the night before: *Just make sure you get your story straight. The boss is on the warpath.*

'Do we know whether he was in the hotel the morning Jenny Lister was killed?'

'No one can tell me.' Charlie looked at her, cowed, waiting for her to lose her temper. 'He doesn't have to sign in like the employees.'

'Well, we'd better find out then, hadn't we?' Vera looked round at them. 'No, *I'd* better find out. I could do with going back to the hotel anyway. I've lost my feel for that place, but I know it better than the rest of you. Does Morgan have a pass to get him through to the pool area?'

'Yes, he's got a staff pass. He negotiated it when he set up business there. He swims and uses the gym most days he's in.'

Charlie was starting to relax. Vera was tempted to let rip at him to keep him on his toes, but she'd woken up feeling generous, proud of herself because she'd stopped drinking at a sensible point in the proceedings. 'What do we know about Freya Adams?'

He'd even made notes on Freya and read from them now, becoming more fluent as she allowed him to speak without interruption.

'Freya Adams started working at the Willows about two years ago, just a Saturday job at first because she was still at school, then full-time over last summer holidays and at Christmas. By that time she'd started at Newcastle College. She even moved into the staff quarters over Christmas because her parents had gone abroad. They'd fixed up for her to stay with her grandmother, but it seems that didn't quite work out. She found it too restrictive apparently. Her nan treated her like a kid. At least according to Ryan Taylor, the assistant manager.'

'Does she still work in the hotel?' Ashworth asked.

There was a quick look at the notes. 'Not since she moved in with Morgan. He wants her to concentrate on her studies.'

'Not restrictive at all then!' This was from Holly, who'd been trying to put in her two penn'orth since the briefing started.

'Does the management at the Willows know Freya is pregnant?' Vera asked.

'Ryan had heard a rumour, but hadn't discussed it with Morgan.' Charlie paused. 'I got the impression that our Michael keeps himself to himself. He doesn't mix much with the hotel staff. Sees himself as a bit superior. And of course he doesn't drink, and most of the socializing involves alcohol.'

'Why did he go to the Christmas party then? You wouldn't have thought it would really be his thing.' Vera hated the work Christmas party herself. Everyone trying to be jolly. Crap food and crap booze. No way could she face it sober.

'I don't know.' Charlie looked up uncertainly from the scrap of paper in his hand, lost. 'It surprised them all. He wasn't even invited, he just turned up.'

'Maybe he had his eye on Freya even then?' Holly said. 'I have him down as a bit of a predator. The way he picked up Mattie too. He could have been following her and just took his chance when she needed money in the coffee shop. Perhaps he seeks out young innocent girls without much support. There'd have been talk about the way Freya's parents had abandoned her. So he saw the party as a way of hooking into her.'

'And must have got her pregnant almost immediately.' Vera wondered how consensual that sex had been. Had she been drinking at the party? Had it happened then? Too late now to charge him with anything, but all the same it added to the picture . . .

'What do we think about Morgan and Jenny Lister?' Joe Ashworth asked. 'Were they having a relationship? If so, when? Was that before he took up with Freya?'

There was a long silence. They were trying to get their heads round the complexities of the timing, but also unwilling to commit themselves.

'I don't see it,' Holly said at last. 'He's into frail little things. Women who're needy and won't stand up to him. Women he can control. It'd be completely out of charac-ter to go out with someone older, independent, strong. We've only got the elderly neighbour's word for it that Jenny had started a new relationship. There's no evi-dence it was with Morgan.'

'Strong women can be needy too.' Vera spoke without thinking, then saw them all looking at her, drawing con-clusions she'd rather they didn't make. 'And Jenny's friend the teacher thought she was having some sort of affair. A guy she had to keep secret. Well, she'd hardly admit to be having it off with Morgan, would she? A client and someone involved with a notorious scandal. Holly, what did you get out of Lawrence May, the guy Jenny had been seeing?'

'He couldn't have killed her,' Holly said. 'He was at a conference in Derbyshire. I checked.'

'Did he say why she dumped him?'

'No, but I'd guess because he bored her to death. I mean, he seemed a really nice man. But earnest. You know the sort. As if he's saving the planet single-handed. He had a go at me because I chucked a plastic bottle into the bin in his office instead of taking it away to recycle.'

'She didn't tell him she'd fallen for someone else?'

'He said he had the impression there was something new going on in her life,' Holly said. 'I pressed him, but he couldn't be more specific. He didn't know if it was a new lover or a new project.'

'So if Lister was involved with Morgan, we have no proof either way,' Ashworth said. 'So we keep it as a possibility, but don't get hung up on it. In the end, it doesn't matter if Morgan killed Lister because she was meddling in his new life with Freya or because he'd been screwing her. Courts don't really care about motive. We have to show he was at the Willows that morning. We need evidence that he put a string round Jenny Lister's neck and strangled her. Why doesn't have to come into it.'

But I want to know why, Vera thought, as she waited for the other actions to be assigned. *I do care about motive. I'm a nosy bitch and it's what I'm in the job for.*

Driving into the Willows, watching the women arriving all around her with their sports bags and their expensive trainers, Vera couldn't believe that she'd been one of them, a punter snatching a quick fix of fitness between meetings or on her way to work. She wondered if numbers were still down, if any of the women had demanded a refund of their membership fee. It seemed a bit quiet for this time on a weekday. She walked through the lobby and down the stairs to the health club. Using her membership card she swiped her way through the turnstile. Almost invisible, she thought, even without her bag and towel. Another middle-aged woman with delusions that swimming a few lengths would make her healthier, more beautiful. If the staff were shown her description, even a photo, she doubted if anyone would remember she'd been there.

Ryan Taylor was sorting out a crisis with an exploding coffee machine. There was a pool of brown liquid dribbling from the machine onto one end of the tiled kitchen floor. Chefs and waitresses were walking it through the room. The place was hot. There were steaming pans on the gas hobs and someone was screaming at a young woman in whites: 'Are you cremating that piece of meat? What do you think this is? Some cheap fast-food outlet.'

Taylor was standing beside the pool and shouting into his mobile. 'We're coming up to our busiest time. I need an engineer here now! And get the bloody cleaner to mop up the mess.'

'And I thought at least I'd get a decent cup of coffee.'

He must have received the assurance he needed, because he switched off the phone, turned to her and grinned. 'Come into my office, Inspector, and I'll make one for you there.'

'The cleaner you're waiting for, it wouldn't be Danny, that student?'

Ryan looked at her sharply, wondering if the question had particular significance. 'No, he works lates. Anyway, it's his day off. Why?'

'No reason, pet. Just curious.'

She followed him to his office and watched him fill the coffee machine before she started talking.

'When you're in this place,' she said, watching the water drip through the filter, 'it's hard to believe there's any life outside at all. Must be worse for you. Do you live here?'

'No. I've got a flat in town with my partner, Paul. There's a room here I can use if I need to stay over.'

'It's an odd sort of community, a big hotel.' She saw him wondering where she was going with the idea. She wasn't quite sure herself. 'Especially for the staff who live in. Everyone on top of each other. Like a monastery. Does it lead to tensions?'

'It can do. And not much of the monastery about it.'

'Romances, then. Love affairs . . .'

'Sometimes.'

'Michael Morgan and Freya Adams.' She took the mug he handed to her, sniffed it appreciatively. 'What was going on there?'

Ryan shrugged. 'They're both adults. I know some of the staff were a bit concerned. Karen, from health-club reception, had a motherly word with her. "Do you really know what you're playing with?" That sort of thing. But there was nothing I could do to stop it.'

'Had Morgan been sniffing around younger women before?'

Ryan took time to consider. 'There was nothing that came to my notice, but I'll ask around.'

'Do that. And I need to know if he was here the morning of the murder. It wasn't a usual clinic day, but I understand he came in sometimes to use the gym. He's not on the list of members who went through the turnstile we got from your IT people, but he'd find a way through that. He's not a stupid man.'

'You think he's a killer?'

Vera could tell his first thought was for the hotel, the publicity and the implications of the arrest of a man who was almost an employee. Ryan didn't consider Michael Morgan a friend. There was no personal concern. 'No, nothing like that. I'm talking out loud, telling stories to myself. That's what my job's all about. Mostly that's all they are: stories.'

'We nearly asked him to leave last year, when there was all that publicity about the little boy.' Ryan was staring out of the window. 'But in the end he talked Louise round.'

'He's got a way with women, has he?' Vera gave a little laugh to show there was no real significance to the question.

'Must have. Louise is as tough as old boots when it comes to the business.'

'Did he ever bring Mattie Jones, the boy's mother, here?' Vera asked.

Ryan shook his head. 'Not as far as I know. And once he and Freya set up home together, Freya kept away too. The girls she used to work with invited her back for lunch one day, but she didn't come.'

'Have you got a key to the room he uses as a clinic?'

'Of course. But Michael doesn't keep any equipment there. He brings it with him each time.'

'Does he make his own appointments, or do the girls on reception here do it for him?'

'He sees to all that himself,' Ryan said. 'If anyone expresses an interest in consulting him, we pass on his mobile number.'

'So no appointment book.' Vera should have known it wouldn't be that easy. 'No way of getting hold of his client list.'

'Sorry.'

She gestured towards the closed door, the way from Ryan's private room to the outside world of the hotel. 'Tell you what, pet, while you're out there doing my job for me, asking your people about Michael Morgan, find out if anyone ever saw him with Jenny Lister.'

Ryan nodded his head, another young man eager to please her.

'I thought I'd just have a bit of a wander round myself, chat to folk. That's all right with you?'

'Of course.' But Vera could tell that he'd be very pleased when he'd got rid of her, when she was finally off the premises.

Chapter Twenty-Two

She wandered through the hotel, going through doors that said *Staff Only*, looking into cupboards and a laundry, hitting at last on the staffroom. A small square box with hardly any natural light, one bright electric bulb in the middle of the room, furniture discarded from the rest of the building. A stack of lockers against one wall.

Lisa from the pool was there on her lunch break, eating chopped-up fruit from a Tupperware box, reading a paperback novel. Vera nodded towards the book. 'Any good?'

A couple of middle-aged women were gossiping in a corner. They looked up briefly and went back to their chat. Ears flapping.

Lisa set down the book and ate the last piece of melon. 'It's OK. Escapist, you know.'

'Aye, well, we all need a bit of that. Have you got a few minutes? I wondered if you'd give me a behind-the-scenes tour of the place.' By now Vera thought she had it pretty well sussed, but she didn't want the old bats in the corner listening in.

'Sure.' Lisa pushed the lid onto the box and put it into her bag. She'd always been pale, but it seemed to Vera today that all the colour had drained from her face.

'Do the staff have passes?' They'd left the staffroom, but were still backstage. Grey walls and dust, occasional piles of unidentifiable equipment.

'Yeah. Electronic fobs that let you in from the public areas. Very high-tech.'

'God,' Vera said, 'what a nightmare! I'd lose mine in a week.'

Lisa smiled indulgently. She was the sort of woman who never lost anything.

'And once you're into the staff areas you have free access everywhere?'

'That's right.'

'What about to the pool?' Vera was developing the germ of an idea. They'd assumed that the murderer had got to the pool through the public changing rooms, but if there was staff access, that wasn't necessarily the case. Again she thought she'd cocked up here, hadn't concentrated on the basics. She should have demanded a floor plan right from the start. No, she thought. Charlie should have sorted the floor plan. It occurred to her that all the stuff about Elias Jones could be a distraction.

'Yes, that's this way.' Lisa led her down a small corridor and into a space that was half storeroom and half office. In one corner there was a half-sized desk with a computer and phone. The rest of the room was taken up with floats and the bendy rubber strips used by the members of the aqua-aerobics classes. She opened another door and they looked out onto the poolside, only yards from the sauna and steam room.

Lisa pulled a packet of blue plastic overshoes from a drawer. 'If you want to go out, you'll have to wear these.'

Vera pulled them on and walked out onto the tiles. The bootees were exactly the same as the ones she wore at a crime scene. The pool was quiet. There was that strange echo that reminded her of aching limbs and a pounding heart. A few determined swimmers ploughed through the water and a couple of women sprawled on the deckchairs. From outside, when it was closed, the office door looked like another wall panel. It wasn't surprising that they'd missed it. Lisa must have been following her thoughts. 'The architect wanted clean lines,' she said. 'There are a couple of other storerooms, but they're hidden too. This is the only one you can access from both sides.'

Vera joined her back in the office. She leaned her backside against the desk. 'Do you know a guy called Michael Morgan?'

'He does the complementary therapies?' The question was innocent enough, but Vera wasn't deceived. Lisa knew him all right. She was suddenly more alert.

'Works here once a week. Got one of the young waitresses pregnant. That's the one.' Vera looked directly at Lisa. 'Did he ever try it on with you?'

'No! Nothing like that. He wouldn't.' Lisa seemed horrified by the idea.

'Why wouldn't he? He has a history of it.'

'I was his client,' Lisa said. 'Our relationship was professional.' A wash of colour was spreading from her neck into her cheeks.

Maybe it was professional, but you'd have liked it to be more than that. What is it about Michael Morgan and women who should know better?

'Tell me about it.'

'It was hard, working here. I mean, I'm good at the job and I love it, but I've never really fitted in.'

'You were bullied,' Vera said.

'That sounds a bit harsh, but it's what it felt like. I didn't go into town clubbing with the other girls and I'm not interested in the same stuff. They could be dead cruel. It got that I dreaded coming into work, started having these panic attacks. My GP couldn't help, so I tried Michael.'

'And he could help?'

Lisa nodded. 'I don't know how it works, but it made me feel really calm. Like I really stopped caring about what the rest of them thought about me. I looked forward to coming into work again.'

'Did you ever see him away from here?' Vera asked.

'No.' Lisa was playing with one of the soft rubber floats, twisting it in her hands. 'Look, none of the other staff know I consulted him. There's always been a lot of gossip, first when the little boy was killed and then when he took up with Freya. It's as if he's some sort of freak. If they knew I'd seen Michael, they'd love that. It'd just give them more ammunition to have a go at me. But he was kind to me, gentle, and I'm grateful to him.'

'Did you ever catch him in the places where the public has no access?'

Lisa frowned. 'No. Only in the office he used as a consulting room.'

'But he would have had one of those magic fobs that would let him back here?'

'I suppose so.' Lisa looked at her watch. 'Look, I'll have to go. My shift started ten minutes ago.'

'Did any of the other staff consult him?' Lisa was already halfway through the door, but turned back to answer the question.

'I wouldn't know,' she said, 'would I? They wouldn't admit to it any more than me.'

Vera drove along the narrow back roads from the Willows to Barnard Bridge, timing the journey, for no reason other than it seemed a sensible thing to do and she wasn't ready yet to go back to the police station in Kimmerston. She had no specific village resident in mind for the murder. Connie Masters wouldn't have left her child alone in the cottage to drive ten miles to kill her previous colleague, and though Vera still loved the idea of Veronica Eliot in the dock, she could see no reason for it. It was more likely, given her new knowledge of the layout of the health club, that they were looking for a staff member. She thought she should pin down the student cleaner whose employment had coincided with the thefts at the Willows. Maybe she'd call into his house that afternoon, catch him by surprise. Once she'd had some lunch.

The fog of the previous day had cleared and it was sunny, unusually warm for so early in the spring. Turning a corner, she saw a couple in the middle of the road. Hannah Lister and Simon Eliot walking hand in hand. Hannah wore jeans and a white muslin top; Simon seemed large and clumsy in comparison. *Beauty and the Beast*, Vera thought. Even from the back and from this distance she could sense the connection between them, like some sort of electric charge, and felt the old stab of envy. Was she a miserable cow, that lovers always made her feel that way? Did she want everyone in the world to be as lonely as she was?

The young people stepped onto the verge to allow her to pass, but she slowed down. 'Do you want a lift?' Immediately she saw she should have continued driving without acknowledging them. This had been a brief moment of happiness for Hannah, a time of escape. Opening the car window, Vera was aware of the birdsong from the woods by the side of the road, found herself unpicking the tangle of sound for individual species. Her father had tested her on her knowledge whenever they were out together: 'Come on, Vee, don't be such a duffer, you must recognize that!'

She'd expected an immediate rebuttal from the young people and was surprised when after some hesitation they got in, Simon in the back seat, although he was so tall that his knees almost touched his chin, and Hannah in the front.

'Where would you like to go?' Vera asked. 'Are you on your way home?'

'Where shall we go, Simon?' The girl turned in the seat to speak to him. Her voice was brittle, almost manic. 'Rome? Zanzibar? The moon?'

He reached out and took her hand in his. 'We'll do Rome in the summer,' he said easily. 'Or Zanzibar, if you prefer. But now, Inspector, yes, we'd better go home. To my place please. It was such a lovely day that we got up very early and we've been walking all morning, but now I think Hannah is very tired. Just as well you appeared to save us. Mother has offered to make us lunch.'

'You must be feeling better if you're up to facing the mother-in-law,' Vera said with a smile.

'The doctor gave me some pills and now I don't feel very much at all.' Hannah had drooped after the flicker of her exchange with Simon. She lay back in the seat with her eyes half closed.

'But you do have to eat, and neither of us can face the supermarket.' He was still leaning forward, the seat belt stretched to its limit, rubbing the back of her hand with his thumb.

'I never did ask you,' Vera said, talking to Simon's reflection in the mirror, 'where were you the morning Jenny died?' She had a sudden horrible thought that he might be implicated in some way. She hadn't checked, after all, that he had an alibi. But she hated the idea of it, of Hannah's saviour as killer.

'At home,' he said. 'Hannah wanted to revise, so we hadn't planned to meet up until the evening.' He must have realized why she was asking, but he didn't seem at all offended.

'Was your mother in?'

'Dunno,' he said. 'I'd been out on the piss the night before, catching up with some of the lads I was at school with. I didn't surface until midday. Mum was out then, but she came back soon after.'

By now they were approaching the crossroads, the turn-off to the village. Connie Masters's cottage was on one side and the big white house was on the other. 'Do you know the woman who lives there?' Vera nodded towards the cottage.

'No, I've seen people in there. A mother and a child. Are they permanent tenants? It always used to be a holiday place.'

'Her name's Masters,' Vera said. 'Connie Masters.'

Hannah stirred. 'Wasn't she the social worker super-vising Mattie Jones?'

'That's right. Did your mother talk about her?'

'I didn't realize she lived here. Mum felt sorry for her. About the way she'd been treated in the press. Because she screwed up over Elias Jones.'

As she watched the young people walk away, Vera wondered what *she'd* have made of Hannah's mother if they'd met. Vera disliked good-looking women as a matter of course, and Jenny's competence, her certainty that she was right in every situation, would have irritated her too. It seemed to Vera that Jenny, apparently so admired and respected, could have had many secret enemies. A book that would have exposed her clients' and colleagues' frail-ties would surely have added to the list. Connie, for example, would almost certainly have appeared in it. She definitely had an interest in ensuring that Jenny's work was never published.

Chapter Twenty-Three

Vera parked in the main street of the village and went in search of food. The pub was open and she was tempted, but she knew how word got around in small places: *that big boss policewoman was drinking at lunchtime.* And besides, she wanted more than a bag of crisps and it seemed there was nothing else on offer. Walking down the street, she got on the phone to Ashworth. 'Lister's handbag. It still hasn't turned up. A big red leather affair that she used as a briefcase.' Knowing that shouting at him would serve no real purpose, because the team already had it as a priority and most of Northumbria Police were already looking for it. She had low blood sugar and it always made her radgy. 'Any chance you can meet me at Danny Shaw's place? I thought it was about time I met him.'

She found the Tyne Teashop and decided that would do. All the windows looked out on the river, and the place had a calm green light from the trees and the reflections of water that had seeped out onto the flood meadow. Most of the tables were occupied. Older couples: big bossy women and slight subdued men for the most part. *You should have carried on working, pet*, she thought, directing her sympathy to the men. *Bet you never thought early retirement would be like this, acting as chauffeur to the wife, and endless cups of tea.*

Then she turned her attention to home-made corned-beef pie and the whereabouts of Jenny Lister's handbag. Had the murderer taken it from her locker? Did that mean she was murdered for what it contained: notes for the book she planned to write. And what had happened to it since? It would be hard to destroy a substantial bag, though of course the paper inside could have been burned. She shook her head and moved on to a meringue filled with cream and covered with grated chocolate. The meringue was crisp on the outside and slightly squelchy in the middle, as near perfect as was possible for an object that was a work of art, not science. The bag—along with the notebook—was probably in a landfill somewhere and would never be seen again.

Joe Ashworth was already waiting for her outside Danny Shaw's house and she got into his car to talk before they went in. The house was grander than she'd expected, an extended detached cottage with a bit of an orchard at the back. Move it halfway up a mountain and she'd have been prepared to live there herself. It stood in a valley on the edge of a hamlet halfway between Barnard Bridge and the Willows, surrounded by established trees.

She nodded towards it. 'I thought you said they'd fallen on hard times since the recession.'

'Probably mortgaged to the hilt,' he said. 'Maybe they see it as an asset to hold on to. But that's why the mother got the job at the Willows.'

'She'll be at work now?'

'I assume so.'

Out of the car, there was that cacophony of woodland birdsong that seemed to be a soundtrack to this case. She tried not to hear it, refusing to take her father's test. The garden was wild; the lawn hadn't had its first cut of the spring and there were weeds poking through the paving stones of the path that led from the front gate. There was the remnant of an untidy bonfire in one corner. Maybe once they'd had a weekly gardener, but that had probably been one of the expenses to go. Nearer the house they heard music.

'Bingo!' she said. 'Not a wasted trip then.'

Danny was sitting outside on a paved terrace, a portable CD player on the table beside him. His legs were stretched so that his feet rested on another wooden garden chair and there was an open book on his knee. But that was lying page-down. And although his face was turned away from her, she sensed that he was sleeping. There wasn't much warmth in the sun and he was wearing a big grey jersey, his chin buried in the collar.

'You've got to make the most of it this time of year, haven't you?' Vera perched on the table. It rocked under her weight. The boy didn't reply.

There was a moment of anger. Cocky little bastard. Even if he'd been asleep the question would have woken him.

'Talk to me, lad!'

Still no response. It seemed to take her an age to realize what had happened. She reached out to feel for a pulse, had the sensation of cold, dead flesh under her fingers, but still she didn't believe it. She lifted his eyelids and saw the red pinpricks in the whites of his eyes and pulled back the deep collar of his sweater to see the line around his neck. Only then did it hit her, like a punch in the gut, that Danny had been killed too. Strangled in the same way as Jenny Lister. This time, the death was her responsibility, her failure. The music from the CD player thumped in her ears, taunting her, drowning out the sound of the birds. She knew better than to touch it. There could be a partial fingerprint on the flat plastic switch. But the noise was driving her crazy and she walked away from it, back towards the road, just pulling herself together sufficiently to shout to Joe, 'Stay there. I'll call it in.'

Standing by her car, waiting for the CSIs—the hoopla of experts who gathered at a murder like raptors over a dead sheep—she wished for the first time in ten years that she still smoked. She hadn't known Danny Shaw, but his death moved her more than any she'd encountered professionally. She'd been cruising on this case. It hadn't even crossed her mind that there might be another killing. Now her mind raced. Why was Danny Shaw murdered? For something he'd seen? For something he'd known?

There was the sound of a car in the road. Vera expected it to be the community officers she'd requested to secure the scene, but it was small and green, and Danny's mother was inside.

Karen Shaw was out of it like a shot. 'Can I help you?' Prickly, ready to pick a fight, assuming Vera was there to hassle her son. Which of course she had been. Then she seemed to sense Vera's mood. She stood in the middle of the road. 'What's happened? Where's my boy?'

Vera couldn't find the words to answer. Before Vera could stop her, Karen had let herself into the house and was running through it screaming for her son.

By the time Vera reached her she'd gone into the garden through a French window in the dining room and Joe Ashworth had her in his arms. She was very small; her head just came up to his chest. He held her there and let her sob. Vera stood watching, helpless, useless. At least by then the CD was over and the music had stopped.

Later, the three of them sat in a neighbour's living room. Karen hadn't wanted to leave her own house, but Joe had explained. 'We have to let the scientists get on with the work. You do understand?' And Karen had nodded, not understanding at all, but without the energy to fight. They'd phoned Danny's father, who was on his way home, but Vera wanted to talk to Karen now. This minute, before the man arrived. The last thing she needed was an overprotective alpha male hovering in the background.

'How was Danny, Karen? The last few days, I mean.
Since we found Mrs Lister's body in the pool.'

'I don't know what you mean.'

'Did he seem anxious, worried? Scared?'

'Are you saying he committed suicide?'

Vera had considered that briefly. It would be a tidy
explanation of the case: Jenny seeing Danny stealing,
Danny killing her to keep her quiet, and then himself
because he couldn't stand the stress. But nobody committed suicide by strangulation.

'No,' Vera said gently. 'We believe he was murdered.'

'Danny was never scared,' Karen said. 'Not even as a
child. He'd climb the biggest trees he could find, swim too
far out in the sea. Reckless. We always said he'd kill himself one day.' She stared bleakly at Vera. 'They'd play
Dare, the bairns in the village. He was always the last one
in the game.'

'Anxious then.' Vera tried to keep the impatience from
her voice. 'Would that be a better word to describe it?'

Karen was holding things together remarkably well, in
a state of shock, but the reality of her son's death hadn't
really kicked in. Vera wanted to get as much information
as possible from her while she was thinking straight.

'More unpredictable,' Karen said. 'Moody. He hated
the job at the Willows, but he only had five more days
before he went back to Bristol.'

'What subject was he studying there?' At the moment
Vera just wanted to keep the woman talking.

'Law.'

Vera imagined the sort of lawyer Danny would have
become. A flash barrister, with an expensive suit and a
bonny little female junior hanging off every word. But he
wouldn't have got very far with a criminal conviction. If
Jenny Lister had caught him with his hand in someone's
purse, that might have provided a motive for murder.
Danny might have had the arrogance to think he could get
away with thieving, seen it as a way to supplement his

income, almost his right. She'd known middle-class crooks like that. Now, though, he was the victim, and none of that seemed relevant. Vera felt as if she were lost in a fog, no point of reference and no idea where to go next.

'Did Danny know Michael Morgan?' Ashford had taken up the questions. He leaned forward, so that his hand and the bereaved woman's were almost touching. 'The acupuncturist working out of the Willows. Did Danny know him?'

Karen didn't answer and Joe continued talking, the words soft and easy, keeping her calm. 'Because I thought they might become friends of a kind. There was a difference in age, of course. But two educated men in a workplace full of women, they might come together.'

Karen looked up. 'I told Danny he was no good. I told Danny to stay away from him.'

'But our kids never take our advice, do they?' Joe might have had teenagers himself, the way he was speaking. Vera sat back in admiration and let him get on with it. 'They always think they know best.' He paused. 'How did they meet?'

'Drinking fancy coffee in the lounge at the hotel. Danny said he couldn't stand the muck in the staffroom. Since he moved to Bristol he'd developed pretensions. We only ever have instant at home.' Karen gave a wry little smile, mocking her son—and herself for minding the change in him. 'He went to the lounge before he started his shift. Morgan was often in there after he'd finished his.'

'I can't see Danny being taken in by all that new-age stuff.'

'He said Morgan wasn't either. Not really. It was just another business opportunity for him, a way of getting what he wanted.' Karen seemed exhausted by the exchange. The shock was catching up with her.

'And what *did* Morgan want, pet? Did Danny say?' Vera thought this was important. What was going on between the student and the older man? She willed Karen to hold it together long enough to answer.

'The same things as anyone else, apparently. A decent income. A nice home. A wife and kids.'

'But his potential wives were so young!'

'I know, and Danny spoke as if Morgan was someone to admire. I couldn't stand that. "Look at the way he treats his women!" I'd say. And Danny would just smile. He said Morgan was a man who liked beautiful things and young women are usually more beautiful than older ones. He could see nothing wrong in it.' Karen stopped abruptly, narrowed her eyes, looked like a cat about to hiss and spit. 'Do you think Morgan killed Danny? Is that what these questions are about?'

'No.' This was Ashworth playing it safe, coming up with the old platitudes. 'We have to ask questions, make connections.' Vera wouldn't have minded letting Karen loose on Morgan. She'd have paid to see her rip the man apart, whether he'd killed Danny or not.

'Did your son have any other close friends at the Willows?' she asked.

'I don't really know about any of Danny's friends, not any more,' Karen said. Her voice was cold and quiet. 'When he was at the high school in Hexham, we used to be close. Like friends. But lately he stopped talking to me. Since he went away to university it felt as if he had a completely new life. I only knew he was meeting Morgan because I saw them together at work. I suppose it was natural, that he should drift away from us when he left home. But he was our only son and it was/hard to feel we didn't have any place in his life. And now he's left us completely. We'll never have the chance to make things right again.' She began to cry.

Chapter Twenty-Four

It was a playgroup day, the weather sunny enough for Connie to walk Alice to the hall. The gossip on the pavement was all about Jenny Lister's death, which made a pleasant change from the usual bitching about Connie and Elias Jones. Because Connie had worked with the murder victim, she was included in the discussion as they waited for the doors to open. There were small tentative questions at first, but after a few minutes Connie found herself in the centre of a bunch of excited young women. 'What do you think happened? The newspapers don't really tell us anything. What have the police said to you?' Connie felt like a tart, but she gave them just what they wanted, little snippets of information about Jenny and her work with social services. When the hall opened they were hanging on her every word and there was none of the usual rush to get inside.

Veronica Eliot was there, taking registration for the following term. She sat at a small table with a clipboard and pen, shiny-lipped and immaculate in a black linen shirt, its collar so stiffly ironed that Connie wondered it hadn't slashed the back of her neck like a blade. Connie joined the queue. When things were really bad she'd considered moving Alice to a pre-school in the next village, or even bullying her ex to pay for a private nursery, but Alice would start at the primary in September and it would be madness to move her just for one term.

When she reached the desk there was a moment of awkwardness. She assumed Veronica wouldn't want their lunch together to be mentioned. It would signal such a U-turn in relations between them that it would be hard for Veronica to explain the shift in attitude to the other play-group mums. How complicated were these oblique communications between women! Surely men were much more straightforward in their dealings. But Veronica gave her a friendly smile. 'I did enjoy the other day. We must do it again sometime.'

Connie was quite thrown. She looked at Veronica, suspecting sarcasm or other, more sinister motives. Was this the start of a joke at her expense?

'It was kind of you.' She looked around. She was the last in the queue; the other mothers were drifting away. She thought Veronica would never have made the comment if she'd had an audience. 'Why don't you come to me?' Connie wondered why she'd felt the sudden impulse to reciprocate. 'What about today? Come for tea. You won't get home baking, but I bought a cake from the Tyne Teashop the other day for a treat and they're always good.'

Veronica looked up from her paper and Connie expected a put-down, at best a polite excuse. The village had a hierarchy and, even without the complication of her notoriety, they moved in different circles.

'Thank you!' Veronica said. Then there was a brief, almost triumphant smile, as if she'd been hoping for the invitation all along. 'Shall we say about four? I'll see you then.' She took the cheque from Connie's hand and set down her pen.

Connie walked back to the cottage, wondering what had brought about this recent change in Veronica. Really, what was this all about? What could Veronica Eliot possibly want from her?

While Alice was at playgroup, Connie tidied the house. As she polished and vacuumed, she saw it through the older woman's eyes, imagined the disdainful glances at the tatty furniture, the cobwebs and the grime. But when Veronica arrived a little earlier than expected, surprising Connie by turning up at the kitchen door and carrying a bunch of flowers cut from her garden, she was gracious: 'Goodness, what a difference you've made to the cottage! I came for dinner one night when the owners were here and it wasn't nearly so cosy then.'

In the end, though, they sat outside, which despite the breeze was more pleasant than the damp house. Alice was wearing her wellingtons and paddling around in the mud and sand that formed a little beach between the burn and the river. Connie poured tea from a china pot she'd found at the back of the larder and cleaned for the occasion. She was reminded again of the young man who'd turned up on the afternoon of Jenny's murder. She'd had tea outside that day too.

Veronica was talking about her son.

'He says they still intend to marry in a year's time. He'd offered to take Hannah away, somewhere abroad, and do it immediately, though I can't imagine how he thinks that would compensate for her mother's death! Jenny was no happier about the marriage than I was. Imagine, some sordid ceremony on a beach, surrounded by package tourists. I'm pleased Hannah had the sense not to go along with that plan. She says she owes it to her mother to keep her word and wait until Simon's got his MA. At least that buys him some time. Who knows how either of them will feel in twelve months?'

'I suppose he's due back at the university in a couple of weeks for the start of the new term.' Connie wasn't much interested in Simon Eliot's plans, but she knew the rules of the game. Each woman should allow the other to speak of subjects close to her heart. Soon Veronica would allow Connie to talk of Alice, of how bright she was and how well she'd settled into the area. The primary school in the next village was well considered and over-subscribed. Veronica was a governor and might have influence if there was competition for places. Veronica might have her own agenda for this meeting, but Connie had one too.

'I've told Simon he has to go back to college.' Veronica was firm. 'Of course he wants to be around for Hannah, but he has his own life to live. She has a father, for God's sake. I know they've never particularly got on, but I think he should take some responsibility.' A pause. 'Don't you?' The question was fierce and a little unexpected.

'I suppose she wants to stay in Barnard Bridge until she's finished her A levels.' Connie didn't want to alienate Veronica now that this new accord had been struck, but she thought Simon should be admired for his loyalty. If anything should happen to *her*, she wasn't certain she'd entrust Alice to her ex-husband. How could she possibly fit into his new family?

'Apparently so. And then, if you please, she's going to move in with Simon in Durham. We bought him a little flat, which was a bargain the way the housing market is, and an investment. Durham's such a popular city. But we wouldn't have done that if we'd realized the consequences.'

Alice had waded further into the burn. The water was still shallow there, despite the swollen river beyond, and it hardly covered the feet of her boots, but Connie called after her, glad of an excuse not to answer Veronica. 'Take care! We don't want you slipping and getting wet.'

Veronica looked up then, distracted from her own pre-occupations, it seemed. 'Oh yes, dear, do come back and play here. That seems rather dangerous. You'd be much better on dry land.'

'She's fine,' Connie said brusquely. She thought Veronica had probably over-protected her child. Besides, what right did the woman have now to interfere?

Alice had found a stick on the bank and was poking at the vegetation on the opposite side of the burn. There were huge heads of cow parsley that were higher than the girl; the lacy leaves and ribbed stalks must have seemed like a forest of trees to her, exciting and mysterious.

'Come back!' Veronica called, her voice seemingly close to panic. 'Oh, do come back, please.'

Alice turned and frowned, but ignored the stranger.

'She's fine,' Connie said again. She remembered the way Veronica had looked at Alice when they'd been invited to lunch. 'Really, I think children need to feel they're having adventures. They have to learn to deal with some risk, don't you think so?'

'How can you say that?' Veronica was almost beside herself. 'You of all people! You allowed a child to die in your care.'

Alice must have heard the shrill voice and turned back again, troubled by the tone, though she hadn't taken in the words. There was a moment of quiet. Water running over pebbles. The distant rumble of a tractor. Connie couldn't trust herself to speak. She wouldn't lose her temper in front of her daughter.

'I'm sorry,' Veronica said at last. 'That wasn't fair.'

Perhaps infected by the tension between the adults, Alice began to lash out at the cow parsley with her stick, beating down the plants and stamping on them to make a path into the middle of the vegetation, her furthest foray ever away from the cottage. Connie started to pile up cups and plates. Now she just wanted Veronica to leave. She could see that really they would never do more than tolerate each other. The notion that they might be friends—that she could be included in the charmed circle of people invited for delicious lunches in the big white house—was ridiculous.

'Look what I've found!' Alice was almost hidden from view and her voice had a strange, muffled quality. Connie stood up, glad to leave Veronica's side. She walked towards the water, the movement shaking the stress from her muscles. She crossed the burn, balancing on a large, flat rock in the middle so that she didn't get her shoes wet.

Alice was standing in an untidy clearing in the patch of weeds, looking down. 'Would you like it, Mummy? Could we keep it?' And she bent to pick up the squashed leather bag.

Chapter Twenty-Five

Vera called the whole team back to the incident room in Kimmerston to brief them on the Danny Shaw murder. Joe Ashworth wasn't sure what had got into her. There was a sort of fury that ran in spasms through her body. It was as if she thought the boy had been strangled just to taunt her. Ashworth decided this evening that she was more mad than usual. She was there before the rest of them, pacing up and down at the front of the room. He knew better than to speak to her. He waited in silence for the team to gather.

Charlie was next in. Eyes like a bloodhound and a paper cup of coffee in one hand, some sort of pastry wrapped in greaseproof paper in the other. Charlie was always on the edge of some crisis, a major depression or breakdown. When his wife had left him, they'd thought for a couple of months that he'd lose it completely. She'd always done the practical stuff—washed his clothes and ironed them, cooked his food and cleared up his mess. Like she was his mother. They couldn't see how he'd cope without her. But he'd pulled himself through it and still he survived, and each day he turned up was a little miracle. He'd even worked out how to use the washing machine, and these days he managed a shave before leaving the house.

Tenacious. That was how Vera had described Charlie to Joe Ashworth: 'You can't expect him to do much under his own initiative, but give him clear instructions, then all you have to do is wind him up and let him go.'

Holly was last in, and something about her, the way she looked round her, the self-satisfied smile of apology to Vera for keeping them waiting, let Ashworth know she had something important to share. She'd wait until the end and then make her announcement. Like some bloody conjuror pulling a rabbit from a hat.

Vera glowered at them. She wrote Danny's name on the whiteboard, stabbing out the letters with the marker.

'Our second victim. Danny Shaw. Mother Karen works on reception at the health club at the Willows. Father Derek, builder and developer, going through hard times financially. Danny was their only child. Spoilt rotten, then he grew up, went away to university and turned moody on them. Stopped talking. He wanted to be a lawyer and he had a kind of motive for the Lister murder. *If* Jenny Lister caught him stealing from his colleagues.'

'You think his killing could be a revenge attack?' Charlie said. 'Because he strangled the woman?'

Vera stopped, frozen, her arm still outstretched towards the board. Ashworth thought she might have a go at Charlie, call him stupid for dreaming up such a notion. One way of relieving the pent-up tension. But instead she nodded. 'I hadn't thought of that, but it's worth considering. Who cared for Lister enough to kill for her?'

'Her daughter,' Holly called out from the back of the room.

'Or her daughter's boyfriend,' Vera said. 'Just because he's besotted with the girl. I can see him committing murder if she asked him to do it. We mustn't forget him.'

'How would Hannah know Shaw?' Ashworth was all in favour of brainstorming, but this was madness, fantasy time.

'Wouldn't they have gone to school together? Only a year between them. We know Simon went to a posh place in town, but Danny and Hannah were both students at the high school in Hexham. Let's check that out with the teachers, other kids. It's another connection between the Shaws and the Listers. Holly, you sort it, you're good at that stuff and nearer in age to the kids than the rest of us.'

She stopped for breath, took a gasp of air. 'Some more news. I got the call while we were with the Shaw family. They've found Jenny Lister's bag. No news yet on the notebook, though. We're still waiting to hear. Guess where the bag was found! Barnard Bridge. Just across the burn from Mallow Cottage, Connie Masters's place.' She looked around the room. 'Any ideas?'

Silence. In another office someone burst out laughing. The noise seemed to tear at Vera's nerves, and Ashworth expected another outburst about their lack of intelligence and about how crap they were as detectives, but she held it together. Instead she nodded towards Charlie.

'What have you got on Morgan? According to Shaw's mother, he and Danny were mates. At least Morgan seemed to have some sort of influence on the boy.' She had set Charlie off to re-interview the people who had been working or playing in the health club the day Jenny Lister had died. Had any of them seen Michael Morgan that morning? He hadn't had a clinic there that day, but had he used the gym or the pool? Ashworth imagined that Charlie had spent his day drinking tea in living rooms in tidy houses all over the Tyne valley, interviewing the wrinklies from the aqua-aerobic class. The sort of task he loved.

Charlie slumped into a seat near the front, licked his fingers and crunched into a ball the greaseproof paper he'd been holding.

'A few sightings that day of young men who *could* have been Morgan, but nothing specific and nothing consistent. They're so eager to help, you get the feeling they'd say anything to make you happy.'

'Morgan's not that young.'

Charlie managed a quick smile. Progress, Ashworth thought. He couldn't remember the last time his face cracked. 'Believe me, to most of them, anything under fifty's young. I'm young.'

Vera looked at Holly. 'Well? What have we got on pretty little Freya? Any evidence that Freya knew Danny Shaw would be helpful.'

Holly sat very straight, waited until Charlie was looking at her too. God, Ashworth thought, she was such a drama queen. Like an eight-year-old in a tutu desperate to show off a new dance.

'Well?' Now Vera was really on the verge of losing it. Ashworth couldn't wait for the storm to break.

'No information on that, I'm afraid.' Holly gave one of her *you-are-never-going-to-believe-this, how-clever-am-I?* smiles. 'But I did find out that Freya was in the Willows the morning Jenny Lister was killed.'

'Why didn't you tell me as soon as you knew?' Vera demanded.

At least, Ashworth thought, Vera wasn't going to give Holly the satisfaction of applause.

'I wasn't sure myself until just now.'

Vera ignored that. 'What was she doing there?'

'There's an exercise class for pregnant mums. Half pilates, half yoga. You know the sort of thing. It was her first week. We'd already checked that Freya wasn't a member of the health club, but non-members can go to the specialist classes. They just pay on the day.'

'How did you find out about it?' Joe couldn't help himself. 'Did one of the staff see her there?'

'Nothing like that. I saw the class advertised and it just seemed like Freya's thing. It took me until half an hour ago to track down Natalie, the teacher. That's why I was a bit late.' Holly was about to launch into a detailed explanation of her cleverness in getting hold of the woman, but Vera interrupted her.

'Go back to the hotel first thing tomorrow. See what time the girl left the health club that morning. It must have been before I found the body, because we'd have noticed her among the other witnesses. Did she drive there or get a lift? And let's make absolutely certain Danny Shaw wasn't around. We know his shift didn't start until later and he wouldn't have been working, but maybe he had another reason for being in the hotel. If he saw Freya commit the murder, we've got a motive for that killing too.'

Ashworth could sense ideas fizzing around Vera's brain. She couldn't stop talking, like his kids after too much sugar, too many e-numbers. 'When you've got everything straight, call me and we'll go to Tynemouth and talk to Freya. Or if the college has started for the new term, we'll see her there. Better if we can catch her away from Morgan. There are too many bloody coincidences here.'

'You don't think Freya's a plausible suspect?' Ashworth interrupted her. 'Why would she kill Jenny Lister?'

Vera spat the words back at him. 'Because Morgan told her to. Because he has a way of making vulnerable lasses do what he wants. He got Mattie Jones to kill her own son, for Christ's sake!'

Joe wanted to say they had no evidence for that: Vera should be careful. But he could tell she was in no mood to listen.

Chapter Twenty-Six

It was almost dark. Joe Ashworth stood next to the unsteady wrought-iron table in Connie Masters's garden and watched the CSI examine the patch of weeds where Jenny Lister's bag still lay. Though he thought it would all be a waste of time. It was nothing more than an elaborate show: the investigator in his suit and bootees, looking like a giant Teletubby. He was working by the light of a strong torch now. What more could he hope to find? It seemed obvious to Joe that the bag had been thrown into the vegetation from the road, otherwise how could the cow parsley have seemed undisturbed from outside? So there would be no footwear prints, no traces at all left by the murderer, if indeed it had been the murderer who had dumped the bag.

Vera had decided they should drive here once the meeting in Kimmerston was over. He'd agreed reluctantly, partly because he was scared that she'd ask Holly instead if he refused, partly because he didn't have the energy to put up a fight. He found himself depressed by his own cynicism. Usually his enthusiasm for work, his place as Vera's second-in-command, her confidant and her surrogate son, kept him going through the tedious phases of an investigation. It was his role to motivate and encourage her, to tell her she was a genius, to keep her on track. This time he felt as if all the enthusiasm had been sucked out of him. Vera would put that down to the landscape, inland, low and waterlogged: *What you need, Joey boy, is a good east wind to blow away the cobwebs.* Ashworth thought it would take more to lift his mood than a walk on the beach with a wind from the sea.

In contrast, Vera was still fizzing. She stood beside him, yelling to the man on the other side of the burn.

'Can you tell how long it was there?'

'Not precisely.' This CSI was new. Joe hadn't seen him before. He seemed bemused by Vera's antics, regarded her rather as if there was a hostile wild animal, pleased she was trapped on the other side of the burn. 'Not yet.'

'I'm looking for a notebook,' she shouted. 'A4 hard-back. I need it before the water gets in and it rots away to nothing.'

Joe knew the notebook wouldn't be there. The murderer was no fool. It was hard maybe to dispose of leather, but paper and cardboard could be burned away to nothing. Why risk dumping it?

He saw the CSI squat to look in the bag. Now the vegetation surrounded him, so all they could catch were glimpses of his blue suit, and he looked like a great blue bird on its nest.

The CSI stood up and shook his head. 'No notebook,' he said. 'You can have the other contents when we get it back.'

Vera took the news more philosophically than Ash-worth had expected. There was no ranting. Her fury seemed to have left as soon as it had appeared. It never suited her to be caged inside the incident room. 'Aye, well, you can't always get what you want. And that would be too easy, wouldn't it, Joe? We always like a challenge.'

She shouted across the stream again. 'Were you working the scene at the Shaw murder?'

'Nah. Billy was in charge of that one.'

'I'll pester him then. There was a bonfire, and I want any paper that was left fast-tracked for examination.'

The CSI looked at her as if she were mad. She stamped off, round the back of the cottage to the kitchen door, turning to call Ashworth to follow her. 'Don't stand around there. The man knows what he's about. He can work without an audience.'

Vera seemed to fill the small room. Connie was sitting on the floor watching television. The child must already be in bed. Vera had knocked on the kitchen door, then gone straight in. Connie got to her feet. 'Would you like some tea?'

'Well done, pet!' Vera took no notice of the question. 'You did all the right things once you'd realized what the lass had found. I wouldn't have handled it better myself.'

Ashworth saw Connie give a little smile of pleasure. It seemed everyone wanted to please Vera Stanhope.

Vera leaned forwards, resting her huge hands on her bare knees. In the background the theme tune to a soap had begun. Connie switched the television off at the set.

'You do realize how important this is.' It was Vera in confiding mode. 'If we find out who dumped the bag, we're on our way to an arrest. And you live here, you're around most of the time, the bairn plays in the garden. You might have seen someone.'

'The murderer would hardly dispose of evidence in front of us!'

'Maybe.' Vera made a pantomime of considering the matter. 'But we have to think about why they chose this particular spot. When they have the whole of Northumberland to pick from, why leave it just outside your back door?'

'You don't think it was me? If I'd killed Jenny Lister I wouldn't be that stupid.'

'Of course you wouldn't, pet, and if I really thought you'd killed your boss we'd be speaking in the station with a tape running, not here over a nice cup of tea.' She flashed a smile. 'I think you did mention tea.'

'I'll make it,' Joe said, knowing that was what Vera wanted. For him to be pottering away with kettle and pots, so that Connie had the sense the conversation was just between the two women. But for him to be keeping his ears open in case he picked up something Vera might have missed. After all, they were a good team.

'So perhaps it was a coincidence,' Vera went on. 'But you're not on the main road here, and this sort of place people notice strange cars. So I wonder if someone's having a bit of fun with us. Like playing games, making mischief. *Let's throw a spanner in the works by dumping the bag next to Connie Masters's cottage. Light the blue touchpaper and see what happens.* Because I have the sense that our murderer enjoys playing games. So have you had any visitors lately?'

'There was that man who called in, asking the way to the Eliot house on the afternoon of Jenny's death.'

'So there was,' Vera said easily. 'You told Joe here all about him. It didn't seem very significant at the time, but looking back, it could be. Would you recognize him again if we show you some photos?'

Connie frowned. 'I'm not sure. So much has happened since then.'

'Worth a shot though, eh?' Vera reached out and took the mug Joe handed to her. 'I'll send Joe round with a few pictures tomorrow. Was he carrying a bag?'

'I think so. Not anything smart like a briefcase, but a holdall. Perhaps a rucksack.'

'Big enough to hold Jenny Lister's bag?' Vera asked.

'Yes.' This time Connie sounded more certain. 'If it was empty, it would squash up very small.'

'Did you see him come and watch him go? Would he have had time to hoy the bag across the burn without you seeing?'

'I didn't see him either time,' Connie said. 'He just appeared when we came out into the garden. Alice saw him first. Later I went into the house to make him tea, and when I came back outside he'd disappeared. He could have done it before we spoke or after.'

'You say he was looking for the Eliot house?'

'Yes. It seemed kind of odd. I mean, if he was a friend

of Christopher and Veronica's, wouldn't he know where he was going?'

'Did he seem like a friend?' Vera asked.

'No.' Joe saw Connie hesitate. She was reluctant to commit herself, but in the face of Vera's barrage of questions she thought she should give an answer.

'We understand you can't be certain,' he said. 'Not after such a brief conversation. We won't make too much of it. But what we're after is an impression. In your line of work you must be good at summing people up, making a judgement about them.'

Connie looked up at him and smiled. 'But I was a crap judge of character, wasn't I? It never occurred to me for a second that Mattie Jones would kill her son.'

'I bet you were right more often than you were wrong,' Vera said. 'And like Joe says, we're after your best guess. That's all.'

Connie took a deep breath. 'My best guess, thinking about it afterwards? That he was working. It wasn't a social call.'

'He was selling something?' Joe saw Vera was trying to rein herself in, so that Connie wouldn't be intimidated by her enthusiasm. But still the question came out like a firecracker. It seemed to light up the room.

'Perhaps.'

Connie sounded doubtful, but Vera got to her feet and started pacing the small room. It seemed to Ashworth that if she'd sat still much longer, she'd have exploded. She was muttering to herself, throwing out occasional questions to Joe and Connie, but not really expecting answers: 'Who else might visit a customer or client in their own home? Solicitor? Estate agent, if he was doing a valuation? Come on, Joey, help me out here!'

'He didn't look like that,' Connie said. 'He wasn't wearing a suit.'

Then Vera reached the point Joe knew she'd been aiming for all along. She looked directly at Connie. 'Could it have been Michael Morgan?'

'No! I'd have recognized him.' But Ashworth could see that Vera had thrown in a seed of doubt. And Connie wanted to please Vera, to get once again that beam of approval. 'Anyway, why would Morgan be visiting the Eliots?'

'Perhaps Veronica likes having pins stuck into her. Or perhaps he didn't go there at all and it was just an excuse.'

'He wouldn't come here,' Connie said. 'Not if he knew I lived in the cottage. He'd be scared I'd know him. I only met him twice, but his photo was everywhere in the papers.'

'Like I said . . .' Vera grinned. 'We're looking for someone who likes playing games, who enjoys taking a risk. And it wouldn't be such an enormous risk. You see someone out of context, how often do you recognize them?'

Nobody answered.

'Veronica was here this afternoon,' Connie said. 'She came for tea, but left soon after I called you.'

They all realized the implication of the words, but Vera didn't pick up on it immediately. She was delighted, though, Ashworth could tell that. There was that shiver of anticipation, the sort she got when she was standing at the bar and he was getting in the first round. 'I wouldn't have thought you two would be best mates,' Vera said, keeping it as calm as she could manage.

'We haven't been.' Connie's face seemed to close down and become expressionless. 'Veronica was rather a bitch actually, as soon as she realized who I was. She made my life hell in the village with her gossip and her rumours.'

Joe could tell Vera didn't really get the significance of what Connie was saying. Vera had always been an outsider: she was used to being considered the eccentric, the mad cop. It was only since she'd made pals with her druggie neighbours that she'd belonged to any sort of community. But Joe's wife had found it a nightmare to fit into their estate when they'd first moved. A couple of nights she'd cried herself to sleep. Something about the babysitting circle and unused tokens, about the PTA committee. The small, unkind digs that stick in the brain and suck out all the confidence, made worse because the insults were so petty and she'd known she shouldn't care.

'What happened to change things between you and Veronica?' he asked.

'Jenny Lister's death,' Connie said. 'Suddenly Veronica wanted my company. She invited me to lunch. Maybe it was just the voyeurism you get when things hit the papers. People seem attracted by that strange second-hand celebrity.'

'And you asked her back here.' Vera was grinning like a wolf. 'Very neighbourly.'

'It's been lonely,' Connie said. And Joe, catching the bleakness in her voice, understood how miserable she'd been, and thought how brave she'd been to hold things together. 'Yeah, I asked her back. She was here when Alice found the bag.'

'And what did she make of that?' There was a glint in Vera's eye: the wolf was sensing her prey.

'She was anxious about Alice playing so close to the water,' Connie replied. 'Then later, when I said I was going to call the police, she said she'd go home, that she didn't want to interfere. She'd only be in the way.'

'Tactful.' Vera nodded again. 'It's a real nuisance for us when folk hang around to watch the action.'

'She offered to take Alice with her.'

'Kind,' Vera said. 'Thoughtful.' There was a pause. 'I suppose you saw her coming. You've got a view down the track from the big house.'

'No.' Ashworth thought Connie understood where this was leading, but she pretended ignorance. 'Veronica was early. I was still clearing up at the back of the house. She came to the kitchen door and gave me a bit of a shock.'

Vera gave the huge grin of approval that made everyone included in it feel like the most important person in
the world. 'So, hypothetically of course, Veronica could
have hoyed the bag into the weed patch on her way round
the side of the cottage. She wouldn't know the bairn would
be playing out there this afternoon.'

'Hypothetically,' Connie said, 'I suppose she could.'

They stood up. 'Does the name Danny Shaw mean
anything to you?' Vera asked.

Connie frowned. 'No. Should it?'

'You'll see it on the news first thing in the morning. He
was a student. He was strangled this afternoon at his
home just up the valley.'

Connie was suddenly tense. Ashworth could see that
her instinct was to gather up her child and run away with
her, to take her somewhere safe.

'The same killer?'

'Not necessarily,' Vera said. 'But the cases are linked.
We're sure the cases are linked.'

Of course the cases are linked, Ashworth thought. But
proving the connection was another matter entirely.

Chapter Twenty-Seven

Ashworth had expected Vera to drag him to the Eliot house immediately, although it was so late. He'd sensed her excitement when Connie Masters had described Veronica's visit, and Vera had never been the most patient of people. But standing by the cars outside the cottage, she surprised him by saying they'd call it a day.

'You don't want to speak to the Eliot woman?'

Vera looked up to where the big house gleamed white in the darkness. 'Do you think she was staring at us earlier? Is she wondering what we've found out about her? I bet she was upstairs at one of the bedroom windows with a pair of binoculars.'

'Maybe.'

'We'll let her stew then, shall we? Give her a sleepless night and go to see her tomorrow.'

'Do you fancy a pint?' he asked. His way of making his peace with Vera. He'd sensed her antagonism earlier in the day. They were like a bickering married couple, he thought. In the end, they couldn't survive without each other and one of them had to give in. Usually, it was him.

'Thought you'd never ask, pet. Tell you what, it's my treat. I got a few bottles of Wylam in last time I was in that shop in Hexham where they do the fancy local produce. Come back to mine and I'll do you a sandwich too.'

And that way you don't have to drive home after we've been to the pub. But he didn't say anything. He'd have to drive back anyway—Sarah would kill him if he turned up pissed in a taxi. He'd already phoned her to say he'd be very late. She wouldn't be expecting him yet. 'Yeah,' he said. 'Why not?'

Vera's house was the most inconvenient place to live in the whole county. Stuck halfway up a hill along a track that was always blocked by the first snow and that turned into a river as soon as it rained. For her personal use she still drove Hector's Land Rover, and he'd never known her not show up for work because of the weather. Joe suspected the dippy hippies turned out with shovels to dig her out, in recompense for her turning a blind eye to what went on in their house, or maybe she camped out in the pub in the nearest village if the forecast was bad. She would never move now. She'd grown up in the hills and got twitchy and bad-tempered if she had to leave them for more than a day.

But the view was fantastic, Joe had to give her that. Too dark to appreciate it now, but he remembered it from previous visits. Open moorland as far as you could see, and a small lough where the geese came in winter. In the valley, the River Coquet that ended up at the coast, and from her house a bird's-eye view of a small grey village and a peel tower. Her neighbours had been through lambing and, even inside, they could hear the ewes. There was never any traffic noise. Nothing but the occasional jet on a training flight from RAF Boulmer as it flew low, following the line of the valley.

They sat in her house and talked about Jenny Lister and then about Danny Shaw. He took a bottle of beer and drank it slowly; she'd had three by the time he'd finished. As good as her word, she made sandwiches and between munches she talked, hardly giving him a chance to speak. Occasions like this, that was his role: to be an audience, her sounding board. It was how she best processed information. Once, exasperated after a late night of listening to her holding forth, he'd asked her why she needed him there at all. 'You take no notice of anything I say. You'd do just as well without me.'

She'd been astonished. 'Nonsense, lad. If you weren't here, I wouldn't bother to think things through. You make me focus.' She'd paused. 'And now and again you come up with a few good ideas.'

So he sat and listened, as outside the moon rose and the breeze dropped. She broke off briefly to throw a match on the fire and turn on the standard lamp with its tatty parchment shade, but soon she continued, ordering her thoughts, reaching conclusions, planning future actions. During the team briefings she used the whiteboard to make her points clear, but Joe could see that she had no need of written notes or charts. It was all in her head; all the links and apparent coincidences seemed fixed in her mind.

And she spoke about the dead woman as if she'd known her. 'Jenny Lister. The way I see it, she was a *proud* woman. That was what motivated her. She was good all right: a good mother, a good social worker, a good boss. A good-looker too for her age. We've heard that from all the people who knew her. But she thought she was a bit better than everyone else. Clever enough not to show it, but deep down that was what she believed. That's what the planned book was all about. She thought she had something to teach the world about compassion.' Vera looked up from her beer. 'If I'd known her, she'd have got right up my nose. I can't stand perfect people. And she didn't have many friends, did she? Not real friends. There's that teacher, but she was more like an admirer than a friend, and Jenny didn't confide much in her. She just threw out a few hints to make herself interesting.'

Joe said nothing. When Vera was in full flow it was best to let her get on with it. The inspector continued. 'So why was she murdered? And why in such an elaborate way? You don't strangle someone just because they get on your tits. And if you want to kill, you choose somewhere private. Not the swimming pool in a flash hotel, where anyone could walk in on you at any minute. This looks like a game to me, a show. And which of our suspects makes the best showman?'

Most of Vera's questions were rhetorical, but this time, it seemed, she expected an answer.

'Well? Are you falling asleep here? Am I talking to myself?'

'Danny Shaw?' His response was tentative and he was ashamed of that. She always made him feel like an eight-year-old desperate not to make a fool of himself in front of the teacher.

'Our second victim? So we're back to Charlie's theory that Danny was killed in revenge. Nah, I don't buy that. Oh, I'm sure Danny was a show-off all right, and cocky with it. But maybe lots of lads are at that age. No, I'm thinking of Michael Morgan. Seems to me that his acupuncture business is more about theatre than medicine. He likes to create a scene, cause a distraction. People believe in the magic and that makes them feel better.'

'Why kill Danny?' Joe was playing the stooge again, feeding her the lines.

'We know they met. Maybe Morgan let slip something of what he was planning. Danny was desperate for money. I wouldn't have put it past him to try a bit of blackmail.'

'Why would Morgan choose the Willows for his stage set in the first place? He must have realized we'd find out he worked there. And surely he'd be the last person to dump Jenny's bag in Connie's garden. He wouldn't want us raking over the Elias Jones case again.'

Vera sat for a moment in silence. 'Bugger,' she said cheerfully. 'You're right of course. I can't stand the bastard and I'd like to see him charged for something. Wipe the arrogance off his face. No way to run an investigation, that. You should never let it get personal.' She grinned at him, aware that she let it get personal all the time. The flames caught one side of her face; the rest was in shadow and for a moment she looked very young, almost flirtatious. 'What's your theory then, Joe? Where am I going wrong?'

'I think Jenny Lister was killed by someone close to home,' Joe said. He'd only had one beer, but it had given him the confidence to throw out a theory without thinking it through. It had just come into his head as Vera was speaking. 'The Willows was chosen to throw us off the scent. Unless it was an impulse killing, you wouldn't choose the place where you worked to commit a murder. So I'm thinking one of Jenny Lister's contacts from Barnard Bridge. That's where her bag was found, after all.'

He'd expected her mockery, some comment about him reading too many old-fashioned detective stories, but she took the comment seriously. 'Well, that limits the field. Are you including Hannah in your suspects?'

That threw him. 'No! Well, maybe.'

'We've only got her word that she didn't go with her mam for a swim that morning,' Vera said. 'Nobody saw the girl in the health club, but that means nothing. Jenny could have used her card to swipe the girl through. I've seen it done.'

'How would Hannah have got back to Barnard Bridge?' Joe asked. 'Lister's car was still at the Willows, and with public transport it'd take you about a fortnight. It'd be quicker walking.'

'Simon Eliot could have picked her up. They'd have worked it between them. She wouldn't have done it without him, however it happened.'

'Motive?' Joe couldn't believe they were considering this. He pictured Hannah Lister as Holly had described her, numb with grief and shock. But maybe killing your mother would do that to you.

'We know Jenny wasn't happy about the marriage and had asked them to wait. That relationship is so intense.' Vera frowned. 'You have a sense that both the kids are a bit crazy. If Jenny had something on Simon—some way of putting pressure on him to ditch the girl—Hannah would go mad. Literally.' Vera narrowed her eyes and painted the picture so that Joe was there too. 'They're together in the steam room. Outside there's the noise of the pool, but in there just the two of them, cut off from the world. Almost naked. It's a place for confidences and serious conversation. Nowhere to hide. If Jenny told the girl there was no way the marriage could go ahead, I can see Hannah losing it and killing her mother. Then phoning Simon and getting him to bale her out.'

'Danny Shaw?'

'Same theory as with Morgan? He was there, saw what happened and tried to blackmail them.' She looked up suddenly. 'We still don't know if he and Hannah knew each other at school. But I think he'd certainly recognize her. Not that many young folk living in the valley.'

'Why would Hannah dump the bag next to Connie's cottage?'

Vera gave a sudden loud laugh. 'God knows. To throw us off the scent? I really don't believe any of it. No way did Hannah kill her mother. You just have to be with her to see she's grieving. We're in *Jackanory* territory here, bonny lad. The land of make-believe.'

'The rest of the Eliots then?'

Vera didn't answer. She went to the window and looked down the valley, then walked unsteadily upstairs to the bathroom. Joe heard the toilet flush, the gurgle of water in old pipes. He stood up too. There was a half moon and a clear sky. A dizzying view of points of light in the village below. It was like looking out of a plane at night. He could feel the chill through the glass. Vera came back.

'The Eliots,' she said as if she hadn't left the room. 'Not lords of the manor. No real land and no old money. Not any more. Local, you can tell that by the name. One of the Border Reiver clans, the Eliots. But seems to me Christopher Eliot's family would have been tradespeople or farmers, not aristocracy. Veronica's a bit different, though. She likes to play the role of lady. Status is important to her. And once her granddad did have a grand house, servants and a big estate. It's still rotting down by the river, and that's odd too. Worth following up. Does she care enough about her good name to kill? I'm not sure, but people have committed murder for less.'

She returned to her seat by the fire and Ashworth followed.

'Our Veronica's hiding something,' Vera said. 'But that doesn't make her a killer. She could have nicked a few quid from WI funds and be shitting herself that we'll find out. I'd love to know why she's become so pally with Connie Masters all of a sudden. I really don't get what's going on there. Can't see that there'd be any connection with Danny Shaw, though, unless she'd chosen him for her toy boy.'

'Shaw could have been the man who called at Connie's cottage the afternoon of the murder.'

'So he could.' Mocking him gently, because of course she'd already thought of that.

'Is that the plan for the morning? Head off for Barnard Bridge. Show Connie Danny Shaw's photo, and chat to Veronica.'

'Aye.' Vera yawned. 'That'll do for a start. And if we can get a recent photo of Morgan with his hair shaved off, get Connie to look at that too.' She looked over at him. 'Are you planning on staying all night? I don't know about you, but I need my beauty sleep. And your missus will have forgotten what you look like. Off you go.'

Joe was astonished. Usually Vera was desperate to keep him there until the early hours. Many times she'd offered him the bed in her spare room: *Don't be a spoilsport, Joey lad. Have a few drinks and keep an old lady company.* 'We haven't talked about Elias Jones,' he said.

'Nor we haven't.' She grinned at him. 'Now what's that saying?' She appeared to drag the phrase from her memory. 'The elephant in the room. That's what Elias Jones is in this case. We all know he's there, but we've stopped talking about him.'

Joe suspected she was pretending to be drunker than she really was. She could drink most of the men he knew under the table. Anyway, he thought, best to go now before she changed her mind. He got to his feet and made his way to the door, half expecting her to call him back. But she stayed where she was, staring into the fire.

Outside it was so cold that for a moment it took his breath away. The metallic smell of ice in the air, maybe the last frost of the season. He stopped for a moment and looked back through the window at Vera, slumped in her chair, her eyes closed. Even from here and seeing her half asleep, he could feel the force of her personality.

If anyone's the elephant in the room, he thought, *it's Vera Stanhope.*

Chapter Twenty-Eight

It was still cold when they met at Barnard Bridge. Dew on the grass and a low mist over the river. In Mallow Cottage the curtains were drawn and there was no sign of life, so they went to the Eliots' first. Vera didn't mind disturbing Veronica, but Connie might have had a bad night with the bairn and Vera thought she could do with a lie-in.

When Vera arrived, Ashworth was already in the village. He was standing outside his car, wearing a duffel coat so that he looked like a student from the days when Vera had been a girl, and was looking down at the bank of the burn where Jenny Lister's bag had been found. 'You'd be able to throw it from here,' he said. 'No bother.'

'You might. I wouldn't get it more than a couple of yards. Never got picked for the rounders team at school.' She turned and led him up the gravel drive to the white house.

Inside the Eliots were having breakfast and, to her surprise, Hannah was there too. They sat round the table in the smart kitchen where Vera had been taken on her first visit: Veronica, a smartly dressed grey-haired man, whom Vera took to be Christopher the husband, Simon and Hannah. Hannah was still wearing a dressing gown, her hair was matted and she looked barely conscious. Simon had come to the door. No one else made any move. No expression of shock or hostility. It was as if they'd been captured in a photograph. There was the smell of good coffee and warm croissants. A jug of garden flowers stood on the table. The scene could have been a photograph in a smart Sunday supplement.

Vera was thrown by the presence of the young people. She hadn't been expecting it. But she wasn't going to let on. She pulled up a chair next to Christopher, leaving Ashworth standing behind her.

Simon seemed amused by the disruption to the family routine and by his parents' dumbstruck stillness. 'Coffee, Inspector? Or would you prefer tea? Hannah decided she was OK to stay here last night, so we thought we'd give it a go.' He reached over and touched the girl's hand.

Vera thought Hannah didn't look up to making any decisions of her own. 'Tea, please, pet. Strong as you like. My sergeant here likes coffee.' She turned to Simon's father. 'We've not been introduced. My name's Vera Stanhope. Inspector with Northumbria Police serious crime squad.' When the man made no answer she added: 'I know you've been away, but you have heard there's been a murder in the valley?'

'Of course.' He was shocked at last to speech. 'Hannah's mother. A terrible tragedy.' The voice was lovely, deep and resonant. A singer's voice.

'Did you know her well?'

'Not well. We'd met a few times of course, through the children.' He stood up, brushed a crumb from the grey suit trousers and took his jacket from the back of his chair. 'I must go, I'm afraid. A meeting at nine.' His body was younger than his face. Vera wondered if he went to the gym. She hadn't asked if he was a member of the Willows, but surely the name would have been flagged up when the list had been requested. Assume nothing, she told herself, and made a mental note to check. It seemed that everyone involved in the case had a link to the Willows. The place was like the centre of a spider's web.

'Does the name Danny Shaw mean anything to you?'

He stopped with his hand on the table. She could smell his aftershave. His fingernails were obsessively clean. 'No,' he said. 'I don't think so.'

He left the room then, without waiting to find out why she was asking. She found his lack of curiosity very odd and stared after him through the open kitchen door. She'd expected him to go upstairs to clean his teeth, perhaps to collect papers for work. There were still questions she had to ask him. But instead he stooped to pick up his briefcase, which was standing in the hall, and left the house. It seemed to her that he was running away. She was tempted to call him back, but after all they knew where he'd be and the gesture would have seemed ridiculous. Much better to go to his office and talk to him alone. She'd already checked that he was out of the country the day Jenny Lister died. They heard the sound of his car, the tyres crunching on the gravel.

With his departure, Veronica came to life. 'What's so urgent, Inspector, that you're disturbing us at this hour in the morning?'

'Murder,' Vera said, enjoying the moment of melodrama. 'That's what's so important.'

'We've told you all we know about poor Jenny.' The *poor* added at the last minute because of Hannah's presence, though it seemed to Vera that Hannah was hardly aware they were there at all.

'There's been another death.' At last Vera had the response she wanted. Even Hannah looked up, her eyes blurred. Ashworth's mobile rang, spoiling the moment. Vera glared at him as he left the room to take the call.

'Who else has been killed?' Veronica had her palms on the table and had half risen in her seat.

'A student called Danny Shaw.'

Silence. Again no sign that the name meant anything to them.

Vera leaned across the table towards Hannah. 'You were at school with him, pet.' Her voice so low that the others had to strain to make out the words. 'Can you tell us anything about him?'

Hannah pushed her hair away from her face, made an effort to concentrate. 'He was older than me.'

'That's right.'

'In the sixth form when I was doing GCSEs. We met up on the school bus sometimes.' She gave a sudden bright smile. 'He asked me out.'

'Did you go?'

'A couple of times.'

Vera wished Ashworth were still in the room. She needed her eyes to be everywhere. Just now she looked at Simon Eliot. Had he known about this previous relationship? Was this the sort of thing young people in love discussed while they walked hand in hand down country lanes in the spring? Had he been jealous, or had the details of previous lovers added spice to their own love-making? Because turning her attention back to Hannah, seeing the smile again on her face, Vera thought she and Danny had probably been lovers. Now, it was impossible to tell what Simon thought about that. His arm was around Hannah and his only concern seemed to be for her.

Vera directed the next question to the boy. 'Did you know Danny? You went to different schools, but you were about the same age.'

'Yeah, I knew him. I was a bit older, but we had friends in common, went to the same parties. We weren't close, though.'

'Have you seen him this holiday?'

Simon hesitated. Because he was trying to remember, or because he had something to hide?

'Once perhaps. A couple of weeks ago in a pub in Hexham.' He turned to Hannah. 'Do you remember, sweetie? You were there.'

'Yes,' she said immediately. 'Yes, of course.' But Vera thought she would have said anything to please him.

'Why did you only go out with Danny a couple of times?' Vera asked her. Hannah was so frail that she wondered if she would manage to answer even something as simple as this.

'Nice body, shame about the personality,' Hannah said. It wasn't the first time she'd used the phrase. Perhaps that was how she'd described Danny to Simon. 'I fancied him like crazy, then I realized he was an arrogant little shit.'

'So you dumped him?'

'Yes.' Again there was the brief flash of a grin. 'I think it was a new experience for him.'

'Did he ever meet your mother?'

Vera asked the question as gently as she could, but still she felt the girl's sudden pain at the memory.

'Once. At least once. Mum asked him to Sunday lunch.'

'How did it go?'

'It was rather hideous actually.' Hannah pulled a face. 'You know how it is when you suddenly see a person through someone else's eyes? I'd been taken in by Danny. He'd impressed me with his talk, his dreams and his plans for the future. He tried the same stuff with Mum, only he couldn't impress her. She was perfectly pleasant and tactful, but it was obvious to me that she couldn't stand him.'

'That's why you dumped him?'

'I think so. Not because Mum didn't like him. But because she made me realize that I didn't like him much either.'

'How did he take it?' Vera realized that Ashworth had slipped into the room again and she felt more confident for his being there.

'No one likes rejection, do they?'

'Did he give you any hassle?' This was Joe's question.

'Only enough to give my ego a nice boost. A couple of love letters. Some soppy emails. Just a case of wanting what he couldn't have, I think.'

'Has he been in touch recently?'

'Not for ages. I saw him about, of course. Someone told me he had a girlfriend in Bristol.'

Her voice had become stronger as the conversation progressed. For a couple of minutes she'd forgotten about her mother, felt sympathy instead for this stranger in Bristol who had lost her boyfriend.

'Did you ever meet Danny Shaw, Mrs Eliot?' That was Joe Ashworth being suitably deferential.

'No, how would I?' Brisk to the point of rudeness.

'He never came to this house, for example?' Joe widened the question to include Simon.

'Of course not!' Veronica answered for them both.

'Because someone answering his description asked for directions to your house on the afternoon of Jenny Lister's death.'

Vera smiled at this. They had no real description of the guy who'd called at Connie's cottage to ask his way. But it was fine with her if Ashworth chose to stretch the point.

'I don't know who gave you that information, Sergeant, but nobody came here.' Veronica, mouth clamped, was determined not to give in. Danny could have danced naked on the lawn that day, but Veronica wouldn't tell them now. She was a woman who never admitted to making a mistake.

'Perhaps you know Danny's father?' Vera thought it was time to change tack. 'Derek Shaw. He's a builder and developer.'

'I know of him.' Veronica's response was immediate and hostile. 'Horrible man. He built that disgusting estate on the edge of Effingham. I have a friend with a property there. She said it halved the value of her home.'

'Ever thought of developing that land where your grandfather's house once stood?' Vera asked. 'That's close to Effingham. Greenhough, isn't that what you said the place was called? The land would be worth a fortune, wouldn't it, even these days?' The question had been niggling at the back of her mind since she'd wandered through the cormorant-headed gateposts.

'We wouldn't get planning permission,' Veronica snapped back. 'And we like it the way it is. Even if it were possible to build, I wouldn't get Shaw involved.'

'He's lost his son.' Simon spoke softly, but they all looked at him. 'Whatever you think about him, he's lost a child.' Did he really care about the young man's loss? Or was he simply warning his mother to be more tactful?

'Of course!' And now Veronica did seem stricken. 'I'm so sorry, Inspector, that was unforgivably heartless.'

Ashworth and Vera walked slowly away from the house. Vera insisted on going to the cafe for breakfast before they called at the cottage. The smell of food in the Eliot kitchen had driven her wild. She wouldn't be able to concentrate without a bacon stottie inside her. The cafe wasn't open, but the Yorkshire woman was already there, took pity on them and let them in.

'That was Holly on the phone,' Ashworth said. He'd tried to explain before, but Vera's focus had all been about finding food. 'There's some interesting information on Veronica. Might explain why she gave Connie Masters such a hard time when she first moved into the village.'

'Go on.'

'She lost a child. A toddler. A little boy called Patrick. He drowned in the river. He was playing down on the beach near Connie's house and he wandered under the bridge and slipped into the river. Veronica was there, but Simon, who was a bit older, was with her too. He'd run off towards the road and she'd chased after him, worried that he might get in the path of a car. When she got back, the little one was face-down in the water. She tried to resuscitate him, but it didn't work.'

'Poor woman.' That stopped Vera in her tracks. 'Poor, poor woman.' Vera tried to think what that sort of guilt would do to you. How could the family still live in that house, looking down every day at the point where their son had drowned? The memory of it must have eaten into Veronica's brain and her bones, scarring her forever. Her upbringing would have prevented her from seeking help. No counselling for her. No getting pissed with her friends either. Stiff upper lip and life must go on. Or had that been impossible in the end?

Then Connie Masters had moved into the village: another woman who had allowed a child to drown.

And what had the accident done to Simon? The son who had distracted his mother and indirectly caused the death of his brother. Had he ever been told about his part in the tragedy?

Vera found herself near to tears. But she was exhilarated too. Perhaps this was the breakthrough in the case they'd been waiting for. If Veronica blamed Connie for Elias Jones's death, had she held Jenny Lister ultimately responsible for it? In killing the social worker, had she found a sort of redemption for her own child's drowning?

Nah, Vera thought. *Real life doesn't work like that.* She'd never been one for psycho-babble, and the death of a strange child wouldn't move a woman to murder. Veronica would only have cared about her own son's drowning.

But all the same, Vera felt she was inching towards a solution. The Eliots were hiding something. If Connie Masters could identify Danny Shaw as the man who'd called at the cottage, then they had a link between them and Shaw, and that should be enough to move the investigation forward. She finished the last mouthful of sandwich, took a slurp from her mug and almost ran from the cafe, leaving a ten-pound note on the table. At the door she paused only to make sure Ashworth was following her.

But when they arrived at Connie's place, the cottage was empty and her car was gone. They knocked on the door, knowing there would be no answer. Vera felt under the plant pot near the front door. No spare key. She walked round to the back of the house and moved the wheelie bin that stood just outside the kitchen. A key lay on the bare soil and they let themselves in.

'Is this strictly legal?' Ashworth knew Vera wouldn't care, but he wanted to make a point.

'We're worried that Connie's had an accident,' Vera said, all mock concern. 'It's our duty to check.'

The house looked as if it had been left very quickly. There were dirty bowls in the sink and the kettle was still warm. Upstairs neither of the beds had been made.

'Maybe she's just taken the lass to playgroup?'

Ashworth shook his head. 'It's not on today.'

'Gone shopping then?'

'She knew we were coming to see her with the photos of Shaw and Morgan. And she'd have seen our cars parked out in the road.'

'So she's run away,' Vera said. 'Why would she do that?'

She lifted the phone in the living room and dialled 1471 to trace the last call made to the number. A distant female voice told her that the caller had withheld their number.

'Or maybe,' Vera said, staring out at the river where Patrick Eliot had died, 'maybe she's been frightened away.'

Chapter Twenty-Nine

Vera and Holly met Freya from Newcastle College at lunchtime. 'Important to keep our options open,' Vera had said, though she couldn't stop thinking about Connie and her daughter. Another child to worry about. Patrick, Elias and now Alice. Somehow that must be relevant. She wished she were cleverer and could make sense of it. She blamed herself too, of course, for missing Connie that morning, for putting her belly before the investigation. She knew that Ashworth blamed her too.

So they'd driven into the city and parked illegally in one of the little streets near to the Rye Hill campus, outside a wholesale warehouse stocking Chinese food. The scent of spice in the air. They were on their way into the drama department when they saw Freya coming towards them, alone among the other students, who were giggling on their way to find lunch. Vera recognized the girlish way of walking that was close to dancing and the printed frock, this time worn over jeans with a jacket on the top. Freya didn't see them until the last minute. She had her mobile phone to her ear, chatting to a friend as she walked about some play they'd been to see. Her face was bright and Vera could have wept for her.

'Hello, pet.'

They swept her with them into a coffee shop, a greasy spoon with pretensions. Now the smell was of frying and of coffee from the big silver espresso machine.

'You'll be peckish,' Vera said. 'Now you're eating for two.'

And it seemed that Freya was hungry. Morgan might be vegetarian, but the girl managed a full English breakfast and a mug of tea. The sausage and bacon disappeared in seconds.

'You never told us you were in the Willows the morning the social worker died.' Vera struggled to get the words out. She'd gone for a piece of flapjack, so sticky that it worked like superglue around her teeth.

Freya looked up. Big eyes, suddenly scared, over the mug. 'You didn't ask.'

'Howay, we shouldn't have needed to ask now, should we? A clever girl like you, you'd have guessed we'd be interested.'

'Michael said you might draw the wrong conclusion.'

'He was there that morning too, was he?' Holly chipped in, out to prove she wasn't just here for the ride. Vera couldn't blame her for that. Nothing wrong with a bit of ambition in a woman. 'Was the session for partners too? Great that he wants to be so involved with the baby.'

'It was an exercise class.' Freya seemed to have relaxed. Perhaps after all she was just as stupid as Mattie Jones had been, but she hid it better. 'Not for the fathers. Michael will come along to the antenatal group, of course. We've planned a completely natural childbirth. One of his friends is an independent midwife and we're having the baby at home. Hiring a birthing pool and everything. But he just gave me a lift that day.'

'I suppose he used the time to catch up on some work.' Holly gave an encouraging little smile. Vera thought she was as bored by the details of motherhood as Vera herself and was glad to move the conversation on.

'I guess so.' But Freya was suspicious again. Had Morgan warned her on the subjects to avoid, if she were questioned alone?

'Where did you meet up?' Vera asked. 'After the class, I mean.'

Silence. It seemed Morgan hadn't given her the answer to that one.

'Was he waiting in the car for you?'

'I can't remember.'

Vera paused until a waitress in torn jeans had swung past carrying a plate of bacon and eggs for a couple of labourers at the next table.

'Of course you can, hinny. And we'll find out anyway. A place like that, there'll be CCTV in the car park and a load of witnesses.' Although the CCTV tape had run out the night before the murder and nobody had bothered to replace it. 'Much better if you give us the information yourself.'

Freya looked cornered. She made Vera think of the traps gamekeepers used in the hills. A wire mesh cage with a crow inside to lure in other raptors. Was it right to be using Freya as their decoy?

'We'd arranged to meet in the car,' Freya said. 'But when I got out of the class he wasn't there.'

'What time was that?'

'The class finished at ten.'

'So what did you do?' Holly asked. 'Did you go to look for him? It'd be a good chance to bump into your old friends from work. Maybe grab a coffee, catch up on some gossip?'

'I don't have much in common with those people any more.' That was Morgan, Vera thought, speaking through Freya's lips.

'So where *did* you go? To Michael's office? Perhaps he'd got caught up in his paperwork and lost track of the time?' This time it was Holly who was putting words into the girl's mouth.

Poor child, Vera thought. *She's nothing but a ventriloquist's dummy.*

'I phoned his mobile,' Freya said. 'I knew he wouldn't want me wandering round the hotel. He says some of the girls there are a bad influence. So I phoned him.'

'And?' Holly was close to shaking the girl now. Vera thought she'd have to learn some patience. Vera was more concerned by the substance of Freya's answer. What right did this man have to choose her friends?

'And nothing. He didn't reply. I waited. He turned up not long after and drove me home. I didn't have college that day. It was still the Easter break.' She sounded sulky, like a spoilt child. Vera thought there'd probably been a row in the car on their way back to the coast.

'Did he explain why he was so late?' Holly asked.

'He said it was none of my business. Something to do with work. I thought perhaps Mattie Jones was hassling him again. She'd started phoning from the prison and it drove him crazy.'

No, Vera thought. *Not Mattie. She was in hospital having her appendix pulled out. Jenny perhaps? Had she seen him, maybe while he was drinking posh coffee in the lounge, waiting for Freya's class to finish? Had she asked for an interview for her book about the Elias Jones case, told Morgan she would write it anyway? Did he watch her go into the steam room from the viewing gallery, quickly change into his swimming trunks and kill her?*

She was so caught up in speculation that she didn't realize the others were staring at her. She saw herself through their eyes: ageing, ugly, slow. Felt their pity. And then experienced an energizing surge of confidence. I might not be young and bonny, but I've got brains, she thought. More brains than the pair of you put together. Another couple of days and we'll have this sorted.

Early afternoon she was back at the Willows, powered by pride and caffeine and sugar. First she sat in the lounge, drinking more coffee, watching the punters. There were deep armchairs of leather and chintz. Easy to hide away from fellow guests, to carry on a conversation that wouldn't be overheard. The waiters came to take the orders. No need to stand up or to queue at the bar. This was as anonymous a place as it was possible to imagine.

Her waitress was elderly, a caricature from a bygone age, stooped and almost deaf. Vera bellowed at her.

'You'll have seen photos of Jenny Lister, the woman killed here last week. Did she ever come into the lounge to have coffee?'

The waitress shook her head and walked off, but Vera wasn't even sure she'd heard. Later, though, a lad turned up. Black trousers, white shirt, black waistcoat. An explosion of acne, made worse because he was blushing and nervous.

'Doreen said you were asking about the woman that died.'

Vera nodded. She couldn't trust herself to speak because she might cheer.

'I think she was here that morning. I didn't tell the police because I wasn't sure. You know, I couldn't swear an oath that it was that particular day.'

Vera nodded again. 'But you *think* it was.'

'Yeah,' he said. 'Yeah. She came in quite often and always drank the same thing. Small, black decaff americano. I got it ready whenever I saw her coming.' The blush deepened and Vera thought he'd fancied Jenny Lister, that he'd had adolescent fantasies about the older woman.

'Did she meet anyone that day?' Vera asked. 'You'd remember that, wouldn't you? Because there'd be another order too, besides the decaff, and that would be unusual.'

'Yeah,' he said. 'I'd remember that. But she didn't meet anyone.' He paused. He didn't want to stick his neck out, hated the idea of being wrong.

'Anything you can tell me would be useful. An impression even.'

'I thought she was waiting for someone.' The words came out in a rush. He needed to speak before he lost his nerve.

'Did she tell you she expected a friend to join her?'

'No. But she looked up whenever anyone came into the room, kept looking at her watch.'

'What time was this?' Vera asked.

'Early. Before nine o'clock. That was unusual too. Usually she came in after she'd been for a swim.'

'How could you tell she hadn't?'

'Her hair was still dry. Usually it was a bit damp at the ends. Like she hadn't bothered to use the hair-dryer. And there wasn't that smell of chlorine about her.'

'Thank you.' Vera gave him her biggest grin. 'You should think of joining the police. You're wasted here.'

Then she was off on the prowl again. No Karen on reception, of course. She was at home mourning her son. A skinny young woman who recognized Vera sat in Karen's place and let her through without a word. She found Ryan Taylor in his office.

'You'll have heard about Danny Shaw.'

'Of course.'

'What's the word in the hotel? They'll all be talking about it.' Vera perched on the corner of his desk. Looking down on his small round head, she saw his hair was thinning at the crown.

'They're scared,' Taylor said. 'Mrs Lister's death, that was a bit exciting. Nobody really knew her. It's like watching a horror movie on the telly, isn't it? I mean, you quite enjoy being scared, but you know it's not real.'

'But Danny's death was real?'

'Yeah, we didn't all like him, but we knew him. I suppose people are wondering who'll be next. We're all selfish bastards at heart, aren't we?'

'Anything else unusual here?' Because something about his manner had made her suspicious. A bit like the young waiter, he was weighing up whether he should talk to her or not.

'Lisa didn't come in this morning. She was due in at eight. She rang in sick. I can't remember the last time she was ill. Probably a coincidence.'

'Sure,' Vera said. 'Bound to be.' But that sent her on the move again. Back to her car with Lisa's address on a scrap of paper in her hand. Another trip east towards the city.

Lisa lived with her mother in a small red-brick house on a council estate in the west end of the city. There was a view from the end of the street across a business park to the Tyne. Perhaps the father still technically lived there and was in prison, or perhaps he'd moved out. In any event there was no sign of him. Half the houses in the street were empty, boarded up, and it looked as if kids had been inside setting fires. Some of the gardens were piled with rubbish. But Lisa's home was spotless. The grass on the small patch of lawn had been cut and there were pots along the path, planted with primulas. Inside, a smell of furniture polish and disinfectant that hit Vera as soon as the door was opened.

A woman stood there. She had Lisa's small features and her hair might once have been blonde. Now the colour came out of a bottle and it hadn't taken properly. Blotchy and uneven, the result was piebald, part chestnut and part brass. But who was Vera to criticize?

'Is Lisa home, pet?'

The woman was only small, but she stood her ground like a fighting dog. She could smell police a hundred yards away.

'She's at work.'

'No, she's not.' Vera let her tiredness show in her voice. The sugar rush and effect of the caffeine had worn off. 'I've just come from there. Don't piss me about; I'm not in the mood. Tell her it's Vera Stanhope, and then let me in so that I can take the weight off my legs.'

And perhaps it was that last phrase that worked the magic. Lisa's mam recognized the exhaustion of the working woman, stood aside and showed Vera into the smart front room, never used during the day except for visitors. At the same time there were footsteps on the stairs and Lisa was there. She'd been listening in. She was pale and thin.

'I didn't do it,' she said. The words were out before she reached the foot of the stairs, spoken through the open door of the living room. 'I didn't kill Danny Shaw.'

'Oh, pet, I didn't think for a moment you had.'

'I heard it on the news, and I thought everyone would believe it was me. Want it to be me.'

Vera saw then that this had been a wasted trip. Lisa had thrown a sickie because she couldn't face the accusations of her colleagues. 'Look,' she said, 'I'll arrest the killer, then they'll have something else to talk about.'

'Will you? You know who it is then?'

Christ, Vera thought, *what can I say?* 'Another couple of days and it'll all be over.' She hoisted herself to her feet. Lisa's mother was talking about tea, but Vera had a sort of promise to keep and she didn't have the time. On the doorstep she paused and turned back to Lisa.

'It was Danny Shaw doing the thieving, wasn't it?'

Lisa nodded. 'I saw him once in the staffroom. He didn't know I was there.'

'Why didn't you tell anyone?'

She only shrugged, but Vera knew the answer anyway. Lisa had been brought up not to grass and, anyway, who would believe her?

Vera was getting into her car when her mobile rang. It was Joe Ashworth to say that Connie still hadn't returned home and he was starting to worry.

Chapter Thirty

Joe Ashworth spent most of the day trying to track down Connie and Alice. First he went into town and found Frank, Connie's ex, at work in the theatre close to the Quayside. Sarah had dragged Joe there to see a couple of plays before the arrival of the kids and he'd usually had a good time despite himself. And despite the arty clientele hanging around in the bar, posing before the show.

Frank was sitting outside with a group of other people smoking. He was dark and thin, with the sort of brooding good looks that Sarah went for. When Joe asked for a word in private, he stubbed out his cigarette and took Joe inside. They sat in the back row of the theatre itself. The stage was being dressed for a play and occasionally someone would wander on to shift a bit of furniture, but the stagehands took no notice of the two men in the audience.

'So you haven't heard from her?' Ashworth couldn't tell what the man beside him was thinking. He seemed to be preoccupied and Ashworth wondered if his mind was more on the production than on his ex-wife and daughter. Certainly his attention was fixed on the stage.

'Not since I phoned her to tell her about Jenny Lister. Alice was going to come to stay with me and Mel this weekend.'

'And you have no idea where she might be?' Ashworth thought if his wife and kids had disappeared, he'd be a bit more concerned than Frank seemed to be.

'She's only been gone for a couple of hours, hasn't

she? She could be anywhere. Shopping. Coffee with a mate.'

And Ashworth realized that he was the one behaving strangely. It was true after all. He was overreacting. 'Could you let me have Connie's mobile number? We didn't get it from her.'

Now Frank did turn towards him to stare. Ashworth felt uncomfortable under the gaze, almost as if he'd been caught propositioning Connie. Perhaps he should explain that his interest was purely professional, but that would make the situation even more embarrassing. He would be seen to be protesting too much. Frank jotted a number on the corner of a sheet of paper torn from his notebook. 'The press made her life torture,' he said. 'And now the media circus is back again. You can hardly blame her for wanting to escape for a while.'

'Could you give me the names and numbers of people who might be putting her up,' Ashworth said. 'We need her to identify a suspect. If she gets in touch, tell her we'll be discreet.'

'Yeah, right.' Frank obviously had little faith in the discretion of the police. 'Just like last time, when you threw her to the wolves and then did nothing to protect her.'

For the rest of the day Joe tried calling Connie whenever he had a moment free. Her landline at the cottage and her mobile. Knowing, after the first few attempts, that it was a waste of time, but still giving it a go in a way that was almost superstitious. The mobile was either switched off or the battery had run down. The first few times he left a message. After that he didn't bother. He didn't want her to feel cornered by him too. There was no answering service on the landline. He let it ring for ten seconds each time, then replaced the receiver.

After the meeting with Frank, he left Newcastle and drove inland. He thought he needed to stay close to

Barnard Bridge while Vera went chasing all round the county following her instincts and her need for perpetual movement. *His* instinct told him that the answer to both murders was here in the lush green fields of the Tyne valley.

Karen Shaw had been allowed back to her house. Joe found her there with her husband. They welcomed him with a warmth he hadn't expected. It was as if they saw him as some sort of medium or magician, as if he provided a means of communicating with the boy they'd lost. Or perhaps it was simpler than that. The young detective was a distraction. They'd been blaming themselves and each other for the loss of their son, and now they had someone else to talk to. There was the guilt that always lingers with survivors. He listened to their confessions, knowing there was nothing he could do to make them feel better.

'He wanted to go back to Bristol a few days ago,' Karen said, the words spilling out like tears. 'His girlfriend had gone early. She does drama and there was a film they were making. She asked him to act in it, just a small part. Her family's got money and she doesn't need to do paid work in the holidays. They'd been skiing in Colorado over Easter; they'd invited him too and he could have gone with them, if he'd been able to find the fare. A couple of years ago we'd have been able to give it to him, no problem. Now it was impossible.'

She paused for breath and Joe tried to take her back to her first sentence. 'That was the only reason he wanted to go back before the start of term? The film, I mean. Jenny Lister's death hadn't upset him?'

'No.' She stared up at him. He'd never seen her without make-up before. 'Why would it?'

'Well, he knew her, didn't he?' Joe gave an encouraging little smile. 'Met her once at least. He'd been out with her daughter, Hannah.'

'Hannah. I remember her. Bonny little thing. I never knew her surname, didn't make the connection. You know her, don't you, Derek? She was the little redhead. He was very keen on her for a while. His first real love.' She gave a gasp of anguish, grieving perhaps because there would be no last love, no wedding, no grandchild.

Derek nodded, though Joe wouldn't have bet that he really remembered Hannah Lister. He didn't want to admit to a gap in the shared experience of bringing up their only son.

'Why did Danny stick around in the end?' Joe asked. 'Why didn't he go down to Bristol to be in the film?'

'That was about money too, wasn't it, Derek? He'd have lost a week's pay if he hadn't worked out his notice. And I told him he couldn't let them down. I'd got him the job, and I'd have looked bad if he'd just quit.' Her own confession. 'If I hadn't been so bothered about what they'd think about me at the Willows, he'd still be alive.'

The couple sat looking at each other.

'It was just as much my fault.' The husband was determined to shoulder his share of responsibility. 'I told him he had to pay his way now. We spoilt him when he was a boy, Sergeant. Our only son. Money no object. We gave him whatever he wanted. It came hard to him when that had to stop. Especially when he hooked up with all those rich southern kids in uni. I could tell he blamed me. He was bored silly in that job in the health club. Sometimes I could see him looking at me and I knew he thought I'd let him down.'

'Is that why he started stealing?' Joe knew all about that now. Vera had called him as soon as she'd left Lisa's house. *Find out from the parents what was going on there. Did Jenny Lister catch him thieving?* 'Because it wasn't for the cash, was it? He'd have hardly made enough to buy a couple of pints in the uni bar. Was it because he was bored?'

Now both parents turned on Ashworth. Fierce looks. A stony silence broken by Derek. 'You can't accuse the boy. He's dead. He can't fight back.'

'If you want us to find his killer,' Ashworth said, 'you have to help me here. We have a witness who saw him take money from the staffroom. Did he know he'd been seen?'

Another silence.

'You don't seem surprised,' Joe said gently. 'If it's not relevant, his stealing will never be made public. The witness won't talk. But you must tell me what you know.'

'I didn't *know*,' Karen said.

'But you guessed? Suspected?'

'He'd been moaning about being skint one morning and then suddenly there was a ten-pound note in his pocket and he was buying coffee in the hotel lounge before his shift started. I wondered.'

'That must have been terrible,' Joe said. He imagined finding out that one of his own kids was a thief. 'It must have eaten away at you. Did you discuss it with anyone at work?'

'No!' The thought appalled her. 'He was going to be a lawyer. If anyone found out, he could ruin the whole of his life for the sake of a cup of coffee. A few more days and he'd be in Bristol and we could forget the whole thing.'

It occurred to Joe that this woman had spent her life protecting her son and had created a monster. Would she kill to protect him? Perhaps, but there was no possibility that she would have stood behind him in the garden and strangled the boy, who had been, he saw now, her passion.

'Did you discuss it with Danny?'

This time there was a hesitation. 'No. I know I should have done. But I didn't want the last few days of his holiday spoiled. I wanted us to be happy, the family we'd once been. I pushed the idea out of my head. I told myself Danny wouldn't behave like that.'

Ashworth turned to her husband. 'Did you know anything about this, Mr Shaw?'

The man shook his head, apparently baffled by the events that had run up to his son's death.

'Where was Danny the morning Mrs Lister died?' Ashworth kept his voice gentle. Not a hint of accusation there. 'I know his shift at the Willows didn't start until late afternoon, but is there any chance he was in the hotel that morning?' No reply. 'Mrs Shaw?'

She didn't speak for a long time, but this time he didn't prompt her. 'He didn't come home the night before,' she said at last. 'Often when he was working late Derek would go and pick him up at the end of his shift. There are no buses in the evening and he didn't have his own car.' *Something else for the boy to complain about.* 'But occasionally he'd stay over. There was one of the staff bedrooms he was allowed to use. If he'd swapped to work an early shift the following day, or if he'd started drinking with some of the lasses working there.' She looked up. 'Usually it was the lasses he stayed up chatting to. They all fell for him.'

'And that was what had happened the evening before Mrs Lister was murdered?'

She nodded. 'Derek would have gone to get him, but Danny phoned and said not to bother. He'd stay at the hotel.'

'Did you see him the next day? The day of the murder?'

'No,' she said. 'He wasn't around when I turned up for my shift, so I thought he'd got the first bus home, that we'd missed each other.' She looked fiercely at Ashworth. 'He probably wasn't even in the hotel when the woman died.'

'You didn't ask him? Later, after the woman's body was found, you didn't ask if he'd been there?'

'No!' she said. 'How could I? That would have been like accusing him of murder!'

After her outburst, they sat again in silence. In the garden a red squirrel balanced on a branch of one of the mature trees that lined the road. A clock in another room chimed the half hour. Time was moving on, and Connie and Alice still hadn't been found. Ashworth found himself distracted, realized he'd lost the focus of the interview.

'Greenhough,' he said. 'That estate not far from here. Land ripe for development, I'd have thought. Did you never try to get hold of that, Mr Shaw?'

Shaw looked at him as if he were mad. 'What's that got to do with this?'

'Probably nothing.' *Another bee in Vera Stanhope's bonnet.* 'But just humour me, eh?'

'I nearly bought it at one time,' Shaw said. 'Christopher Eliot seemed close to settling. But in the end the rest of the family wouldn't agree.' He stared out of the window. 'If I'd got that, we'd have been set up for life. Fifty executive homes. Danny would have had everything he'd wanted then.'

'I'd like to see Danny's room,' Ashworth said. 'Would you mind?'

'The police have already been in,' Karen said angrily. 'They were there for hours, going through his things. He'd have hated that. I was never allowed in there, not even to change his sheets.'

'I know. And I won't disturb anything.'

She stood up and he followed her, expecting to be led upstairs. Instead they went along the corridor and into the ground-floor extension. Danny's space was almost like a self-contained flat, its own shower room, its own outside door.

'We built this when he was thirteen,' Karen said. 'When we still had the cash. Derek's idea. A place he could have his friends to stay without disturbing us.'

Spoilt brat, Joe thought. *Most kids would give their eye-*

teeth for a place like this, and he still wasn't happy.

The room was long and low. It had the feel of a rather grand student bedsit. A guitar lay on the floor next to a pile of CDs. There was a television and PC. At one end a workbench with a kettle and microwave, a small fridge. Flat-pack bookshelves. The posters on the walls seemed to date back to school days. Rock musicians and weird prints that meant nothing to Joe. On one wall a huge collage made of scraps of fabric and shiny paper in vivid colours, arresting and vital. At first it seemed to have no apparent form, but staring, Joe made out a huge, smiling face. Karen saw him looking at it.

'Hannah did that,' she said. 'She made it for her GCSE exam. Danny said he liked it and she gave it to him for a birthday present.' There was a pause. 'Sometimes I think things would have been different if he'd stayed with Hannah. That's when we started to lose him: when she told him she didn't want to see him any more. It was as if he gave up on us then.'

'But he had a new girlfriend in Bristol?' Joe wanted to believe that Danny had been happy at university.

'Oh, yes.' Karen walked around the room, picking up small objects. 'And she was lovely too. But more like a trophy. Something else for him to possess. He'd never have been able to possess Hannah.'

Chapter Thirty-One

Sitting in the car outside the Shaw house, Joe Ashworth tried to imagine what it must have been like living there for the last few years. Derek, the strong man, who'd built houses, made money, provided well for his family, suddenly seeing himself as a failure. Living with dreams of what might have been. The woman, forced to give up the easy life and take work she despised. Had she blamed Derek? Secretly, and hating herself for it, had her resentment eaten into the marriage? Led her to find a lover, start an affair? Ashworth wouldn't have been surprised. Then there was the boy, bright and charming and used to getting everything he wanted, thwarted first by Hannah and then by the change in his parents' fortunes. Ashworth wished Vera had been with him for the interview. She would have teased out the implications of the situation. She would have made more sense of it.

He started the car and drove along the valley towards Barnard Bridge. Connie's Nissan was still missing from outside the cottage, but he stopped there anyway, knocked on the door and looked through the windows. The post was sticking out through the letter-box. He pushed it through. Sitting in the garden, he worked through the names of Connie's friends given to him by Frank, calling each in turn. It didn't take long. There were only three of them, all women, and none had seen Connie for a while. 'We sort of lost touch when she moved out west,' one said, and that was the gist of each of the responses. They felt awkward because they hadn't been better friends. Joe realized again how isolated Connie had become, too proud to keep up with the friends from her old life and ignored by the women in her new one. He tried Connie's mobile once again, but the call was immediately transferred to the answering service.

On impulse he walked across the lane and up the drive to the big house where the Eliots lived. One time he'd have been nervous. He hadn't liked policing when work took him into smart houses, was happier in the council estates, the small miners' cottages. But Vera had worked on him: *You're as good as any of them. Don't be intimidated by money. It doesn't mean they're brighter than you, and it certainly doesn't make them better people.*

Veronica Eliot opened the door. She didn't invite him in and he felt about as welcome as a double-glazing salesman. At least the Shaws had been pleased to see him.

'I wondered if you have any idea where Connie Masters might be?' he asked.

'Why would I?'

'You were at her house yesterday afternoon when Jenny Lister's bag was found. Being neighbourly. She's having a tough time at the moment. I thought she might have told you. If she was hiding out from the press.'

'I don't think the press have got to her yet.' Veronica seemed less hostile. Had she thought she might be the subject of his attention? 'She didn't mention anything to me about going away.'

'Is there anywhere in the village she might be?'

Veronica appeared to consider, but he could tell she had already dismissed the idea out of hand. 'She hasn't made any close friends here. I must say, it seems unlikely.'

Perhaps because she was so offhand, Joe stayed on the doorstep. Vera had taught him to be stubborn, to face down the snotty middle classes. 'It must have been hard,' he said, 'to see another child in the cottage down there.'

She looked at him with distaste. If he'd farted at one of her smart dinner parties, she couldn't have despised him more.

'I'm not entirely sure why you think you have the right to dig around in my family's personal tragedies.'

He ignored that and continued, as if he were thinking aloud and no response were required. 'There would have been an inquiry, I'm sure. A sudden death and the police would have been involved. Social services too, I expect. People must have talked. It can't have been easy.'

Veronica lost control. The disintegration was sudden and completely unexpected, and it made him feel like a worm. Her face was flushed and she ranted at him, the words beating against him, making him flinch. 'Do you really think I cared about that? I'd just lost my son. Do you imagine I worried that people might be talking?'

'I'm sorry.'

'And it wasn't just me. Christopher had lost his baby boy. I knew I couldn't bear to have any more children after him. Simon had lost his brother. Have you any idea what that did to us?'

'I'm sorry,' Ashworth said again.

It was as if he hadn't spoken. 'We never blamed Simon for what happened that day. Never. He was a child. But he was old enough to remember it. He knew he shouldn't have run away from me. He thinks it was his fault. He's had to live with the knowledge all his life. Do you think a bit of gossip is worse than the pain of that?'

'No,' Ashworth said. He had to stop himself putting up his hands to protect his head from the violence of the words. 'No, of course not.'

The outburst ended as quickly as it had begun. Veronica became distant, icy, once again. 'To answer your question, Sergeant, of course it was difficult to see a child playing where Patrick died. I had mixed feelings. Perhaps my response to Connie was coloured by my experience. I was unkind. But I've had nothing to do with her disappearance. I don't know where she is.'

She made to turn away from him and shut the door, but Ashworth called her back.

'Would it be possible to speak to Hannah?'

'Hannah's not here. She and Simon left soon after you did this morning. I assume they're back in her house, but they didn't say where they were going.' She stood on the doorstep, a lonely and dignified figure, watching the detective walk away.

He found the girl in the garden behind the little house she'd shared with her mother. There was no answer when he knocked at the door and he was about to give up when Hilda waved at him from her living-room window, pointing to an arched gap in the terrace between their two houses.

Hannah was alone. Her red hair was tied back in an untidy plait and she was wearing wellingtons, a big hand-knitted sweater with a frayed rib and holes in the elbows. She was digging over the small vegetable patch. When she saw him she stopped and leaned on the fork. She was flushed and breathless.

'Mum always planted a few new potatoes over the Easter holiday. Broad beans too. I didn't want to let it go.'

'You've been going at that like a dog at broth.' One of his grandda's sayings. 'You'll wear yourself out.'

'I hope so.' She smiled at him. 'It'd be good to get to sleep without a pill. They make me feel lousy the next morning.'

'Simon not with you?'

'He's taken Mum's car to the supermarket in Hexham. I couldn't face it—the supermarket or the car—so I said I'd stay here. We have to eat, I suppose, and I don't want to go to the White House for meals every day.' She bent absent-mindedly and pulled a strand of goose grass from the soil and threw it onto the wheelbarrow, then straight-ened. 'Do you know who killed my mother yet?'

He shook his head. 'Are you up to answering some questions?'

'If you don't mind doing it here. I feel better outside.' And it seemed to him that she was much better, almost cheerful in the spring sunshine. She'd lost the pallor and the doped indifference.

'Did your mum mention seeing anything unusual about the health club lately? We think one of the staff had been stealing from guests and other employees. It might be a motive.' He wanted to start off with something imper-sonal, not too close to home.

'No. Nothing like that. But that doesn't mean she didn't see something. We were both busy. Often she didn't get back until late from work, and by then I'd be out with Si or holed up in my room revising. We were close, but there wasn't a lot of time for chat.'

'I'd like to talk again about Danny Shaw.' Joe hesitated. This was more sensitive, but he wanted to broach it while he had Hannah to himself. 'There's a collage on his wall. His mother said you gave it to him. It sounds as if there was more between you than the fact that you went out together a few times. Karen says you were his first love, that he never quite got over you.'

She stooped again to pull out more weeds, avoiding his eye.

'I fancied myself in love with *him* for a while. I gave him the picture while I was still a little bit besotted.'

'What went wrong?'

'Nothing really. I hooked up with Simon and saw that Danny was basically a bit of a prat.'

'So you dumped Danny for Simon? That wasn't the impression you gave yesterday.'

'Wasn't it?' She smiled. 'I don't know. All that stuff seems so important when you're going through it, but later it hardly seems to matter. This is a small place.

There aren't that many people of our age. You tend to have been out with most of the available boys by the time you hit seventeen. It's like one of those Scottish country dances. *Change your partner when the music stops.* In the end we just all become good friends.'

Joe supposed that was true. It had been the same for him. He'd been out with a couple of his wife's friends before hooking up with her; one had been to dinner at their house with her husband the week before. Teenage passion soon faded.

He wanted to ask Hannah if she'd slept with Danny, if they'd been *that* close, but resisted. His reluctance was more a matter of knowing the question would have seemed ridiculous to her than of not wanting to pry.

'Was Danny upset? You said yesterday he emailed and phoned you after you dumped him. Did he make a nuisance of himself?'

She shrugged. 'Nah. He soon got over it. He started going out with his new lass in freshers' week, so he can't have been that heart-broken.'

She pushed the wheelbarrow to the end of the garden and lifted the weeds onto the compost heap. 'Is that all you wanted to know? I don't think I've been much help.'

'Did Simon ever talk to you about Patrick?' Joe hadn't meant to ask her about the dead brother, but he thought it was important: the child drowning, the effect on the adult Simon.

'Of course.' She wiped a stray hair away from her face and left a streak of mud. 'We tell each other everything.'

'What did he say?'

'That Patrick was like a ghost in their lives. Nothing of him remains. Veronica threw away all his toys and his clothes, and they hardly ever mentioned his name after the accident. Simon said that sometimes he felt as if Patrick had never existed, that he'd created the whole incident in his imagination.'

'Would your mother have been working as a social worker then?' Ashworth felt as if he was groping towards a connection, an explanation.

'I suppose so.' Hannah looked up sharply. 'Do you think she worked with the Eliot family after the tragedy? I suppose she would have qualified by then, and we'd be living here.'

'It just crossed my mind,' Joe said. 'But that would be too much of a coincidence. Your mother would surely have remembered the case, happening so close to home. She would have mentioned it.'

'Oh, I don't think she would.' Hannah was quite certain. 'She had a thing about confidentiality. She said work had to stay in the office, where it belonged.' She leaned the empty wheelbarrow against the wall. 'Look, I probably won't do any more of this now. Do you want some tea?'

'Does Simon feel responsible for his brother's death?'

She'd already started walking towards the back door of the house, and his question made her stop in her tracks.

'Of course.' She pulled out the band that was tying up her hair and shook it loose. 'It's made him the person he is.'

Chapter Thirty-Two

Vera wanted to talk to Michael Morgan. She'd never admit it to Joe Ashworth, but she'd seriously cocked up that last meeting when they'd barged into the flat. Something about the man—his ease with his body, his assumption of superiority—had got under her skin and made her lose the plot. He was into mind-games. That was how he made his living. He depended on the gullibility of his clients. This time she'd be calm. She'd take him through the facts, box him into a corner.

She met Joe in the cafe in Tynemouth where they'd taken Freya. He was already waiting for her, jotting notes in his Filofax, frowning a bit like a schoolboy doing difficult homework. Vera ordered coffee and a slab of chocolate cake. She hadn't eaten since breakfast in Barnard Bridge.

'How did you get on at the Shaw house?'

'Danny was in the Willows the morning Jenny Lister died.'

'Was he now?' Vera wasn't sure if this was good news or if it just complicated matters. 'So he might have seen what happened, even if he wasn't implicated himself.'

'I asked Shaw about Greenhough.'

'And?' Vera looked up sharply from her cake. Something about that place still haunted her.

'Christopher Eliot came close to selling it for development, but the deal fell through in the end. I had the impression that Veronica vetoed it.'

'I wonder why she's so attached to it. An overgrown garden and a few statues. A boathouse. If Patrick had died there, instead of in Barnard Bridge, you could understand it.' Vera realized she was talking to herself and turned her attention to Ashworth. 'Still no news of Connie?' She knew the woman's disappearance was on his mind.

'I've put out a search for the car. If she's not home tonight, I think we should go public, get the press involved. If she just wanted some breathing space she'd have told us where she was going. She's not a stupid woman.'

'You do realize,' Vera said, 'that some folk will see her disappearance as evidence of her guilt. Go to the media, and she'll be the awful witch that caused Elias Jones's death *and* a multiple murderer. Her photos all over the paper and the television. Just what she'd want before the lass starts school. Not.'

'Do you think she's a killer?'

'Nah.' Vera had just poked the last bit of cake into her mouth and the crumbs went everywhere when she spoke. 'I think she's scared. And not just of the press. Someone's told her to make herself scarce.'

'It could be more sinister than that.'

'You think someone's killed her to keep her quiet?' Vera licked her fingers to pick up the crumbs from her plate and the surrounding table. 'It's possible. But if she's dead, we can't help her and going to the press will be bugger-all use.' She paused. 'What does she know that makes it so important that she shouldn't talk to us?'

'She could recognize the bloke that turned up at her house the afternoon of Jenny Lister's death. We were going to show her photos of all the male suspects this morning.'

'Aye,' Vera said. 'Maybe. But if he wanted to be discreet about visiting the Eliots, he'd hardly have asked directions from a stranger. And if he was the person who dumped Jenny's bag, the same applies.' She thought the guy was

probably some door-to-door salesman. Surely Connie
would have recognized Morgan if he'd turned up at her
cottage. No way would she have invited him in for tea. But
then with his new haircut Vera herself hadn't recognized
him.

'Something about the Elias Jones case frightened her
off then?' It was clear Joe wasn't going to let this go.

'That takes us back to Michael Morgan again, doesn't
it? If we discount Connie, he's the only person implicated
in Elias Jones's death who could be the killer. Mattie
Jones was in hospital. So for now let's concentrate on him.
After that we'll go back to Barnard Bridge. It'll be the little
girl's bedtime. If they're not back by then, it's time to
worry.'

She looked up at Ashworth, realizing that she might
have sounded callous. He could be sentimental, especially when women and children were involved. But he
nodded to show he agreed.

'So,' she said. 'Morgan. I wondered if we should bring
him in to the station.'

'Have we got enough on him to do that?'

'I'm not talking about an arrest,' she grinned. 'An invitation, that's all. He's an upstanding member of the
community. I'm sure he'll be delighted to help. He'd be
less comfortable on our territory. What do you think?'
Usually that sort of question was rhetorical, but this time
Vera really wanted Ashworth's opinion.

'I'm not sure.'

'Come on, Joey. Spit it out! You're allowed to disagree
with me. Every now and again.'

'He's good at playing the game, isn't he? They had him
in for questioning after the boy died. An interview at the
station won't be anything new to him. Probably not even
very scary. He'll make sure his solicitor's there.'

'What do you suggest then?' She could hear the annoy-
ance in her own voice. *It's all very well pulling holes in my*

ideas. More difficult to come up with a suggestion of your own.

'What about taking him to his office at the Willows? That'll inconvenience him, pull him out of his home just as he's about to have his tea. While we're picking him up, we can have a quick scout round the flat for evidence of Connie or the girl. It'll be a neutral space, his office, but unsettling. I know he doesn't keep any of his records there, but we can imply we have a specific reason for wanting to see it. Send him home in a taxi, and we'll be . . .'

'. . . almost in Barnard Bridge, to call in to Connie's cottage before close of play.' Vera grinned. 'Eh, lad, I've taught you a couple of things at least while you've been working for me.'

She decided to phone Morgan in advance to tell him they'd be collecting him. That would be more formal than just turning up on the doorstep. And phoning from her mobile from the end of his street, she'd see if he or Freya appeared suddenly with Connie and her daughter. Though that was never going to happen. Morgan might be a bastard, but he was too bright to keep them there.

He was rattled by her insistence that they go to the Willows. 'Is that really necessary, Inspector? There's nothing at all to see.'

'Of course we could always get a search warrant, if you'd prefer, Mr Morgan. That might take a few hours, though, and I wouldn't really want to drag you out in the middle of the night.'

He was alone in the flat. No Freya. When Ashworth asked, Morgan said she'd gone to a film with some friends. He tried to make out that he was pleased for her, but it sounded to Vera as if he was sulking about it. She asked to use the bathroom and had a sneaky look at the rest of the flat. One bedroom with a futon instead of a bed. Like sleeping, Vera thought, on a sheet of hardboard. Everything very clean and ordered. No room to hide a mouse.

In the bathroom the towels were folded, the mirror shone. She couldn't imagine Morgan taking his turn with the Hoover and wondered if that was down to Freya or a cleaner. If it were Freya, she'd be defecting soon enough without any intervention from outside.

They drove to the Willows in complete silence. That was Vera's idea. Morgan liked talking. It made him feel in control. Once, just as they came to the A69, he tried to start a conversation. 'Has there been any development, Inspector?'

But Vera responded immediately, breaking in before he'd finished the sentence. 'We'll leave that until we can talk properly, shall we?'

During the drive she felt the tension rise in the man sitting behind her. At the Willows they made sure he was walking between them, not because they thought he'd try to escape, but to make him feel like a suspect. He used his electronic fob to get to the area closed to the public, and then again into the small room where he saw his patients.

'Is that what you call them?' Vera asked. They were sitting across a coffee table. There was a high bed against one wall, but these easy chairs must be where Morgan took the histories. She'd chosen the chair that she assumed he used. 'Patients? Do you have any medical training?'

'The training to become an acupuncturist is long and rigorous.' He was determined not to be provoked, but he was finding it hard to keep the relaxed, amused tone he'd used with her before. There was a touch of petulance that made her want to cheer.

'You're not a doctor, though?'

'Western medicine doesn't have all the answers, Inspector.'

'You'll have heard about Danny Shaw.' Changing the subject so abruptly that she saw Morgan blink. There wasn't a seat for Ashworth and he stood, leaning against the door, blocking any escape. 'Of course you will. No

telly, I know, but it would have been in that fancy newspaper you read. No doubt about that. A second murder
connected to the Willows. The press is loving it.'

'It's very sad,' Morgan said, 'but I can't see what you
think it might have to do with me.'

'You were very close to Danny.' Vera fired the words
back at him. 'Or so his mother says.'

'That's somewhat of an exaggeration.'

'He admired you,' Vera went on as if there'd been no
interruption. 'Admired your drive and the way you went
for what you wanted. It must have been flattering to have
a bright lad like that hanging off your every word.'

And Morgan couldn't help giving a little smile. Even
here, with the two cops watching on, he couldn't help
being pleased with himself. 'We had a couple of interesting discussions. As you say, he was a bright lad. Working
in a place like this, you can miss intelligent conversation.'

'Of course,' Vera said. She had to bite her tongue to
stop herself from asking if that was why he'd taken up
with Mattie and Freya. For the quality of the conversation. 'When did you last see him?'

'The afternoon before he died,' Morgan said. 'It must
have been then.'

'Tell me about it.' This chair was comfortable, more
comfortable than any of the furniture in Morgan's flat.
Vera had to force herself to concentrate. Suddenly she
thought it would have been very easy to drift off to sleep.

'We met for a coffee in the lounge. Something we did
most of the days when our shifts coincided.'

'How did Danny seem?' She shuffled her bum forward
so that she was in a more upright position.

Morgan took time to answer and that made Vera suddenly feel wide awake. Was he putting together a story in
his head? That would mean he had something to hide.

'I thought he was a bit jumpy,' Morgan said at last.

'In what way, jumpy?' She leaned forwards, elbows on
her knees, right in his face.

'You know, tense, wired up. Perhaps he'd just had too much coffee. There could have been no more to it than that.'

'Mr Morgan, you're used to interpreting people's physical responses. It's how you make a living, how you persuade unhappy people to trust you. People like Lisa, who works here. People who can't really afford your charges. And then you get your *patients* to confide in you. I want to know exactly what you made of Danny's state that afternoon. And exactly what he said.'

The room was very small and there was no natural light. It had a background smell that was faintly aromatic, a result of incense perhaps or scented candles. But now Vera could smell fear on the man who sat so close to her.

'Like I said, he was wired up,' Morgan said. He wouldn't meet her eyes. 'Hyper. At first I thought it might be drugs, but I think it was just adrenalin.'

'And what did he say?'

'Nothing specific. Really. Nothing that would help you find his killer.'

'I really don't think you're qualified to make a decision about that.' Vera's voice rose in volume so that it filled the room.

'He was asking questions,' Morgan said. 'About Jenny Lister and her part in the Elias Jones case. "You knew her, man. What was she like? Was she as prim and self-righteous as the papers made out?" It was rather distasteful actually. I'd have thought Danny would be above that sort of gossip.'

'Did Danny tell you that he'd met Jenny? That Jenny's daughter had once been the love of his life. That he blamed Jenny for splitting them up?' Vera hadn't put this thought into words before, but she was sure it was true. And it gave Danny a motive for murder.

'No,' Morgan said. 'He didn't tell me any of that.' His voice was quiet and measured.

'It doesn't surprise you, though!'

'No, it doesn't surprise me. The interest he was taking in the Jenny Lister murder sounded like more than voyeuristic prurience. It seemed to me that it was personal.'

'Do you think he killed her?'

There was a pause. Morgan looked at her, said nothing.

'It must have crossed your mind. All those questions.' Vera waited again for an answer. At last it came.

'He could have done,' Morgan said. 'Yeah, he was so wound up that he could have done.'

But you would say that, Vera thought. *If you were the murderer, what else would you say?*

Morgan looked around the room, like some performer, Vera thought, waiting for applause after a particularly dramatic moment. Well, she wasn't going to give him the satisfaction. She continued the interview in the same tone as before. 'Do you remember anything else about your conversation with Danny the day before he died?'

Morgan frowned. 'He went on about friendship. About how important our friendship was to him. He'd met lots of people in Bristol, but no one he could really be himself with. There was so much posing at university. I suppose I should have felt flattered, but by then I was just keen to get home and didn't even take in everything he said. I'm afraid I cut him off and told him I had to rush. I feel very bad about that now. If I'd listened more carefully, been a true friend, perhaps his death could have been avoided.'

Vera allowed him a moment of self-satisfied and mournful reflection before continuing. 'You didn't tell us you and Freya were in the hotel the morning Jenny Lister was strangled.'

It was the last thing he was expecting and the look on his face made her feel like singing.

She went on, 'I know you have a very low opinion of the police, Mr Morgan, but you must have realized that we'd find out.'

'Freya attended one of the exercise classes for pregnant women.'

'Very nice.' She looked at him, waiting for him to continue, eventually running out of patience. 'And you, Mr Morgan? What were you up to?'

'I was here,' he said. 'In this room. Catching up on some paperwork.'

'Why didn't you tell us that before?'

'Because, Inspector, you didn't ask me.'

Walking back to the car, Vera wanted to talk to Joe about the interview. She felt she'd handled it almost perfectly and with remarkable restraint, would have liked that recognized. But he'd switched his mobile back on and had it stuck to his ear, listening to the missed calls.

'Well?' When at last he put the phone back in his pocket.

'One from forensics. They found some scraps of paper unburned on the bonfire in the Shaws' garden. Thought we might be interested. They reckon it's Jenny Lister's writing.'

'Her notebook,' Vera said, her thoughts firing away in all directions. 'Maybe the outline of the stuff she was writing about Mattie.'

'They've transcribed it and sent it as an email.'

'And the other?' Because Ashworth was tense and troubled, not as excited as he should have been by the forensic news.

'From Connie Masters. Saying she's OK, just taking a couple of days away.'

'Well,' Vera said. 'That's good, isn't it? A bummer because we can't show her the photos, but at least we know she's safe.'

'I'm not sure.' He'd reached the car and stopped, looking back to the hotel. It was dusk and all the lights were on. 'She sounded odd. I'd like you to listen to it.'

Chapter Thirty-Three

That night it rained, a sudden torrential downpour like a tropical storm. It began as Vera was running towards her house from the car and she was drenched by the time she'd got the door open. She stood just inside and shook herself like a dog, in her head blaming Ashworth, who'd kept her standing in the Willows car park, listening over and over again to the voicemail left by Connie. Maybe the woman did sound a bit strained, but Vera always felt flustered when she found herself talking to an automated voice too. She thought her sergeant was over-reacting, making a fuss about nothing. He'd insisted they go to the cottage in Barnard Bridge and they'd even looked inside again, but of course there was nobody there. Connie had explained in her message that she'd be staying away for a while. Without all that fannying about, Vera would have been home in the dry.

Driving north, she'd thought she might call in to see her hippy neighbours for an hour to wind down. They were always welcoming. There'd likely be a pan of soup on the range and some of the home-brew that was a more effective relaxant than anything a doctor would prescribe. Now she couldn't face the idea of wrapping herself up in waterproofs and paddling through the mud. Instead she lay in the bath listening to a gloomy play on the radio, then changed into the faded tracksuit she wore instead of pyjamas in the winter.

Because she had the idea of soup firmly in her mind, she went in search of some and found a tin at the back of the larder that must have been there since Hector was still alive. Oxtail. His favourite. Heating it in a small pan, the smell brought him vividly to life. Hector, big and bullying, picking away at her confidence. Blaming her, she thought now, for being alive when her mother was dead. But what sort of parent would Vera have made if she'd had the chance to have children? Crap, she thought. She'd have been crap too. Much worse than Connie, or Jenny Lister, or even Veronica Eliot.

There was a small room at the back of the house that she used as an office. Piles of paper that she had to climb over to get in, a computer that would soon be fit for a museum. She fired it up and went to make a cup of tea while it chugged into life. It still hadn't quite made it by the time she returned with her mug and a packet of chocolate digestives. She had a quick memory of the child doctor who'd sent her to the health club to get fit, imagined her disapproval, then dismissed it. Digestives were wholewheat, weren't they? Healthy enough.

There was time for her to eat three biscuits before her email account was displayed on the screen. She opened the message from the scientist who'd been looking at the scraps of paper found in the bonfire burning in the garden at the Shaw house. Vera had asked Karen about the bonfire during the first interview in the neighbours' house. 'Did you or Derek light it before you went to work?' It had seemed odd to Vera even then. Bonfires were for weekends, when you had the time to keep an eye on them. And Karen had looked at her as if she were mad, obviously had no idea what she was talking about. The bonfire had been nothing to do with her or Derek.

Vera had persisted. 'Danny then? Did he help you out in the garden sometimes?'

At that, Karen had shaken her head sadly. 'Danny didn't really do helping. In the garden or anywhere else.'

So the bonfire had been started by the murderer. That was the way Vera saw it. A mistake. Better to take any incriminating paper away with him and dispose of it carefully. So why the hurried fire in the garden? What was that about? Why the rush?

There were really only scraps of text. Handwritten. By Jenny Lister. The forensic handwriting woman had been certain of that. It said so in the email: *I'd be quite happy to appear in court. I'd stake my reputation* . . . Blah, blah. Very dramatic. But good enough for Vera.

They'd retrieved three different pages containing text, it seemed, and all three were partially charred, one so severely that they'd been lucky to get anything. The first page was the most intact, but contained what looked like a final paragraph. At least, the writing stopped a third of the way down the page. According to the lab, one corner was burned so the ends of some of the sentences were lost, and they'd re-created the pattern of the writing as accurately as they could on the screen. Vera thought that it wasn't hard to make out the sense.

> *and the importance of learning to build relationships early i*
> *The patterns of behaviour developed in childhood can oft*
> *no reason why another adult shouldn't play this role. The child can then*
> *to sustain a normal and healthy relationship with his or her own children. However, in the case study described, we see deep problems that were never properly addressed and which would be impossible at this point to solve.*

Social-work bollocks, Vera thought. If Jenny had been hoping to write a popular book to explain her job to the layperson, she wouldn't achieve it with stuff like this. Was she talking about Mattie in this piece? Vera assumed so. In that case, Vera had learned nothing from the notes on this page. Still, assumptions were always dangerous. There was no indication here about the gender of the subject of the case study, and Jenny could have been writing about somebody quite different. Besides, she'd been working with Mattie since she was a child. Would the model social worker really admit that she hadn't 'properly addressed' Mattie's problems during all those years of intervention?

Vera moved away from the computer and stretched. In the lean-to at the back of the house she could hear rain dripping. The flat roof there leaked when the wind blew from the west. Usually it did blow from the west. She fetched a bucket and a bowl to catch the drips and went back to the office. Outside it was raining more heavily than ever.

The second piece was certainly about Mattie, at least to some extent, because she was named. If the piece had finally achieved publication, Vera assumed that Jenny would have chosen a pseudonym for her, but at this early point of the process she clearly hadn't seen the need. There was one complete sentence, then a number of gaps. It seemed that sparks had burned isolated little holes in the paper, without setting the whole sheet alight. That at least was how it looked from the scanned image that the lab had attached, along with the words within the body of the email on the screen.

The complete sentence still read like an official report or undergraduate textbook: *It is sometimes a mistake to blame an outsider for disrupting the balance of a family, when other factors could be in force.* Did this mean that Jenny was making an excuse for Michael Morgan? Was she implying that Mattie was solely responsible for the death of her son? The rest of the words were scattered apparently at random as short phrases, separated by the burn marks.

> *Death by drowning is never t stice system   substitute*
> *mother can someti*
> *happiness   s then the trigger   n alternative way of*
> *Sometimes it's best not to intervene.   illness*
> *tie Jone*

Vera stared at the screen. She felt suddenly cold and realized that the timer had switched off the heating. It was already late. She fetched her outdoor coat and sat in that, would have fancied a whisky, but couldn't be arsed to get up again and fetch it. Still there was the background sound of rain, like shingle hurled against glass. The snatches of text tantalized her. Death by drowning surely meant Elias. But Veronica's son was drowned too. What was the word that Jenny had written after 'never' in the first phrase? Vera printed off the scanned image of the charred and blasted paper, held a ruler across it so that she could see which words were written on the same line, but still it made no sense.

In frustration she turned to the third sheet of paper. This was the most damaged. In the email, the technician had said she thought it might have been torn in half before it was burned: there was one ragged edge. It seemed clear to Vera, even from the brief fragments, that the tone was different, less formal. This wasn't a note from an official report, but more like a personal diary entry.

What the helling friendship

That word 'friendship' again. Vera had heard it that evening as Morgan had tried to scrabble his way out of the hole he'd dug by not telling them earlier about his meeting with Danny Shaw. It seemed to Vera that Jenny had had few real friends. There was the teacher, Anne, but that was more an arrangement of convenience. Two women of a similar age who enjoyed each other's company. The relationship satisfied Anne's need to admire, and Jenny's to be admired. Friendship surely implied something stronger than that. Friendship was what Vera had with Joe Ashworth, but not yet with the hippy neighbours. And had Michael Morgan and Danny Shaw really been friends? The idea was improbable. They fed each other's egos, nothing more, so why the sentimental drivel from Danny in his last conversation with Morgan?

Vera looked at her watch. Past midnight. The questions were too difficult for this time of night, and tomorrow would be an important day. She felt that she was grappling towards some sort of solution. Ashworth was right; they needed to find Connie. She shut down the computer and sat for a moment listening to it grind and chug to a close. When this case was over, she'd treat herself to a new machine. Perhaps Joe would come with her to buy one.

Lying in the bed she'd slept in as a child, between the sheets grey with washing, which had probably been in use since then too, images and ideas floated into her head and then fluttered away from her, like the charred tatters of paper blowing from a bonfire. Outside, it was still raining.

Chapter Thirty-Four

Joe Ashworth hated the rain. It meant his kids were trapped indoors and his wife moaned about mud and mess. He thought she had that illness, SAD—seasonal affective disorder. She seemed to wilt without the sun, to become crabby and ungenerous. Mornings like this, he envied Vera's solitary life. It would be great to be selfish without the guilt. He drove away from the house, from the damp children's clothes stretched over radiators, the toy-strewn living room, the whining baby, and told himself he was the breadwinner, that he couldn't be expected to do it all.

Travelling towards the police station for the morning briefing, he hit a traffic jam. It was still raining and the standing water had caused a minor accident on the way into town. His windscreen-wiper blades were faulty and squeaked at the same pitch as the baby's cries. He switched them off and couldn't see, put them back on and got the noise that set his teeth on edge and made him feel like putting his fist through the glass.

It didn't help that, when he reached the incident room, Vera was at her most jaunty. She'd blagged a proper filter machine from somewhere and the smell of the coffee hit him as soon as he walked in.

'Where are the others?' His question. Usually Vera hated people to be late, one of the reasons why he'd been so tense when his way had been blocked by the crawling traffic. Now he hoped to hear her slag off the rest of the team. After all, he'd made the effort to be there.

But she only shrugged. 'This weather's a nightmare, isn't it?' She poured him coffee. 'Have you tried Connie this morning?'

He looked at her, suspecting she was mocking him, but she seemed serious enough. 'Yes, it went straight to voicemail again. I left a message asking her to get in touch.'

'I'd like her opinion on these.' Vera pinned a series of sheets onto the board. Copies of the charred paper rescued from the bonfire in Danny Shaw's garden. 'More than anyone, she'd know the way Jenny thought about her work.'

'You've dismissed Connie altogether as a suspect then?'

'Eh, pet, I didn't say that. That's another thing entirely.' She gave the smile that was supposed to be enigmatic, but only made her look constipated.

He carried his coffee to look at the burnt paper more closely, but found it hard to make any sense from the words, even to concentrate on them. He couldn't understand why Vera was so happy. Holly and Charlie came in together, laughing at a shared joke, and again he felt isolated, an outsider, trapped in the gap between Vera and her troops. *I need to move on*, he thought. *I'll always be in her shadow.*

Vera regarded the latecomers indulgently, waited until they'd fetched coffee and then swung into her performance. It occurred to Ashworth that from these scraps of text she'd deduced some meaning or motive for the murders. That would explain her good humour. In that moment his envy was so intense that he almost hated her.

Vera set out the events of the previous day: the interviews with Veronica Eliot, Lisa, the Shaw family, Freya and Morgan. Joe had to admit that she was bloody good at this summing up, at pulling out links and meanings that would probably have passed him by, at laying out the facts in a way that was easy to follow.

'It seems to me that the only intended victim was Jenny Lister,' she said. 'At first, at least. Danny Shaw was killed because he knew something or found out something about the first killing. The fact that the bonfire in his garden contained documents belonging to Lister suggests that he'd found her notebook.'

She paused for breath and Holly took the opportunity to stick up her hand. 'Could Shaw have killed Jenny then? How else would he have her notebook?'

'How else indeed? It seems that Danny and Hannah had a bit of a fling before he went away to university. By all accounts it meant a lot more to him than to her, but of course we can't get his take on that. We might assume that the fragments in the fire were stolen at the same time as Jenny's handbag, after the murder, but I think we have to keep an open mind.'

'What do you mean?' Charlie, hunched over his coffee, seemed almost alert.

'Maybe Hannah's not telling us the truth, and Danny visited her when he was home from uni.' Vera looked at her audience. 'Maybe she thinks she's too young to be settling down after all.'

'No!' Holly was horrified. 'She's devoted to Simon. No way would she cheat on him.'

'We know Danny was in the Lister house a couple of years ago when he and Hannah were going out together,' Vera went on. 'But it's unlikely he stole any material from Jenny then. What would be the point? It would have been before Elias's death, so there'd have been no press interest.'

Ashworth lifted his hand from the desk in front of him. 'It'd be interesting to find out if Morgan and Danny knew each other before they met at the Willows?'

'It would, wouldn't it?' Vera gave no sign whether or not this idea had occurred to her. 'I'd have thought Karen would have mentioned a previous connection with Morgan when we talked to her about him, but she was all over the place. Could you follow that up, Holly? With the mother and with any of Danny's mates we can track down.'

Holly nodded and scribbled a couple of lines in her notebook.

Vera turned to Charlie. 'Any joy in tracking down witnesses around the Shaw house the day Danny died?'

'Nah. That place is like a dormitory village. Most people work in Hexham or Newcastle. During the day it's quiet as the grave. I found an elderly gent who was taking his dog for a walk at about the right time. He was passed by a small car he didn't recognize, but it could have belonged to anybody and he can't even remember the colour of the vehicle.'

'Anyone else got any bright ideas?' Vera looked around the room. There was silence apart from the rain still gushing from a blocked gutter outside. 'Actions then.' She paused for effect, but Ashworth thought she'd had these worked out from the moment she stood up. Before that even. Who knew what she dreamed about at night?

'Holly's to follow up on Danny Shaw and Michael Morgan. Check out possible previous points of contact. Joe, I'd like you to go to Durham nick. Have another chat with Mattie. She's back there now, recovering in the hospital wing. You're good with helpless females. I need more details of the visits Jenny Lister made to her. What exactly did they talk about? Charlie, see if you can track down Connie Masters. Her car must be somewhere, and it's not easy to hide a four-year-old girl. They haven't been in the cottage in Barnard Bridge since yesterday morning. She left a message on Joe's phone saying she was fine and needed a bit of space, but he thinks there's more to it than that.' Another pause, even longer than the first. 'And so do I. I want to speak to her.' Ashworth wasn't sure what to make of that. Did she think Connie was in danger? If so, why would she leave her in Charlie's unreliable hands?

Vera stopped speaking, made a sort of shooing gesture with her hands. 'Go on then. This is a murder inquiry, not a mothers' union meeting. You haven't got all day.'

'What about you?' Charlie said, verging on the rude.

'Me?' She gave another of her self-satisfied grins. 'I'm management and I don't go out in the rain. I'm doing some strategic thinking.'

Joe Ashworth liked Durham city. Only twenty minutes down the A1, he thought you could have been in a different world from the centre of Newcastle. This was an old town, classy, with its huge red sandstone cathedral and the castle, the smart shops and the fancy restaurants, the university colleges and the students with their posh voices. Like a southern city, he always thought, lifted up and stuck on the Wear. The prison was quite a different matter. Joe hated most prisons, but this was one of the worst. It was grim and old and made him think of dungeons and rats. It didn't belong in Durham. It had a unit for long-term and dangerous female prisoners.

Seeing Mattie now, it was hard to think of her as dangerous. He talked to her in a small office, reluctantly relinquished by staff, on the hospital wing. She was already there when he arrived, escorted by a male officer who'd brought him from the gate. She was dressed in a prison-issue tracksuit, but there were slippers on her feet and she seemed very young, reminded Joe of his daughter when she was ready for bed. He'd wanted to bring Mattie something. He always came with a small sweetener on his prison visits—cigarettes usually, especially if he was coming to see a man, cigarettes that were chain-smoked throughout the interview because prisoners weren't allowed to take anything away with them. Most of the men smoked. Cigarettes hadn't seemed appropriate on a hospital visit, so he handed over a small box of chocolates, not sure about the rules.

Mattie seemed disproportionately grateful and held the gift-wrapped box on her lap.

'Did that fat cop send you?'

She could only be talking about Vera. 'Aye, she thought you could do with the company.'

'She was canny, like.'

Not when you really know her.

Mattie looked at him. Huge blue eyes in a wide, smooth forehead. 'But what do you really want?'

'A chat,' he said. 'About Jenny Lister.'

She nodded. 'But I told the lady everything I know.'

Vera would like that, being called a lady!

'You were ill,' Joe said. 'You had a fever. We thought you might remember a bit more now.'

'It still knacks,' she said and lifted her tracksuit top, quite unselfconsciously, to show him the wound on her abdomen covered with a dressing. Again he was reminded of his daughter showing off a scab on her knee.

'It must be very painful,' he said gently. He could understand why Jenny had been so taken with Mattie, why she'd come each week to visit, even though really she'd no longer had any formal responsibility for her. 'Tell me about Jenny's visits,' he went on. 'Was it the same every week?'

'Yes. Every week. Not in the main visits room—you know, where you see your family and they have toys for the bairns. She said it was too noisy there and we wouldn't be able to talk properly. Though if you're there, they bring you a cup of tea and there are biscuits—chocolate if you get in early.' She looked at the chocolates he'd brought her.

'Why don't you open them?' Joe smiled. 'I don't have much of a sweet tooth, but you could have a couple.'

She ripped the wrapping off and took one out.

'So where did Jenny see you?'

'In those little cubicles where you talk to your lawyer or the cops.' Her mouth was already full of strawberry cream.

Did that mean that Jenny hadn't wanted to be overheard? 'What did you talk about?'

'Like I told the lady, it was about me. Jenny was going to write a book.'

'Did she make notes?'

'Yeah, mostly. Sometimes we just chatted.'

'Where did she write the notes?'

'In a big black book.' Mattie was already getting bored. Maybe she was missing something she liked on the television in the ward.

'Did she talk to you about Michael?'

'She said I had to forget about him.' Mattie reached out and took another chocolate, unwrapped the silver paper carefully and put the sweet into her mouth. 'She wanted me to talk about when I was little, what I could remember about growing up.'

'Where did you grow up?' he asked.

'In the country,' she said. 'That's what I remember. When I was very little, before I went into care. At least I think it was before I went into care. Or maybe I went there for a visit. It was a little house by the water. That's what Jenny wanted from me, my memories. I wanted to talk about Michael, but she said I wasn't to speak of him.' Mattie paused, reached out greedily for another chocolate. 'I didn't think that was fair. Jenny never even stayed for very long. She was in a rush to get back to her real work, the other kids she was looking after now. Sometimes it was like she didn't even care about me. All she wanted to know about was that house in the country, and she'd make me close my eyes and picture it and tell her what I could see.'

They sat for a moment in silence and again Mattie closed her eyes. Ashworth was going to ask her to tell him what she saw, ask her perhaps to sketch it, but in the ward a woman started screaming and the spell was broken. Mattie opened her eyes. 'Stupid cow,' she said. 'She's always doing that. Makes you want to slap her.'

'Why did you go into care?' Joe asked.

'I dunno.' Mattie stared into space. He thought she was about to cry, but she turned back to him, dry-eyed, and said in a matter-of-fact way, 'I think my mam died. Or maybe that was just what I wanted to think. I asked a bit when I was growing up, but I kept getting different stories. In the end you don't know who to believe.'

Chapter Thirty-Five

The gate officer handed him back his phone and he switched it on, running back from the prison to his car in the rain. It rang immediately. Not the answering service with a message from Connie, but Vera. He thought either she'd been phoning him every five minutes or she had an instinct for how long these prison visits took. It occurred to him in a moment of whimsy that she could have a sort of telepathic link to him, but that idea was so scary that he forced it out of his head.

'How did it go?' Her voice was cheerful, but he wasn't deceived. She was crap at delegating. It would have been a nightmare for her to be sitting in the office while he was doing the real work.

He sat in the car with the rain battering the roof and she made him take her through the entire interview almost word for word.

'Good,' she said in the end. 'In fact, bloody brilliant. I could have talked to her, but I knew what I was looking for and I'd have asked leading questions. She was always going to be a suggestible witness.'

He knew better than to ask what was so significant. Vera would tell him without the question, if she'd wanted him to know. 'Any news on Connie?'

'Not exactly.'

'What do you mean?' Ashworth demanded. 'Where is she?'

'Oh, I don't know that.' She sounded impatient. 'But I have some ideas about who might be hiding her.' This was Vera at her most infuriating.

'What do you want me to do now?'

'Come back to the Tyne valley,' she said. 'I'm on my way there now.'

They sat in the lounge at the Willows looking out at the river. It had spilled over its banks and the raised driveway into the hotel was like a drawbridge over a moat, the only way in. A pile of sandbags stood in the car park. Ryan Taylor met Ashworth in reception and pointed him to the lounge where Vera was waiting. He said there'd been a flood alert. If it continued raining that night, the whole valley would be under water. There was a big tide forecast and that always made things worse, even this far inland. The hotel was on high enough land to be safe, but the last thing they wanted was guests stranded or health-club members not able to get in, so he planned to build a wall of sandbags by the side of the drive.

After Vera's response on the phone, Ashworth had expected her to be in high spirits. It had seemed from her words that the case was all but over, that they'd have an arrest before the day was out. But seeing her now, crouched over her coffee, a plate of shortbread on the arm of her chair, he thought she seemed tense. Almost unde-cided. Like a gambler unsure which call to make. Or as if she didn't trust her judgement after all. There was a fire in the grate, but it was giving out more smoke than heat, and the room was cold. Her mobile phone was on the table in front of her. She glared at it.

'Bloody social services,' she said. 'I've been on to Craig, the big boss. You'd think he'd be able to help track down where Mattie Jones was born. Apparently it's a nightmare going back that far. Nothing computerized. He said he'd ring as soon as he had something.'

'What's going on then?'

'If I knew that, pet, I'd ride in like a knight in my trusty Land Rover and rescue the fair maiden.'

'Are you talking about Connie?' Ashworth couldn't stand it when Vera went all weird on him. It was her way of keeping her thoughts to herself. As if she didn't trust him enough to share her ideas.

'Well, her for one.' She looked up at him. 'Did you get any more details from Mattie about the place she grew up? Apart from the fact that it was in the country and near water? That wasn't what I sent you in for, but it's significant, isn't it? It's set me thinking . . .' And she lapsed into silence. Joe was reminded of an old woman in a care home, rambling away to herself, losing her thread in the middle of a sentence. It came to him that if Vera did end up that way, he'd be the only person to visit her.

She looked up at him and he saw that she was far from senile and was expecting an answer.

'No,' he said. 'I think there could have been more, but some woman kicked off in the ward and she lost concentration.' He paused, added pointedly, 'It would have helped if I'd known what you were looking for.'

'No,' Vera said, 'that wouldn't have helped at all.'

'So what are we going to do now?' He was starting to lose patience. He'd feel happier if he knew Connie and the child were safe. He had the feeling that it was their lives Vera was gambling.

She didn't answer immediately and again there was that sense of uncharacteristic indecision.

'The place by the water Mattie was talking about,' he said. The idea had come to him suddenly, looking out over the sodden parkland. There was no reason for it, apart from his instinct that the killer was linked to Barnard Bridge. 'Could it be Connie Masters's cottage? We know it's a holiday let now, but someone must have lived there once. A family? Mattie's mother?'

'No point guessing, is there?' she said, dismissing the idea without even considering it. 'Could be anywhere. I need to make some more phone calls.'

It seemed to him that her decision had been made. The dice had been thrown. He waited for her to elaborate, but she sat back in the deep chair, her eyes half closed. 'What do you want me to do?' he said after a while. He wanted to shake her. He wanted her fizzing with energy again, indomitable, taking on the world. He hated to see her so frail.

'Go to Barnard Bridge,' she said, 'and keep an eye on Hannah Lister.'

'You think she might be in danger?'

Vera didn't answer directly. He wasn't even convinced she'd heard the question. 'Jenny Lister and Danny Shaw,' she said. 'Someone's covering his tracks.' She looked up at him and gave one of her old wicked grins. 'Or her tracks. I thought I knew what had been going on here. Now I'm not so sure.'

In Barnard Bridge there was a sense of a community under siege. There were sandbags piled outside all the doorways in the main street. The burn that had been just a trickle outside Connie's cottage was more than a foot deep and the Tyne was brown and fierce, frothing under the bridge, covered with a cream-coloured scum. The place was deserted. Ashworth phoned Connie's mobile again and left a message. 'If it continues raining tonight, the river will flood. You should come and move your belongings while you can.'

But, he thought, few of her belongings remained in the cottage. When he and Vera had checked her wardrobe, most of her clothes, and those of the child, had gone. The furniture was the property of the owner, not of Connie. After all, she had no reason to return. His message would have no effect, even if she picked it up.

In the Lister house he found Hannah, Simon and a vicar, who was there, it seemed, to discuss Jenny's funeral. Her body had been released to the undertaker and arrangements could now be made. The vicar was wearing jeans and had a Barbour jacket over his clerical collar. Hannah invited Ashworth in and offered him coffee, but the detective felt he couldn't stay. Hannah would surely be safe in the company of these men, and religious people always made him slightly uncomfortable. There'd been a stern Sunday-school teacher in the Methodist Chapel where his mother had taken him as a boy. Instead, he went next door and knocked at Hilda's house.

She was there on her own. Maurice had been banished despite the weather.

'Don't worry about the boys,' Hilda said, when Ashworth made a comment. He smiled to think of her husband and his friend as boys. 'There's a shed like a palace on that allotment of theirs. They were in the house all morning, but it's cleared a bit now and they could do with some fresh air.'

She was in the middle of cooking tea, but she invited him in anyway and he sat in the kitchen on a tall stool by the workbench while she rubbed fat into flour to make pastry.

'That cottage by the burn where Connie Masters lives,' he said. 'Who lived there before it became a holiday let?'

He'd been going over this in his head since his meeting with Vera in the hotel, trying to picture it. He wanted to prove to Vera that he had ideas too. Veronica Eliot would have been visiting the cottage when her son Patrick was drowned. Must have been, because the only access to the burn was through the cottage garden. So surely a woman of about Veronica's age would have been staying there then, if they were friends, on visiting terms. A woman perhaps with young children. It could have been the mother of Mattie Jones, the mother who had given her up to care. Mattie would have been older than Veronica's children, but not so much older. If she'd seen Patrick die in the water, had the image stuck with her? It would perhaps explain why Mattie had disciplined her own son in that way, why eventually she'd killed him.

It occurred to him that this link was just what Jenny Lister had been looking for when she'd questioned Mattie for her book. It would make a good story after all, and social workers liked neat and tidy motives, just as some detectives did. Vera would say he was back in *Jackanory* land and fairy tales were just for bairns, but she was always taking leaps into the dark and it seemed to work for her.

He waited now for Hilda to answer. She finished rubbing the fat into the flour, washed her hands under the tap and wiped them on a towel.

'Mallow Cottage,' she said at last. 'It was never a happy house. Folk never seemed to stay there. They'd move in full of plans to do it up, but they all seemed to sell up before the work was done.'

'I'd never have had you down as a superstitious type,' Ashworth said.

'Nothing to do with superstition!' She fired the words back at him. 'Damp and dark and too expensive to renovate—that was it, more like.'

'But there was a tragedy there,' Ashworth said. 'A little boy died.'

'Aye, Patrick Eliot. That would have been twenty years ago, almost to the day. We all turned out for the funeral. The whole village, though we didn't know the family really then. And after that Veronica refused to speak about the boy.' She shrugged. 'People thought it was odd, but everyone has their own way of coping, I suppose.' She paused again. 'There's another funeral for us to go to now. I saw the vicar in next door.'

'Who was living at the cottage at the time of the accident?' Ashworth found he was holding his breath as he
waited for the answer.

She was standing at the sink, dribbling water from the
cold tap into the bowl, mixing it into the pastry with a
knife. She turned to speak to him.

'Nobody,' she said. 'The place was empty. There was a
For Sale board outside; I remember it. It was in all the
newspaper pictures. That's why Veronica could take the
boys into the garden to poke around in the stream. The
White House didn't have much of a garden then. It was
more like a builders' site. The Eliots had only just moved
in.'

When Ashworth went back next door and knocked at the
Listers', that house was empty too. Perhaps the vicar had
taken the couple to the chapel of rest, or to the rectory to
continue the conversation about hymns and eulogies
there. Ashworth phoned Vera to bring her up to date, but
he could tell she was preoccupied. She gave him a list of
instructions without explaining the reason for them.

The rain stopped by mid-afternoon and people meeting each other in the street laughed at the sandbags and
said that the Environment Agency had over-reacted this
time. But as it got dark it started raining again, this time a
soft drizzle that folk still didn't take seriously.

Chapter Thirty-Six

Vera spent all day in the hotel lounge at the Willows. Most of the guests had left, despite Ryan Taylor's reassurance that the sandbags would keep out the flood. The place was silent and gloomy; there was little natural light from outside despite the long windows. She'd shouted at him to switch off the background music after 'Walking Back to Happiness' had come round for the third time on the taped loop; she felt as if the tune were mocking her for her inability to get the case right.

She'd decided on inaction, at least for today. Waiting was always torture to her and she understood it was a risk. If he knew what was in her mind, Joe Ashworth would be horrified. He'd recommend arrests, dramatic chases through the countryside. And of course she could be wrong. The idea had come to her sitting here, listening to the young waiter describe how Jenny Lister had waited here on the morning of her death for someone who never turned up. It wasn't much to build a case on. And even if she were right, Vera thought, there'd be no guarantee of a conviction. A guilty plea would be better for everyone. The decision to wait having been made, it was better that she stay here where she would do no harm. If she went out, she might put in her huge, wellie-clad foot and upset the delicate balance that she sensed now existed. There was always a danger of further violence.

So she sat in the big floral armchair by the window and occasionally summoned her team members to her. More often she spoke on the phone, sometimes persuading and sometimes swearing. Once she threw it across the room, and she had to retrieve it from the silk chaise longue where it had landed. Doreen, the elderly waitress, brought her cups of coffee, cheese sandwiches, hard scones and butter. Every hour or so Vera would pull herself to her feet and stamp around the room to bring the feeling back into her limbs. She'd stand in front of the fire, which at last seemed to throw out some warmth, or waddle to the toilet, then return to her seat and continue to scribble notes that charted the progress of the case.

Once she stopped for ten minutes to stare outside at a rainbow that spanned the valley. But the sun, which had come out briefly, was soon covered again by cloud and the rainbow faded and then disappeared.

Holly was her first visitor. She arrived in the early afternoon, starving. Vera fed her crisps and cake and listened to what she had to say about Hannah and Danny. Holly had been to the high school and talked to a couple of teachers, and through them she'd managed to meet up with some of the kids who'd been friends with Danny and Hannah. They'd met in the bar in Hexham, where one of them was working to save up to go travelling. He'd called up another couple of cronies. 'Not that Danny had many close friends,' Holly said, her mouth still full of cake. 'Apparently he was a bright lad, but cocky. A tad arrogant. The teachers wouldn't say, but you could tell they couldn't stand him. The kids were a bit more forgiving. He was like leader of the gang. The show-off. But they admired him more than they liked him. I had the impression he was considered very cool, but a bit self-centred. Good for a fun night out, but not for a long-term friendship.'

That word again.

'What about the relationship with Hannah?' Vera was still taking notes. She wanted this clear in her head.

'She wasn't his first girlfriend, they were all clear about that. But she was the first girl he really cared for.

And the first time he'd been dumped, apparently. It came as a shock to the system. Not what he'd been expecting at all.'

'Did he blame Simon Eliot?' Vera thought this could be important. She looked at Holly and hoped she was taking the question seriously. 'It does look as if Hannah dumped him for Simon.'

'Danny was probably pissed off at the time, but more recently they seem to have got on OK. People have seen them knocking around together in the university holidays. It's not really a big deal at that age, is it?'

Which was what Hannah had said too.

'So nobody thought Danny had a grudge against the Eliot boy? He could be one to harbour a grudge.'

'Nah,' Holly said. 'I didn't get the impression there was anything like that.'

Vera gave a little sigh, which reminded Holly of her nana playing patience. Sometimes, when she played out all the cards, she made a noise that was exactly the same as the one Vera made now.

'Any of them heard of Michael Morgan?' Vera asked after a brief pause. 'Do we know if Danny had contact with him before he started working in the hotel?'

'They didn't recognize the name.' Holly set her plate on the floor beside her. 'But that doesn't mean anything. They said that Danny liked to be mysterious about what he got up to. Part of his image. Sometimes he disappeared off the radar for days and nobody knew what he'd been up to.' She looked at Vera. 'Sorry, it's not much, is it? I can carry on asking around if you think it's important.'

'Why don't you get home early?' Vera said. 'It'll be a bloody nightmare on the roads with all this standing water, and you'll have a long day tomorrow.'

She had the satisfaction of seeing Holly lost for words. For once.

Vera hadn't heard from Charlie all morning and she summoned him in to the Willows after Holly had gone. She saw him walk from his car and up the steps, with that stooped posture he always had, as if he were looking out for dog shit on the pavement before he put down his feet. By now the sunshine and the rainbow had gone and it was almost dark, though it was still only the middle of the afternoon. Doreen had padded round the lounge switching on small table lamps. Charlie stood at the entrance to the room, peering into the gloom, and Vera called him over. She'd always had a bit of a soft spot for him. Perhaps it was something to do with the fact that his private life was even more of a failure than hers. He made her feel good.

'Tea?' she said. 'Or could you use something a bit stronger?'

'What are you having?' Charlie had never really mastered the art of being gracious and the words came out as an aggressive grunt.

'Oh, it's a bit early for me,' she said virtuously, 'and I'm drowning with tea, but I'll get you something.'

'Tea then.' He looked at her suspiciously.

'Have you found Connie, that social worker, yet?'

'I found her car. Or at least I saw it a couple of times on CCTV. There's a camera in Effingham, the village east of Barnard Bridge. A little lass was killed on the zebra crossing and the parish council paid to have one installed.' Doreen had brought him a plate of biscuits with his tea and he dipped one in the cup before eating it whole.

'And where was the other camera?' Sometimes, Vera thought, patience was the only way to deal with Charlie.

'There was only one, but the car appeared on it twice.' The second biscuit crumbled and fell into the tea before he had a chance to eat it. He swore under his breath and scooped it out with his spoon.

'Why don't you explain to me, Charlie? Words of one syllable. I'm a bit brain-dead after spending most of the day in this place.'

'Yesterday, nine o'clock in the morning, the car goes east.'

'So towards Newcastle.'

'Aye, but if she were going into Newcastle, wouldn't she just cut onto the A69 and go down the dual carriageway?'

'I don't know, Charlie, maybe she wanted to go on the scenic route!' But would she? Vera wondered. If Connie were scared and had somewhere in mind to run to, wouldn't she just choose the quickest road?

Charlie ignored that and continued. 'Then an hour and twenty minutes later she drove back west, past the same camera.'

'So where was she going?' Vera was talking to herself now. 'Certainly not into Newcastle. There'd hardly be time to get there and back, never mind do whatever she wanted while she was there. Unless she just wanted to drop off her daughter for safekeeping. But that would be with the father, and he says he's not heard from her, and why should he lie? To Hexham then? To pick up a load of food from the supermarket, if she's planning to go into hiding. I had an idea, but I must have got everything wrong.'

'If she carried on driving she'd end up in Carlisle,' Charlie said. 'From there, Scotland or anywhere in northwest England.'

'I don't need a geography lesson, man!'

And I don't need reminding that this is needle-and-haystack territory.

They sat for a moment in silence. Doreen threw a log onto the fire and it must have been damp because it hissed and oozed sap.

'Holly said an early finish might be in order.' Charlie gave her a look, hopeful, almost pleading. It reminded her of one of those big, soft, slack-jawed dogs, the sort she'd always hated and felt like kicking under the table when the owner wasn't looking. The sort that drooled.

'Not for you, bonny lad.' She flashed him a smile. 'You've still got that car to find. I know you're not one for leaving a job half done.'

Now it was quite dark outside and though she thought the rain had started again because the lights that lined the drive were misty, filtered by the moisture, she couldn't hear it. If there were still guests in the hotel they must be hidden in their rooms. No cars approached the house, though she watched Charlie's leave. She thought she should be kinder to him. There was no real sport in having a go at him. But at this sort of job he was the best on the team, and she'd told him that too, before he'd shrugged on his stained raincoat and walked away from her.

She shouted to Doreen to bring her a bowl of chips, maybe a burger if they could run to it. When the food arrived she had her eyes shut and was lost in thought— not relaxed at all, but the ideas bouncing around in her brain, random images colliding and connecting and almost making sense. She ate too quickly because she didn't want to lose the thread of her deliberations and ended up with indigestion that stayed with her all night.

Later she made a call to Durham prison. 'Yes, I know what time it is. But this is urgent. I need to get a message to Mattie Jones. Even better, let me speak to her.'

But the governor was unsympathetic. He'd been called in on his night off. There'd been a suicide and then trouble on one of the wings. They'd done an early lock-up in the hope of calming things down. He implied that he wouldn't put the safety of his officers and inmates at risk on the whim of a policewoman. Vera pressed him, but without success. There was surely nothing, he said, patronizing and unmoving, that couldn't wait until the morning.

As soon as that call was ended, Ashworth rang. Hannah Lister was back home, he said. He didn't know where she'd spent the afternoon, but he'd seen her arrive. Simon was there too now. Did Vera want him to chat to her?

'No,' Vera said. 'Best leave things be, for tonight.'

For the last time she stood up and halted in front of the fire. There was a temptation to stay where she was, to curl up in the big armchair and sleep the night there. But she went out into the soft, dark evening, intending to drive home.

Halfway there the idea came to her, sudden, like a light bulb flashing above her head in the cartoons she read when she was a child. In comics bought for her by Hector because he loved them too. She did a U-turn the next place she came to and went south and east towards the coast.

Tynemouth was hidden by the misty drizzle and she came on it suddenly, the lamps on the wide main street hardly throwing enough light to park the car. Outside there was a smell of salt and seaweed. The foghorn was sounding, as it had that first time she'd come to interview Morgan.

There were no lights on in his flat. She looked at her watch. Nine o'clock. Too early, surely, for the couple to be in bed. All the same she rang the bell and banged on the door. No answer. Someone appeared in the mist at the top of the street. Tall as Morgan and wearing a long coat, a snug hat that gave the same outline as a bald head would. But it wasn't him, she saw as he approached. This man was younger, a student.

Still she refused to give up and she walked through the village, checking all the bars and restaurants, looking for Morgan or his woman. Looking quite mad, she realized, as she grew more desperate. All she wanted was confirmation, for Morgan to dig into his memory, to relive his conversations with Mattie Jones and Danny Shaw. A few words to make sense of the whole drama. There was no sign of them and at last, after trying the flat for one last time, she went back to her car. When she arrived home, she saw it was midnight.

Chapter Thirty-Seven

The water rose silently in the night. There was no wind, no rain like pebbles against the window, but, instead, a persistently steady downpour. When Vera woke it was to quite a different landscape, a countryside dominated by water. Looking down from her house, she saw that the banks of the lough had breached in places and become indistinct, almost lacy in outline, ditches had become rivers, then seeped into low meadows and formed a string of pools. But the sky was lighter now and the rain had stopped.

It was just dawn and she was woken by her phone. Charlie. *My God, he's been up all night.* 'I've found the car.' His voice was hoarse, as if he'd been speaking all night too, but triumphant.

'Where?'

'Not far from where the CCTV picked it up in Effingham. There's a small business park on the Barnard Bridge side of the village. It's in the car park there.'

'Bloody hell, man, how did you find it?'

'I looked.'

And she imagined him driving round in the dark and the rain, checking every side street and lay-by in the Tyne valley.

'Are you still there now?'

'Yeah, I found it about an hour ago, but I reckoned you needed your beauty sleep.'

'You shouldn't have bothered about that!'

'Aye, well, I was so knackered I dropped off myself, before I got round to calling you.'

She laughed. 'You're too honest for your own good, Charlie. You'll never make management. Can you give me the names of the businesses?'

There was a pause and she heard him shift in his seat. She pictured him looking at a noticeboard at the car-park entrance. She knew exactly the sort of place this would be: half a dozen units in tidy brick buildings, housing insurance companies, IT firms, some local businesses, some household names. After all, the rents would be lower here than in the city.

He reeled them off for her: 'Swift Computing, Northumbrian Organic Foods, Fenham and Bright Communications, General—'

'Stop there, Charlie. Christopher Eliot works for Fenham and Bright. Treat the car as a crime scene and don't let anyone close to it, but don't call in the CSIs until I've spoken to the man. Watch him come in to work, and only stop him if he tries to leave.' Then she remembered he'd been up all night. 'I'll get Holly to relieve you.'

'Nah,' he said. 'Don't bother. I can hang on for as long as it'll take you to get here.'

'But I'm not coming straight to the Tyne valley. I've got to see Morgan first. I need to get a few facts straight before I have a go at the Eliots.' She was already dressing, rooting in the drawers for clean underwear, deciding that the skirt she'd had on the day before would be fine. Just as well Crimplene didn't crease. No time for a shower. All the way south she was on the phone, using the hands-free kit she'd transferred into Hector's Land Rover, choosing that over her own car because she thought it would make it better through the flood.

At first she thought Michael Morgan had done a runner. The curtains to the flat were still closed and though it was still too early for his clinic to open, she'd have expected some sign of life. She'd imagined him and Freya break-fasting on organic muesli and yoghurt after an hour's yoga. Whale calls as background music.

She banged on the door, aware of neighbours looking from windows across the street. They'd remember her from the night before. Any minute now they'd be calling the police. Neighbourhood Watch would be big in Tynemouth. It was that sort of place. Just as she was thinking she'd cut her losses and head straight off to meet up with Charlie, she heard footsteps on the stairs and the door was opened.

She saw immediately that Morgan had been drinking. Maybe all night, or maybe he'd had a couple of hours' sleep and woken up with a hangover that hadn't quite kicked in yet because he was still pissed. She was an expert. He was wearing loose jogging pants and a hooded sweater and he stank of alcohol and sweat.

'My God, man, I thought you were into clean living.' She pushed the door further open and he stumbled back a little before following her upstairs. She drew the cur-tains and opened windows at both ends of the room. There was an empty vodka bottle on the floor, a tumbler beside it. Without speaking, she went into the kitchen and made two mugs of instant coffee.

'Did Freya buy this?' She held up the jar of Fairtrade instant and shook it at him. 'You're into the real stuff, aren't you? You and Danny Shaw were both snobby about your coffee.'

'Freya's gone,' he said.

'What happened?' Inside she gave a little cheer, but she kept her voice sympathetic. You could have taken her for a social worker.

'She's fallen for someone else. One of the other drama students. Brilliant actor, apparently. Destined for star-dom.' With each phrase he grew more bitter. Vera wondered how much of his reaction was grief that Freya had left him and how much was shock that she'd dared choose someone else over him. Like Danny, when Hannah had dumped him. Pride was something else the two men had in common.

'Well, she's very young,' Vera said. 'Too young to settle down maybe.'

'But I wanted to settle down!' It came out almost like a scream. 'I wanted a home and a family. I wanted all those things everyone else has.'

'It's not all about what *you* want though, is it, pet?' She thought he was like one of those toddlers she saw occasionally in the supermarket, lying on the floor and kicking and shouting because his mam wouldn't buy him an ice cream. 'Besides, I've got more important things to talk about than your love life. Drink that coffee and get yourself sorted. I need some questions answered and I haven't got all day.' She lowered herself on the futon in the living room and waited for him to follow her.

Later, when the interview was over and she'd heaved herself to her feet ready to go, he said: 'I really cared for Freya, you know. It wasn't just about me.'

And Mattie Jones really cared for you. But she didn't spend a night getting pissed on cheap vodka; she killed her child. Vera looked at him and said nothing. Perhaps after all she couldn't blame him for that.

Charlie was still in the business park when Vera arrived there. She slid into his car on the passenger seat. Holly and Joe were already in the back. The complex was smart and landscaped, the visitor parking hidden from the office blocks by a row of trees and shrubs.

'That's Connie's car.' Charlie pointed to a far corner, which was still in shadow. 'I nearly missed it.' He didn't smell quite as bad as Morgan, but he was on the way. It looked as if he hadn't shaved for days and there was a mound of cigarette ends in the ashtray.

'Has Eliot gone in?'

'Well, I've never met him, but the car you described arrived at eight-thirty, parked in a reserved space near the door and a tall gent with grey hair went inside.'

'That'll be him then.' Vera looked at her watch. It was not long after nine. 'Joe, you come with me. Holly, you stay here and get the CSIs all over that car like a rash. Charlie, you go home and shower.'

He started to argue. 'You're the hero here,' she said, 'and we won't forget it. Shower, shave, an hour's kip and you can come back. You won't miss anything exciting. We'll keep you posted.'

'What do Fenham and Bright do then?' Ashworth asked. She was walking fast towards the office building and Joe was trotting to keep up with her, so his question came out in short bursts.

'Set up phone and Internet services, mostly in developing countries. That's why Christopher Eliot travels so much.' She'd googled the company after meeting Eliot in the White House.

'You think he's involved in Connie's disappearance?'

'I won't know,' Vera said, 'until I ask him.'

They walked through a swing door into the office reception. Two glossy women were sitting behind the desk and talking about the floods, loving the vicarious drama of it. 'Did you see the local news on the television? That car being washed away? Some places the electric's down.' There were plants in big tubs on either side of the desk and they were glossy too.

'Can I help you?' The accent was Ashington with a posh veneer.

'I hope you can, pet. I need to speak to Christopher Eliot.'

The response was immediate and automatic. 'Mr Eliot's tied up all day, I'm afraid. Perhaps his secretary can help.'

Vera put her warrant card on the desk. 'Like I said, I need to speak to Mr Eliot. Just point us in the direction of his office. No need to let him know we're on our way.' Swinging through the door into the corridor, she stopped and turned back, enjoyed seeing the look of outrage on the woman's face. 'Some of our colleagues will be working in the car park very soon. Teas and coffees all round, please. Much appreciated.' Hearing Joe chuckle at her side, Vera felt on top of the world.

Eliot's office was on the first floor with a view of woodland and the hills in the distance. She thought he seemed more at home here than he did in the White House. He could have been a soldier, she thought. An officer, of course. One of those ordered men who can pack up all their worldly goods into a backpack and function equally well in Afghanistan or South Georgia. His passport would have stamps from all over the world. But this was his HQ for the moment. There was a map on the wall, red pins stuck throughout the continent of Africa. On the desk a photograph of two small boys.

'Is this Patrick?' Vera pointed to the smaller. He was slight and fair, took after his father more than his mother.

Eliot still sat at his desk. He'd risen briefly when Vera had come in. 'Inspector Stanhope?' A greeting, as well as a chilly enquiry about the intrusion. Now he looked at the photograph. It was impossible to tell from his face what he was thinking. 'Yes, that's Patrick. It was taken on his second birthday. He died a week later.'

'No photographs of him at home.' Not a question.

He frowned. 'We all grieve in our own way, Inspector.'

'You never considered having another child?'

Vera thought he was going to tell her to mind her own business, which is what she'd have done in the circumstances, but perhaps he was grateful for the opportunity to discuss it, even with a stranger like her.

'I'd have liked another baby, but Veronica wouldn't hear of it. She said she couldn't take the risk. What if something were to happen, to go wrong? She couldn't bear another lost child. It would kill her.'

'Did that seem like an extreme reaction to you?' Vera kept her voice low and gentle.

He shrugged. 'As I said, Inspector, we all grieve in our own way.'

'Of course.' *And yours is to keep moving: hours spent in airports, drives in trucks on dusty roads, new faces, new places. No attachment.* 'Where did you meet Veronica?'

This time he did question her reason for asking.

'Humour me,' she said.

And he did, perhaps as used to taking orders as to giving them.

'It was at the Willows Hotel. An engagement party. Through friends of friends. I think I'd known her as a child. You know how it is when you grow up in the same region. Her parents were rather grander than mine, but they had no money. There was a very sad story about a fire and the house being uninsured. But the party at the Willows was the first time we really spoke. She'd been away, I think. Some au-pair job up in the Borders for friends of her parents. She was lovely. Still is, of course, but then she was stunningly beautiful.'

Loyalty. Another of a soldier's virtues.

He took a small photograph from his wallet. There was Veronica in her early twenties. Very slender and pale. Long dark hair, pushed back from her face. Serious. No hint of laughter.

'Was Simon Veronica's first child?' Vera asked.

'Of course!' He gave a little laugh. 'It was a very uncomplicated pregnancy. There'd been no problems, no history of miscarriage. Nothing like that. He was a bit early and I missed the actual birth, arrived in from the Middle East when all the messy bits were over. But it was quite straightforward. That was why I thought we could risk another baby after Patrick had died.' He looked up. 'What is all this about, Inspector?'

'Background.' She kept her voice light. 'More likely just plain nosiness. Not what I'm here for. I'm here because there's a car outside that belongs to a missing woman.'

'Oh?'

'Connie Masters. She lives in Mallow Cottage, just over the road from you.'

'I've heard my wife speak of her, but I've never met the woman.'

'So you don't know what her Nissan Micra's doing in your car park?'

'I'm sorry, Inspector, I haven't a clue.' He looked up at her with clear grey eyes and for once in her life she couldn't say if he was telling the truth. She imagined him in business negotiations. Or playing poker. He'd be good. He could be bluffing, but his face would give nothing away.

She stood up and saw that Ashworth was surprised that she was prepared to leave things at that. At the door she stopped and turned back to face Eliot. 'Was Patrick buried?' she asked. 'Is there a grave?'

If the question shocked him, the man gave no sign of it.

'No. He was cremated. Veronica's decision.'

'And the ashes were scattered at Greenhough, her old family home.' A statement this time, not a question.

'Yes.'

'And that's why the place is so important to her?' Vera said.

'It's important to us all.'

This time Vera left the room and shut the door carefully behind her.

Chapter Thirty-Eight

On the short drive from the business park to Barnard Bridge, Vera didn't open her mouth except to take one phone call. Joe Ashworth thought it was the chap in social services because Vera called him Craig, but he couldn't tell what it was about. It was all Craig talking and Vera listening, and it lasted the whole journey. They were still using Vera's Land Rover, which was completely against all regulations because it was about a hundred years old and likely to clap out at any time, but she'd said if there was floodwater on the road, at least they'd get through. The windows didn't close properly and the engine was so noisy it felt as if they were riding in a tank. There was a stink of diesel fumes.

They rolled onto the gravel drive at the White House and at last she did speak. 'You keep your mouth shut here, OK? And you take notes. Detailed notes. We're going to need this in court.'

Veronica opened the door to them on the first knock. She looked pale and tense, and Ashworth was reminded of the photo Christopher Eliot had shown them in his office. The hardness had gone and she was a vulnerable young woman again. She was dressed in a long waxed coat and wellingtons.

'I'm sorry, Inspector, I was just on my way out.'

'We need to talk.' Vera walked straight in past her and into the kitchen as if it were her place, not Veronica's. Ashworth followed. When Veronica hesitated, Vera barked at her, 'Now! I'm in a hurry here.'

They sat at the kitchen table, Vera and the woman facing each other, Ashworth at the far end, his notebook discreetly on his knee. Veronica slipped her coat off her shoulders, but was still wearing the boots.

'Where have you hidden Connie Masters?'

'I don't know what you're talking about.'

'Don't piss me about, lady. Her car was found in your husband's office car park. I need to know where they are. That lass of hers'll be scared stiff by now.'

Veronica said nothing. She stared, haughty and impassive, into the garden.

'I know it was you who left the Nissan, and if I need to I'll prove it. A call to every minicab firm in the Tyne valley and we'll find someone who picked you up there and brought you back to Barnard Bridge. Because you couldn't ask your husband for a lift, could you? You couldn't have him asking questions.'

Still the woman remained silent. But Ashworth saw that the white hand resting on the table was trembling. Soon she would crack, he thought.

Vera leaned forward and when she spoke her voice was quite different. So low that Ashworth at the other end of the table could hardly make out the words. 'Tell me about your baby, Veronica. Your first baby. Tell me about Matilda.'

Veronica remained completely still, but her eyes were full of tears. She blinked and they ran down her cheeks. Ashworth realized she was wearing no make-up; perhaps that was why she looked so different.

'How old were you when you had her, Veronica? It's in the records. The social-work records. I'll be able to check.'

Oh, she's already checked, Ashworth thought. *That's what the phone call was all about.*

'Fifteen,' Veronica said. 'I was fifteen.'

'Teenage pregnancy was a bit different then, wasn't it? A stigma. Especially to a family like yours. Tell me about it.'

'The baby's father was older than me,' she said. 'A mechanic. He drove a big motorbike and wore leathers, and I thought he was the most glamorous man in the world. I'd told him I was seventeen and he was horrified when he found out how young I was.' She gave a brittle little laugh that made Ashworth want to weep. 'He offered to marry me as soon as I was old enough. But of course that would never do for my family. Think of the disgrace.'

'Bad enough to lose all their money,' Vera muttered. 'They couldn't lose their good name too.'

'Anyway,' she said, 'it would never have lasted. They were right about that.' They sat for a moment in silence and Ashworth could hear the swollen river churning over the boulders and under the bridge.

Veronica went on, her voice quite calm now. 'By the time I realized what was going on and found the nerve to tell my parents, it was too late for an abortion. I had to have the baby. Everyone was perfectly kind about it. My parents blamed the man and would have got the police to prosecute, only then it would have become general knowledge and they couldn't face that. They treated me as if I were an invalid, so ill that I couldn't make decisions for myself.'

'So you were sent away to friends up in the Borders.'

She looked up. 'You know about that?'

'Christopher told us you worked there as an au pair for a while.'

She looked horrified. 'Christopher doesn't know anything about this!'

'Maybe you should have told him,' Vera said. 'Maybe he wouldn't care.'

Veronica shook her head.

'Anyway,' Vera said. 'The plan was that the baby would be adopted. Is that right?'

'That was what everyone told me would be for the best.'

'But it didn't feel that way to you.'

'I wouldn't let them take her away straight after she was born.' Veronica gave a flash of a smile. 'I was bloody-minded even then. I kept her and I fed her. I didn't make a bad job of looking after her.'

'But eventually your parents talked you round?'

'They said it would be better for the baby. There were lots of couples who would love to have a child of their own. Two parents to care for her properly. I'd have my life back.'

'But she never was adopted, was she? She was taken into care, but never officially adopted. Why was that?'

'There's a process,' Veronica said. 'It's done through the court. Somebody called a guardian *ad litem* is appointed to look after the interests of the child. A formality. Usually.'

'But not in your case?'

'The guardian came to my parents' house. Matilda was nearly eighteen months by then. Because I wouldn't give the baby up immediately, things were more complicated and the process had taken longer. It was all very messy. Matilda was in care with a foster family, who'd asked if they could adopt her. She wasn't what I'd expected—the guardian, I mean. I'd thought she'd be old and stern. "Guardian" made me think of a workhouse. But she was young. Nearer to my age than my parents'. She wore the sort of clothes I wore. She was the first person I could really talk to about the baby.'

Ashworth caught Vera looking surreptitiously at the kitchen clock. She was thinking of Connie Masters and *her* child, of time moving on. But hearing his boss speak to Veronica, you'd have thought she had all the time in the world.

'The guardian woman encouraged you to think you could look after the baby yourself?'

'Not even that. She asked if I was ready to sign the form. The form consenting to the adoption. When I hesitated, she talked through the options. If Matilda were fostered rather than adopted, she said there was a chance I could stay in touch with her, maintain contact. And maybe I could have her back one day.'

'So you refused to sign the form. Bet your parents were delighted. Not!'

'They were horrified and said it was the most selfish thing I'd ever done in my life.' Veronica looked straight at Vera. 'And they were right, of course. The family who were looking after Matilda couldn't face the uncertainty of knowing whether or not they'd be able to adopt her. She was moved. When she was three and a half I signed the consent form, but by then it was too late. Adoption never happened for her. There was no stability throughout her childhood. That was all my fault.'

'More likely the fault of that soft bloody social worker who talked you out of signing the consent form!'

Ashworth thought his boss was going to give them her usual rant about social workers, but she managed to restrain herself.

'Matilda came on visits,' Vera said. 'During that time when you were making up your mind. She remembers.'

'Does she?' Veronica said, and Ashworth couldn't tell if she was terrified or delighted by the information. 'She was so young that I didn't think she would. I remember every detail, of course. What she was wearing, what she said. She was so small. Very pretty. And good. An obedient little girl.'

Ashworth thought: *So obedient that she went on to do whatever men told her to.*

'She told Jenny Lister about the visits to you,' Vera went on. 'But Jenny would have had access to the records anyway. She must have known you were Mattie's natural mother.'

'I hated thinking about that,' Veronica said. 'I kept expecting Jenny to say something. I thought she might tell Simon. He never knew he had a sister.'

'Why would she have done that? Confidentiality was important to her.' Vera paused for a moment, looking at the woman, seemed to give the question more significance than it deserved. 'Did she tell you she planned to write a book?'

There was a silence. 'Simon mentioned it one day,' Veronica said at last. 'Hannah had told him of her mother's dream to tell her clients' stories. As if that were a noble thing to do.'

'She would have changed names, of course, if a book did get written, but people close to you might have guessed.' Vera looked directly at the woman opposite. 'Is that why you were so against the relationship between Hannah and Simon? You thought Jenny might share your secret if she got too close to him.'

'Elias Jones was my grandson,' Veronica said. 'Those women let him die.'

'You let Patrick die,' Vera said, her voice quiet and matter-of-fact.

There was a shocked silence; again the sound of the river running high intruded into the house. Ashworth imagined a young child being swept away by it, rolled by the current until his face was under the water, being carried all the way to the sea.

'That was an accident!' Veronica cried at last. 'Not the same at all.'

'One child given away,' Vera said, as if Veronica hadn't spoken, 'and one child lost. And the child that was left fell for your enemy's daughter. Is that how you saw it?'

'Simon could have done better for himself,' Veronica said. But the reply was automatic and meant nothing.

'Where did you take Connie Masters?' Vera demanded.

Veronica ignored the question. It was as if each woman was hardly aware of the other's words: each was pursuing her own line of thought, a monologue occasionally interrupted. It seemed to Ashworth that it was like watching one of those odd modern plays his wife took him to see at the Live Theatre sometimes. Two characters rambling on without making any connection.

'Did Matilda really remember those visits?' Veronica's question came suddenly from nowhere.

This time Vera did answer. 'Aye, she talked about them. To Jenny and to Michael Morgan. I went to see him this morning to check I had it right. They meant a lot to her.'

'How much can she remember?'

'The social worker bringing her in the car. She talked about a house with its legs in the water. That must be the boathouse by the lake? The place in the picture in your hall? The one at Greenhough.'

'I always met her there,' Veronica said. 'My parents wouldn't have her in our house. It was still a shameful secret.' She looked up and asked the most important question. 'Did Matilda remember me?'

But Vera had already leaped to her feet, almost tripping in her haste. 'And that's where you took Connie and the child. God, I have been such a fool! But why? Couldn't you stand seeing them happy together?' Then she fell silent and was still, her body twisted towards the woman, like a massive granite sculpture, and when she did speak it was quietly and to herself. 'No, of course that wasn't it at all.'

Ashworth was standing too. He wasn't sure what Vera expected from him. To follow her? To arrest Veronica Eliot? After her final words the inspector had moved surprisingly quickly. She was already in the hall close to the front door, the keys to the Land Rover in her hand.

'I would never hurt them,' Veronica called after her. 'I would never hurt a child.' But her voice was thin and unconvincing.

Ashworth left her sitting where she was.

Chapter Thirty-Nine

Connie lay awake all night, thinking she'd been a fool. How had she allowed herself to be trapped like this? At first she'd thought she'd been so clever. She'd panicked, of course, when she first got the phone call. It had come early in the morning, threatening, insinuating, demanding. The voice disguised, she'd been sure of that. She'd had threatening phone calls following the publicity of Elias's death. They'd been malicious and mindless, but not like this. Not terrifying. There'd been letters then too. In the end she'd burned them without reading them. The police had said to give the letters to them: it might be possible to prosecute the writers. But Connie hadn't been able to bear the thought of a stranger seeing them. They might believe the dreadful accusations. *This* phone call had been more horrible than the letters, and Connie had taken it seriously. She'd known she had to leave Mallow Cottage. She had to take Alice and get away. She couldn't be seen to be talking to the police.

Then Veronica had arrived. Connie hadn't been able to tell her the truth, of course. That would have been unthinkable. She could hardly tell this respectable woman that she was running away from the police! She'd said the press were on her back and she needed to disappear for a while. They'd tracked her down, connected her to Jenny Lister's murder. And Veronica—who had been so hostile, who had poisoned the village women with her stories— had suddenly become helpful. She'd understood the need for utter secrecy. Of course the tabloid press were ruthless and devious. Veronica had read how they searched dustbins and put taps on mobile phones. Veronica said she had a holiday home, not far away. Connie and Alice could stay there for a little while until the police had found the real murderer. It was basic and it had been empty over the winter, but she thought it would do. There was a Calor gas stove and they could stock up on supplies. She'd camped out there when she was a child and had always loved it.

They'd taken Connie's car to the supermarket to buy food. They couldn't use Veronica's because it had no child seat for Alice. Then they'd driven down a grassy track and had arrived at the boathouse. Alice had been enchanted. Any child would be.

'You'll have to be very careful close to the water, dear,' Veronica had said to the little girl, kneeling down so that her face was very close to Alice's. 'It's very deep here, even so near to the shore.'

Then they'd gone inside and thrown open the windows to let in the air, because at that point it still hadn't started raining. Veronica had found linen in a painted white cupboard and they'd hung the sheets over the deck rail to air.

Inside there was one big room, with two sets of bunks built into the wall. At the end without windows there was a wood-panelled cubicle with a sink and toilet and a candle on a saucer standing on a shelf. Veronica had shown them how the stove worked and they'd cooked sausages for lunch. It had been Veronica's idea to phone Joe Ashworth, when Connie had shown her how often he'd called.

'You don't want them thinking you've got something to hide! Really, I would phone him, dear, or they'll be looking for you all over the county.'

Then she'd driven away in Connie's car, saying she'd leave it where no reporter would find it. She'd come back in two days' time with more food. Though by then, of course, the murderer might have been arrested and it would be safe for Connie to move back home.

That first afternoon, after they'd watched Veronica drive away, they'd gone for a walk in the wood and Alice had loved it, balancing on the fallen logs and picking flowers that later they'd put on the windowsill in a chipped enamel mug. They'd come across a cairn made of small white pebbles that looked like a shrine, a small bunch of primroses laid carefully on top. In the evening Alice had fallen asleep immediately in the bottom bunk and Connie had read by the light of a tilley lamp, listening to the rain and imagining herself in her father's shed at home.

The next day it had been raining and Alice had been fractious and bad-tempered. There was no television to distract her. Connie would have phoned Veronica, but the battery on her phone was flat. She'd brought the charger with her, but of course there was no electricity in the boat-house. There was a box of games on the table and they played Snakes and Ladders and Snap. The rain battered on the roof and Alice put her hands over her ears.

'I want to go home! I hate it here!'

'Tomorrow,' Connie had said. 'Tomorrow Auntie Veronica will come and we can go home. Then perhaps you could visit Daddy for a couple of days.'

There was no fridge in the hut and the fresh food had all been eaten. She cooked pasta and mixed it with a tin of tuna. Afterwards she let Alice have a whole bar of chocolate for pudding. As soon as the girl was asleep, Connie climbed into the bunk and lay flat on her back, awake for most of the night. She thought this must be what it would feel like to be in prison. Though she supposed there would be odd and frightening noises in prison. Here there was complete silence. Eventually she slept.

She woke the next morning at dawn, gritty-eyed and still tired. The curtains at the windows were very thin and it seemed, even lying in her bunk, that there was something strange about the light. It was the same light as waking up to snow, brighter than it should have been. She got up quietly, pulling the blanket from her bed around her shoulders, and looked outside. The water level of the lake had risen in the night and the house was surrounded. Little waves lapped against the decking. Everything was still, and the trees on the opposite bank were perfectly replicated in the water.

She saw at once that they were in no immediate danger of drowning, but still she felt panic rise in her stomach and almost turn into a scream. She could see how beautiful everything was—the reflected light that had made her think of snow, the composition of trees and hills in the water—but that didn't stop her being frightened. The notion of imprisonment had become a reality. She understood how people caught in a burning building could become so desperate that they would jump to almost certain death. It wasn't a fear of the flames, she thought, but of being trapped. She could hardly swim, but the temptation to let herself out of the door to slide into the water was almost irresistible.

She heard a noise behind her and then she did give a little whimper of fear. Perhaps it was a rat. She'd heard that rats were pushed out of their natural homes during floods. Could rats swim? But of course it was Alice, who'd climbed out of her bunk and was standing shivering beside her. And then Connie had to turn their plight into an adventure.

'Isn't this fun! It's just like being on a boat. Where shall we imagine we'll sail away to this morning?'

Even to her own ears her voice sounded desperate. Alice climbed into her arms and began to cry.

Connie heard the car driving down the track after they'd had breakfast. They were so far from anywhere, hidden by the trees, that the sound carried and seemed very loud. Once she might have worried that it could be the police. That fat female inspector, with her huge hands and her filthy feet and her questions. Now she'd have been glad even to see Vera Stanhope. But perhaps it would be Veronica. This was her territory after all. The boathouse must have flooded before. She'd know the best thing to do. Connie leaned out of the window and caught a glimpse of the car through the branches. Not *her* car. It was the wrong colour for that, and her little Nissan wouldn't make it through all the water. But it might be Veronica all the same.

It was still early in the year and the sun, which had come out now, was very low in the sky. The emerging sun made the figure on the shore nothing more than a silhouette, appearing suddenly from the high wall surrounding the old garden. Perhaps the car had got stuck, or perhaps they'd decided to walk the last part. Connie had to squint even to see the figure as a person. It was a shadow with waterproofs and boots. She could tell no more than that.

A small dinghy that had once rested on the bank now floated on the pool, tethered by a rope. The man tugged on the rope and pulled the boat towards him. Because it *was* a man, Connie thought. The action seemed too strong and purposeful for her visitor to be a woman.

She called to Alice. 'Look, sweetheart, we're going to get rescued.' And the two of them waved like mad things. The man on the shore only raised his hand in greeting.

Now he'd pulled the dinghy onto the bank and had taken out a couple of oars that must have been stowed under the seat. He pushed it back into the pool and waded in as far as his calves, then he climbed aboard.

He rowed towards them, circling towards the boathouse. The light was no longer behind him, but as he approached he had his back to them and still Connie couldn't make out who it was. Even when he'd reached them, and tied the rope around one of the planks that made up the rail of the deck, she didn't recognize him. Then her attention was elsewhere, stuffing all their belongings into a bag, making sure that Alice was with her and not too close to the water.

'Just wait a minute!' she shouted and some of the panic returned. Though that was ridiculous because their saviour wouldn't just turn round and row back to dry land without them.

She heard him climb onto the boathouse deck. There was the creak of the planks, the splash of displaced water as his weight left the dinghy, then footsteps. He stood in the doorway and she saw him properly for the first time and recognized him. She'd seen that face before.

Chapter Forty

Vera told herself that there was no hurry. The social worker and her daughter would be in the boathouse. It would have been an adventure for them, like camping out. The girl would probably have enjoyed every minute. Vera hadn't minded a bit of an adventure herself when Hector had first taken her on his expeditions. It was only as she got older and realized the implications of the night-time raids into the hills that she'd disliked and then come to hate them. Perhaps that was why she drove so fast, because she didn't want the girl to have the same sort of memories of childhood that she'd been left with: the fear in the pit of the stomach and the longing to be home in a familiar place. Because there'd always been people chasing Hector: the police, the National Park wardens, the RSPB. Absorbed in his passion, he'd enjoyed the game of cat-and-mouse. It hadn't bothered him that Vera had been terrified.

Vera felt a sort of sick excitement now as she coaxed the ancient Land Rover to greater speed. Just before the turn-off through the stone pillars with their cormorant carvings there was water across the road. A sign saying: *Way Closed. Flood.* An elderly man was trying to do a three-point turn in the narrow track to get back to the village. Or a forty-point turn. Vera pushed the Land Rover into four-wheel drive, drove it so that two wheels were on the steep verge and the vehicle was tilted at an angle of forty-five degrees, then ground past the pensioner's Volvo. The water was deep enough to seep in through the doors.

She wasn't sure the old man noticed they were there until the spray caused by their movement splashed onto his windscreen. Beside her Joe Ashworth swore.

The grass track past the formal gardens of the old house was much boggier than it had been when she walked down it a few days before. Even in four-wheel drive, she felt the vehicle slide. She kept the pace slow. It was most important now not to get stuck. She wanted to get the mother and daughter back to safety, and then she had an arrest to make. Before anybody else got hurt.

She knew Ashworth had questions, but she couldn't concentrate on getting them to the boathouse in one piece and chat to him at the same time.

'What's that?' Ashworth's question annoyed her because she was just navigating a tricky patch, but she looked all the same. A small car stuck, water up to the bumper, the driver's door wide open. Ashworth had the righteous indignation of the careful driver; he always seemed old before his time: 'They must have been mad trying to get down here without four-wheel drive.'

Then Vera knew that the little girl was in danger, not of having bad dreams and tarnished childhood memories, but of not growing old enough to remember anything.

'Out!' she said. 'Quick! We haven't the time for this.' She was wearing wellingtons, but Ashworth was still in his work shoes, newly polished every morning. He looked at the mud and slime surrounding the vehicle and hesitated. She'd already gone four paces down the track, slithering and swearing at every step. She glanced back at him, still in the Land Rover. 'Do you want another child drowned? Get out here, man. That's an order.' As she spoke, she knew she was being unfair. If she'd shared her fears with him, he'd have been there before her.

They ran together past the garden with the strange statues and the tall wall covered in ivy and, reaching the edge of the pool, she thought they were too late. She saw the rowing boat, the man inside, bent over his oars and so intent on pulling his way across the water that he didn't see them. And she saw the mother and her child on the deck, following his progress.

'They're all right then,' Joe said. He was frosty with her and had every right to be. 'He's gone to save them.' Implying that there was no need for the fuss and the ruined shoes.

'No, pet, that's the last thing he wants to do. He hates happy families.'

Vera stood watching. She was completely powerless. The boathouse was on the other side of the pond, too far away for her to shout, so she couldn't warn Connie. Besides, what could the woman do if she heard? She was imprisoned there.

And, Vera thought, the man in the boat would be impossible to scare now. With the second murder he'd gone beyond reason. This was like one of those nightmares when you scream and no sound comes, when you try to run, but your feet won't move.

'It was *him*,' Ashworth said. 'All the time? Of course. I should have recognized the car.'

She didn't answer. They watched the man climb onto the boathouse deck. They couldn't see Connie or the girl, who were still inside. Ashworth slipped away from her and made his way through the undergrowth, following the line of the floodwater to the point where the boathouse was closest to the bank. No thought for his shoes now or for his Marks and Spencer suit.

I owe him an apology. He'll never want to work with me again.

There was a high-pitched scream, so loud that Vera could hear it even at this distance. The man appeared on the deck with Alice in his arms. Connie followed. She was the person screaming. It seemed to Vera that the child was silent, frozen perhaps with fear, her only survival tactic to shut off all emotion. Frozen as Vera had been. But the scream had woken Vera up. Suddenly she found herself on the phone demanding back-up, an ambulance, a rubber dinghy and a helicopter. Screaming herself, into her mobile: 'Now! Get them here now!'

On the deck the man was holding Alice above his head. It occurred to Vera that he must have strong muscles in his upper body to lift her so easily. Did he work out at the gym? Then she thought he looked a little like a priest. One of those grand priests in the fancy robes that you found in cathedrals, lifting the chalice for the congregation to see as he blessed it during the communion service. Or did they call it the mass? She'd never got the hang of the different denominations.

The man held his hands apart and dropped the girl into the lake. She disappeared without a splash.

Ashworth had reached the closest point to the boathouse and was already wading out towards it. Now he started swimming, his hair slick like an otter's. On the decking Connie was struggling to get past the man, shouting and scratching at his face. But Vera kept her eyes fixed on Ashworth. He dived into the water and emerged, shaking the water from his head, holding the child. He swam on his back, clutching the girl's body to his chest, until the water was shallow enough for him to stand. Then he held her over his shoulder and wrapped his arms around her. Vera thought she would never be rude or snide to him again. Half walking and half swimming, he carried the child to the shore.

Chapter Forty-One

From the boathouse Simon Eliot watched impassively. Then he turned deliberately, did a perfect swallow-dive from the deck, and began to swim away to the far end of the pool. A show. Like the fit lifeguards at the Willows, when they were showing off in front of the yummy mummies. He must know now that there was no escape for him.

Vera decided to leave Joe Ashworth in charge of the operation to pick up Eliot. There was some satisfaction in knowing she'd been right about the killer. It had come to her suddenly, thinking about the teenage waiter's blushes when he spoke about Jenny Lister. Jenny had talked about her unsuitable lover. Who could be more unsuitable than her daughter's fiancé? And who was more likely to fall for an older woman than Simon Eliot, whose own mother's energies had been taken up with grieving for her two other lost children? But Vera felt ill when she thought how close they'd been to losing a child. She found her sports bag in the back of the Land Rover. A towel and a brand-new tracksuit, bought after she'd first joined the Willows Health Club and never worn.

'Put this on,' she said to Ashworth. 'You'll catch your death.'

'I can't wear that!' He'd always been vain.

'Suit yourself.'

In the end the cold convinced him. He went behind the high wall and came out, his hair tousled like a bairn's and in the tracksuit. The legs were a bit short, and the joggers looked odd above the sodden work shoes. If he hadn't been such a hero, Vera would have taken a photo on her phone and sent it to the rest of the team.

'Be grateful I'm not a girlie type and I don't wear pink,' she said. Relief was making her a bit giggly and flighty. 'What'd you have looked like then?'

Connie and Alice sat in the passenger seat; Alice had changed into dry clothes already and was wrapped in Connie's coat. Ashworth had pulled Connie ashore in the dinghy after handing Alice to Vera. Vera could still remember the feel of the soaking child in her arms, the fragile bones and the fluttering heart. It was like holding one of Hector's birds, she thought. An owl perhaps. And as close she'd get now to cuddling a bairn of her own.

'You don't want to stay and see this through?' Ashworth asked. 'We can get a patrol car to take Connie home. The water's already gone down a bit.'

'Nah,' she said. 'This is more important.' And she knew it would only take a matter of minutes for Ashworth to track Eliot down. The man had no car, he was wet through and there was a helicopter buzzing overhead. Joe deserved the glory of the arrest.

She dropped Connie and Alice at Mallow Cottage. 'You're sure you don't want a lift to A&E?'

'The ambulance crew checked her over and said she's fine.'

'Aye, well then.' Vera thought it was for the best, but she wouldn't have minded putting off the next interview for a bit longer.

She parked outside the Lister house. The elderly woman next door was watching through the nets and gave Vera a little wave when she recognized her. Reassuring that there was someone to keep an eye out for Hannah.

Vera rang the bell and heard footsteps. The door opened and the girl was already speaking.

'Where have you been? I thought you'd only gone to the supermarket.' Not nagging. That one would never be a nagging sort of woman. Just concerned. Then she saw Vera and it was like a rerun of the first visit to the house, the time when Vera had to tell Hannah that her mother was dead.

'Oh, it's you, Inspector. I thought you were Simon. He's taken my mother's car to get some food. He's been ages, but perhaps he's got stuck in the floods. Do you want some coffee?' She walked through to the kitchen and Vera followed.

'Maybe later, pet. We need to talk first.'

Something about Vera's face made the girl stop in her tracks.

'You've found him, haven't you? The man who killed my mother?'

'Aye, we know who it is. Not in custody yet, but only a matter of time.'

'Is it someone I'd know?' Hannah looked up at her, sensing perhaps that there was more to this than the official notification that the killer had been found.

Vera paused. The girl had been through so much already. How could Vera tell her that the man she adored was a murderer?

'It's Simon.'

'No!' She forced a laugh. 'This is a terrible joke, right?' Her face was grey. She pulled out a chair and almost fell into it.

'No joke. Do you want me to tell you about it? Should I get someone to be with you first? Friend? Teacher?' Vera had asked much the same question on that earlier visit too and Simon had come rushing in. Hannah's knight in shining armour. Her boy fiancé.

'Tell me. I don't believe it, but tell me your story.'

'She fell in love with him. Your mother fell in love with him.'

There was a silence, which wasn't what Vera had been expecting. She'd thought there would be tears, denial, rage, even that Hannah would throw her out of the house.

'You're not surprised?'

'She fancied him,' Hannah said quietly. 'You could tell. But Simon and I made a joke about it. Why wouldn't she? Why wouldn't a middle-aged woman fancy a fit younger man? But she wouldn't do anything about it. My mother was a good woman.'

And she was getting older, body clock ticking. It's a powerful sensation, lust. Easy to convince yourself that you're in love when the hormones start working. Love gives us licence to do what we like. Love is honourable and brave, even if we're screwing our daughter's fiancé. All bollocks of course, but that's what we're brought up to believe. And after being good for so long, the temptation to be wicked must have been overwhelming. I understand all that.

'What about Simon? Did he fancy her?'

'He liked her. Admired her. He didn't have much of a relationship with his own mother, so I was pleased Mum and Simon got on so well.'

'They were lovers,' Vera said. It was best the girl heard the details from her. No doubt the story would dribble out over time, even if Eliot was persuaded to plead guilty. 'Have been for months. They met an afternoon a week in Durham. Her excuse was that she went to Durham prison to meet Mattie Jones, but she always kept the visits very short. Mattie confirmed that with my sergeant. Then they spent the rest of the day in Simon's house. His parents had bought it for him. An investment. Very handy.' She looked at Hannah. 'We showed Jenny's photo to the neighbours. A few recognized her. The pair of them were about as discreet as it's possible to be, but there's no doubt, I'm afraid. One afternoon they left the curtains open and a nosy old lady saw them kissing.' This was another of the operations she'd planned from her seat in the Willows the day before: a house-to-house in the street where Simon lived. She had a couple of friends who worked for County Durham police. They'd owed her a few favours, paid back now.

'Thursdays,' Hannah said slowly. 'Mum was always late home on Thursdays. And I knew not to contact Simon then, because he said he had rowing practice. Followed by a few pints with the boys, of course.'

'Then your mother must have started feeling guilty,' Vera said. 'Not about the relationship with Simon, I think, but about lying to you. She wanted it all out in the open.' *Stupid woman. Some things are best kept secret.* 'Simon hated the idea of your knowing. If he loved anyone, it was you.'

'So he killed Mum just to stop her telling me?' Now Hannah was horrified.

'Oh, pet, nothing's quite that simple, is it?'

Because Simon Eliot was certainly a complicated young man. He was someone else with disturbing childhood memories. Pictures in his head. First, of a small brother who disappeared in a river in flood. Then who seemed to disappear completely from the family's life. No toys. No clothes. No photographs. Simon must have been left with a sense of guilt, confused that nobody would acknowledge it. Had he believed himself mad? There would have been times when he'd thought the whole incident was imagined. Maybe the care of a compassionate social worker was just what he needed.

Hannah was staring at her. 'Tell me,' she said. 'I want to know.'

'Simon had a half-sister,' Vera said, 'called Mattie Jones.'

'That woman who killed her child?'

'That woman.' Vera looked at the kitchen tiles and saw that her mucky wellingtons had left a trail of footprints. She should have taken them off at the door. 'Veronica had a child when she was still a schoolgirl.'

'But my mother wouldn't have told him about that!' Hannah's voice was so high-pitched that it came out like a shriek. 'She never discussed her work with anyone.'

But with Simon, Jenny Lister had broken all her rules.

'Perhaps she didn't tell him,' Vera said. 'Perhaps he found her notes. The plan for the book she intended to write.'

They sat in silence.

'Simon and Danny were friends, weren't they?' Vera had done what she'd come for, but Hannah was so calm and composed that she felt she could ask more questions.

'Sure, I told you they were.'

'But close friends?'

'Yeah, we were all in Folkworks, the scheme for young musicians at the Sage. Danny was a mean fiddle-player. Great on guitar too. He didn't get on so well with the kids at school; he was more comfortable with the older guys he played music with.'

'Even though he'd lost you to Simon?'

'I told you. Things like that happen all the time. It's no big deal. Danny liked heroes. Simon was older, cleverer.'

But I was distracted by it. I saw the young men as rivals, not allies. That threw me entirely off track.

'Where is he?' Hannah asked suddenly. 'Where's Simon?'

'Last time I saw him he was soaking wet. He'd just swum across the pool at Greenhough, trying to get away from us.'

'That was where we first made love,' Hannah said. 'In the boathouse. This time of year, but it was sunny. Birdsong in the woods. He took me out on a boat on the lake and we drank champagne.' She looked out into the garden. Next door Hilda was pegging sheets onto the line. Hannah, though, was lost in thought and didn't notice her. 'I could always tell he was damaged. He had these weird silences and sometimes he'd get angry for no real reason.

But I thought I could heal him. I thought I could make him whole.'

'Oh, pet, nobody could do that for him.'

'Except my mother,' Hannah said. 'Perhaps *she* could.'

'No! She was going to spoil everything!' The voice was loud and sharp and startled them both. It was like someone shouting in church. Simon had let himself in through the front door. Vera had been so focused on the girl that she hadn't heard him. His dark hair was still damp, but he'd changed into dry clothes.

'How did you get here?' Vera said. Then immediately, 'Your mother, was it? The one child that she has left she wants to protect. You gave her a ring and she drove out to rescue you? Took you home to get changed, then let you on your way? Very responsible, I'm sure, to let a murderer on the loose.'

'You can't blame my mother,' he said. He sounded suddenly weary. 'She doesn't know what's been going on.'

'She knows enough,' Vera snapped back. 'She guessed it at least. Why else would she get Connie and Alice out of Mallow Cottage?'

'Because I asked her to.'

'And why would you do that? What danger could Connie Masters be to you?

'Jenny was planning to interview her for the bloody book. Maybe she already had. What if she'd told the woman we were lovers? I couldn't risk Masters talking to the police again. She could give me a motive for murder.'

The words were rambling, incoherent, and Vera thought Simon was deceiving himself. That wasn't the real reason for the abduction. From the big white house he'd seen Connie and Alice together. Playing happy families in the garden where his brother had been drowned. She could tell from the bitterness in his voice that he'd hated them.

'I want to talk to Hannah,' he said. 'I want to explain.'

'Yeah, and I want to win the Lottery and not deal with people like you ever again. But it's not going to happen.'

'Please,' Hannah said. 'Give him a couple of minutes.' She stood up and the two young people were facing each other across the room. Again, Vera thought how calm she was. It had been the uncertainty surrounding her mother's death that had fractured her confidence and personality. Knowledge had put her back together. 'So tell me, please, Simon, why did you feel the need to kill the woman who'd been so good to you?'

'How can you say that?' He was screaming. 'How can you say that when she tempted me? When she took me away from you?'

'That was your choice, I'd say, Simon. Your responsibility. Why did she have to die?'

'She was going to tell you. Then everything would have been over between us. I couldn't bear it.' Tears were running down his cheeks.

'Oh, Simon, you're such a child. You make me feel as old as the world.' The words were cold and deliberate. Hannah walked towards him and Vera expected a gesture of violence. A slap on the face. She was ready for that. Instead the girl took him in her arms and held him for a moment. He rested his head on her shoulder and she stroked his hair. Then she pushed him away and turned to Vera. 'Now take him away. I never want to see him again. If he stays here any longer I might have to get a bread knife and kill him.'

Chapter Forty-Two

To mark the end of the investigation Vera treated the team to dinner at the Willows. She didn't see it as a celebration—the memory of the encounter between Hannah and Simon was too fresh for that—and the Willows, with its large echoing dining room, seemed to suit the mood. Besides, this was where the whole case had started.

Ryan Taylor had given them the best table in the room, next to a long window and looking out over the garden and the river. The water had gone down, but still there was a feeling of being on an island, of being cut off from the rest of the world. The place was almost empty. In a far corner an elderly couple sipped coffee in silence. At a table near the door a businessman was spooning soup into his mouth and reading the *Telegraph*.

'Tell me, Joe, how *did* you let Simon Eliot get away?'

They'd finished eating. Vera had insisted that there'd be no talk until after the meal. And they'd drunk a lot of wine. Vera had said the taxis home would be on her. Or, she said, winking at Joe Ashworth and Holly, who seemed to be getting on better this evening than she could remember, they could stay the night here if they preferred. Charlie had just gone outside for a cigarette. They could see him in the security light on the terrace, his hand cupped round the flame as he tried to light it. He must have seen them looking, and waved at them through the window to wait until he got inside before they started talking.

Vera was teasing Joe, a habit she'd probably never get out of. Even if he became her boss, which wasn't beyond the realms of possibility, she knew she'd still have a go at him. Her resolution at the pool not to bait him was completely forgotten.

'So come on!' she said. 'All that back-up, the cars and the chopper, and he could just ring his mam and you let him drive away.'

Joe, mellow on Merlot and a brandy with his coffee, didn't allow himself to be provoked. 'You told us he spent every summer camping out there. He knew all the places to hide.'

'Banged up now, at any rate,' Vera said. She'd taken Eliot to the police station herself, breaking every rule in the book yet again, letting him sit beside her in the Land Rover. Hannah she'd left in the care of Hilda. 'He'll plead guilty. No need for Jenny's daughter to appear in court. That was what I was afraid of, that was why I wanted to wait.'

They sat for a moment, and Vera knew they were all thinking about Connie and Alice and what might have happened if Joe hadn't got there on time. Charlie appeared in the doorway and walked across the polished wooden floor to join them.

'So talk us through it then, boss,' he said. He was already unsteady on his feet, but he poured himself another glass of wine. He'd already told them he didn't do spirits: *the slippery slope*. 'Beginning to end.'

Vera had been waiting for the invitation. She'd have given them the story anyway, but it was much more gratifying to be asked. She sat back in her chair at the head of the table, a glass in her hand, and began. She spoke slowly. This wasn't for rushing.

'The beginning was simple,' she said. 'A frustrated middle-aged woman fancying a good-looking young man. And a student choosing experience over innocence. Or wanting his cake and eating it. It happened one night when Hannah was out. Simon came to visit her, but she'd been held up and Jenny asked him in to wait. Offered him a glass of wine.' She shrugged, held up her glass. 'Terrible stuff, alcohol.'

She looked round the table and saw that she had them hooked, like bairns listening to a bedtime story.

'Simon kissed her,' she said. 'Nothing else then and he apologized, but that was the start of it. Jenny became obsessed with him and an affair developed. He was flattered by her attention, I think. Why wouldn't he be? She was still lovely. They met every week in Durham. Jenny wanted to see Mattie anyway to get information for the book. She went first to see Mattie. The prison visits were short. Jenny was there as much to make herself feel better about screwing her daughter's man as to collect information for her great work of literature. Really she was desperate to spend time with the boy.'

She paused, topped up her glass, and imagined herself as Jenny Lister, counting off the hours until she could spend time with Simon Eliot in his student house. 'Then guilt set in, as it always does.' Again she looked at Ashworth. 'It's a terrible thing, guilt. Not everyone can cope with it.' Another grin.

'So why did Simon Eliot kill her?' Charlie could understand the sex part, Vera saw that; it was the violence he didn't get.

'Eh, Charlie man, give a woman the chance to tell a story in her own time.'

Vera had asked Taylor to leave the whisky bottle on the table and tipped a little more into her glass. Bugger the doctors and their healthy living—tonight she needed to get pleasantly pissed.

'While Jenny Lister was besotted with her young lover, Michael Morgan had taken up with pretty little Freya. About the same sort of age difference between both couples, though we don't talk about Jenny corrupting Simon, do we? Then Jenny found out from Mattie that

Freya was pregnant and she became involved in the Morgan case again. It all got a bit close to home, didn't it? Suddenly it would have hit her that she was screwing Mattie's half-brother . . ' Vera half closed her eyes and thought about chance and the coincidence of Jenny Lister and Veronica Eliot living in the same village. But Northumberland was the least-populated county in England and in small communities there were always connections. 'She decided it had to stop. And being honourable and *really* stupid, she decided she'd have to come clean to Hannah. Simon couldn't stand that. Hannah worshipped him. They were engaged, after all, a big commitment for a couple that young.'

'Where did Danny Shaw come into it?' Ashworth was suddenly getting impatient. Maybe there'd been a text from his wife, read surreptitiously under the table, asking where the hell he was.

Vera opened her eyes and sat forward. 'Ah, Danny Shaw, wild boy and charmer. And thief. Never got on with boys of his own age, always wanted to knock around with older people. If I were some sort of social worker I'd maybe diagnose a conflict with his father, but luckily I don't go in for all that crap.' She paused and tried to put into words the friendship between Danny and Simon. 'Simon was everything Danny wanted to be: he went to the posh school in town, his father was a successful businessman, and Simon had the girl Danny had fallen for. But that didn't make Danny resent Simon. It just made the younger boy admire him. Weird.'

'So?' Ashworth demanded. 'I still don't see why he had to die.'

In the corner, the elderly couple got to their feet, and holding hands like teenagers they walked slowly out of the dining room.

'That's because you're not very bright, pet. You don't have a logical mind.'

'Did Danny help Simon with the murder?' Holly asked. 'He was working there. He could get Simon through the turnstile and into the pool. He knew too much.'

'Right!' Vera gave Holly a little clap of approval because she knew it would wind up Ashworth.

'But why would he do that?' It was Ashworth, fighting back. 'Why make himself an accessory to murder?'

'Because he's young and daft,' Vera said. 'Because he liked taking risks. Because his hero asked him to.'

And maybe because he still blamed Jenny Lister for break-ing up his relationship with Hannah. Or maybe at that point he didn't even know Simon intended to kill the woman. Per-haps he thought it was a joke, a big game.

'Talk us through that day,' Charlie said. 'Tell us what actually happened. No more psycho-babble.' He slumped forward across the table.

'Jenny came here a couple of times a week to use the pool before work. Not dead early, but before the cheap sessions started. Simon wanted to make sure she would be there that day, so he arranged to meet her for coffee before she went for her swim. Of course he didn't show. He'd gone beyond the stage of deep and meaningful talk-ing. She got changed as usual, leaving her clothes and bag in her locker, and went into the steam room as usual, but Simon was waiting for her.'

'Danny had let him in,' Holly said. 'We know he'd stayed here overnight and was in the hotel that morning.'

'Yes, Danny had let him in. Another anonymous swimmer. Who would notice? Simon's a strong young man, a rower. He could strangle her and make no noise. There would always be a danger that someone would interrupt him, but I suspect Danny was keeping watch. Again, who takes notice of a cleaner? You see the mop, the bucket, even the overalls, but you don't see the man. And nobody noticed Jenny's body for more than an hour until I found her, which gave them both time to leave the hotel.'

Vera leaned back in her chair. Had the two young men considered the enormity of what they'd planned? Or had it been an intellectual challenge for them? Like some project set at university?

'Simon went into the gents' changing rooms to get dressed, but of course there was a problem. Jenny's bag was in her locker in the ladies'. And in her bag was her diary, her notes. Probably some reference to her infatuation with Simon. The solution was easy.' Vera looked up, became again their mentor and teacher. 'Anyone?'

'Danny,' Holly said, jumping in ahead of Ashworth. 'He had a pass key.'

'Right! Simon cleared out of the hotel as soon as he could; he was too bright to be seen hanging around there. Not so concerned, you notice, about Danny. He left him to collect the bag and get rid of it, and to bring the notes back to him in Barnard Bridge. But Danny was curious. Who wouldn't be?'

'So he checked out what was in the bag before he dumped it?'

'Of course. And he wasn't as cool as he pretended either. He didn't know Barnard Bridge and got lost on his way to the house. He'd thrown the bag into the weeds at Mallow Cottage before Connie saw him.'

Ryan Taylor came up to clear the table. By now all the waiting staff had left and they were the only guests remaining. 'I'm sorry, pet,' Vera said. 'You'll want to be away home. Just throw us out when you're ready for us to go.'

'No rush,' he said. 'I'm staying here tonight.' He flicked a switch and dimmed all the other lights in the room so that they were spotlit by one dusty chandelier. Vera felt like an actress; she'd always enjoyed performing for an audience and looked around her to make sure she had their full attention. Perhaps when she retired she'd go in for amateur dramatics, though she didn't see there'd be nearly as much fun in the made-up stuff.

The background music had been turned off now. Vera thought this was not so much like being on the stage, but in one corner of a huge film set, one of those big dusty hangars, where fantasies were created with bits of hardboard and scraps of velvet and silk.

'So Danny Shaw? If the lads were such friends, why did Simon kill him?' Ashworth leaned across the table and took Vera's bottle, poured a large measure into his glass. *Oh, Joey boy*, Vera thought. *What will the perfect wife make of you turning up pissed? You'll be changing the mucky nappies for the next fortnight.*

'Danny started to think he deserved more than a thank-you for helping Simon commit murder,' Vera said. 'And maybe he didn't even get that. If Simon hadn't taken him for granted, I don't think he'd have made demands. For him it had all been about friendship.'

He talked about friendship to Michael Morgan. Michael was preoccupied and not listening properly and, self-centred bastard that he is, he thought Danny was talking about him. Until I asked him about it again this morning.

'So Danny started to blackmail Simon?' Holly said. Even after a week with little sleep and a bucketful of alcohol, she still looked poised and lovely. Some things in life weren't fair.

'He was probably more subtle than that. But Bristol's a university that attracts wealthy folks' kids. His girlfriend's parents were minted. He wanted enough cash to feel that he belonged.' Vera paused. 'I don't think he ever would have gone public on Simon, he probably didn't even threaten to, but Simon couldn't risk it. That day he borrowed Jenny's car. He told Hannah he was going to the supermarket and he must have gone shopping on the way home. Cool customer! More like his father than his mother. I'd guess Christopher could be pretty ruthless too, and Veronica just lost it at the end. Did she suspect her son had killed the social worker? Maybe she saw some of the notes he brought home. Maybe she heard the end of a phone conversation with Danny. That was her worst nightmare, that her son was a murderer. That's why she suddenly became best buddy with Connie Masters. She wanted information, reassurance.'

'Can we get back to Danny Shaw?' Charlie was struggling to get the words out without slurring. 'Don't know about you guys, but I'm going to need my bed pretty soon.'

'Simon strangled him and lit the bonfire with the files from Jenny's bag. Taking out anything that might point to him first, of course. To implicate Danny in the first murder and just generally muddy the waters.' Vera beamed to herself and realized how drunk she must look, but she didn't care. *Muddy waters. Good image.*

'Then things got to him and he lost all that composure, started to do the "what if" thing, and that's always dangerous. What if Jenny *had* gone to interview Connie for her book? Simon hadn't even realized she was living in the village until I told him. That must have really freaked him out. What if they'd been best mates and Jenny had confided in her about the relationship? The anxiety ate away at him. First he threatened Connie by phone, then he persuaded his mother to take them to the boathouse.' Vera looked up at them. 'But deep down he was just jealous of the care Connie gave to her daughter. This case was always about kids and their parents. Simon Eliot was like a little lad in a tantrum, smashing what he knew he could never have.'

'Eliot almost killed a four-year-old child because he was jealous of her?' Ashworth was incredulous.

Vera shrugged. 'We'll probably never know exactly why he threw her in the water. His brother had drowned, and so had his sister's son. Maybe there on the boathouse deck he saw it as payback time.'

'Is that what you think this was all about?' Charlie raised his head far enough from the table to speak.

'Doesn't matter what I believe, does it? The CPS has got him for two murders that he's admitted. They probably won't push him on the child. And Connie won't want to go through another court case, so I imagine she'll be happy to let it drop.'

'Another child that'll be terrified of water all her life,' Holly said.

'Aye, maybe.' But Vera wasn't sure about all this cause and effect. Life was less predictable and more messy than that. Best leave the theories to the shrinks and social workers. 'Or she could turn out to be an Olympic swimmer.'